3 0117 0344

C000180333

PLUNDER
WITH
INTENT

PLUNDER WITH INTENT

J. E. D'ESTE CLARK

ember

First published in hardback in the UK in 2017
by Ember Press

Digital edition converted in 2017 by Tutis Innovative E-Solutions Pte. Ltd
and distributed in 2017 by E-Book Partnership

HB ISBN 978-1-9997701-0-5
EB ISBN 978-19123173-4-9

1 3 5 7 9 10 8 6 4 2

Cover by Emma Graves

Illustrations by Joey Everett

Print and production managed by
Jellyfish Solutions Ltd

This book is dedicated to the Hellenic people. It is time to repay the people of Greece – those who have given so much to the world

Part One
Fifth-Century BC Athens

Chapter One
The Morning of the World

That morning, all that could be heard echoing in the dusty, drowsy silence was the gentle rhythmic sound of a solitary sculptor's chisel ringing out, striking a chorus of iron and stone.

Clear blue skies and dazzling bright sunlight had returned once more to the ancient, walled city-state of Athens, blazing a trail of burnished gold across the eastern sky. Apollo seemed to delight in his god-given status as the Hellas 'god of light' because the purity and the clarity of the light was truly astonishing. Athens virtually radiated with golden sunlight – it shone with such luminosity and such brilliance that at times a little of the pain and the misery appeared to fade from the haggard weary face of the lone sculptor. For him, the glorious sunlight went unnoticed, the morning began like any other: labouring on relentlessly, inside his shabby workshop; chiselling deeper into the marble, in the fading, flickering light of a single oil lamp, *without much oil*. He cursed miserably to himself, while a host of ghostly amorphous shadows dancing on the rough-hewn, dimly lit limestone walls bounced off the stone statue, his yet unfinished masterpiece.

CHAPTER ONE

Nikodimos had worked throughout the night without respite or sleep, chiselling down to the penultimate layer, using all the genius in his hands to transform the cold, lifeless block of stone into the statue of the virgin goddess, Athena Parthenos.

As he chiselled deep into the marble, Nikodimos became one with the stone. He became one with the dust from the stone. He worked in dust. He breathed dust. He ate dust. He choked on dust. Every pore in his body was clogged with fine white dust and so too were his eyelashes and his long curly hair. However, he was so intent on completing his sculpture of the Greek goddess, Athena, that he just kept on chiselling, ignoring the thick cloud of dust swirling about inside his workshop like sand in a desert storm. He paid no heed to the marble chips gathering in clumps on his himation, the threadbare cloak that he wore flung over his right shoulder and he paid even less heed to the clods of marble dust clinging on to his woollen tunic, encrusting his sleeveless shirt with dust, sticking to the shaggy woollen cloth like glue. His leather buskins, relics from his past as a tragedian actor, were also weighed down with dust and chipped marble newly wrought from the Pentelic stone. Although it mattered not to this brilliant sculptor, because as he chiselled deep into the marble, Nikodimos truly became one with the stone.

Yet, despite his fierce unbending resolve, any hope of completing the larger-than-life marble statue of the virgin goddess, Athena Parthenos, was gradually slipping away.

Everything had been going according to plan, until late yesterday afternoon, when Themis, his young slave, came bounding into the workshop and thrust a rolled-up papyrus into his hand. The message had come directly from Pheidias, the site-manager in charge of building the Parthenon. With great trepidation Nikodimos unrolled it and, squinting through the dust, read the following missive informing him in no uncertain terms:

Nikodimos,

Work on the Parthenon is progressing well beyond our expectations. Please have all of the remaining statues and metopes ready for collection at dawn tomorrow as the stone-masons have progressed way ahead of schedule. As the roof is now on we will be ready to begin installing the marbles in the east and west pediment sooner than anticipated.

A hastily written postscript had been added at the bottom of the page, penned in the most elaborate scrawl imaginable which Nikodimos found even more disconcerting:

As you can well imagine Nikodimos, it is absolutely crucial that the statue of Athena be ready, otherwise the entire building project will be placed in jeopardy. As you well know Pericles has set down a rigorous building schedule that must be adhered to at all costs. Meaning: 'at your peril', my honoured friend.

With respect,
Pheidias

Dawn had broken. The first light of day had come and gone. And, thank god, the wagon-master and his ox-cart had yet to appear. Nikodimos hastily scanned his workshop. All the metopes Pheidias requested were ready. He counted seven leaning against the wall.

He breathed a sigh of relief, knowing all of them were ready. The colossal stone statues were ready, all except one. The statue that he had been working on throughout the night and, what seemed like, every night, for the last one thousand and one nights. In fact, so

FRIEZE *METOPES* *PEDIMENT*

Plate I: An architectural drawing of the Parthenon showing sculptural decoration.

exhausted, he imagined he might actually succumb from overwork right there in his workshop.

Nikodimos shrugged his powerful shoulders. He tugged wearily on his dusty silk snood. The moment he had been dreading for weeks had finally come. Reality was staring him in the face. His statue wasn't ready. He had failed to complete his commission. The Parthenon was nearing completion, so any grandiose ideas he may have indulged in of furthering his career as a great Athenian sculptor were about to end, because if he were to win any further commissions from Pheidias, his statue of Athena needed to be spectacular – and it wasn't.

Nikodimos cursed aloud. He abhorred the thought of carving elaborate gravestones for dead warriors or wealthy nobles for the rest of his life; those who wished to have enormous, allegorical-type steles erected to commemorate their families' dearly departed loved ones. To spend his days carving memorials for the dead overwhelmed him to such an extent that he had even contemplated digging himself a massive grave and climbing in.

Nikodimos pondered further. Because of his age he could be called up by the military to do garrison-duty, a two-year stint patrolling the frontiers, protecting the city of Athens from the ever-encroaching infidels threatening to invade. Admittedly, his future looked a great deal bleaker than he had hitherto imagined, as it was a case of either: be killed in battle, which he didn't really fancy – as death on a battlefield was a grisly, often gruesome affair, although it was considered an honorable thing to do amongst Athenian society – or endure a life of boredom, carving marble sculptures he thought worthy of the living not the dead.

Of course, all this was exacerbated by the simple fact that Pheidias, under whose aegis Athena's sacred temple was built, had very graciously awarded Nikodimos this last commission purely as a favour. And to disappoint Pheidias would be a tragedy like no other, thought Nikodimos, stomping his buskins in the goo, indulging his theatrical tragedian-self in waves of self-pity.

Pheidias had been his inspiration for most of his life. Since the great man had agreed to take him on as an apprentice at the tender age of eight. For the next four years he had been kept busy doing simple tasks: filling the oil lamps, sweeping the dust and the goo from the floor, and feeding Pheidias' horses, which was a great honour as only the great and the good within Athenian society kept them. Sadly, the closest he actually ever got to a marble statue during those early years was when he was asked to clear the workshop overflowing with corpses (chipped, broken or battered marble statues no longer of use), assisted with the loading of the donkey-cart with corpses and took the marble to the dump at the foot of the Hill of the Pnyx. He also recalled running messages to and from Athens until his small, calloused feet bled.

Under Pheidias' expert tutelage Nikodimos soon flourished and at the age of twelve he became a fully-fledged apprentice. Needless to say he was delighted, although his delight didn't last long, because his dream of carving a marble statue remained just that – a dream. He spent the next year sitting cross-legged on the dusty floor making moulds from clods of wet clay or chipping away at small blocks of stone, making roof tiles for the Parthenon. The number of roof tiles required to build the Parthenon was staggering.

His thoughts drifted back to the day he got his chance to carve his very first statue and how excited he had been at the prospect of actually carving a stone, so much so, that he had been unable to eat or sleep. The day that he had visited the quarry was even more memorable, because he had been nearly crushed to death by a falling block of stone. However, his passion for stone-carving never wavered. Until now.

The statue, which had taken him two solstices to complete, was still standing in the shed. Of course, he had had the benefit of a muse at the time, which was more than he had now. He would never forget his first muse, Cassandra, who lived in the same deme as he did. He may have only been a young apprentice at the time, yet Nikodimos was no stranger to the exquisite natural beauty of the female form and Cassandra epitomised this within the inner recesses of his young imagination.

Thinking back, something odd had happened to him that day and it was truly astonishing. Suddenly, in the flickering lamplight the statue appeared to come to life – right there, before his very eyes – standing on her plinth. Nikodimos had imagined that the statue *was* Cassandra and she had come magically to life. This thought evoked such wild, euphoric passion within him that he, quite frankly, forgot himself and began rubbing his small sensitive hands very gently over the smooth surface of the creamy white marble. After all, it wasn't uncommon for an apprentice to do this, considering his chosen field. On this occasion, however, he imagined that he was actually caressing the young maiden's soft, supple flesh...her arms, her legs, her pert young breasts.

Just prior to this totally absorbing flirtation with the subtleness of virgin flesh, Nikodimos had been filling the oil lamps. Some of the residual lamp oil was still on his hands and it rubbed off on to the soft stone, causing ugly, yellow oily patches to bleed into the skin of the marble. Sadly, no matter how hard he rubbed, he could not remove the stains. His statue was ruined, much to the chagrin of Pheidias.

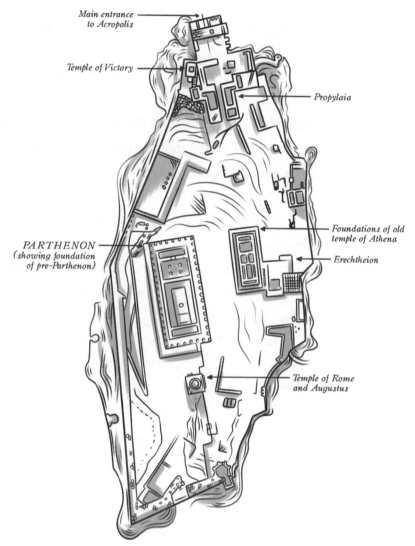

Main entrance to Acropolis

Temple of Victory

Propylaia

PARTHENON
(showing foundation
of pre-Parthenon)

Foundations of old
temple of Athena

Erechtheion

Temple of Rome
and Augustus

Plan of the ancient Acropolis

Plate II: Plan of the ancient Acropolis showing the main entrance, Propylaia, Temple of Victory, Erechtheion and the foundation of the Parthenon.

His thoughts returned to the present. Pericles was no fool. 'Old Squill Head' – as he was referred to by the Athenians, after the comic-poets had had a go at him because of the elongated shape of his head – chose Pheidias for good reason, for he proved to be a truly gifted genius. Nikodimos never ceased to marvel at the sheer magnitude and majesty of the newly constructed Parthenon whenever he gazed upon the colossal structure, with its north and south porch, and colonnades comprised of long rows of massive Doric columns that quite simply *glowed* in the bright sun. The marble used to build the Parthenon had a translucent quality that reminded him of a beautiful woman's flawless complexion, like Casandra's fine white skin. He truly believed that the Parthenon was the most breathtakingly beautiful building in the world. Like a goddess's temple ought to be. The purity, symmetry and simplicity of the building he imagined, bordering on the divine. The reason the Parthenon was so spectacular, thought Nikodimos (having spent hour-upon-hour gazing at the citadel), from a purely design point of view, was because Pheidias had had the foresight to leave unencumbered void spaces between the fluted columns, which greatly enhanced the design.

Nikodimos had never openly expressed his views about the Parthenon to anyone. The other masons might think he had lost his head. Perhaps he had, although it was considered fashionable to think, to question and to reason and Nikodimos enjoyed indulging in all three of the aforementioned. Lately, however, he didn't have much time to think, although he strongly believed that the sublime beauty reflected in art and architecture came from a much deeper source that began with a greater understanding of the natural world.

CHAPTER ONE

Pheidias had captured this in the Parthenon and in so doing Nikodimos believed that he had quite simply perfected Athena's shrine. All the more reason why he couldn't disappoint Pheidias who, lately, had obtained a god-like status in Athens and one could not possibly upset a god. Mortal or immortal.

Chapter Two
Inside the Stone-Carver's Shabby Workshop

Nikodimos' workshop comprised numerous stone-masons, various and sundry stone-carvers from various demes and three aspiring young apprentices. Although they were all absent that morning because every available mason, aspiring or not, had been commandeered by the master stone-masons to assist with the installation of the enormous metopes in the Parthenon frieze. However, there was one bright star in the workshop and it was his young cousin, Menelaos, who was showing signs of having an immense talent, even though he was only twelve years of age. Another of his protégés was Syrinx, a barbarian slave girl who might prove to be the best sculptor ever. He also kept one personal slave, Themis, who was supposed to keep the workshop neat and tidy, although he rarely had the time, because, that morning, like every morning, as soon as the cock began to crow, his young slave boy rose from his straw mat, which he slept on by the door of the workshop, and set off on foot taking messages to 'The Great One', the name Themis used to describe Pheidias.

There was another stone-carver, however, who worked alongside Nikodimos. His name was Orestis and he lived in squalor on the beach, not far from the workshop. Orestis had been born on the sacred island of Delos, near Mykonos, in the Aegean Sea, living there until being forced into exile. Orestis had managed to flee the idyllic island famous for being Apollo's birthplace, with his life and not much else. Now, Orestis lived in constant fear of his life, hidden away at the far end of Kantharos harbour. In his prior life Orestis had been a brilliant bronze-sculptor, working under the famous bronze-sculptor, Myron.

Nikodimos had encountered Orestis hobbling along the dusty back streets at Piraeus begging for scraps of food, and he quite rightly assumed that he was a beggar-man. However, the beggar showed up outside his workshop one morning, sat crouched by the door and refused to go away. Orestis didn't speak, not a word, and Nikodimos assumed he had been tortured, had had his tongue gouged out. This escapade went on for days until early one morning the beggar-man seemed quite agitated as Nikodimos hurried past and scrambling to his feet, with his hands shoved deep in the folds of his himation, begged Nikodimos to provide him with work.

Nikodimos was reluctant to take him on at first, convinced that this shabbily dressed beggar hunched before him, shrouded in rags and with filthy bare feet; this broken man with a broken nose, wizened face, stooped back and badly butchered hands would be incapable of carving stone. In fact, he thought it nigh impossible for a man without thumbs to do anything, let alone a thumbless sculptor be able to wield a mallet, carve stone.

Not so.

When he, finally, out of sheer necessity, offered Orestis a job, (due to desperate and ongoing need for stone-masons and sculptors required in building the Parthenon) he soon discovered that even

Plate III: The Parthenon frieze showing the young apprentice Menelaos and fellow stone-masons hard at work, finishing their carving of the enormous marble metopes.

without his thumbs Orestis had managed to carve the enormous metopes. Even more remarkable was that, unlike his wretched self, Orestis had finished carving all his metopes...on time, which Nikodimos thought truly amazing.

As this poignant recollection began to fade he spied Orestis' metope leaning against the stone wall and, not for the first time, cast a critical eye over the marble slab. The metope comprised two figures: a young maiden about to be ravaged by a grisly centaur, an ugly monster with a human torso and body of a horse. According to legend the metope depicted a scene from the wedding of Peirithous, King of the Lapiths, when a centaur got very drunk and tried to abduct a beautiful young Lapith girl. However, any further examination of the metope ended when Orestis, on cue, pushed open the door and hobbled in.

'Good morning, master!' boomed Orestis, smiling broadly, spitting through his missing teeth. 'It's such a beautiful morning!' he cried cheerfully while dragging his left leg through the marble dust. 'Apollo is shining on us once more!'

'*Kalimera*!' replied Nikodimos trying hard to gather some of the old man's optimism.

'*Ti kaneis*, Nikodimos?' asked the aged sculptor as he nodded at Nikodimos.

Whether Orestis had ever been in possession of any redeeming facial features was debatable; however, he had one outstanding characteristic that never diminished and that was his mischievous grin – even with his missing teeth. Orestis' grin never faded even when he happened to bash his hand with his mallet – which was quite often. A lifetime of misery should have reflected upon his countenance, but, strangely, it did not. His jet-black eyes encased in crinkly, leathery eyelids glowed with warmth and tenderness, a remarkable quality indeed for a man who had experienced such terrible cruelty in his lifetime.

'I hope you don't mind, master, but I wanted to give the metopes one last polish before being taken away.'

As Orestis spoke he stood winding long dusty rags around his butchered hands to compensate for the missing thumbs. 'I want *my* metopes to be perfect for Athena's shrine!'

'Please do,' replied Nikodimos, eying Orestis' metope in shards of bright sunlight filtering through the cracks in the roof, reflecting on to the pure white marble. He thought that the maiden's dress was a little *too* wrinkly for his liking and the facial expression of the centaur really rather wooden, not at all what it should be, although the young maiden's girlish figure and breasts were exquisitely carved.

'I must say, Orestis,' said Nikodimos, teasingly, 'you certainly have captured the young girl's charms.'

Orestis glanced up, beaming, from his bandaging although he did not say a word.

'Are you sure you didn't use a muse, Orestis?' asked Nikodimos quizzically, rubbing his scruffy beard, 'because the Lapith girl's breasts are so exquisitely carved that I find it impossible to think otherwise!'

Orestis stopped bandaging and his broad, almost impish smile filled the room. However, he still refrained from speaking.

Was Orestis shy?

'Master,' said Orestis as he slumped down on the floor in front of his metope, staring down at his stumpy hands as he so often did when holding something back, 'Perhaps...its...time...to...reveal... the...truth.'

'Please!' offered Nikodimos, impatiently, 'yes, please do!'

17

CHAPTER TWO

'Well...master....'

'Go on, Orestis I beg of you, please stop stammering!'

Orestis shook the sand from the beach off the tunic gathered in shreds around his crooked, spindly legs which were curled under him.

There was a pause, adding to the drama.

'Hurry up man!' Nikodimos shouted impatiently, 'What have you done?'

A loud whistle came whizzing through Orestis' missing teeth. Then he blurted out: 'Syrinx...I used Syrinx...as my muse!'

'You mean Syrinx, our very own slave girl?' Nikodimos flailed his arms wildly in the stuffy air, kicking his buskins in the marble dust gathering on the floor.

'I used Syrinx because she is what I imagined the Lapith girl looked like. She was perfect!'

'I don't believe you!' Nikodimos was peeling his snood from his head and tossing it in the air, watching it land on his unfinished statue. He could not stop shaking his head. 'I don't believe it. You used our slave girl?'

'Was I wrong to do so?' asked Orestis, obviously crestfallen as he sat polishing the metope for last time.

'Of course not!' exclaimed Nikodimos, 'I'm surprised that's all.'

Suddenly, Nikodimos knew he had the answer after dithering over the fate of Orestis' metopes for weeks, asking himself whether he had done right by allowing Orestis to carve the metopes in the first place, knowing that his stone-carving wasn't quite as good as it ought to be.

However, by using Syrinx as his muse he had done something extraordinary. Without realising it, Orestis had left a legacy in the stone. The Lapith girl was Syrinx. Nikodimos concluded that it mattered less about technical ability and more about this once brilliant bronze-sculptor's lasting contribution to Athena's sacred temple. Athena would agree, he was certain, as the goddess inspired those who suffered to triumph over their misfortune, and she would have wanted Orestis to flourish in an otherwise unforgiving world. He considered Orestis to be a hero among men, as he refused to allow his spirit to be broken by bloody tyrants.

Nikodimos found the horrors of war incomprehensible. What he found even more incredulous was that Athens' greatest statesman, Pericles, could have waged such horrid wars against his fellow man. He had asked himself many times how 'Old Squill Head' would have felt having his thumbs hacked off.

Nikodimos watched Orestis polishing the stone and he never failed to be overwhelmed by the man's desperate struggle to hold a mallet and chisel. To stand by and watch Orestis trying with all his might to complete one of life's simple tasks, either that of breaking a *koulouri* or drinking from a beaker, was excruciating.

This was all the more reason to engage in rhetoric. Study philosophy. Every young man in Athens loved a debate, strove to become enlightened. Sophocles, Aeschylus and Euripides came swiftly to mind. Once upon a time Nikodimos had aspired to be a great orator. He had also aspired to be a serious tragedian actor; however, stone-carving had won his heart and now all that remained of his theatrical pursuits were his dog-skin buskins minus a whole lot less fur.

The Agora was a favourite place to hear Athens' greatest philosophers debate issues pertaining to the modern world. However, it was the search for truth and the need to look beyond the material world that had captured Nikodimos' imagination. Socrates had become his mentor. The fact that he happened to be the ugliest man that he had ever set eyes on was of little consequence; his gruesome countenance – not dissimilar to the ugly centaur in the metope Orestis was polishing, with his sparse, receding hairline, pock-marked skin, snub-nose and bulging eyes – belied an astonishing truth as he also happened to be the wisest man in Athens.

The gods were a cynical lot thought Nikodimos. Tricksters, who delighted in playing games on mere mortals like himself, because that is exactly what had happened to Socrates who questioned the inner beauty of an ugly man's soul and/or the beautiful man without a soul. Meaning, appearances could be very deceiving. Nikodimos concluded that the Athenians were desperately in need of philosophers like Socrates, because without these highly enlightened men there would be no hope for the humble man who spent his day carving stone, while debating the meaning of truth.

—◌℞ ℼ◌—

Nikodimos left Orestis to finish his polishing. There was nothing more he could do except wait. What he needed was a change of scene and he decided to take a walk down to the harbour, get some air, no matter how foul it might be. He hurried out of his workshop, an enormous flat-roofed building constructed entirely of limestone, and headed in the direction of Athens' major port. After the ravages of war Piraeus was *the* place to be. He sped along the water-front past newly erected enormous sheds and vast warehouses used by Athens' Imperial Navy and local merchants. The port had become the centre of trade and commerce with Asia Minor and the Far East, and all three harbours virtually throbbed with Metics, non-resident aliens like himself, searching for reasonably priced rental accommodation;

Plate IV: This is the rather crudely sculptured metope carved by Orestis, the stone-carver who had badly butchered hands with no thumbs. It is remarkable, nonetheless, and much loved by all in the Quimby Gallery because the young girl's breasts are exquisitely carved.

Phoenicians, Corinthians, Egyptians and the Athenians coming from Athens to shop at the market stalls lining the quay mingled with the sailors.

The bustling streets echoed with the sounds of everyday life. Piraeus was an ideal location for self-employed artisans because of the extensive building programme going on within Athens itself. It meant that goods and services were in constant demand, and every aspiring craftsman in Hellas had set up shop, selling ceramics, pottery, textiles, leather-goods and foodstuffs. He sped past a metal-works and a tannery near the water's edge, en route to the small bakery that had just opened at the end of the quay. It was a blessing, as Nikodimos, being a bachelor, hadn't the slightest idea how to bake bread. The putrid smell emitting from the tannery was vile; however, the tantalising aroma of freshly baked *koulouri* offset the horrid smell rising from the foul waste gathering in the street.

Eventually his workshop faded from view. The local tradesmen referred to it as 'Nikodimos' Shabby Workshop', which it was, of course; although this location was not without good reason, as it was the only rental accommodation in the area with a small loft above the shop. Upon reflection he deemed the loft a complete waste. Most nights he fell asleep at his workbench. The fact that the property belonged to his cousin Alcibiades was a moot point because he was forever hoisting up the rent. This did nothing to relieve the tension between the two young men. Alcibiades was a wealthy aristocrat whereas he himself was a lowly Metic who lived off his meagre commissions.

He wasn't enjoying his walk and returned to the workshop. While en route, however, he was reminded: the main reason for choosing this less salubrious location over something more appropriate just happened to be braying loudly in a small paddock, the only one on the street. Even more importantly, the dusty, sparse, most miserable patch of grass was street-facing which was of vital importance to the beast screeching loudly, as Dora was extremely gregarious by nature and thoroughly enjoyed people-watching.

Dora always provoked a smile and rushing towards her, leaning over the fence he gave her a scratch between her ears. Dora, his nimble-witted donkey, could, if provoked, even venture a nibble or two of clothing if one happened to stand too close. Straw baskets were her favourite. In fact, Dora would eat absolutely anything, even the wooden bucket if left in the paddock.

Despite Dora's constant obsession for nibbling she was irresistible. The most loveable creature ever. There was, however, an altruistic side to Dora. She thrived on donkey-work; like all the beasts of burden who worked from dawn till dusk, carrying panniers of building material from the stone quarry to the Parthenon. Nikodimos praised these humble creatures because the donkeys had played a vital role in the building of the Parthenon.

Dora hadn't come with a name. And, as he had been lacking in female companionship at the time, a situation that hadn't improved in the least over the years, he had called her Pandora after the first woman on earth. Why she was 'the cause of all man's woes' was a mystery as he believed the opposite, that men were the cause of all her woes. What he associated with Pandora was hope and he needed great gobs of it. He also desperately needed a muse; however, neither had been forthcoming.

Athens was heating up. By midday it would be unbearably hot inside his workshop and by late afternoon the heat would be so intense, he would feel like he was being roasted alive in a charcoal oven. A sacrificial lamb sprang to mind. Nevertheless, no matter how miserable or hot this shabbiest of workshops had become, like all aspiring stone-carvers he had only one thing on his mind: completing his sculpture of Athena.

He said goodbye to Dora, then walked into his workshop, banging the door; then sped past enormous sections of the Parthenon frieze leaning against the stone wall. The frieze told the amazing story of the Pananthenaic procession. The Hellenes referred to this deeply religious festival celebrating Athena's birthday as the Great Pananthenaia. It took place every four years, during Hecatombaion (roughly August) and was the most sacred of all festivals. Therefore, the Parthenon's interior frieze represented a highly significant and much-loved part of the goddess's temple.

Although they were unaware of it at the time Nikodimos' team had actually participated in carving the most important section of the east frieze where a young child is seen presenting Athena's peplos to a high priest. This robe was woven by young priestesses. All the young girls in Athens dreamed of becoming a priestess. Nikodimos had glimpsed many of these nubile young creatures while en route to the Acropolis. One maiden in particular had captured his imagination, although sadly she had vanished for ever from his midst and she had never been seen again. She was divine.

Nikodimos surveyed the metopes that were being installed between triglyphs on the Parthenon's frieze. Many of the metopes comprised violent scenes. The battle between the Lapiths fighting the centaurs was a favourite. For the first time ever, Pheidias had incorporated immortals and mortals in his designs. Hence, gods became more like men and men, more god-like. Nikodimos agreed with this modern way of thinking as the gap between the mortals and the immortals diminished, meaning virtually everything in life was possible.

Meanwhile the cock had stopped crowing, reminding him of the passing of time. In a frenzy Nikodimos continued with his stone-carving, chiselling through the layers of stone. He sought perfection in everything he did, although he was never satisfied with his work, berating himself constantly for the lack of finesse he deemed necessary to be a great sculptor, failing to recognise his own immense talent. His teammates believed he was a truly gifted genius. Nonetheless, the self-flagellation continued...a 'hair-shirt' pending.

'Must all the gods rage against me?' Nikodimos roared aloud and his chisel flew. One Olympian deity after the other was offered up; he knew from past experience that offerings were a complete waste of time, nevertheless he called upon all the gods he could think of: 'Hermes...Iris...Dionysos...Hera...Apollo!'

The problem was it was neither a special occasion nor a religious festival, therefore a sacrifice was out of the question. And he had neither a bull ox, pigeon or goose nor a blazing hearth in which to send the smoke billowing forth towards Olympus, that hallowed place where immortals lounged on soft comfy cushions all day while sipping ambrosia, the nectar of the gods.

Perhaps an olive branch would do or a floral tribute of some kind. He had even resorted to calling upon Athena herself, which he did, to no avail, of course. However, there was no further time to partake in idol worship, ever fearful of committing piety or impiety. He understood the penalty for heresy was death so he kept his pious thoughts to himself.

He carried on with his carving like all good Hoplite warriors, relying on what little strength remained in his powerful arm, struggling against time to round out the stone, mould the soft contours of Athena's face, give her countenance quiet dignity and a calm repose, give her owl-eyes more depth, more brilliance. However, as a dazzling sun rose higher in the midday sky he was forced to accept defeat.

'I will never get it right!'

No matter how hard Nikodimos tried Athena's countenance evaded him; whether the length of her nose, the arch and shape of her brow, style of her hair and the depth of her eyes. He was incapable of carrying on, not forgetting for a moment, as he stood chipping away at the statue, that he had run out of time. Although he didn't realise exactly how much time he had run out of until his young Thracian slave banged open the door of the workshop and rushing in shouting.

'Master, Master!' cried Themis while spluttering and gasping for breath, as one would expect after running four and a half miles from Athens. 'Master! I have news from…The Great One!'

'Calm yourself,' said Nikodimos, wiping the sweat dripping from the end his nose, tearing impatiently at his sweat-soaked snood.

'Sit down,' he said, pointing to a small stool in the corner of the workshop, 'I will get you some water from the bucket.'

'Yes, Master,' puffed Themis collapsing in a heap on to the dusty floor. Like all slaves he had become accustomed to sitting on the floor, as that was where he belonged. He was a slave. He knew his place.

'Master!' Themis shouted at Nikodimos, who had disappeared into a small closet where the bucket was kept. 'I have an important message from the stone-man!'

'What is it?' Nikodimos rushed back with a half-filled bucket. 'What–'

Themis sat slumped at his master's feet, gulping water down his parched throat while sputtering:

'The stone-man...told me... (gulp) ...to tell you...that the wagon-master is on his way. The stone-masons are ready.... (sputter) ...to install... the statues...and the metopes...on...the side...I...can't... remember...which...side...now...I'm sorry...master...and he...told me to tell you that the ox-cart should be here at noon...!'

Themis sat dousing his head, his coarse woollen tunic – the typical garb worn by slaves – soaking the sheepskin trim. While this was the only garment that he wore, the elaborate tattoos on his neck made up for his lack of clothing.

'Noon...today?'

'Yes...Master!' Themis jumped up. He stood on one leg, rubbing his bleeding blistered right foot. 'That is what he said although I couldn't hear very well over the clanging and banging going on around me and...'

'Did you pass the ox-cart en route home?'

'No, Master, no!' cried the slave.

Nikodimos rushed towards the open door and peered out. There was no sign of the wagon-master or his enormous ox-cart.

Time was on his side.

'Listen to me, Themis. You must return to the Acropolis at once. All the metopes are being installed on the south-west side of the Parthenon this morning. Find the sculptors and tell them to return to the workshop at once. We will need all the man-power we can get to move the statues out of the workshop. Do you know which side of the Parthenon is west?'

'Yes, master,' replied his slave, puffed up, thrilled at the prospect of being sent on another urgent mission. 'West...is where...the...sun sets, Master.'

'That is correct, Themis. Menelaos should be there too. Tell him that he is to return to the workshop at once. Do you understand?'

'Yes, Master,' breathed his slave, shaking his head like a shaggy dog, water dripping from his long, stringy hair.

'Now, make haste!' Nikodimos shooed his young slave out the door. 'Be off with you!'

Nikodimos watched his slave race down the narrow winding street, disappear in the throng of passing trade, estimating the length of time it would take for his slave to return with his team of sculptors. What on earth was he going to do?

Pheidias' words, 'at your peril' came swiftly to mind.

Chapter Three
Menelaos, the Legend Begins

The young apprentice, completely unaware of the drama unfolding in his cousin's workshop that morning, had risen long before the cock began to crow, and leapt out of bed as if nothing on earth would keep him in it. So overly enthusiastic was he about his first day on the job, Menelaos set off, riding his donkey as fast as the beast would go, which wasn't very fast, towards the Acropolis. The master stonemasons were installing the last batch of metopes along the southeast corner of the Parthenon, and one of the metopes being installed was *his*. Menelaos had been praying for this day for months, never dreaming he would be allowed to witness such a spectacle. It had happened by chance, all because he had completed his carvings of the metope ahead of schedule. Nikodimos had granted him special permission to assist the masons on the day they were installing *his* metope.

He was thrilled to be part of the team responsible for installing the enormous metopes, as it was a great privilege for an aspiring young apprentice such as himself. What he was not thrilled about, however, was being told that he had to remain on the wobbly wooden

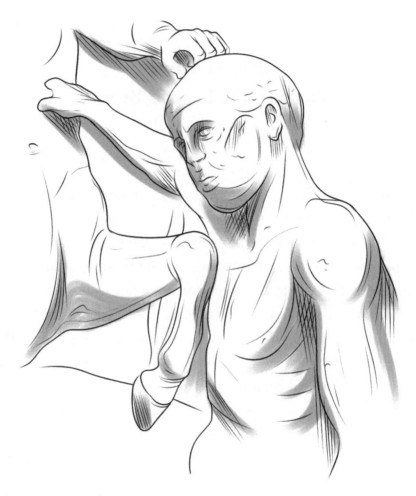

Plate V: A metope of a Lapith in mortal combat with a grisly centaur. The sculpture, carved by Menelaos, becomes one of his imaginary friends, and is also exactly the same size as Menelaos!

scaffolding until he finished work at sunset. The site-manager didn't know that Menelaos was terrified of heights or that every time he glanced down from the scaffolding he felt dizzy, as if falling over the edge. His fear was forgotten, however, when he heard:

'Hey! You there,' barked a big burly stone-mason standing directly in front of him, 'I need a claw chisel!'

'I need a riffler!' shot another, wiping sweat streaming from his brow.

'Boy Get me a mallet!' shouted a master stone-mason, looking down below, where his mallet lay, having slipped from his hand.

'I need more sand cloth.'

'Water...more water, boy!'

Menelaos rummaged through his tool basket. He was so nervous he didn't know what to do first. He could only do one thing at a time, he thought, while squeezing past an army of slaves crowding the scaffolding.

'Hurry up, boy,' shot a mason. 'I need more emery stone!'

'Menelaos, get me a chisel, please!'

On and on it went.

Menelaos thrust an emery stone into a stone-mason's enormous paw, pressed a chisel into the hand of another scowling mason, then carried on along the scaffolding delivering tools.

However, as the day wore on and Menelaos had been racing back and forth on the scaffolding since dawn without a respite, he started to feel woozy from the scorchingly hot sun beating down on the back of his neck, making his skin tight. Sun-blisters were bubbling up on his arms and his forehead. Even his nose was raw. Why hadn't he remembered to bring his *petasos*? By mid-morning he felt faint and if he passed out he might fall over the edge, which would be disastrous, he thought, while choking in a cloud of swirling marble dust.

CHAPTER THREE

That morning, the scaffolding was swarming with slaves, stone-carvers, master stone-masons and young apprentices like he himself. Menelaos recognised quite a few of the apprentices from other workshops but he did not speak to them. He was much too shy. What he did relish, however, was the thought of a drink of water. Unfortunately, there was only one water bucket and it just so happened to be dangling over the railing, swinging back and forth on a long rope. This meant that every time he needed a drink, which was often, he was forced to glance over the railing. But he was dying of thirst so he had no choice. Very gingerly, Menelaos made his way along the scaffolding towards the bucket. Just as he was leaning over the railing, at the same time his metope was being hoisted through the air. He was so excited he forgot both his fear and his thirst and watched awestruck as the enormous slab of marble was hoisted with lanyards and long ropes on to the scaffolding directly in front of him, then slowly wedged into place by the master stone-masons. Tears of joy streamed down his sunburned face as an army of masons wedged his metope of the Lapiths fighting the centaurs into place.

The site-manager in charge of installing the metopes stood next to Menelaos, barking orders at the slaves.

'Gently, do it gently!' he shouted, 'These are extremely precious metopes! The slabs are more valuable than gold!'

Instructions poured forth from the master stone-masons although it was so unbelievably noisy it was a wonder that anyone could hear.

Then a master stone-mason called Menelaos shouted,

'Hey! Boy! This metope could do with an extra polish.'

Menelaos squeezed past the slaves. He couldn't believe his luck. He couldn't tell the masons that he himself had carved the metope. They wouldn't believe him. Menelaos could hardly contain his excitement as he placed his tool basket down on the scaffolding and set to work. Stone-polishing had to be his favourite thing. He was always fascinated by the way in which polishing the dull lifeless stone brought the marble to life. However, as he sat polishing the metope he wondered how long it would take for his dream of becoming a great stone-carver like his cousin, Nikodimos, to come true, because at the rate he was going he would be a wizened old man, like Themis, before he actually achieved his goal.

Yet something was holding him back.

Menelaos had a problem. He suffered from debilitating shyness. At times, he had difficulty getting his words out; it was a problem even talking to his tutors who came to the villa every morning to give him lessons in reading, writing and reciting poetry. When asked to speak to his elders he became tongue-tied and his face glowed bright red. This he found most annoying. Even his ears glowed red and they looked like lumps of burning charcoal. Sometimes he stammered when he was spoken to, especially when he was in the company of his brother's friends. This annoyed Alcibiades terribly, and he teased him, which caused him to feel even worse.

Menelaos had become so inhibited that he preferred not to speak at all and hence he sought refuge in stone-carving. Besides, the noise was so unbelievably loud inside his cousin's stone-carving workshop, with the constant sound of hammering and chiselling and singing, no one could hear themselves think, let alone talk.

As Menelaos polished the stone he muttered quietly to himself. No one could possibly imagine that what he was actually doing was talking to his 'imaginary friends'. The marble figures had become real to him. He told his imaginary friends everything. He shared his inner-most secrets with the Lapith boys who had become part of his imaginary world, a world without debilitating shyness. When he spoke to his imaginary friends he never bumbled or stammered. He wasn't embarrassed and, more importantly, his ears didn't burn. What he loved most of all about this unique relationship with his marble friends was that they were never annoyed when he sang or when he made silly mistakes reciting lyric poems, which he did a lot of while carving the stone. His imaginary friends never complained when he played his lyre, which he loved most of all, no matter how often he struck a wrong note.

Menelaos forgot his shyness as he sat curled up on the scaffolding that morning polishing the stone, losing himself completely in the gentle rhythmic sound. He forgot the sadness that overwhelmed him at times, forgot to secretly pine for his older brother who had been killed at sea while fighting the Persians.

Playing his lyre also helped alleviate some of his shyness. He loved his lyre, which he had carved from an empty tortoise shell that he had found washed up on the beach at Piraeus. His lyre went everywhere with him. In fact, it was stashed inside his goat-skin bag in case he had time for a tune, although the young apprentice's happy thoughts were interrupted when he heard his name being called above the sound of the hammers and the chisels.

'Menelaos! Menelaos!'

'Turn around, Menelaos,' said a squealing voice from below. 'Look at me!'

Menelaos turned his head ever so slowly and looked down. Themis was standing on the ground, beneath the scaffolding, waving his arms wildly about in the air. He kept shouting, 'Menelaos! Come down!'

'No I will not come down!' shouted Menelaos, remaining his stubborn self.

'You must come down. Now!'

'Go away, Themis. Can't you see I am busy!' shouted Menelaos, as he leaned over the railing, feeling sick.

'Look at me!' Themis, becoming more and more agitated, stood yanking on the frayed edge of his frayed tunic.

'I get dizzy whenever I look down,' shouted Menelaos.

'Please listen to me!' the slave yelled loudly above the noise going on around him. 'Nikodimos told me to tell you that you are to return to the workshop at once. The wagon-master is on his way to the workshop to collect the stones.'

'Why can't the stone-masons help? They are much bigger than me. Anyway, can't you see I am busy!'

'Do you know where the stone-masons are?' asked Themis, while he stood on one foot, scratching bug bites on his bare leg.

'No, I do not,' boomed Menelaos, emphatically. 'Are the metopes going too?'

'How should I know,' replied Themis, his hands planted firmly on his narrow hips.

Themis could not see how exasperated Menelaos was from where he was standing on the ground because Menelaos was so high up.

'Fine, I'm coming down!' Menelaos shouted from the scaffolding and, grabbing his basket of tools and his goat-skin bag, very slowly edged his way towards the end of the scaffolding. The site-manager was so busy he failed to notice the boy slithering down the rope, obviously greatly relieved to be on firm ground.

Chapter Four
Nikodimos' Unfinished Masterpiece

After his slave's hasty departure Nikodimos found himself once again alone in his workshop, standing before his unfinished statue of Athena, without realising that he was glaring at the goddess with such malice and such open hostility that had the statue been made of wax it would have surely melted; dissolved on to the dusty floor, slithered out the door. This thought prompted the mythological figure of Daedalus to come to mind. The boy had flown too close to the sun and his wings had melted.

However, the myth vanished swiftly from his mind.

Nikodimos was at his wits end.

He was all too aware of his bad temper that flared at the least provocation and he suddenly turned his back on Athena, pacing back and forth in his worn leather buskins until the leather straps uncurled, the dust fell away. He could feel the anger rising deep from within and as he paced back and forth in the goo he became more and more enraged until he could stand it no more. He picked up a hammer on his workbench and hurled it at the statue with such force that it chipped the stone Then, he flung the chisels at his sculpture, no longer giving a damn.

He looked around. Thank god there was no one else in the workshop. His outburst went unnoticed. In fact, there wasn't a sound except the scuffing of Nikodimos' buskins trudging back and forth in a rising tide of marble dust.

Time passed. Then, suddenly, he stopped trudging, imagining he heard a loud grating sound. Who could it be? He called out. When no one answered he assumed it was the rats nesting in the junk and thought nothing more about it, and because he was quite frankly at his wits end, and could not proceed further without the aid of his men, he decided to take his mind off it by making himself useful. He began scrounging underneath his workbench for lengths of rope and sailcloth to cover the enormous statues, as the marbles needed to be protected from prying eyes while en route to the Parthenon.

When he found what he needed he set to work covering the metopes leaning against the stone wall; amongst the collection were his young cousin's metopes. He was pleased Menelaos had had an opportunity to watch one of his metopes being installed in the Parthenon frieze. Menelaos had an exceptional talent. He had also finished carving his metopes way ahead of schedule, which was not bad going for a young apprentice. Nikodimos took his time wrapping the metope, finding it impossible to believe that the figure of the Lapith boy was attached to the marble slab because Menelaos had carved the figure in such high-relief that the sculpture looked as though it might fall off the metope itself at any moment. Before he covered the marble slab completely he stood back, and took a closer look.

The carving was not only brilliant, it was exceptional.

The day Menelaos told Nikodimos that something extraordinary had happened to him while he had been carving the metopes came racing back. Apparently, as he carved the marble day after day he became more and more intrigued with the Lapiths, and by the time the stone figures gradually emerged from the marble, Menelaos had developed a real affinity with the Lapiths; sympathising with their plight, fighting in mortal combat with the grisly centaurs. This affinity with the Lapiths overwhelmed him to such an extent that it was almost as though, he himself, had become a Lapith boy.

Then, Menelaos revealed something even more extraordinary. He explained to Nikodimos that once he had finished carving the metopes he realised the young Lapith boys looked similar in size to himself, and to verify this, he lay down on the floor beside one of the figures when no one was looking – just to make sure he had got his calculation absolutely right – and discovered the figure was exactly the same size. This finding made him feel even closer to the Lapiths.

Menelaos was his protégé, no doubt about it, thought Nikodimos proudly, as he finished wrapping his cousin's precious carving, tucking the sackcloth in gently around the outer edges of the stone, making sure that the metope was safe and secure for transport in the ox-cart.

Next to Menelaos' metope was the larger-than-life marble statue of Hermes – the envoy of the gods – standing on a large round plinth. He had carved the statue himself, although he didn't want to be reminded and looked away, always critical of his work; convinced that his carving wasn't as good as it ought to be. The sculptors who had assisted him thought Hermes was a masterpiece, believing Nikodimos had captured Hermes' youthfulness and charm to perfection. Hermes wore a *petosas*, a large, broad-brimmed travelling hat, a short cloak and winged sandals, all necessary for a quick flight. For added drama he held a winged staff, wrought in metal, entwined with two serpents. Nikodimos harboured extreme disdain for his work, convinced his statue looked more like a wayward Athenian youth than an immortal god.

'Where the devil are my men?' blared the disgruntled sculptor while scrounging underneath his workbench for more sailcloth to cover Poseidon.

Poseidon was colossal. A sculptural force of epic proportions. When installed in the gable-end of the Parthenon he would, like Athena, represent one of two main figures in the west pediment. Poseidon had been Athena's arch-rival in their competition for Athens and had met her on the Acropolis where they both laid claim to the land. Poseidon was the brother of Zeus, who became supreme ruler of the sea. Nikodimos related to Poseidon because he was a tempestuous god, subject to sudden and violent rages, just like himself.

Poseidon was a masterpiece that unfortunately had been carved by his cousin, Alcibiades, his arch-rival in the art of stone-carving. He had also finished the statue weeks ahead of schedule, which Nikodimos found, frankly, irritating.

Poseidon looked formidable with his enormous head thrust out in a determined fashion, mass of leonine curls, bulging eyes, square jaw, noble forehead, magnificent torso and a god-like stance while clutching a metal trident (his symbol) in his hand, as though he had proclaimed Athens his own.

The next statue needing covering was Iris who stood in the corner of the workshop, apart from the rest. The statue provoked a smile; after all, she was one of his favourite goddesses. Thinking back, he was truly amazed how quickly he had carved the statue. For once, stone-carving had come easy to him. Perhaps it was because he simply adored rainbows and rainbows were her symbol. Whenever he caught sight of a rainbow after a violent thunderstorm, glimpsed vibrant colours of red, orange, yellow, green, blue, indigo and violet arched across the heavens, he never failed to be awestruck by Iris' dexterity with a paintbrush. He believed that all the colours he had ever seen on earth were reflected in the rainbow. Rainbows had to be one of the wonders of the natural world.

There was a certain vitality in his statue of Iris, an *élan vital* that radiated from within the stone itself, reminding him, once again, of his deep relationship with stone, with the earth. He felt energy coming from within the marble. Perhaps he was mad, but it was as though he had brought Iris to life.

According to Homer Iris was 'wind-footed'. The poet's words had had a profound effect on his stone-carving and he had modelled the statue of Iris with her chiton blowing against her thigh, 'pressed against her body, rippling in a myriad of tiny folds', against the firm outline of her perfect breasts. The Hellenes believed Iris had an amorous side. He liked to believe that *his* Iris inspired those who gazed upon her to feel amorous too. Of course, this was expected was it not, from a hapless tragedian actor like himself with a fiercely romantic heart? A mere mortal who absolutely adored goddesses, especially those made of flesh, unlike his rendition of Athena Parthenos standing next to Iris, listing sideways. The gormless statue looked as though it was about to topple over at any moment but, as he grabbed hold of the headless statue, tried to right it, the sailcloth bunched at the side of the statue slid away to reveal…

'Syrinx!' cried Nikodimos, nearly jumping out of his buskins.

'Nikodimos!' Syrinx screamed from under the sailcloth. 'Master!'

'By Zeus, Syrinx, you frightened the very life out of me!'

'Forgive me, master!' Syrinx cried, crouching on the floor, with her slender arms flung tightly around the neck of her statue of Selene's horse.

'I'm so sorry. I didn't mean to frighten you,' breathed Syrinx with her eyes cast down in slave-girl fashion.

'What on earth are you doing...hiding under the sailcloth?'

'I heard Themis telling you that the wagon-master is coming.'

'Yes, that is correct.' Nikodimos sounded deflated.

Syrinx sat quietly patting the head of the horse as though the statue were a live stallion and not made of stone at all.

'Yes, Syrinx,' said Nikodimos. 'The wagon-master will be coming any minute now to collect the marbles.'

Syrinx' small voice grew tight. 'I wanted to give *my* horse...because *he* is *my* horse...one last polish...before *he's* taken away!'

Nikodimos could hear the emotion in Syrinx' voice. Words failed him. It was obvious his slave had developed a great affection for the stone statue of Selene's horse.

Although, what he found even more astonishing was that his young slave, a mere wisp of a girl with long slender arms and small delicate hands, had carved the enormous statue in the first place, and what a truly brilliant rendition of Selene's horse it was. The horse looked utterly exhausted, its energy spent after pulling the moon goddess's golden chariot across the night sky. Perhaps Syrinx, in her naivety, had imparted some of the terrible sadness she had experienced in her own tragic life into the lifeblood of the stone. The horse was so true-to-life he could not believe his eyes. It was the first time that he had taken a really close look at the carving. How could he have been so selfish.

This is the section that drops off

Plate VI: The horse's head was originally carved by Syrinx, a young Athenian slave girl in the fifth century BC. In the nineteenth century Selene, the moon goddess's horse, becomes the most beloved marble sculpture of all in the Quimby Gallery. However, it shatters and the nose mysteriously drops off, just like Lord Quimby's nose.

Worldwide dismay follows when, much to the horror of the British public, it is revealed that the statue is a fake!

'Master...please...will...you...help...me?' Syrinx begged as she held out a chisel in her small hand. 'Please, I want to leave my mark in the stone, just like all the other stone-carvers do. I have been trying to teach myself how to write the alphabet; however, there so many letters I can't remember them all, so I can't spell my name yet!'

'Of course, I will help you, Syrinx, I would be delighted,' said Nikodimos taking the chisel in his right hand. 'Would you like me to carve your name on the bottom of the statue or somewhere else?'

His slave's deep-set, dark eyes, the colour of jet, grew darker. 'I would like to have two of my favourite letters carved inside the horse's nostrils,' said Syrinx, 'because I don't want anyone to know my name. Please, master, could you carve the letter α for alpha and an Ω for omega. I like the meaning of these letters, don't you, Master?' Then she laughed, 'They are the only two I remember!'

As Nikodimos carved the stone he glanced down at his slave's small delicate hands flung around the neck of Selene's horse, and not for the first time was he struck by the size and shape of her hands. He decided that one day he was going to carve Syrinx' hands, believing that her hands were worthy of being carved in stone because Syrinx was not only a truly remarkable human being, she was also a brilliant sculptor.

—◁ ▷—

Syrinx didn't talk very much, hardly a word. She kept her thoughts to herself. Her deep-set, dark eyes, to the point of being black, revealed nothing to the outside world, nothing at all.

To her master, Syrinx remained an enigma from that very first day, when, disguised as a young slave boy, she had come to work for him in his workshop, as an errand-boy, helping out with the chores, sharpening tools for the master stone-masons and the stone-carvers or fetching water from the well. It was a mystery how she had managed to maintain her disguise for so long after becoming an apprentice, yet, she had. By the time her true identity had been revealed, however, that the slave boy was, in fact, a slave girl, she was accepted by her fellow workers and had been treated as an equal ever since.

Although the slave had been in desperate need of a name, as she could no longer be called 'boy' or recall her birth name. Nikodimos had given Syrinx her name not only because she was extremely slender, like the reeds, but, also, because of the extraordinary circumstances in which he had found her hiding in the long reeds, near the water's edge down by the River Ilissos. He had come upon Syrinx by accident, one hot summer's day while bathing in the river, and was reminded of the ancient myth about a nymph, beloved by Pan, who had run away, fled down to the water's edge and sought solace from the river nymphs, as his slave had done. So Syrinx it was.

Syrinx' secret identity remained locked away within the confines of Nikodimos' workshop. To the outside world she was 'boy'. The local merchants were unaware that the stone-carving shop at the end of the street had a female apprentice within its thick limestone walls, and that the only sculptress in Athens had carved the head of Selene's horse, the statue that was about to be installed in the Parthenon that very afternoon. The Athenians would be horrified if they knew a slave-girl had carved the stone. A slave, perhaps, but a girl? A barbarian? Never. It was absolutely forbidden.

Nikodimos had placed his reputation on the line when he agreed to teach Syrinx how to become a sculptress, although something unexpected had happened along the way, and it had nothing whatsoever to do with stone-carving.

Rivulets of perspiration trickled down her back, soaked through the coarse wool of her tunic, and it had nothing to do with the intensity of the heat. Her hand shook as she glimpsed Nikodimos from afar as she sat curled up beside her statue, polishing the stone for the last time. All she had to do was *think* about her master and her heart raced.

Syrinx was a natural born slave. She had been born into slavery and she had never known anything other than slavery all her young life. This wasn't unusual for a large percentage of the population were slaves, Thracian or Skythian slaves, many of whom were skilled craftsmen, like herself. There was one overriding difference between Syrinx and other slaves, however, and this could very well be her undoing. She didn't think like a slave. Slave girls were thought of as nothing more than low-life slatterns and Syrinx refused to think of herself in that way.

Once upon a time she had been owned by a noble Athenian family. However, at the age of six, after her mother and father had been murdered by Persians, she was bought by a famous Athenian general as a house slave for his wife. For the next five years she learned to sew and to weave. Then one day her innocence was taken from her by force, and she learned that the term 'house slave' had an altogether different connotation, and no longer meant sweeping the kitchen floor, or weaving cloth. Over the next several years life for Syrinx became intolerable as she was sexually abused, raped by the general, whose wife, like all obedient Hellas wives, turned a blind eye, and failed to acknowledge her husband's licentious behaviour towards women.

But Syrinx never lost faith in herself, and one day she ran away. She was found hiding in the stable and after a severe lashing by her master, was left to die. Somehow she managed to flee, but not before stealing the brute's donkey, as the poor beast had also been thrashed to near death.

After years of torture she had finally escaped her life of hell, rescued by a handsome stone-carver who discovered her asleep in the long reeds. Nikodimos had become many things to Syrinx. Saviour. Mentor. Teacher. Could she help it, now that she was full-grown, albeit a slave girl, that she dreamed of being with the one who had taught her the art of stone-carving?

Syrinx could not take her eyes off him.

Nikodimos looked like a god. Exactly how she imagined Apollo or Dionysos. His athletic body was honed to perfection. There was a grace and elegance in every movement that quite simply took her breath away. She was convinced he was related to the gods as he seemed to have a life-force deep within that came directly from the gods themselves and it was reflected in every fibre of his being. While Syrinx didn't know much about divinity, there was something in the way he moved, a rhythm in every movement, in his shoulders, his arms, his thighs, in the tautness of his belly, and the positioning of his limbs as his buskins gripped the floor, that could only be described as divine.

Syrinx was haunted by all these nuances as she snuggled up to her statue, while Nikodimos stood right next to her, chiselling the stone. She was so close to him that she could smell the earthy musk of his skin. Stone-carving was one passion, and Nikodimos had become the other. Being allowed to carve the horse's head had been pure luck, thought Syrinx to herself, as she polished the horse's mane one last time. Syrinx loved horses and donkeys and puppy dogs. Animals never abused her or caused her harm. They didn't rape her just for the fun of it. So, as you can well imagine, dear reader, carving the statue of Selene's horse was the absolute best thing that had *ever* happened to her.

When she chiselled the stone she forgot all those horrid memories from the past. The art of stone-carving had captured her imagination and her heart. One day the citizens of the world would discover that the best-loved marble of all – the statue of Selene's horse – had, in fact, been carved by a slave girl. Syrinx was leaving her mark, not only in the stone, but, also, in the history of the world.

Chapter Five
The Rent Collector

As the day wore on and his men failed to appear, Homer's words blasted out the door of Nikodimos' shabby workshop, and caught passers-by unaware outside in the street: 'below to Hades' realm... where the dead live on ..without their wits...as disembodied ghosts'.

'Indeed!' the sculptor boomed while scowling at his statue. He stared at his rapidly expanding collection of corpses, battered and broken statues, hapless phantoms without an ear, an eye, a nose, a chin that Themis needed to take to the dump. Statues reminiscent of disillusioned thespians – tragedian actors like his former self, those he had encountered loitering by the Odeion theatre without a part to play – rather than statues of gods and goddesses.

The rant continued and so did the sweat streaming from the end of his nose – it dribbled down his face, soaking his silk snood, and mixing with the marble dust on his skin to create an unsightly thick goo – a dirty mud daub – that caked on his handsome face.

It was obvious from the way he tugged angrily on his snood, scowled at the sculptural mass, that this nimble-witted sculptor was not a happy man. How could he be, when his failings as a master stone-carver were reflected in the blank expression of Athena's face? Nikodimos did not need reminding that *his* Athena had yet to emerge from the cold lifeless block of stone.

He had to admit defeat.

He could not continue without a muse. Those malevolent gods had won. He had been rendered incapable of giving his statue of Athena the qualities he imagined worthy of her. Athena was a goddess with grace, dignity and charm and his statue had none of these qualities.

'Athena was the daughter of Zeus. She had been endowed with many creative powers. Well. Damn it, Athena! Why can't you endow this poor wretched stone-carver with a few creative powers?'

He cried aloud while staring grimly at a face carved in rictus. Athena was one of his favourite goddesses. She had captured his imagination at a very young age. He worshipped her on feast days and religious holidays. He bought garlands of flowers from the flower sellers, the *stephanoi*, and offered them to her at her shrine. His singular devotion to Athena stemmed from her being the goddess of the humble artisans, craftsmen, weavers, spinners and textile makers. However, he was beginning to doubt Athena, as she had failed one of her most loyal subjects by omitting the art of stone-carving in her list of goddess-manships.

Athena refused to come to his aid when he needed her most and as teeming rain poured down outside and Zeus' thunderbolts tore the heavens apart, he was completely overwhelmed by his failings as a sculptor.

There was only one thing left to do, however, and that was to soldier on. Although fighting the bloody Spartans or the Persians seemed preferable, because the battle raging within him had already been lost.

A family of rats were scurrying beneath his feet, leaving faint tracks in the marble dust. He loathed the vile pests nesting in an unsightly and rapidly expanding accumulation of junk. A rather sad and sorrowful collection of busts with broken noses and shattered faces, many with wayward glances and hastily lopped-off ears, statues he couldn't possibly part with after so many years. Enormous piles of cracked and broken marble plinths deemed useless to all but himself. Sadly, three previous failed attempts of Athena's head, that never ceased to remind him of his own abject failings as a sculptor; a motley collection of tools used for cutting and working the stone; buckets, used for grouting and masonry work, a vast assortment of wedges, wooden buckets containing pitch and mortar, solidified and no longer useable. However, there was one precious object in this war-torn collection, resembling Marathon after the battle, and the said object was his actor's mask, all that remained of his career as a tragic actor, other than his buskins, of course. How befitting, he thought to his weary self, and spotting his lunch on his workbench. A large beaker, a *koulouri* and a small plate of honey cakes – bought at dawn, from the bakery – were hiding in dust. It was almost noon. And as there was still no sign of his men, and he was greatly in need of sustenance, he sat down on a small wooden stool and poured a much needed *kafeneion* of wine from the goat-skin bag.

No sooner had he sat down, when Dora stuck her shaggy head through the open window in the limestone wall. How could he possibly refuse Dora? As they shared his lunch, his thoughts drifted back over the years, before he had moved to Athens.

Once upon a time he had lived in Miletos, a thriving Ionian city on the coast overlooking the Aegean Sea. This was before he was forced to leave following the tragic death of his father, Demetrius

Poliorcetes, a distinguished Ionian general who had been killed in battle fighting the blood-thirsty Persians. He could not remember his mother, who died from the plague when he was a small boy. After his father's tragic death his uncle, a widower who lived in Athens, took Nikodimos into his care. This arrangement proved successful. He absolutely adored his uncle, and his young cousin Menelaos. However, his relationship with Alcibiades had been difficult right from the start, as the two boys were the same age and so competed against each other in everything they did, be it swimming, wrestling, running, lessons, even knucklebones. The competition continued long after Nikodimos had moved out of the villa in Athens.

Alcibiades never let him forget that he was a lowly Metic and not a true Athenian like himself. This really niggled Nikodimos but what he found even more niggling was that to his eternal dismay, he would never be allowed to become a citizen of Athens, no matter what, all because he had not been born in Athens.

While Dora nicked Nikodimos' honey cakes, his thoughts returned to Alcibiades who only visited the workshop to collect the rent. Perhaps he deliberately avoided the place, which was completely understandable, he thought, with his buskins knee-deep in chipped marble and dust.

Alcibiades had become Pheidias' protégé, as, not only was he a brilliant master stone-carver, he was also Pheidias' golden-haired boy, which gave him a god-like status in the community. Nikodimos' humble station in life paled in comparison, hence, Alcibiades treated him abominably, worse than his slaves. Alcibiades owned many slaves, whereas Nikodimos owned only two – Themis and Syrinx. He had granted Syrinx her freedom, although she said that she didn't know what to do with it. He had no desire to own slaves, although it was de rigueur in Athenian society.

Alcibiades had been blessed at birth. He had inherited wealth, whereas Nikodimos remained penniless, especially after paying his cousin extortionate rent money. His cousin owned several small estates, with citrus groves, olive groves and huge vineyards in Attica and beyond. He also had the luxury of indulging in every kind of hedonistic pleasure befitting an Athenian nobleman, be it gambling, carousing or idling away his days at the baths or private clubs. Whether he ever discussed politics, religion, the arts or affairs of state was questionable, as Nikodimos very much doubted Alcibiades' rhetoric worthy of debate.

On numerous occasions he had encountered Alcibiades staggering home at dawn, after an all-night orgy, as he had been on his way to work. Was he jealous of Alcibiades? He was forced to work for a living, whereas Alcibiades was not, even though he was a master stone-carver and Pheidias was desperate for sculptors. Alcibiades was, without doubt, the most singularly handsome, eligible young nobleman in Athens, and captured everyone's heart. He was so charming, intelligent and quick-witted that people found him irresistible. Especially the ladies; the most beautiful young women in Athens fell at his feet, women he called upon at the drop of a drachma, whereas Nikodimos' wretched self had not had the pleasure of female companionship for so long, he doubted he would know how to behave if he were to encounter a member of the opposite sex. Alcibiades' loose, licentious lifestyle had no appeal whatsoever. But what really irked him most was that his cousin had only received one commission in the last five years, whereas he had been given twelve commissions and had worked himself to near exhaustion in the attempt to finish his carvings. His cousin made him feel like an ass.

He didn't need to be reminded, as Alcibiades threw open the door and strode into the workshop with such aplomb it was as though a god had descended from Olympus.

Was it any wonder he imagined himself to be a descendant of Zeus? Most Athenian nobles also believed this was true.

'Niko! Make haste!' the god said, as he paraded through the marble dust in his soft-soled sandals, trailing his fine white woollen cloak within an inch of the floor, resembling a famous eponymous hero returning from war. He had a monkey on his shoulder, while a retinue of young slave boys followed close behind with puppy dogs in tow. The puppies were yelping and scrambling about, creating a terrible fuss, racing around the workshop, peeing on every stone with which they came in contact.

'I have been to see Pheidias. The masons are ready to install the metopes and the rest of the statues in the gable-ends of the Parthenon.' Looking around he spat, 'Where is your statue of Athena?'

It was difficult to imagine that the weary stone-carver dripping in sweat and caked in marble dust and Alcibiades were related.

'The stone-masons are ready to install my statue of Poseidon this morning. Athena is next!'

Alcibiades spoke with such enmity, warring Spartans could not have sounded more hostile. Although the warring faction seemed more preoccupied with his pet monkey as it scrambled up his arm, leapt on to his head and played with his long curly hair.

'We are waiting!' Alcibiades tilted his magnificent head as he spoke to accentuate his magnificent profile, drawing attention to himself.

'Where is your statue of Athena, Niko, as it doesn't appear to be here in the workshop?'

'Athena is ready!' Nikodimos replied flatly, lying, not for the first time that morning.

'Really,' Alcibiades exclaimed, wiping marble dust from his dark blue eyes smudged with black shadows, hinting at the previous night's escapade, gambling the night away at his favourite club.

'Where is *your* masterpiece?' Alcibiades asked, pointing in the direction of the shed. 'Keeping Athena well hidden are you, Niko?'

'Sarcasm is so unbecoming,' Nikodimos shot back, grinding down hard on his back teeth, and despairing, accustomed to his cousin's constant ridicule.

'Pheidias has invited us to dine with him at his club tonight. You will come, won't you?'

'I think not,' said Nikodimos, knowing that it didn't really matter whether he attended or not.

Alcibiades didn't wait for a response. He couldn't have cared less and pranced around the workshop until stopping directly in front of the heavily draped statue of Athena. When he got close enough he pulled the cloth from the statue, snickering under his breath: 'Good god, Niko! With those lips Athena looks more like a whore lingering near the docks than a goddess!'

Nikodimos stomped his buskins in the dust. 'Can't you see I have yet to finish the statue, Alcibiades!'

'An idiot can see that, Niko!' Might I also add that a full-lipped pout is a most unenviable characteristic for a goddess, especially a virgin one, would you not agree?'

'How dare you mock my work!' Nikodimos stood towering over the magnificent head of Alcibiades, hissing in his face. 'Come here.

Look at your masterpiece! Why, I think it resembles Dionysos more than Poseidon. Furthermore, may I remind you Athena represents a young woman, so why not give her full, sensuous lips? She had brilliant flashing eyes too...but—'

Alcibiades interrupted: 'How do you know Athena had brilliant flashing eyes? How do you know what she looked like?' Alcibiades suddenly turned his head, ignoring his puppy as it pooed at the base of Nikodimos' unfinished masterpiece.

'Get that vile dog out of here!' Nikodimos raged, glancing down at his badly worn leather buskins about to fall off his feet. 'I'm in desperate need of new buskins. In fact, a bit of dog skin would not go amiss!'

Alcibiades clapped his hands twice and his slave rushed forward and, gathering the squealing puppy in his arms, hastened out the door.

'Have you failed to remember Homer's *Odyssey*?' asked Nikodimos. 'I expect so, since you have so little time to read. Is it whoring, drinking or gambling, Alcibiades, that occupies your leisure?'

'Insults are so lower-class!' Athens' boy beautiful snapped as he waded through chipped marble, stroking the long skinny tail of his pet monkey.

'Allow me to refresh your memory,' offered Nikodimos. 'According to Homer, Athena had exceedingly clear, bright eyes.'

'Her eyes don't look very bright to me.' Alcibiades said, as he ran his hand over the statue of Athena, and peered into her eyes. 'In fact, she looks dead. Her eyes look cold, dull, uninteresting. Not at all what a finished masterpiece should be, Niko.'

There was no response from Nikodimos.

'The wagon-master will be here any minute to collect your statues from this utterly disgusting place and nothing is ready. Whatever will I tell Pheidias?' Alcibiades asked, smirking.

While the cousins hurled insults at each other, Alcibiades gathered up his cloak, and strode further into the workshop. Something had caught his eye. He waved his arm.

'Why not send *this* statue, Niko?' Alcibiades asked, examining yet another statue of Athena with lopped arms, minus her head. 'Is this your first attempt or your fifth?'

A heavy iron bar lay in the dust next to the statue. Fratricidal thoughts sprang to mind. Death was the penalty for killing one's brother. Did it apply to killing one's cousin? Nikodimos debated, as he stood within an inch of the crime scene, marble dust blurring his vision. He had a powerful arm. He was capable of murder. He could kill Alcibiades in one blow. However, the iron bar remained buried in the dust.

'Perhaps you need a muse. Is she hiding, Niko?' Alcibiades inquired, waving his small, aristocratic hands that had not lifted a hammer or a chisel in months – since he had completed the statue of Poseidon – impatiently in the air, and sporting the largest gold signet ring imaginable. 'I'm sure I can find you a muse, Niko!'

'Don't bother.'

'Whatever is the matter, Niko? Have you no time to entertain a few local virgins in your back shed?'

Nikodimos could not find his voice.

'Not to worry. Leave it with me. I'll ask around at the club, Niko. I'm sure I can find you a whore or two who would be suitable.'

'A muse is a luxury I can ill afford,' said Nikodimos glaring at his cousin. 'I do not have the time to stroll the market in search of a muse. Furthermore, I doubt there is a woman worthy of the job. I have neither money nor time to invest in one.'

'You don't have to get so huffy!'

Nikodimos brushed the dust from his bare shoulders. 'I am very busy. I barely have time to think!'

'Well, I think Athena looks positively hideous!' Alcibiades shook his head, disgusted. 'That is all I have to say,' he said, as he strode towards the door with his aquiline nose held high. His departure was thwarted when suddenly the god turned, hovered on the threshold and while bending down, and shaking the dust from his soft-soled sandals, his beautiful mouth etched in superciliousness, said, 'I know exactly what you should do with your statues...all of them. Scrap them! Start again. You should smash Athena to bits, Nikodimos.

'We desperately need rubble to bulk up the walls; as you know the stone makes excellent building material. We could use your statues as filler for the new road. You know, the one I'm building through the neighbour's olive groves, as the bastard never pays his rent on time. That reminds me. What about the rent?'

'Go to Hades!' Nikodimos spat from the very depth of his buskins. 'Get out!'

Alcibiades took his leave.

Nikodimos watched the most beautiful boy in Athens walk out the door. He was shattered. He had never been more aware of his failings, both as a man and as a stone-carver, in his entire life.

There was only one thing left to do.

The need to destroy the very thing that he had created took hold. He had killed many a man on the battlefield so this would not be a problem. He grabbed hold of a large wooden mallet sitting on his workbench and clutching it in his fist strode towards his unfinished masterpiece, glaring at the statue as though he were about to commit murder. He raised his powerful arm and in one fateful blow Athena's head went flying across the workshop, hitting the stone wall, smashing the marble into a thousand pieces, until nothing was left but a faint stirring of dust. He flung his mallet on the floor. He had destroyed his creation. He was a ruined man, albeit a much calmer man on the inside. So why was he shaking uncontrollably on the outside?

But something extraordinary was about to happen...

Suddenly Dora started up. The donkey kept on screeching in her paddock until Nikodimos rushed out of his workshop to see what the fuss was all about.

Chapter Six
The Muse

'Pandora!' He reverted back to her full name when cross with her. 'Pandora, whatever is the matter!'

Nikodimos ran towards the paddock only to find an elegant young woman leaning over the fence pulling bunches of headless flower stems out of Dora's clenched jaws.

'Is *this* your donkey?' she asked, with her hands full of stems.

'Why...y...e...s!' replied Nikodimos shyly. 'Dora is mine.'

'Well, your donkey is a very naughty donkey indeed!' exclaimed the young woman close to tears. 'Not only has Pandora munched her way through my basket, she has devoured *all* of my freshly cut violets...violets I bought from the market!'

Nikodimos didn't know what to say and just stood there, dumbstruck, like a blasted fool.

'Just look what Pandora has done!' The young woman was trying to rescue what little there was left of her flowers dangling from Dora's drooling mouth.

Meanwhile Nikodimos had leapt over the fence into the paddock, and began gathering the stems that, sadly, were no longer in possession of their tiny blooms.

When Nikodimos had found his voice he asked, 'How on earth did this happen?'

'Well, I'll tell you,' huffed the girl, hotly. 'Your donkey started braying as I was walking past and I felt the need to comfort her. She was making such a terrible noise!'

As the young woman related what happened she kept her hands firmly planted on her hips, accentuating the lovely curvature of her waist.

'She is such a pretty donkey...and...so adorable that I couldn't resist stopping to comfort her; but when I leaned over the fence she gobbled up all my flowers.'

'Goodness gracious me!'

'Now look what your Pandora has done. The flowers were for my bedridden auntie.'

'I am truly sorry,' said Nikodimos, apologising profusely, thinking that he had never felt so awful in his life. 'I would be only too happy to—'

The young woman interrupted him again.

'Not only has your donkey eaten all of my precious violets...she has also destroyed my new basket that I bought from the market this morning!'

Nikodimos wasn't listening. He could not take his eyes off the young woman standing before him. And as he glimpsed beads of perspiration gathering on her upper lip he realised it was the lip of a goddess. Her hair was the hair of a goddess...

The heat was intense; however, he did not feel a thing.

'I am soooo sorry!' Nikodimos begged forgiveness from the goddess. Aphrodite paled in comparison and the immortal goddess slipped from his mind. He could not believe that the beautiful priestess he had glimpsed so long ago, near the entrance gates of the Parthenon, had come back into his life and it was all because of Dora. He decided right there and then to have his donkey instated as a god.

This was the young priestess who attended the shrine of Athena and now, here she was standing before him She was without doubt the most heavenly creature that he had ever set eyes on, from the rich, golden coppery colour of her luxuriant hair to the folds of her peplos fastened at the shoulders with elegant amber clasps. As she moved her cloak fell open revealing ravishing long slender legs and small delicate feet, elegantly clad in neat sandals adorned with precious stones.

Apologies poured forth. 'I am so very sorry,' was all he seemed capable of saying. 'Please, allow me to compensate you for the loss of your flowers and your basket.' He was suddenly aware of the goo on his face.

The goddess looked the other way. She smoothed the folds of her long white tunic edged in bright cerulean blue.

The tease!

'Dora has been a very bad girl. You must understand that Dora loves flowers, and violets are her favourite. Dora would nibble her way through almost anything given half a chance. She has even eaten my tunic off the clothesline.'

The thought of Dora eating his tunic brought a faint smile to the priestess's face, that became even more radiant in the bright sunshine. Flashing her brilliant eyes at him, she presented him with the most dazzling smile ever.

'Would Dora eat my hat?'

'Probably.'

'Or my cloak, if I allowed her to get close to me?'

'Yes, I believe she would,' replied Nikodimos, suppressing a smile, enjoying the banter.

He leaned a little closer to his muse. He caught the exotic fragrance lingering on her fair skin, her luxuriant hair, something from the East, an elixir of love perhaps?

'Please, do me the honour of telling me your name,' Nikodimos asked while offering his hand.

'Kallisti.'

Nikodimos thought her name could not have been more fitting as it meant 'the most beautiful' and Kallisti had to be the very embodiment of beauty.

'Pray tell, what is your name?'

'Nikodimos.'

Kallisti looking somewhat bemused asked, 'Nikodimos, what is that thick goo all over your face?'

Chapter Seven
Alpha and Omega
(The Beginning and the End of All Things)

The season of gathering the olives had passed. The night of the winter solstice had arrived once more. From where he stood, high up on the scaffolding, on the west side of the Parthenon, that night Nikodimos glimpsed a faint dusting of snow on the distant hill of Lykabetos and Mount Pentelicus beyond, where he had cut and quarried his very first stone. The stone-cutters had finally finished quarrying the enormous blocks of stone for the Parthenon. Athena's shrine was complete.

It could be said that a truly remarkable metamorphosis had taken place. All the forces that had plagued him for months had finally come together, magically working themselves out in the stone. Reflecting back, his life improved dramatically from the day he had met and fallen hopelessly in love with Kallisti who had finally agreed, after much coaxing and numerous bunches of violets, to become his muse, and, in so doing, she had provided him with the inspiration he so badly needed to complete the statue of Athena Parthenos.

However, it wasn't only his deep love for Kallisti that had inspired his art. It was Kallisti herself, her inner, ethereal beauty that came deep from within that ignited his senses and brought a wild sensuous abandon to his art. As he carved his masterpiece, his hand quivered with some unexplained exalted force, enabling him to complete the intricate details of Athena's face: the defining arch of her brow, the neat plaiting of her hair, bringing a divine remoteness to her gaze. And as he polished the stone for the last time he was overwhelmed by the extraordinary luminosity that radiated from within the marble, especially her eyes (Homer would have approved) and the sensuous outline of her mouth, a full-lipped pout, transforming the cold lifeless stone into warm living flesh like his muse, Kallisti.

Finally, all the statues were in situ. Looking back, he couldn't believe his good fortune. The morning that the marbles were to be collected, the wagon-master had broken a wheel en route and by the time it was repaired Athena was complete.

His senses soared while experiencing the great euphoria, exacerbated by the sight of an extraordinary phenomenon taking place in the descending night sky. Suddenly, all of the marble statues magically came to life in a veil of glimmering violet light, illuminating not only the Parthenon itself but also the Acropolis. Nikodimos was awestruck not only by the light but also by the transformation within the stone. The violet light only lasted for a short while, then, in an instant, the moment passed, the light surrendering to the greyness of the night.

It was time to say goodbye to Athena; however, more commissions would be forthcoming because he had created his masterpiece. The final polish had given a translucent quality to her face and her countenance had all the Classical features befitting a goddess.

Although, rightly or wrongly, he insisted on retaining her full-lipped pout.

He had directed Athena's gaze towards the heavens, towards Mount Olympus, within sight of her father's heavenly abode. She was resplendent in her crested helmet adorned with mythological creatures, a magnificent Sphinx and upturned cheek pieces. Her aegis, worn over her peplos, was the most important part of her battle-dress, and was believed to be immortal and ageless.

Her shield he had kept till last. All the sculptors had taken part in carving Athena's shield, as he had wanted it to be a lasting tribute to those who had worked in his workshop. It had taken months to complete because of their demanding work schedule. The battle between the giants and the Amazons was the overall theme, with a gorgon's head in the centre of the shield causing him to roar with laughter.

He would recognise that face anywhere.

'Pheidias You old devil!'

He took one last look at Athena. He would not have wished to argue with her as she had a formidable presence, as though she might step down from her plinth at any moment, engage in battle, if need be. He was pleased that he remembered to include a perky little owl he had called Thomas, she so adored, sitting by her right foot. He was happy. He had imbued Athena with all the physical qualities he imagined.

Joy filled his heart. His beloved Kallisti was waiting for him. They were planning a small celebration at the Symposium to announce their wedding the following year.

Nikodimos packed up his tool bag and prepared to go. It was getting dark. He took one last look at his creation. He had something on his mind, evident by the way he plunged his hand back into his goat-skin bag.

Riotous laughter filled the air. Of course! How could he have forgotten one of Athena's most endearing qualities. Homer mentioned in the *Odyssey* that Athena possessed a wicked sense of humour. Now that his humour had returned having vanished from the face of Attica for the last five years, he knew exactly what he wanted to do and as his chisel and mallet flew out of the bag he crouched on the scaffolding and carved 'Nikodimos' on the inside of Athena's right toe. He smiled to himself thinking Athena would appreciate his sense of humour.

It was time to go. He tossed his tools into his bag. Shrugged deep inside his himation, and feeling a chill, ran to the end of the scaffolding, calling to his young cousin as he slid down the rope.

'Menelaos!'

Silence.

'Hurry up Menelaos!'

Silence.

'It's time to go. It's time for supper.'

When there was no reply he assumed that his cousin had gone home. He thought nothing more about it. It was time to celebrate.

—ᙅ ᙆ—

Menelaos remained hidden deep in the shadows of the lofty Parthenon. He did not want Nikodimos to know that he had stayed behind on the scaffolding. He was not polishing stones; he did not want anyone to know that he was having one last conversation with his imaginary friends, as the marble statues had proved to be his best friends ever.

As he bid farewell to the Lapiths he kept one foot firmly placed on a narrow stone ledge directly beneath the metope and the other foot firmly fixed on the wobbly wooden scaffolding. Their conversation ended abruptly when Menelaos suddenly panicked, caught in a sudden down-draught, a contrary wind blowing in from the Aegean Sea. He was only too aware of the danger working on the scaffolding, and it wasn't uncommon to fall off. The wind gathered pace and within seconds a fierce storm had blown up. Lightning bolts flashed, close to his head, illuminating an ominous sky. Zeus' thunderbolts crackled in the distance and Menelaos became terribly afraid. Heavy rain pelted down and gathering up his goat-skin bag he ran as fast as he could towards the opposite end of the Parthenon. Before he shimmied down the rope, he turned around one last time and waved goodbye to the Lapith boys. As he did so, however, Menelaos slipped on the wet slimy goo, a mixture of marble dust and rain, and lost his balance. As he fell he grabbed hold of the wooden railing, snapping from the weight of his body. Menelaos plunged to his death.

—CR ℘—

The alarm was raised when Menelaos failed to return home for his dinner. A search party had been called out, although Menelaos' body had yet to be found.

Sadly, Nikodimos made the horrifying discovery while leading a search party the next day. Menelaos' short woollen cloak was found in a pool of bloodied rainwater directly beneath the metopes of the Lapith boys. But there was no sign of his cousin's body or his tool basket or his goat-skin bag anywhere near the south side of the Parthenon. Mysteriously entwined in his cousin's cloak were his open-toed sandals, silk snood and his woollen tunic, torn and stained with blood. Several days later Syrinx discovered his cousin's goat-skin bag near the Hill of the Pnyx. His mallet and chisel and a small lead weight embossed with a tortoise were still inside the bag, yet his lyre, that went everywhere with him, had disappeared. Those Athenians who believed in myths assumed Menelaos had been rescued by a Naiad, as the Hill of the Pnyx was where the water nymphs lived. No one could dispute this, as the body of this brilliant young sculptor was never found.

Chapter Eight
Anima Mundi (Soul of the World)

A day of celebration was taking place on the Acropolis to commemorate the completion of Athena Parthenos' temple. Crowds, anxious to view the Parthenon, could be seen gathering in the distance. Nikodimos ignored the crowds as he walked towards the Parthenon. He had come to view Menelaos' stone-carving in private. His buskins felt like lead, his heart, as though it had been wrenched out of his body, but he carried on nevertheless. As he drew near he noticed a faint shadow gradually taking shape on the Parthenon's south frieze, swirling and eddying around Menelaos' metope like some disembodied presence. The sight brought Nikodimos to a standstill, mesmerised by the phenomenon while staring at the metope of the Lapiths fighting the centaurs high above his head. Suddenly he was moved to the very depth of his being, overwhelmed by what he saw before him – the powerful legacy Menelaos had unknowingly left behind, etched in the stone. It was almost as though part of his cousin's young soul remained in the stone. Even more extraordinary, he thought, part of Menelaos' soul would remain in the stone for an eternity.

Nikodimos sought comfort, meagre though it might have been, in knowing that the metope was a testament to Menelaos and his truly astonishing talent as a stone-carver.

The sky took on a violet hue as Nikodimos walked away. He believed Athena's temple belonged to the people of Athens because the Athenians had built the sacred shrine with their bare hands and nothing on earth would ever change that. He believed that the Parthenon was indestructible and neither earthquakes, plunder by warring factions, nor other unforeseen disasters could ever destroy it. Then, his eye caught sight of Syrinx' carving squeezed into the corner of the east pediment of the Parthenon. The statue was magnificent, causing him to smile in spite of his overwhelming grief. Syrinx' sculpture was an even greater masterpiece, because the statue had been carved by a slave girl.

Nikodimos walked between the colossal marble columns lining the colonnade. A throng of Athens' greatest and good, nobles, aristocrats, philosophers and senators, were gathering on the south porch. He caught a glimpse of Pericles as he strode up the steps, flanked by Hyperbolos, Thucydides and Socrates. However, Pheidias was not there. Rumours were spreading, ugly, malicious rumours that he preferred to ignore.

Nikodimos glimpsed Orestis with both hands thrust deep inside the folds of his himation hiding his thumbs, his twisted body shrugged in the folds of his tattered cloak. He was standing hidden in the shadows of the Parthenon's massive Doric columns, apart from the army of stone-masons, stone-carvers, stone-cutters and sculptors gathering on the mound.

As the crowd gathered they tossed garlands of roses and violets at their feet. Despite the crowd's praise one sculptor remained bitterly disenchanted. He was not in a festive mood. For him it was not a day of celebration. It was a day of remembrance, as several weeks had passed since Menelaos had vanished and all hope of finding his cousin's body was gone. His uncle had consulted the Oracle at Delphi, hoping for answers. None were forthcoming. The crowd's fanfare was tremendous as Pericles took the podium. Nikodimos didn't stay. He walked away. He wasn't in the mood for rhetoric. He and Kallisti were sailing for Patmos later that evening as she wished to introduce him to her parents.

Nikodimos wandered aimlessly along the dusty path lost in thought, while pondering what ironies there were in life. The Parthenon had been built as a shrine to Athena, and yet the reverse was true. In years to come the Parthenon would become a shrine to the Hellenic people. Every chunk of marble had been carved by a Hellas. He truly believed that the souls of all those responsible for building the Parthenon were somehow imparted in the stone; therefore, if anything untoward ever happened to the Parthenon, the Hellenic people would lose their soul. The word *eternal* sprang to mind. Everything about Hellas was eternal. Like the goddess Athena Parthenos. Like Menelaos.

Plate VII: 'The Legend Begins!'

This is the famous metope that Menelaos was polishing when tragically he fell to his death from the scaffolding on the south side of the Parthenon. His body was never found. This is now on display at the Quimby Gallery, Museum of Classical Antiquities, London.

Part Two
The Beginning of Nineteenth Century, Athens

Chapter Nine
'Lord Quimby's Dig'

Maximilian Henry Perceval stood on the verandah in his pyjamas, watching the early morning mist rise above the canopy of date palms lining the drive at the front of Mrs Logotheti's rambling, Turkish-style villa on the north-east side of the Acropolis. The Lauds bell had wakened him at dawn – his favourite time of day – and he raced outside on to the verandah with his new brass telescope tucked under his arm, in the hope of catching one last glimpse of the Parthenon before leaving Athens at noon. He was not disappointed. The view from the verandah was breathtaking.

As Max watched the mist rise slowly above the Parthenon he could not help thinking that the ancient temple of the virgin goddess Athena Parthenos was, without doubt, the noblest pile of ruinous stone that he had ever seen. As the rosy-fingered dawn broke through the mist, illuminating the jagged edge of the fortress, little did he know that years later this image of the golden sunlight touching the honey-coloured stone would cause all of Athens to come rushing back in his memory. During his brief stay in Athens he had visited many ancient ruins, but the Parthenon would always stand out most.

Max pressed his brass telescope – a bon voyage present from dear, sweet Aunt Vrai Viviette, upon their departure from London – tightly to his eye, trying hard to memorise every tiny detail of Athena's temple. He had come to know the Parthenon well, having spent *all* his free time sketching the crumbling citadel looming before him on the lofty outcrop of the Acropolis.

Sketching the remains of the Parthenon had become an all-consuming passion during the summer months. However, to have developed such pathos, such affinity for the Parthenon itself was, well, a bit odd, thought Max upon reflection, as he leaned further and farther over the railing, and peered through the mucky lens of his telescope at the mouldering pile; all that remained of the once mighty fortress slowly emerged in the mist. After all, the Parthenon was *really* nothing more than a clump of ruinous stone with battered columns, a shattered frieze and badly mutilated marble pediments. Sadly, almost all of the magnificent frieze's metopes were now missing; however, most of those that remained in situ were in perfect condition. But for how much longer?

Max understood all about metopes.

Mr Dashiell Hamilton, Max's uncle's London agent, whom Max had simply adored until three weeks ago – mainly because Mr Dashiell Hamilton always had time to talk to him and smiled at him, unlike his uncle, who never smiled at him and more often than not ignored him completely, which most adults seemed to do – had explained the whole business about metopes the day after he had returned from London.

Their conversation had taken place in the morning room, during breakfast, as Max sat buttering his toast. Max could recall just about every word, because he had never seen his uncle's

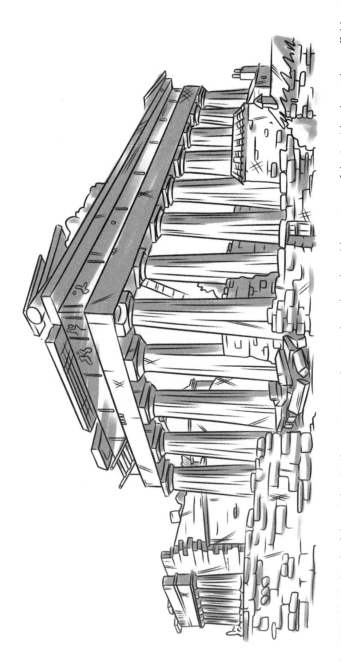

Plate VIII: Max's sketch of the mighty Parthenon in 1802, showing the colossal marble metopes of the Lapiths above the scaffold on the south side. Fighting the centaurs (originally carved by Menelaos in the fifth century BC), they are about to be removed by Lord Quimby's men.

London agent in such good humour. Max had not been party to the goings-on in London, but whatever had taken place had certainly put Mr Dashiell Hamilton in a jolly fine mood and Max, being a true opportunist, plunged in. He had even had the foresight, which wasn't often, mind you, to bring his most recent sketches of the metopes that he had been working on for the last month downstairs to breakfast, and he spread his drawings out on the breakfast table...right under Mr Dashiell Hamilton's aquiline nose.

'I beg your pardon, Sir,' said Max, in a small voice, not wishing to interrupt Mr Dashiell Hamilton at breakfast.

'Please, Sir, if you would be so kind, I really want to know more about the enormous marble slabs on the side of the Parthenon. Metopes, I believe they are called. I was really hoping you could explain what they mean because I think they are fascinating. Could you help me, Mr Hamilton?'

'Well, goodness gracious me!' exclaimed Mr Dashiell Hamilton, smiling brightly at Max, which he always did.

'Of course, dear boy, I would be delighted to tell you what I know about metopes.'

Max had obviously caught Mr Dashiell Hamilton's attention because he suddenly leaned forward in his chair. Max thought this was a really good sign. Mr Dashiell Hamilton rested both arms on the breakfast table, and a host of exclamations followed while he examined Max's sketches, squinted through his pince-nez held tight within the fleshy folds of his right cheek and his bushy eyebrow overhanging the glass like a thatched roof.

While Mr Dashiell Hamilton perused his drawings, Max munched happily on his toast, eagerly awaiting his uncle's London agent to elaborate. Which he did, of course, because he liked to think he had a lovely speaking voice.

'Your first two sketches,' said Mr Dashiell Hamilton, pointing at the metopes with his fork, 'they are from the south side of the Parthenon. They are two out of the original ninety-two metopes that ran around all four sides of the frieze when the Parthenon was built, before being plundered!'

'I want you to look closely at your drawings, Maximilian,' said Mr Dashiell Hamilton, reaching for Max's hand, pulling him closer, pointing to the sketch.

'I want to show you something quite extraordinary. It is important that you understand the difference between high-relief and low-relief.'

'Yes Sir.'

Mr Dashiell Hamilton kept right on smiling and enthused, 'In this sketch the sculptors carved the metopes in high-relief, Maximilian, so that the carvings will have much more depth. Although what I find so fascinating is that the Lapiths and the centaurs have been so brilliantly carved that they are almost free-standing. Do you know what centaurs are, Maximilian?'

'Yes Sir!' Max replied with every ounce of enthusiasm he could muster, wrinkling his nose. 'Centaurs are ancient Greek mythological creatures, ugly, gruesome monsters with the body of a horse and the torso of a man. Exactly the same as I have drawn, here!' Max exclaimed while pointing at his sketch, scattering toast crumbs on to the pristine white tablecloth.

'That is correct, Maximilian. Do you know who the Lapiths were?'

'Lapiths were a tribe from northern Greece.'

'Correct. Well done, my boy. Well done. May I also add that I think your sketches are quite remarkable, Maximilian.'

Max nearly choked on his toast. *Never* in his entire life had anyone *ever* complimented him on *anything* that he had ever done. *Ever.* Although he kept these thoughts to himself, as one did in the presence of one's elders. He was much too interested in what was coming next.

Between sips of steaming Turkish coffee – as thick as mud – Mr Dashiell Hamilton continued: 'The metopes on each side of the Parthenon told a different story, although the theme was the same, and as the ancient Greeks were pagans, mostly illiterate folk who could neither read nor write, the metopes were an excellent means of communication. As these people, mostly heathens, you understand, went about their daily lives, glimpsed the metopes from afar, they were reassured, constantly reminded of the vital part they played protecting their city.'

Enthralled, Max sat very still, quietly sipping his Earl Grey tea, while listening to every word, as though it were written in stone.

'When the Parthenon was built, in ancient times, the metopes running along the east side of the temple represented the battle between the Olympian gods and the giants who tried to expel the immortals from their sacred temple; whereas the metopes on the west side showed the Greeks fighting the Amazons, although most of the metopes have since been destroyed. The north side shows the Fall of Troy, and the metopes that you have sketched, those that obviously captured your imagination, running all along the south side of the Parthenon, Maximilian, told the story of the fierce battle between the Lapiths and the centaurs.'

Mr Dashiell Hamilton drained his coffee cup. He appeared to be enjoying himself.

'The metopes on the south side represent many things, Maximilian. The battle between the Lapiths and the centaurs represents the battle between man and beast. This, in turn, represents the ongoing battle between order and chaos and good and evil. This conflict continues, even to this day, and will no doubt continue to do so until the end of time. Always remember that these battles that I have mentioned exist within all of us, to this day, even within you, Maximilian, even you. There is also another meaning and that is the continual struggle between civilisation and barbarism, the civilised world and the uncivilised world. The British Empire represents the civilised world, and the uncivilised world is this part of the world. In today's modern world the barbarians are the Greek peasants we see roaming the narrow streets of Athens, those irreligious Turkish infidels, heathens really!'

Perplexed, Max rubbed his temples. He didn't want to admit that he didn't really understand what precisely Mr Dashiell Hamilton meant by the continuous battle between good and evil and order and chaos, as he did not see any sign of chaos lurking in the sun-lit morning room; in fact, everything looked in order. Nor did he feel evil nudging him on his shoulder. He did not think that the Greek peasants were barbarians either, but what did he know? After all he was just a boy. However, his uncle's London agent interrupted his muddling thoughts. He had more to say.

'I strongly believe, my boy,' said Mr Dashiell Hamilton, with conviction, 'that the metopes are without doubt one of the finest examples of stone-carvings that the Western world has ever seen.'

'I agree, Sir!'

'It is difficult for us to imagine that the metopes were placed on the Parthenon's frieze so long ago. Sometime during the middle of the fifth century BC, I believe. This means that these enormous marble slabs, those fortunate enough to have survived, have been there for well over two thousand years. What a truly miraculous thing. To think that the metopes have remained in situ all that time. It is unfortunate that so many of the metopes have been plundered by the infidels and the barbarians, to say nothing of blasted by cannon balls!'

Max nodded. He was truly amazed at the extent of Mr Dashiell Hamilton's superior knowledge of the Classical world.

By this time Mr Dashiell Hamilton was in full swing. The morning room was filling up with lodgers, providing Mr Dashiell Hamilton with an even greater audience.

'The metopes played an important role in fifth-century Athens. As you know, young man, Greeks at that time were pagans, illiterate folk, and they could neither read nor write, therefore the metopes were an excellent means of communication. And, as these ancient people, mostly heathens, you understand, as they went about their daily lives, glimpsed the *metopes* of the battle between the Lapiths and the centaurs, situated high up on the Parthenon's magnificent marble frieze, they were constantly reminded of battles that needed to be fought and won, and of the vital part they played protecting the City of Athens. As you know, the Athenians were always at war with their neighbours and still are to this day.'

'Thank you, Sir,' said Max, never failing to remember his manners.

'May I also say,' said Mr Dashiell Hamilton, enthusiastically, while adjusting his pince-nez, 'I find the fine detail in your sketches quite remarkable!'

Max could not believe his ears. He was Odysseus! He had returned to Ithaca.

'And to think that you have sketched the one metope that surpasses all the others, I believe, is truly extraordinary!'

Mr Dashiell Hamilton's smile spanned the morning room.

'Your drawing of the Lapith tackling a fleeing centaur is brilliant, as the Lapith nearly jumps off the page while preparing to strike a decisive blow.'

'Thank you, Sir.' Beaming, Max leapt to his feet and as he leaned over the table grabbed hold of his sketch with buttery fingers. 'This is my favourite too, Mr Dashiell Hamilton!'

'Have you ever tried to imagine why that is, Maximilian?'

'No, Sir.'

'Well, please allow me to explain. The Lapith was so brilliantly carved by the stone-carver, Maximilian, that it's nearly free-standing, like a statue. In fact, the Lapith looks as though it might fall from the metope at any moment!'

The morning room fell silent. Coffee was being served by a young servant about the same age as Max.

Then, after a lengthy pause, Mr Dashiell Hamilton flipped his tailcoat. He sat down. He turned sideways in his chair. Max thought he had something really important on his mind because he suddenly grabbed hold of Max's arms and held on tight, although he kept his eyes glued to the table. He lowered his voice to an almost inaudible whisper, as though he were speaking to the tablecloth. He never blinked, not once, during this brief soliloquy with the table, as his eyes penetrated deep into the linen, into the very soul of the cloth.

'I believe that the metopes, like the Parthenon itself, are of vital importance to the art world, to the Western world in particular. Whether the bloody Greek peasants know it or not, or even care, will soon no longer be the issue.'

Max remained seated on his chair, in silence.

It was evident that Mr Dashiell Hamilton had finished speaking by the way in which he folded his linen napkin, and placed it neatly on the table. His expression changed. His countenance clouded over. There were no more smiles. He tugged on the curled ends of his bristly moustache, that Max noticed for the first time was edged in grey. His uncle's London agent bowed to the elegant ladies seated at the breakfast table and strode out of the morning room without further ado.

Max felt quite chuffed as he rolled up his sketches, and tucked them inside his leather satchel. He was in a hurry. Nikolaos was waiting on the south porch of the Parthenon. Another art lesson pending. He raced out of the morning room, thinking that he had learned a great deal more about metopes than he could have possibly imagined. He was in awe of Mr Dashiell Hamilton, whose knowledge of the Parthenon he thought staggering.

However, his thoughts returned to the present. Since that enlightened conversation with his uncle's London agent, whom Max had privately referred to as the 'dashing' Mr Dashiell Hamilton because of his charm, his wit and his tremendous knowledge of everything Greek, things had started to change. Until three weeks ago he had never once doubted the goings-on on the Acropolis. There was no reason to do otherwise. Now, however, Mr Dashiell Hamilton was not so dashing. He was up to something, and it was not very nice.

Max remained on the verandah, unable to tear himself away. Enthralled by the dazzling sun shining through the colossal fluted columns lining the colonnade – a mere shadow of its former self – shimmering in the brilliant light of the deep blue sky. Nevertheless, even in its ruined state this glorious wreck – once the great sanctuary of Athens – would always be his favourite.

Max had been dreading this moment for weeks. The truth was that deep down in his newly acquired Athenian heart Maximilian

Henry Perceval did not want to leave Athens, at noon, or any other time for that matter. He did not wish to return home to England. Be sent away to prep school for the fourth year in a row. He had enjoyed boarding at Harrow on the Hill very much although it was because his friends all went to the school.

Max wanted to remain in Athens, attend the school for the sons of Franks (as people coming from the West were called) at the Capuchin Monastery next door to the villa, like the other boys that he had met while on holiday in Greece. He was really going to miss Lars, a young Dane from Copenhagen; François and Sébastien, the French Ambassador's sons, even though they were about to return home to Paris, as the war between Turkey and France was heating up; Giuseppe, the son of his uncle's clerk of works, Don Giovanni Battista Belisario; Gunther, a German boy from Munich, and his young cousin, Friedrich, a Bavarian lad from Würzburg. Every morning Max had glimpsed the boys filing into school and he did not think it unreasonable that he should be allowed to go too. If the school was good enough for his friends, why wasn't it good enough for him? However, there was one friend whom he was going to miss more than the others, one who did not attend the school for the Franks, and that was his absolute best friend, Nikolaos.

You see, dear reader, something extraordinary had happened to Max during his visit to Athens and that *something* had crept up on him so slowly and so effortlessly that it had taken him completely by surprise. Lately, Max had begun to feel differently about Hellenic people, although he did not really know how he was expected to feel upon his arrival in Athens at the beginning of April. What had transpired in the ensuing months was startling even to Max. Deep down in his English heart a metamorphosis-of-sorts had taken place and Max was slowly coming to realise that he *felt* more like a Greek and a whole lot less like an Englishman than he could have possibly imagined. What was even more profound was that he was beginning to *act* like a Greek and *think* like a Greek. And, because he felt so strongly about his newfound affection for all things Hellenic, all he could think about was remaining in Athens, for ever. But whether he liked it or not, the East Indiaman was preparing to set sail that afternoon, after his uncle, Lord Quimby, had returned from Constantinople with the badly needed firman and Max was expected to be on board the ship. Like it or not, that was all there was to it.

Several deep, heartfelt sighs echoed forth from the third-floor verandah that morning as Max gazed wistfully at the Parthenon that had emerged fully from the thick mist. He recalled what a difficult time he had had learning how to draw the mouldering ruin, and how his absolute best friend had rescued him from wasting yet more incredibly valuable paper by offering to give him art lessons. That sweltering hot midsummer's day in July returned like a heatwave.

'What is *that?*' Nikolaos asked, as he leaned over Max's shoulder, glimpsing what he considered to be his Frankish friend's absolute worst drawing of a statue, ever. It was of one of the few marble statues remaining within the Parthenon's east pediment.

'Persephone may no longer be in possession of her head but she is still a Greek goddess. Although I think she looks more like your tutor, old Duffy, dressed in his ratty old housecoat, than an important cult-figure wearing her magnificent peplos!'

'Go away!' Max elbowed his best friend in the ribs.

'Don't be so difficult, Menelaos!' Nikolaos said while clutching his ribs, pretending to be wounded, 'I was only trying to help.'

'Well, you are not helping.' Max heard himself shouting at his best friend. 'How dare you make fun of me.'

'I am not making fun of you. I am only telling you the truth, for your own good.'

Max was becoming enraged. 'I don't want to know the truth!'

'Why not?'

'Because telling the truth can hurt people!'

'No it doesn't. Socrates said, "Wisdom begins in wonder." I believe wisdom begins with seeking truth.'

'Then, if that is the case, I will never be able to draw any of the statues because I have been sitting here on this blasted stone plinth all day, in this unbearable heatwave, trying to draw Persephone's robe and I will never get it right!' Max cried, and, in a fit of temper, he ripped his drawings out of his sketchbook and began to tear them to shreds.

'Stop, Menelaos! Stop!' Nikolaos grabbed his friend's sketchbook out of his hands, his drawings fluttering on to the marble steps.

'You English! You must learn to be more patient. You must try harder, Menelaos!'

'Go away. Let me alone, Nikolaos. One day, I will learn to draw,' Max snapped, hiding the tears of frustration gathering in the corners of his eyes.

'Listen to me. Kore's peplos looks more like a bunch of garlic sausages tied together than a magnificent gown,' Nikolaos said, doubling over with laughter.

'Bugger off!' Max cursed, while ignoring the steady stream of sweat dribbling down, running into his eyes and dripping off his sun-burned nose that was raw and peeling.

'How disrespectful of you, Menelaos, to turn our goddess of youth and joy – one of our favourite goddesses into a bunch of Neapolitan sausages!'

'Stop saying that!' Max was waving his hands wildly in the air like a demented soul. He couldn't stop shouting. 'Stop it!'

'Please, Nikolaos, please I beg of you, do not make fun of me,' Max pleaded, staring down at his blistered toes. 'I have been sitting here for weeks, trying with all my might to teach myself how to draw. My pencils are getting shorter by the minute. Now, look what I have done. My last sheet of paper is ruined.'

'I'm going home!' Max was so upset he began stuffing his pencils and crayons and sketchbook inside his satchel. However, his motley collection of art supplies refused to co-operate and fell out of the bag as fast as Max shoved them inside.

Nikolaos was a sensitive soul. He immediately sensed his friend's frustration and offered help.

'I have an idea Menelaos,' Nikolaos said, enthusiastically. 'I will give you art lessons. We can begin tomorrow. When I am not working for your uncle, on the Parthenon, that is. Would you like that, Menelaos?'

'Yes, thank you,' replied Max, 'I would like that very much.' Max had calmed down a little by this time. 'However, what I would like even more, is for you to please stop calling me Menelaos. My name is Maximilian. Do you hear? If you cannot manage Maximilian, call me Max!'

Nikolaos nodded.

'Yes. Max will do nicely!'

'Maximilian is your English name. However, Menelaos is your ancient Greek name. I think your archaic name suits you better.'

The young master stone-carver from Piraeus stood balancing himself on one leg with one arm wrapped around a crumbling colossal Doric column, hugging a chunk of antiquity that rightfully belonged to him anyway. He was nibbling a juicy, fresh fig that he had plucked from his goat-skin bag slung over his bronzed shoulder. Nikolaos could not have looked more like a Greek god, the modern-day version of the male body-beautiful, with his magnificently honed, oiled body glistening in the dazzling bright sunlight, his deep-set, dark eyes raised towards the heavens, towards Olympus, and his long black hair held back with a silk snood.

'Pray tell, what is your ancient Greek name?' Max asked, feeling no affection for his ancient Greek name whatsoever.

'I am not telling you, Menelaos.'

'Fine,' said Max. 'Don't then, see if I care.'

'Don't be flippant!'

'Flippant? Flippant! Is that your new English word?'

'Yes. Do you like it, Menelaos?'

Max was really fed up by this time, listening to Nikolaos pretending to sound English and calling him Menelaos.

'Listen. As you insist on calling me by my ancient Greek name then go ahead I will be Menelaos. Only in private. Do you understand? Otherwise you will confuse everyone, including my uncle. He won't know who I am. Not that it matters.'

'Agreed!'

The boys laughed and hugged each other.

'I think that your ancestors were Hellenes, Menelaos, long before they were English. I mean in archaic times.'

'That makes no sense, Nikolaos!'

CHAPTER NINE

Max was becoming impatient. 'I am an Englishman, through and through. I also look like an Englishman. I have big ears and my thatch of tufted hair looks like a mop. I also have freckles Greeks do not have freckles!'

Nikolaos laughed. He liked to laugh.

'Do you want to know why I believe this?'

'Not really,' said Max nonchalantly. He wasn't the least bit interested.

'You are beginning to act like a Greek. Look at how passionate you are about our stones. Just like us. Soon, you will learn to think like an Athenian. Instead of sitting on the fence, like the Spartans. Your Greek isn't bad either, which is very remarkable for an Englishman. Besides, look at you. You are always in your bare feet. I haven't seen those awful English shoes of yours for weeks.'

Nikolaos tugged the sleeve of Max's threadbare cloak he wore thrown over his right shoulder. 'You are a philosopher!'

'So, as you say, who do you think you are kidding, Menelaos?'

'Homer is your hero. Remember, I have had to listen to your ramblings all summer long, listened to you quoting pithy sayings from Homer and Socrates and Plato, have you not, Menelaos? In fact, that's all I hear when we go walking on the Agora, or while riding our donkeys along the banks of the River Ilissos. So, it's evident, is it not my Hellenic friend, you are Greek!'

'Bollocks!' Max shouted. He walked towards a marble plinth that had toppled over on its side, and he sat down, sweating in the hot sun. 'Don't be daft!'

'Daft? What does daft mean?' Nikolaos asked, although he didn't get a response. His friend had climbed on to the marble plinth and stood gazing out over the Aegean Sea, deep in thought. A few minutes passed. Nothing was said. This didn't happen often, then came:

Plate IX: Sketches of Max's beloved Parthenon during the summer holiday in 1802. These metopes were the first to be removed by his uncle, for 'safe keeping'. These are the same sketches Max finds in his trunk nearly ten years later at the house in St James's Square, London.

'You could be right, Nikolaos,' said Max in a small voice, 'You could very well be right.'

'Drawing was the first thing I learned how to do when I became an apprentice,' said Nikolaos as he walked over, joined Max on the plinth, lying on the ground like a dead warrior. He despaired, as he did not like to see his Frankish friend's drooping shoulders, his hands limp on his lap. His deep husky voice softened. His sensitive dark eyes became serious.

'Pheidias, Michelangelo, Palladio, even my father, had to learn how to draw when they became an apprentice, before they learned how to carve the stone. All great sculptors had to learn how to draw first. Here, Menelaos, please, let me show you.'

Nikolaos extracted a stub of crayon from the bottom of Max's satchel.

'See...it's like this...this is how you draw a peplos,' he said, as he turned the sketchbook over and drew on the back.

Max sat curled up on the broken marble plinth, hugging his knees, as he always did when feeling threatened or unsure of himself. He was fascinated by the ease with which his absolute best friend sketched Persephone using a few brief strokes.

However, these art lessons came with an added bonus. As Nikolaos tutored his young friend, he also shared his vast knowledge of ancient Greece and Greek mythology – and the myths and legends of pagan gods and goddesses magically came to life – while seated on a marble plinth in the shadow of the mighty Parthenon.

Over the summer the two boys became even closer friends, bound by their love of sketching the ruins of Athens' glorious past. Even though Nikolaos was in his seventeenth year, Max didn't mind being the younger boy. Age didn't matter to either of them. He proved to be an excellent student, excelling at linear drawings, and he had mastered the basic techniques of drawing perspectives in no time, although drapery continued to be his downfall.

When Nikolaos wasn't giving his young friend art lessons he worked for Max's uncle on 'Lord Quimby's Dig'. For the last three years Nikolaos, his older brother Alexios and his father, who were master stone-carvers, had worked on the site, making plaster-of-Paris casts of ancient Greek marble sculptures, copies of the statues that remained in situ within the gable ends of the Parthenon. It was difficult to find work at that time, as the Ottomans had no need for stone-carvers. When they weren't making casts, they spent their days helping the *formatori* (moulders) make moulds of the Parthenon's enormous marble statues, metopes and sections of the Parthenon's marble frieze.

One morning, while Nikolaos was busy making moulds and unable to give Max an art lesson, Max sat, where he always sat, on a chunk of broken marble – as there were so much laying toppled over on the ground – sketching the last two remaining statues in the west pediment. For Max, the west pediment was the best of all. It was what he had glimpsed that very first day, on his inaugural visit. The west pediment was what everyone saw when they entered through the gates leading up to the Parthenon and the sight was well, quite simply overwhelming.

Max had sketched all of the marble statues during the summer, gradually working his way along the pediment, from left to right; beginning with Ilissos, a river-god snug in the left corner of the Parthenon's west pediment. There were a few statues that he didn't know; however, he made several drawings of the charioteer's galloping horses rearing up. And Hermes, of course, Athena's consort, was also

93

a favourite. Her charioteer was missing but he had made several sketches of Iris, Poseidon's consort, and his charioteer, Amphitrite. The two protagonists he had yet to finish sketching were Athena and Poseidon, in the centre of the pediment, standing next to each other, although the two divinities were not facing each other. At one time, there had been an olive tree in between the two statues; however, the olive tree was missing.

The noble statue of Poseidon was colossal. He towered above the other statues. A formidable figure indeed. He looked every inch a Greek god. Of course, he was Zeus' brother, so it was to be expected. His magnificent marble head was enormous. His eyes were piercing and his beard was curly. Max was glad that Poseidon was still in possession of his head, as so many of the statues were not. His powerful stance was tremendous. As though he had already struck the ground with his trident. His body was intact. Perfect. Only his arms and a section of his left leg were missing.

It was the statue of Athena, though, that had totally captured his boyish heart. His affection for the goddess had taken hold long before his visit to Athens. Before Max had set one bare foot on Hellenic soil. Max had been introduced to Athena while he was in first form, at Harrow on the Hill, learning to recite from memory verses from Homer's great epic poems, the *Odyssey* and the *Iliad*.

He *really* liked the idea of Athena being a warrior goddess. Max recalled his then tutor, Mr Murgatroyd Jones, expounding in great detail that Athena was fearless in battle, and as Homer had so rightly said, always armed for war.

'Athena was fearless in battle and, as Homer had so rightly said, "always armed herself for grievous war".'

Max tried to envision Athena dressed for battle, wearing her terror-inducing aegis, and her formidable helmet adorned with a Sphinx, fierce creatures and mythical beasts from Greek legends, and up-turned cheek pieces. Her shield and her long metal spear were missing. Her right foot was gone too. The goddess was headless, which was a pity, and he could only imagine what Athena actually looked like. Although he did know that her head had been carved separately and then fastened on to her torso at a later date. Max thought this was most interesting and wondered whether all the statues had been made this way. The reason he knew so much about Athena was because Nikolaos had explained everything during a recent art lesson. It was during this same art lesson that he had confessed that his ancestors were the sculptors responsible for carving many of the Parthenon's marbles. Max thought this was truly astonishing.

His affection for Athena ran deep. He recalled having read in a book on Greek mythology – although he had since forgotten the title – Athena was 'man's ideal of a big sister'. Max liked this idea. Because he was an only child he really fancied having an older sister, and over the years Athena had become just that. She remained the most enchanting goddess of all. Even without her head and with her badly mutilated arms and missing right foot, which had been ravaged by vandals. Revenge was not an admirable characteristic, nor was it something Max considered to be part of his nature. In this instance, however, he felt justified in feeling revengeful towards those persons who had deliberately and maliciously hacked the statue of Athena to pieces. Ravaged her. How on earth anyone could have done such beastly things to Athena, whom he regarded affectionately as his big sister, was beyond belief.

It was an atrocity.

Max tried to envision Athena with entire arms. Her missing foot bothered him too, although her missing head was even more of an enigma. However, Nikolaos had mentioned that he could recall Athena with her head. This meant that her head had only gone missing within the last seventeen years, which wasn't actually that long ago, when considering the age of ancient Greek antiquities. So, someone must have found it. Perhaps it had fallen off in a bad storm or during an earthquake? Max was so eager for Athena to have her head back that he had spent hours combing the rubble on the Acropolis, in hopes of discovering it, but to no avail.

Nevertheless, his adoration for Athena was so great that he overlooked the fact that her head was missing, a tragic anomaly indeed. Enchanted was how he felt and enchanted is how he remained. If he ever had the good fortune of finding Athena's head or any other part of the statue he knew exactly what he would do. He would present his finds to his uncle. It might even provoke a smile. Max would insist Athena's head be glued on to the statue, where it rightly belonged.

Max had spent hours lying on his belly, in the moonlight, sketching all that remained of the marbles in the east and west pediments. His sketchbooks were full of drawings of gods and goddesses, mortals and immortals, horses' heads and horses. One night, on one of his night-crawls, the gods and goddesses appeared to magically come to life in the light of the full moon. A sort-of light-force deep within the stone appeared to shine right through the marbles themselves. The statue of Athena became so luminous, life-like, that in the soft golden moonlight the marble looked exactly like his skin. He was awestruck. And from that moment on, not only Athena, but the entire collection of marbles had come to life. At times, he found this quite unnerving. He told himself, repeatedly, that marble statues were inanimate objects. Stones were definitely *not* living things. Statues could not move about or breathe or talk. Statues were not *real* people.

The marbles did not have souls.

So, how was it possible for him to feel this way – be totally captivated by statues that were made of stone and not *really* real at all? He shook his head ruefully. Trying with all his might to dispel what he concluded – absolute – nonsense from his mind. Was he mad? Had the extreme heat finally got to him? Max could not share his thoughts about the marbles with anyone. However, throughout the long, hot summer, as he sat making detailed drawings of Iris, Amphitrite, Poseidon and Hermes, and in particular his make-believe older sister, he continued to be strangely drawn to them.

Goodness me. I'm thinking like a Greek again.

Athena was a marble statue, a Greek mythological goddess and nothing more. However, he had read, probably in the same book, about Athena being an older sister, that Greek goddesses were imbued with special powers. That is what the ancient Hellenic people believed, so why shouldn't he? Why not believe that his big sister kept him safe from peril? He found comfort in this thought and clung to it. He recalled reading in the *Odyssey* that was exactly what Athena did for Odysseus. He rather liked the idea of believing in a goddess, rather than a god. Perhaps being an orphan had something to do with it, no longer having parents, a mother in particular. In the Christian religion God was an old man who lived in heaven, in the mysterious realm of the unknown and bounced about on fluffy white clouds. Max imagined God to be like Moses, wearing long flowing robes, with a straggly white beard and a stern countenance.

Not altogether someone whom young boys, like himself, envisioned cuddling up to when badly in need of solace or reassurance; confided in, in time of trouble, when he forgot his rhyming elegiac couplets and Latin verse or was unable to do his sums in maths.

Athena, on the other hand, was neither old nor wizened. She was formidable, no doubt about it. Athena was not only youthful, she was also beautiful. Like the enchanting young woman he had glimpsed in the market at Piraeus one day. She looked exactly like a goddess, what Max imagined Athena to be. She had the thickest, most luxuriant black hair flowing down her back in waves. Her skin was so white it appeared translucent and she had magnificently arched eyebrows, etched in black, as though a Greek god had drawn them on her face. She had brilliant grey flashing eyes. He had seen her eyes for himself, when the goddess suddenly turned her head, caught him staring at her.

Yet there was an even greater reason for Max's fascination with Athena. According to Homer, Athena had a great sense of humour. This, above all, was the absolute best reason for worshipping her, as Max's life had become rather serious of late.

Athena had become a mother figure. Perhaps, not having a mother had a lot to do with it. He imagined Athena holding him in her loving arms when he was unwell, rubbing cream on his blisters, his sun-burned nose, tucking him into bed at night, covering him with loving kisses, hugging him tight. No one ever hugged him. This sadly overlooked fact caused Max no end of grief, and, on numerous occasions, when badly in need of comfort he had had to resort to hugging his pillow when curled up in bed at night. People in England *never* hugged each other. English people were reticent. Showing *affection* was *not* done. Max had observed his aunt and uncle greeting each other on numerous occasions and they never embraced. Kisses never touched a cheek. Not like the Greeks or the Turks or the Latins, who were lovers, masters in the art of showing affection. The Latins never stopped hugging each other. Perhaps that was one of the reasons he had such affection for the Europeans and the folk from the Levant. The Hellenic people did not have much money but they certainly loved each other, which couldn't possibly be a bad thing, could it? Max had observed this outward display of affection with great fascination and concluded that these humble people whom Mr Dashiell Hamilton alluded to as uncivilised barbarians, loved each other.

Max wanted to be loved too.

Max adored Athena. There was no question about it. He desperately wanted to have someone to love, and to love in return, and as there was no one else around at the moment to lavish his affection on, other than his donkey, Mopsus, Athena fit the bill. He did not feel that he was a pagan or involved in idol worship. His feelings were real. That was all he knew. Sébastien and François, his Roman Catholic chums from Paris, worshipped the statue of the Virgin Mary. Was there any difference? Max did not think so. He did not believe in the virgin birth so he could not possibly agree to worship something he did not truly believe in. He would be a hypocrite. Athena was a virgin goddess and she remained a virgin He could cope with that. His Roman Catholic chums spent a lot of time on their knees, praying, keeping their souls out of purgatory, for when they passed on, so they believed. According to Sébastien, there was: heaven, hell, and purgatory, where no one on earth wished to retire to after death. To pay to keep one's soul out of this truly gruesome place seemed ludicrous. Although he liked to keep his options open. He desperately needed to believe in something, but it was most definitely *not* the Holy Ghost. Ghosts were ghoulish, scary creatures. Although the Holy Ghost was really popular at the moment, especially at Harrow on the Hill. Every morning at chapel the headmaster mentioned the Holy Ghost. In the Church of England the Holy Ghost was always present, sitting next to him in the pew, inside the church, no less. Although no one could see the Holy Ghost because ghosts were invisible. So, how on earth could he believe in something he couldn't see? Not one of his friends had been privileged enough to glimpse the Holy Ghost, either. Was the Holy Ghost benevolent or malevolent? No one seemed to know.

He did not believe for one minute that he was an atheist. Atheists chose not to believe in God. Perhaps they should consider believing in goddesses instead. Until coming to Athens last April, he wasn't sure what to believe. It was a dilemma and one that had caused him no end of grief. However, after glimpsing the mighty Parthenon for the very first time, standing on the porch, as close as he could possibly get to the colossal structure, touching the marble with his bare hands, feeling the power radiating deep from within the stone, within the ruin of Athena's sacred temple itself, well, thought he to himself, he was no longer confused. The spirit of Athena was there, on the Acropolis. Did this mean he was a Greek?

Max laughed aloud at the mere thought.

His uncle refused to discuss religion, so there was no point in asking him about his new-found belief in Athena or about the Holy Ghost. Aunt Vrai Viviette ignored the subject, entirely, when he had asked her about the fact that a ghost might be prowling around the churchyard. No one ever mentioned the Holy Ghost in polite conversation. He didn't know one single person who prayed to the Holy Ghost so why on earth should he? Besides, ghosts really, really spooked him. Churches did too. They were awfully smelly, damp, musty places like the crypt downstairs in the Capuchin Monastery. Churches were sinister, dark places where priests in odd-shaped hats and long-flowing robes shuffled down the aisles between the pews. Why on earth men-of-the-cloth chose to wear robes when breeches would do the job was a mystery. Priests never smiled either. Although the Capuchin monks next door never stopped smiling. Not the priests. They never smiled, not even when Aunt Vrai Viviette allowed him to put a halfpenny in the money bag used for collection on Sunday morning. Max assumed bumping up the coffers would be worthy of a smile. Not so. Max deemed this ungrateful attitude 'bad manners'. Priests thumped their harpy claws on the pulpit during sermons, rattling the stained-glass windows, candlesticks. Perhaps the congregation had nodded off. The Bishop frightened the very daylights out of him, squinting through his spectacles, examining every iota of Max's attire. Why did the Bishop cause him to feel *so* extremely guilty about absolutely *everything?* Whether it was helping himself to a second slice of cake, picking his nose, which he rarely did, because it was such a disgusting habit, or pulling the girl's pigtails seated next to him in London's Westminster Abbey.

Athena did not make him feel guilty. Not one bit. That is *why* Max chose to believe in Athena. That is *why* he prayed to Athena every time he felt sad or lonely, which seemed to be a lot lately. Max thought that the Christian religion had got it all wrong, inside-out so to speak. He believed that the inside of the cathedral was not the place to worship. One should not be inside the church but outside in the natural world. That was the odd thing about the Parthenon. It worked its magic from looking outside-in rather than inside-out. Max believed that standing on the Acropolis looking towards the

Parthenon, at the sky, through the colonnade, and beyond, was the closest he would ever get to heaven. The god who lived in heaven never answered any of his prayers. Not once. Not ever. So, he prayed to Athena that one day he might return to Athens. Where he belonged. He truly believed that the goddess was going to answer his prayers, although he must be patient, as Nikolaos said he must.

Max enjoyed the simple ritual of making offerings to the shrine of Athena. He didn't need money. An offering could be a stone. He believed that the goddess's spirit lingered outside in the open air. Sometimes he got goosebumps. So it proved that she was there beside him. Violets were her favourite. Nikolaos always bought violets from the flower sellers. When they could afford a bunch or two the boys laid the flowers – that wilted ever so quickly in the hot sun – at the foot of Athena's sacred olive tree, conveniently located next to the Erechtheion, the temple with the six maidens. Max *knew* that Athena liked violets. How he knew was a complete mystery.

There I go, thinking like a Greek again.

Chapter Ten
'Lord Quimby's Dig'...continued

Maximilian Henry Perceval had spent the last year aspiring to become a true Classicist, like his uncle, Lord Quimby, and his uncle's London agent, Mr Dashiell Hamilton, whom Max simply adored until three weeks ago. These men had exalted taste and higher ideals. They appreciated the Classical splendour, beauty and grandeur of ancient Greece. His uncle, Lord Quimby, had explained to Max and to his cousin, Eggy – while standing on the poop, crossing the English Channel, on their outbound voyage to Constantinople – 'that a lifetime was needed to gain the wisdom, grace and lucidity evocative of this once, brilliant race'. Now, that was impossible. They were sailing home to dreary old England at noon and there was nothing on earth that he could do about it.

Being twelve years of age definitely had its drawbacks. So did being a ward of his uncle. Even the word 'ward' sounded nasty to Max. Becoming an orphan at the tender age of four was a horrid fate indeed, but nothing would bring his parents back to life. His father and mother had been killed in a tragic coaching accident, upon returning to their family home in Perthshire, after attending a grouse shoot in the Scottish Highlands. Now, Pagaille House, known as the Shambles, remained boarded up.

Back to the verandah…

For the last fortnight Max had suffered the worst bout of melancholy known to man; however, he never let his thoughts be known to anyone, that he was totally overwhelmed by the thought of leaving Athens. So much so, that hot, salty tears gathered on his thick black lashes. He quickly brushed them away. Mr Twelvetrees, his housemaster at Harrow on the Hill, strictly forbade any outward display of emotion, albeit good or bad. His uncle, Lord Quimby, was always stone-faced. He never showed emotion – other than contempt for Max, which was often – so Max didn't either. However, Being alone on the verandah gave one certain privleges. It allowed his emotions to let rip. Sobs he had gulped down for days, causing his throat to hurt and tightness in his chest, came gushing out. Tears splashed down the front of his newly acquired Egyptian cotton pyjamas – Lord Quimby exported by the boat-load from the Near East – dripped on to the floor of the verandah.

And tears continued to stream as Max leaned over the banister, glimpsed his uncle's servants loading a virtual mountain of luggage, battered trunks and valises, on to the backs of enormous camels, while the bad-tempered beasts whom Max absolutely loathed – because they always spat in his face whenever he walked past – impatiently stomped their big, flat feet on the drive. It wasn't only *his* trunk that was being taken down to the quay at Piraeus, loaded on to the ship. His uncle's luggage was also piled on the drive, and that of his young cousin, Eggy, and Mr Duffy, the boys' tutor, who was really his uncle's aged manservant when at the house in London. It was all loaded on to the backs of the huge beasts by his uncle's servants, evocatively dressed in traditional costume with baggy white trousers, bright red sashes, caps with swinging tassels and pompom shoes. Max really coveted a pair of pompom shoes. Had he been in possession of the required drachmas he would have invested in a new pair of *tsarouchia* shoes. Now, however, it was too late to scour the market stalls on the Agora for pompom shoes, for anything that he had dreamed of while on his Grand Tour of the Near East, because of that blasted East Indiaman sailing home.

His sudden outburst had left him feeling like a silly girl and he turned his head away, shame-faced. However, there was another reason for the sudden re-positioning of his head. He could no longer abide glimpsing the goings-on next door, within the crumbling, cloistered walls of the French, Capuchin Monastery, without making a run for it. Every morning, as the Laud's bell peeled, Max sat on the floor of the verandah and glimpsed the abbot leading the young friars shuffling silently in their Greek sandals out of the monastery. They walked along the well-trodden, dusty path towards the chapel with their hands neatly folded inside their robes and their cowled heads bowed in silent prayer. And every morning for the last week as Max watched this procession he had debated whether to make inquiries, ask the abbot whether he might consider taking him in. Keep him hidden in the crypt until the blasted ship sailed. Would the abbot betray him? Tell his uncle? Or would he do the Christian thing and keep him hidden within the cloistered walls, until he was old enough to become a fully fledged monk? That was the question. Max knew the monks were kind, benevolent fellows, with a great sense of humour because the younger monks were always laughing and giggling, telling each other ribald jokes. For a brief moment Max tried to envision everyday life at the monastery. Praying five or was it six times a day might be stretching it a bit. Although taking a vow of poverty would not be a problem. Max was an impoverished aristocrat. His total net-worth, his uncle called *assets*, Max deemed far below the poverty-level. Bare feet would not be a problem. Living within the high, cloistered walls of the monastery would not bother him either, not one bit, as long as he was allowed to visit his beloved Parthenon and roam freely over the Acropolis. There was one issue, however, that might well be a problem and that was celibacy – not initially – but most definitely in years to come. Max grinned. How many years? Not many.

The villa was also a consideration. Max had become accustomed to everyday life at Mrs Logotheti's rambling villa and it was beginning to feel like home – and to be able to call a place home was a rare thing indeed, because he could not ever recall feeling at home anywhere in his young life. The widow's villa, situated on the north-east side of the Acropolis, was where Max and his eight-year-old cousin, Eggy (short for George Egbert), and his uncle, Lord Quimby (when he wasn't away, buying Greco-Romano *objets d'art* in Naples or Rome, or completing important business deals on behalf of the East India Company in the Far East), and his uncle's London agent, Mr Dashiell Hamilton, lodged when not in London. His uncle's adviser, the highly esteemed Curator of the Museum of Classical Antiquities in London, Sir Archibald Lushington, and the Curator's slaves, lodged there while 'Lord Quimby's Dig' continued to excavate the ruins on the Acropolis. Max was unsure when 'The Dig' would end as it had been going on for the last three years.

It all began when his uncle took it upon himself to do the Greeks a great favour after numerous visits to the Far East. Lord Quimby had announced to the world, to anyone who would listen, that 'the Parthenon's treasures needed to be rescued from further destruction by the heathens and the barbarians or invading infidels!' Max was unsure who these folk were but he did not inquire further.

So, the expedition commenced. Lord Quimby obtained special permission from the Sultan of the Ottoman Empire in Constantinople to search for artifacts on the Acropolis. In other words, he could dig up the ground wherever he chose to do so. He employed a world-famous artist from Naples, Don Giovanni Battista Belisario, who was allowed to make sketches and detailed architectural drawings of the Parthenon or any of the remaining temples on the Acropolis. How on earth he managed to do this, no one seemed to know. Not even his aunt. This happened three years ago.

Since that time 'Lord Quimby's Dig' had taken on an entirely new dimension. Work progressed at an alarming rate when Don Belisario hired the *formatori*. This happened after Lord Quimby's most recent visit to the Levant. His uncle's workforce expanded, as the formatori were allowed to make plaster-of-Paris moulds of all the remaining artifacts on the Acropolis, the Parthenon, in particular.

A virtual army of sculptors, moulders, cast-makers, architectural draughtsmen and landscape painters were employed from every conceivable corner of the British Empire. Many of the artists also came from Florence and Naples. As you can well imagine, dear reader, the villa was a godsend. It had become the one place where his uncle's workforce lodged while 'Lord Quimby's Dig' continued. As there were no coaching inns in Athens at that time weary English tourists on Grand Tours of the Near East were billeted in private houses or lodged at the monasteries, of which there were several.

Max thought that the interior of Mrs Logotheti's rambling villa enchanting. There was an enormous interior courtyard with

Eastern-style loggias and porticoes leading to an enclosed walled garden. The exterior of the villa had a wide wooden verandah on the ground floor that stretched all the way around the house. This was a perfect place for house guests to amble along after dinner on exceedingly hot nights, where gentlemen smoked cigars, water pipes, and Eggy and his friends played tag. The villa was not in any way comfortable or grand like his aunt and uncle's palatial house in St James's Square in London. In fact, quite the opposite. The villa was a total wreck. Not unlike the Parthenon itself. Max assumed that the villa had begun to fall apart after the widow's husband, the previous British Consul at Athens, had died. Murdered in his bed. By his butler, if you please. Max squirmed. Anyway, the villa had shuttered windows; the shutters, many of which were falling off their hinges, were badly in need of a touch-up of blue paint, a favourite colour for shutters in Greece. Terracotta tiles were missing from the roof, a minaret-style affair, more in keeping with a Byzantine church in Constantinople than a private villa in Athens.

Nevertheless, Mrs Logotheti's rambling villa had many redeeming qualities and exuded enormous charm for those with a highly sensitive, poetic nature like his own, thought Max whimsically, and any sign of neglect or decay only added to the romance of the house. The villa was a serene place to be, to dream and to think. And Max dreamed and thought a lot of late, being twelve years of age and all.

The walled garden, however, was a mess. The exotic plants had been allowed to run riot over the years. He hadn't the foggiest idea what the names of the different species were, although it was not only the plants he deemed exotic.

Immediately after lunch, on scorchingly hot days, when art lessons were out of the question, Max took his afternoon siesta in the walled garden, where he lounged on the lawn on a straw mat as the tufted grass had become dry and brittle. Max doubted whether the grass had even been green, as it had scorched in the hot sun. Incapable of sleep, he kept in the shade of a date palm, which was of no earthly good, as spindly palm fronds provided a minimal amount of shade at the best of times. When the air got too hot, or he became exasperated memorising verses from Homer's *Iliad* or tired of reciting lengthy verses from Ovid's *Metamorphoses*, which he promised his housemaster, Mr Twelvetrees, he would do while on his Grand Tour, he practised his flute, an endeavour which drove anyone within earshot racing indoors, as Max was tone deaf.

These interludes, however, were precious. Although Max had an ulterior motive for lounging on the lawn, which will be explained fully a little later, and it had nothing whatsoever to do with reciting poetry, the drawing of perspectives of the Parthenon that even with Nikolaos' art lessons he seemed unable to master, or the heat English tourists complained of incessantly. On these rare occasions Max took no notice of the blistering hot sun. Although the sun's rays had burned every inch of exposed skin in the last year, caused painful blisters to bubble on his lips and his nose to peel continuously.

The best time of all at the villa was in the evening, after dinner. When Mrs Logotheti's house guests, of whom there were many gathered round on the lawn, listened to Mrs Logotheti's three scrumptious daughters play simple melodic tunes on a *rebeck*, an archaic three-stringed musical instrument familiar in that part of the world. The villa was filled with English tourists at the time, aspiring English writers and poets, artists, happy wanderers, roaming travellers on the Grand Tour of the Levant and the Near East, many of whom were guests of his uncle, including Lord Egfrith and his wife, Lady

Hortense, and their eight children, and Lord and Lady Montague and their two daughters, Posy and Charlotte. The girls were English wallflowers if ever there were, and sat stiffly on stone seats, twirling sun-brollies, sweltering in the intense heat because of their reticence to dispense with their English frocks and stiff poke bonnets, while the Latins, Neapolitans and Florentines were totally at ease with themselves, relaxing on enormous silk cushions, thrown helter-skelter on the lawn just for the occasion. The only distraction in this musical interlude came from the Capuchin monks' neighbouring honey-bees zooming in from the monastery next door and feasting on the wild thyme they apparently thrived on.

The crumbling remains of an elaborate marble fountain held centre stage in the walled garden. In its prior life Max assumed that this marble edifice edged in box hedge had been a cherished relic from the dearly departed British Consul's previous life, as the fountain boasted a display of marble statues engaging in intriguing erotica. Max could only imagine. As the marble statues were lacking fig leaves he assumed the fountain was not English. The statues brought blushes to many an English rose's countenance. Max touched his cheeks, checking for heat. The marble fountain was slowly sinking into the ground. On the rare occasion when the fountain was on, water trickled out through the cracks, forming puddles on the lawn. None of the guests seemed to mind that the fountain needed repair or that the rambling porticoes were desperately in need of plastering. In fact, Max had heard Lady Soames commenting on 'the immense charm of the place'.

The most evocative time in the walled garden was twilight, when the garden became an enchanted place, as the light changed dramatically from golden to pink and purple hues merged with shadows casting a magical spell over every inch of it. Max allowed his senses to be swept away by the magic, the air sweet with a fiery mixture of tobacco, the lingering fragrance of lavender and the sweet scent of white jasmine, aromatic plants, basil, thyme, rosemary and exotic herbs from the Far East. These were sublime moments indeed and stayed with Max throughout his lifetime, long after his sea voyage home to England. His vision of England would be forever thus, a dark, dingy place without golden sunlight or crumbling ruins, which was the very essence of ancient Greece. England was a place to which he no longer wished to return.

However, the villa's absolute *ne plus ultra* was the small verandah on the third floor. During the summer, this most halcyon of places was where Max sat with his long legs curled up, hugging his knees, watching the glorious sun rise and set over his *beloved* Parthenon while dreaming of becoming a Greek scholar or a student at the Gymnasium, engaging in rhetoric, discussing modern philosophy. Learning to be a great orator.

However, it was still far too early to go down to breakfast. Max much preferred to sulk in private. His reluctance to quit the verandah was nothing new as it had become his sanctuary when suffering extreme bouts of melancholy, which was often the case with one of nervous sensibilities, an extremely volatile disposition such as his own. Of course, this last bout had been the worst, exacerbated by the fact that his plan to visit the Acropolis one last time, to say goodbye to his absolute best friend Nikolaos on the steps of the Parthenon immediately after breakfast, had been squashed following last night's fiasco after dinner.

Now, his last day in Athens was ruined. As were all his plans for making one last visit to the Acropolis. Max began to fret. Nikolaos would be standing waiting for him on the steps of the Parthenon and his drawings that he had been working on for weeks would be left unfinished.

Although there was an even more poignant reason for making this last visit to the Acropolis – and it was a tricky one. He could not possibly reveal this to anyone – not even his best friend, Nikolaos, or his German friends, Gunther or Friedrich, or his young cousin, Eggy, or his uncle, Lord Quimby, or his aged tutor, Mr Duffy, or even Mr Dashiell Hamilton, whom he had admired greatly, although the esteemed gentleman was no longer the recipient of his trusted affections – the absolute truth was he *had* to say goodbye to the Parthenon. Not only the Parthenon itself, the marbles in the east and west pediments, but all the statues on the Acropolis. Every last one. It was impossible for him to leave Athens without bidding farewell to Selene's horses in the east pediment, and the six lovely maidens standing holding up the Erechtheion with their heads. Especially the statue he foolishly alluded to as his sweetheart, Helen. She needed his support most of all. Otherwise, she would grow weary and tire, and crumble, causing the roof of the temple to collapse and fall down Heaven forbid. The statues had become his friends. The list of goodbyes went on and on, which was sheer nonsense. Pure and simple. The Parthenon could not hear a blasted word he said. The statues did not understand English. This was a moot point. He must remember to speak Greek. How on earth could one actually say goodbye to statues that were nothing more than lumps of bashed-up bits of broken stone? Statues without noses or heads. But, he *had* to say goodbye and that was all there was to it.

Because, you see, dear reader: this Athens is where Max had, for the first time ever in his young life, experienced the *joy* of going bare foot. The delight that came from dispensing with his sturdy

English-made leather boots and roaming the plains of Attica (and he had hard calluses on his feet and open blisters on his toes to prove it).

This Attica is where Max allowed his hair to grow down to shoulders, which infuriated his uncle no end. And, like Socrates, Max had shown his contempt for luxury by forgoing all the luxuries he used in his everyday life, albeit his sensible English shoes and his fine clothes, and he wandered the dusty paths of the Agora with the thinnest, rattiest cloak he could find draped over his right shoulder, clutching a walking stick tightly in his right hand, imagining himself to be the great orator, engaging in rhetoric, although the comic-poets invariably sprang to mind.

This land, the homeland of the Hellenic people, is where Max had strolled aimlessly amidst the battered marble columns of the Stoa, the long marble colonnade; sat sketching Athena Nike's Ionic temple and the Propylaea, the enormous entrance gates leading up to the Parthenon. This is where Max had spent his days and many nights watching the marble statues magically come to life in the light of the full moon.

It was while roaming the dusty paths of the Acropolis that Max imagined himself to be a famous Athenian Hoplite warrior returning from the Battle of Marathon or Odysseus coming home after fighting in the bloody Trojan Wars. On cloudy days, which were infrequent, when the winds were gusty and the sky electric and Zeus' thunderbolts crashed in the heavens high above his head, Max imagined himself as the most nimble-witted epic-poet of all, his hero, Homer. Needless to say, this thought really stretched his imagination. Homer was, without doubt, the greatest poet that ever lived. He was a genius. On rainy days which were even less frequent, when he surrendered briefly to melancholy, his spirits sinking to the very bottom of the 'wine-dark sea', Max and his nimble-footed donkey, Mopsus, whom he loved more than anything on earth, sought refuge from the storm, within the shattered walls of the Erechtheion. The storm may have raged, yet neither he nor Mopsus was ever afraid.

This place, the Erechtheion, is where Max had spent days trying with all his might to sketch the caryatids, the marble statues of six maidens who held up the temple with baskets on their heads. Max grew tired on their behalf, as he imagined holding up a roof with your head a most exhausting endeavour. The statues were beautiful. Because the statues were Hellenic he gave each statue a Hellenic name: Aphrodite, Artemis, Demeter, Leda, Cassandra and Helen, his favourite caryatid of all. She had the prettiest smile, even without her nose. Helen was now missing from the temple. His uncle had had the wit and the foresight to have the statue removed. 'For posterity,' he had said. Lord Quimby had her taken away for safe keeping. She had been stowed in a shed at Piraeus, awaiting steerage-class home to England. Max could not believe his luck. To think that Helen was going home with him to England, on the same ship, was the best thing that could have happened to him, although he did think that the temple looked sad without her, very sad.

There were days when he became desperately ill from the scorchingly hot sun and suffered debilitating bouts of sunstroke or worse – suffered from gastroenteritis, or diarrhoea. Whenever this happened, Max sought comfort in the shade of the walled garden, close to the privy. He sprawled, full-length on a marble slab, like Prometheus chained to a rock, felt relief from the coolness of the marble on his burning hot skin. The marble slab was exactly the same colour as the marble in the Parthenon, leading him to believe that the stone had once been part of the Parthenon itself.

When he was feeling puffed up with his own importance, which was not often, or feeling exceedingly tall and handsome, which was even less often, Max dreamed of being one of the eponymous heroes that he had seen carved in the Parthenon frieze, and like all actors he wore his buskins and his face mask and played the role of a tragic figure, as there were many in ancient Greece.

This 'Eternal Greece' is where Max, when reason failed him, gambled that the guards had fallen asleep from too much Ouzo and escaped the cramped confines of his small room and unbeknown to all dragged a slumbering Mopsus from the stable and ridden up the steep incline to the Parthenon. And, having reached his destination intact, he spent the night sketching the remains of the enormous interior marble frieze of the cella of the Parthenon. Thankfully he had never been caught by the Turkish guards. To be incarcerated in the Tower of the Winds without any prospect of ever being released was a ghastly, hideous thought.

Curiosity would be the death of him.

Drawings from these 'midnight crawls' filled his sketchbooks; detailed sketches of broken capitals and splintered columns, lintels and pediments, chunks of entablature and broken architraves, statues of gods and goddesses with missing arms and legs. He had made so many sketches of Selene's horses that he had lost count. He could not resist, as the two heads of the moon goddess's horses were the most beloved marbles of all by the English tourists.

Max understood that the Parthenon represented the Doric order of architecture. Once again, Max had to thank Mr Dashiell Hamilton for enlightening him on the subject. Now he knew the difference between the five orders of architecture. This, he imagined, greatly enhanced his knowledge of Classical Greece.

CHAPTER TEN

All told, his visit to Athens had been the best part of his Grand Tour. However, there had been one huge disappointment. What Max had longed for most had evaded him – he was beginning to think that the strange phenomenon was pure nonsense. That the lament, as it was called, did not really exist.

Max paced angrily back and forth on the verandah, thinking it was diabolical to be confined to quarters on his last day in Athens. Even worse. Under house-arrest, until the blasted ship sailed. This meant that he did not have time to make one last visit to see Diomedes the old peasant who lived in a miserable little cottage – no bigger than a hut, which blew over every time it rained – not far from where the villa was situated, on the north-east side of the Acropolis.

The day that the old Greek peasant had tried and failed to explain about the lament sprang to mind. It had been one scorchingly hot day and Max had offered to prune his grapevines in a section of his small garden, set amidst bee hives and a score of ancient olive trees.

Flummoxed. Yes. He had been flummoxed as the old Greek peasant told his story and it went something like this:

'Menelaos, my friend [*strange how the Greeks insisted on calling him Menelaos*], now you must listen carefully.

'Whenever a stone is removed from the Acropolis the stones that are left behind on the Acropolis get very upset, and the marbles become so distraught that they start to scream, as you do when you hurt. The sound is a lament. It can be heard throughout Athens, because the marbles are wailing and moaning most piteously. The marbles have been known to carry on something frightful.

'When your uncle removed our precious Kore – the statue of the beautiful marble caryatid – had her taken away for safe keeping, which she was not, because I know for a fact that she is being shipped to England – the statue became so distraught that all of Athens could hear her wailing. And doleful sighs, groans and lamentations were heard long after she had been removed from her home, her rightful place in antiquity.'

'Diomedes!' Max cried. 'Whatever do you mean?'

Max threw down his pruning shears with a loud thump. He crouched on the dusty soil. Had he heard correctly? Perhaps his Greek wasn't as good as it should be.

'My uncle did not have the caryatid taken down without good reason. He would never have done that. It is his wish to save the marbles from further destruction. She was taken down for safe keeping. He told me so, himself!'

Max sat on the ground listening in total disbelief. While tears seeped from beneath the leathery lids of the old peasant's myopic eyes.

'No, Menelaos. Our beautiful Kore was not taken down for safe keeping. Nor did she fall down, as many people believe. She was ravished. Plundered, Menelaos. She was wrenched from her home, the magnificent temple of the Erechtheion, where she has been standing for thousands of years and now, sadly, lies stowed in a wooden crate in your uncle's shed, awaiting deportation to England – like a wanted criminal!'

'No. No! That cannot be!' Max cried, his voice rising.

'Imagine how she feels being separated from her family. Hidden from view,' said the old peasant, 'without being allowed out in the open air and sunlight...without companionship...and family love...' He was choking. The old man was having difficulty finishing his sentence.

'The lament, Menelaos,' breathed the old peasant, wiping the tears from his weather-beaten tear-stained face, 'takes place every

117

single time a marble is removed from the Acropolis. We also grieve for the marbles that have been plundered and are now missing.'

Max, always eager to learn the truth, asked, 'You mean every time a stone is removed from the Acropolis the spirit within the stone starts wailing?'

Max stabbed angrily at the bare rock face with a stick, waited impatiently for Diomedes to reply. As he did so, he happened to glimpse the Parthenon high on the rocky outcrop of the Acropolis. Once again he was overwhelmed by the sheer power and the majesty of Athena's sacred shrine. He could feel the power radiating from within the Parthenon itself. He felt empowered by this force in some unexplained way. It was as though the Parthenon had a spirit within the stone, because every time he glimpsed the edifice, it gave him strength and courage.

At that precise moment Max thought to himself, I must be going completely mad. Bonkers.

Max's thoughts remained elsewhere until the old peasant, brightening suddenly, said, 'Yes, Menelaos', using Max's ancient Greek name, Menelaos, over and over again.

'We Athenians believe that one day Pheidias' masterpieces will come home and our virgin goddess, Athena, will once again reign over the city of Athens. Until that time nothing will ever come right.'

'Do you understand what it means, Menelaos, to lose your soul?' Diomedes asked while leaning heavily on his gnarled walking stick, carved from the remains of his favourite olive tree.

'Do you know how it feels to lose everything that rightly belongs to you, all your belongings, all your treasures, the things you love, hold most dear?'

Max's brain was working fast.

As the honey-bees swarmed around his head, he asked, 'Have you ever lost anything that you loved deeply, Menelaos?'

Max didn't need much time to think.

'Yes!' Max felt his throat tighten as he leapt to his feet, his arms reaching upwards. He cried: 'I have lost my mother and my father, without whom I no longer have the money or reason to live in my boyhood home in Scotland. My grandparents are dead. I loved my grandpapa and grandmama dearly. All my boyhood treasures were disposed of when I was made a ward of my uncle. I lost my rocking horse and my pony and my toy sailboat. So yes, I have also lost things in my life.'

'Then you know exactly how Athena feels without her spiritual home. When the Parthenon is being plundered we Hellenes feel as though we ourselves are being plundered. Every time a chunk of marble is removed from the citadel, another chunk of our soul is lost, torn from us. At the rate we are going, soon we will have nothing left of our sacred temple or our souls.'

A lengthy silence followed. All that could be heard was a blackbird singing in a lone pine tree. Max stood up. He returned to his pruning. However, the old peasant had more to say.

'The Parthenon marbles are exquisite works of art. The statues were designed by Hellenes for the Hellenic people, for the people of Athens. The statues were carved by master stone-carvers who came from all regions of Greece. Do you know something, Menelaos?' Suddenly his gravelly voice became inaudible. 'You will find this difficult to understand, but we Hellenes believe that the souls of all those brilliant sculptors who carved the marbles remain buried deep in the stone, within the marble itself.'

Max shook his head. He didn't want to be rude but he could not imagine this so he thought it best to refrain from comment.

119

'The sculptors were extremely gifted artists. Like your friend Nikolaos' family. Did you know that his ancestors were master stone-carvers responsible for carving many of the marbles in the Parthenon's friezes and pediments? What you may find even more unbelievable is that no one has ever been able to replicate the carvings.'

Max listened carefully, translating every word into English in his mind.

'We are a strong race. We will not be defeated. We are ruled by the Ottomans and have been for three hundred and fifty years but nothing lasts for ever. One day, everything will come right. Athena will once again preside over our city, as Athena Parthenos was meant to do. Only then, Menelaos, will the desolation and the despair of the Hellenic people end.

'Do you understand why this is, Menelaos?'

Max nodded.

'I believe that when the stones from the Parthenon are returned, so too will our lost souls be returned. Because we have been bereft of our souls for so long, we, as a race, no longer care about anything. You can see this reflecting on the haggard, weary faces of our people. We have lost our heritage. When the marbles come home we will rejoice. We will have hope for the future because we will have regained our past. You will feel the same way, the day that you return to your boyhood home in Scotland.'

'Scotland is not my home!' Max reacted quickly. 'My home is here in Athens!' Max could not believe what he had said. His words had tumbled out before he could stop himself. Thinking back to that scorching hot summer's day in the garden, had he perhaps misunderstood Diomedes? He knew that his Greek was not as good as it should be. Perhaps the old peasant was sinking into senility.

Why would he deliberately make up such an outlandish tale? Max had been shocked by what the old peasant had said regarding Kore. Max could not believe that his uncle had deliberately taken the statue down from the Erechtheion.

While debating how to jump ship at Piraeus, Max slumped down on to the warped wooden floor of the verandah with his long scrawny legs curled up under him, hugging his knees. He could not recall feeling so wretched as he peeped dejectedly through the banister's wooden slats. Signs of neglect were everywhere. When he accidentally leaned against a slat, it crumbled like feta cheese, giving way in his hand. None of these things bothered him in the least as he sat in the privacy of the verandah, where unbeknown to his uncle he had slept naked most nights. All the boys in Athens slept and swam naked. Besides, Athens had been scorchingly hot all summer long and his small room had been so claustrophobic by the end of the long hot day that he had even contemplated sleeping downstairs in the cellar. If he could manage this minor caper without being discovered by Mrs Logotheti he would have done so, although he most certainly would not have minded being discovered by one of her three gorgeous daughters.

Mrs Logotheti's girls were Marcia, Allegra and Tatiana, the youngest of whom Max imagined to be the same age as himself. The girls were flower sellers and sold flowers every morning at the Propylaea, the gates leading up to the Parthenon. Perhaps this explained his passion for violets?

In the afternoons the girls returned to the villa. They appeared to float about the villa in a vision of loveliness, swathed in long, flowing gowns, neatly wound around their bodies. All Max could think of was unwinding their robes to glimpse what lay beneath, as the girls were, without doubt, the most beguiling creatures that he had ever set eyes on. Hence he was forever grateful for his uncle bringing him to Greece. English girls paled in comparison. Not that he knew many. The girls in London were dowdy, prissy creatures without an ounce of exotic blood in their veins. English girls buried themselves in layers of cloth, and Max, like the entire male population, was never allowed a glimpse of female flesh. Ever. The girls at the villa were a different species entirely who enjoyed dancing on the lawn in their see-through gowns, leaving a trail of sweet jasmine, incense and heady musk oil in the air. The girls were always laughing and giggling among themselves. Especially Marcia, who flashed her liquid amber eyes at him, and causing more nerves in his tummy. She wore delicate sandals decorated with brightly coloured gemstones, although the straps wrapped around her slim ankles continued up her legs. Max was fixated. He wanted to see where the straps ended. And as she walked her gown gaped open at her hip, revealing long, slender legs that went on for ever. Of course, this prompted more nerves. This provocative display of flesh was his undoing Max did not know whether to look at her legs...or her face...or her thighs...or her neatly wrapped waist. This was understandable.

Although her younger sister Allegra was the seductress because she swayed her hips when she walked. Allegra had a tiny waist and pert breasts that Max would have given *anything on earth* to touch.

Tatiana, on the other hand, wasn't anything like her older sisters. She was a born tease. She pinched Max when she raced past him, then hid in the bushes. Tatiana had the largest, blackest eyes imaginable. Her eyes mesmerised him, as did her thick, luxuriant hair that was so black it appeared blue. The thought of being alone in the cellar with Tatiana, or any of these nubile young beauties, overwhelmed him to such an extent he deemed a cold swim in the sea was badly needed to return his thoughts to reason. Otherwise, he might suffer a fainting spell – as Aunt Vrai Viviette had on many occasion – right there, on the verandah; although the heat was not to blame.

Suddenly, the whiff of burning charcoal ended this fanciful flight with the villa's three vestal virgins. Breakfast was being prepared in the kitchen down below. The pungent smell of burning charcoal was a clear indication that a servant had lit one of the enormous charcoal ovens and the cook was baking fresh bread. When Max had arrived at the villa he had been frightened by the sight of these enormous charcoal ovens, comparing the huge, dark orifices with their raging fires and huge gaping holes to infernos with bottomless pits. Like Hades, the underworld, where strange mythological creatures called Cyclops, sinister, one-eyed monsters, would grab Max and drag him into the raging inferno. Rip his heart out given half a chance. However, his fear of charcoal ovens had diminished greatly after celebrating his twelfth birthday, on the night of the summer solstice. Now, he considered himself to be approaching manhood and grown men were unafraid of everything, including charcoal ovens.

As the smell of burning charcoal wafted past his nose he spied a goat-skin bag containing olive oil lying on a small wicker table. He debated: should I give it a go one last time?

He had attempted the ancient custom of bathing in fresh olive oil on numerous occasions. He had stood on the verandah, pouring lashings of olive oil over his naked body, imagining himself to be a Greek god. Zeus invariably came to mind. Until it came time to scrape the slick oily substance from his tender, sun-burned skin with a sharp knife, as he was without a strigil, the steel blade used by the Greeks.

123

CHAPTER TEN

Yes, thought Max ruefully, life at the villa had been unlike anything he had experienced before and that was precisely what prompted him to feel so utterly wretched about leaving. According to his elders, he was considered 'a young man', or 'just a boy'. Deep down, he felt much older. He had this notion that he had lived long ago, in ancient times, or perhaps even before, in archaic times, as he was convinced he had been born with a very old soul. He could not explain this. There were times, in the past, when he had visited a special place that he was convinced that he had been there before, even though he had never been there in his life. It was uncanny. Déjà vu. Athens was a perfect example of this, the beach at Piraeus, yet another. Nikolaos' father's stone-carving workshop was another. Déjà vu feelings loomed largely in Greece and, sadly, were totally non-existent in London or Scotland or Harrow on the Hill.

He deeply resented being sent back to school in England, especially when his uncle had so little affection for him. He thought that he deserved to be consulted. His uncle would be happy to be rid of him. Although Max would miss his aunt, dear, sweet Vrai Viviette, whom he loved dearly, even with her silly French-sounding name. He wrote to his aunt every day. He had great sympathy for her, left behind in dreary old London, overseeing the refurbishment of their palatial house in St James's Square, a house that was so cold and draughty and exceedingly large that Max hated the damn thing. The problem was the Georgian pile was nothing like the crumbling villa in Athens.

Matins had ended at the Capuchin Monastery but the peeling of bells had been drowned out by the Muezzin calling the faithful Muslims to prayer from the minaret down the street...and Max failed to see Mr Dashiell Hamilton galloping through the gate, at a hellish pace.

Chapter Eleven
Mr Dashiell Hamilton Clinches the Deal

On the opposite side of the Acropolis Lord Quimby's London agent – the tall, elegant, although the no-longer *dashing* – Mr Dashiell Hamilton, stood banging on the door of the Disdar's house. The Disdar was the commandant in charge of guarding the Acropolis, and Mr Dashiell Hamilton, who was expected, was most anxious to get on with the business at hand. Within the soft folds of his fine leather case was the long-awaited firman, a signed document His Lordship had managed to procure from the Sublime Porte at Constantinople, allowing 'Lord Quimby's Dig' to continue. With luck it would be extended indefinitely, depending on how the meeting went. Mr Dashiell Hamilton was in a foul mood. Lord Quimby's ship sailed at noon and all of the metopes needed to be in the hold by twelve o'clock. His backside was terribly sore, suffering from the after-effects of a perilous ride around the base of the Acropolis at breakneck speed on a lumbering great camel, while jolting up and down on a splintered wooden saddle.

He mopped his brow with a fine linen handkerchief, impatiently waiting for a Turkish slave to open the door. As he waited he happened to glance at rows of potted geraniums sitting on the windowsill. The freshly painted blue shutters were pulled shut. There was no sign of poverty here. Then he happened to glance upwards and caught sight of an exquisite chunk of marble set into the stone wall above the door. Why hadn't he noticed it before? Why – it was exquisite!

How many piastres were needed to persuade the Disdar to part from the ancient artefact with a gorgon's head in the centre of the stone and surrounded by allegorical figures?

Everything had a price, he thought smugly, and banged louder, rattling the sun-bleached oak portal. Six hundred piastres would do the trick. Four or five hundred piastres was the going rate for a small piece of marble – even the tiniest piece of stone – which everyone called loot.

Several minutes passed before a young boy quietly opened the door. He recognised Evliya immediately, having made several visits to the Disdar's house in the last three years. Evliya was the Disdar's youngest son. He must be about the same age as Max, thought Mr Dashiell Hamilton, as he was about the same height. Evliya bowed several times before ushering Mr Dashiell Hamilton inside. He was immaculately dressed in typical Turkish-style garb: pristine white silk pantaloons gathered at the ankles, which ballooned out when he walked, and bright blue embroidered Persian slippers with turned-up toes on his small feet. He wore a long white tunic with a stand-up collar and with a single row of pure gold buttons down the front. His collar and cuffs were embossed with gold palm trees and heavy gold braid swung from his right shoulder as he pattered silently down the hall. It was enough to put the entire British Naval Fleet to shame. Completing the ensemble a bright red fez with a long black tassel sat perched on a mass of jet-black curls. Evliya kept his enormous black eyes lowered at all times, perhaps showing his contempt for strangers, even though they had met many times before. Mr Dashiell Hamilton followed the young lad down the hall into a large sitting area – as if he was making a grand entrance into an enormous marquee at St James's Park. The interior walls of the house were painted white; however, the ceiling was lined with striped gold and white satin, and matching gold and white satin curtains billowed through double doors leading on to a terrace. Mr Dashiell Hamilton felt as though he were being led into a circus ring. Was a Bengal tiger about to jump through the hoop?

'Mr Hamilton.' The Disdar held out his arms swathed in richly embossed gold silk. 'Please. Sit.'

'Thank you.'

Sitting cross-legged on a sumptuous bed, the Disdar looked more like the Ali Pasha than a military man. The counterpane embroidered with enormous pearls was swathed in layer-upon-layer of yellow silk. He wore a brightly coloured turban wound tightly to his head that boasted an emerald the size of a goose egg. His snow-white beard hung over an enormous paunch, hidden beneath a yellow silk robe trimmed in ermine and studded all over with brilliants. *The Arabian Nights* came swiftly to mind. The Disdar sat plumped-up on a vast assembly of sumptuous, brightly coloured red, gold and green silk cushions that were also tucked in behind his back, while his hands laden with jewels rested heavily on enormous silk cushions embroidered with gold elephants.

He clapped his hands once, shooing his harem away.

He clapped his hands twice signalling the dragoman to enter. The small man, of no consequence, bowed then sat down on the floor on a large tufted hassock beside the Disdar.

CHAPTER ELEVEN

A three-way conversation began.

'Ask him,' said the Disdar to the dragoman. 'Ask him, did he bring the firman from the Sultan?'

'As promised,' replied Mr Dashiell Hamilton, smiling brightly as he spoke in very bad pidgin Greek, while the interpreter spoke Greek, Turkish, Arabic and Latin, but not a single word of English.

'Begin!' boomed the Disdar, his piercing grey eyes drilling into his guest's.

Mr Dashiell Hamilton read out the terms of agreement and the dragoman then translated every word, very slowly, into Turkish for the Disdar, who coughed and sputtered throughout the entire process because of his extreme poor health. But he still managed to smile. After all, the Disdar was a happy man He had in his hand the long-awaited firman, the document from the vizier, the Ottoman official in Constantinople, allowing 'Lord Quimby's Dig' to continue to further excavate the Acropolis.

'We, meaning, of course, Lord Quimby, will be allowed to enter freely the Acropolis, carry out our excavation, within the walls of the citadel, and to draw and model with plaster the ancient temples there. We will be allowed to erect scaffolding on all four sides of the Parthenon. We will be allowed to dig where we may wish to discover ancient foundations, and we are at liberty to take away any sculpture or inscriptions which do not interfere with the walls of the citadel.'

This translation took quite some time as the dragoman had to keep repeating himself.

'My money, where is my money?'

Mr Dashiell Hamilton opened his fine leather case, a present from his darling, his mistress, sweet Vrai Viviette. He proceeded to withdraw the bribery money – ten bags of piastres.

'I shall make you an offer,' Mr Dashiell Hamilton said, offering his best smile imaginable, 'Five thousand piastres for the lot!'

The dragoman translated.

The Disdar wrinkled his nose. Obviously pooh-poohing the offer.

Mr Dashiell Hamilton tried again. 'One thousand piastres for the horse.'

The Disdar understood. 'No. Not one. Two. Two thousand! Not one piastre less!'

'Lord Quimby wants Poseidon! How much for the statue of Poseidon?'

'Not for sale!'

'Everything is for sale.'

'Five thousand piastres!'

'Done!'

'I want Athena! How much for Athena?'

'She not for sale.'

Mr Dashiell Hamilton opened his case and withdrew a cache of articles of bribery and spread them out on the counterpane right under the Disdar's cauliflower nose.

'This is for you,' he said while holding up a handful of exquisite gold rings set with diamonds and rubies direct from Asprey's in London. He then offered an engraved silver snuff box with the *Disdar's* name, Raschid, engraved on the lid. Also included in this hoard, which had cost Lord Quimby's wife *the earth*, was a diamond box worth 1500 guineas.

The Disdar grinned, parting large leathery lips. He clapped his hands once and his harem entered.

He leaned closer to Mr Dashiell Hamilton and whispered, 'Now, I can afford to keep my harem!' which the dragoman then translated.

'You want marbles?' the Disdar asked, waving his ample arms. 'Bring me more sable, ermine, satin, brocade, velvet, damask, Venetian sequins! Then, my friend, we do much business.'

Mr Dashiell Hamilton had discovered Elysian Fields, ambrosia awaited. He couldn't wait to return to his mistress in England, as he needed to keep her happy. This was not difficult, as her appetite for sex was insatiable. She, in turn, had been supplying him with all the money that he needed. She was funding Lord Quimby's expedition as well. The woman had gobs of money. There seemed to be no end to the damn stuff. She had to be one of the wealthiest women in England. Inherited wealth… There was nothing quite so alluring. Vrai Viviette was a French noblewoman and when she fled at the outbreak of the bloody French Revolution she brought all her money with her, hidden in enormous chests. She also received numerous pensions from the King's Privy Purse that quite frankly boggled his mind. His licentious thoughts darted back and forth across the Channel, dreaming of holding his darling sweet Vrai Viviette in his loving arms. She swooned every time they made love in each room of the empty house in St James's Square. The Shambles in Perthshire was the next bed on sin – the perfect love-nest in which to romp naked. Even if the house was bloody freezing. As long as Lord Quimby stayed in the East there wouldn't be a problem.

Keep it up old chap and you can have all the marbles you want. Lord Quimby be damned!

Needless to say Mr Dashiell Hamilton had even more grandiose ideas on his mind, although he kept them to himself. The Monument of Lysicrates, the temple of the Erechtheion and the Temple of Athena Nike must wait. Acquisition fever had taken hold. There was no stopping him.

Chapter Twelve
Time to Meet Murgatroyd, the Tortoise

'Max Max!' Eggy's squeaking voice blasted loudly through the open doorway. 'Hurry up!'

'Keep your voice down,' urged Max with his finger pressed tight to his lips. 'For heaven's sake, Eggy, be quiet. We're right next door to hallowed ground!'

'Hurry up, Max!' Eggy blasted again, staring quizzically at Max's attire. 'Why are you still in your pyjamas?'

Eggy yanked on the ends of two white linen pillowcases tied in a knot around his bare shoulders, his make-believe version of Hermes' short cloak. He wore the same outfit every day, consisting of a pair of cotton short trousers with a patched seat that were much too small for his fat legs, and a motley-looking straw hat perched on his small round head, which was fringed with a halo of soft blond curls. A cherub if ever there was one. His straw hat had magically sprouted wings over the summer and clumps of wilted olive branches poked through the holes on either side of his hat. Eggy imagined himself to be the embodiment of the youthful god Hermes, the envoy of the gods. He had even persuaded Duffy to glue enormous wings, made of a goat-skin bag, on to either side of a ratty pair of sandals. However, Eggy appeared to be having difficulty keeping his sandals on his feet, as bare feet were *de rigueur* in Athens.

It wasn't only Max who was acting like a Greek.

'Aren't you coming on our treasure hunt?' Eggy asked, becoming more and more agitated while jumping up and down on the verandah. 'You promised. You promised!'

'No, Eggy, I am not coming with you. Furthermore, I never promised to accompany you on your treasure hunt.'

'Yes you did Max-ie. You said so, last night when we were on our way into dinner. Don't you remember, silly?'

'No, Eggy, I do not remember and please do not call me Maxie. And please don't allude to me as silly either!'

Eggy pouted. He picked his nose. He tugged on the ends of the pillowcases as he stared at the ceiling.

'The treasure hunt is on, so I am going to meet my friends at the Acropolis. More metopes are being pulled down this morning. Remember? Father told everyone at the dinner table last night. Don't you ever listen?'

Max looked at Eggy, hiding his disdain. He debated the possibilities of becoming a ward of some hitherto unknown soul as he no longer wished to be associated with his cousin or his uncle.

'Is this not the most exciting thing ever?' exclaimed Eggy, wrinkling his small freckled nose. 'The metopes coming down, I mean.'

Max did not respond. He was too busy ignoring the squeaking sound blasting forth from his cousin's precocious mouth.

'Come on, Max! Come on!' Eggy tugged on the sleeve of Max's pyjamas. 'I demand you come with me. I need help loading the loot on to the back of my donkey. Evliya's father wants us to get as much loot as we can find because he needs more stuff to sell on to tourists before the ship sails, Max...ie!'

'Your trunk is filled with loot,' spat Max, angrily.

'I know but I don't care.'

'Eggy, please, listen to me. You cannot possibly fit any more rocks into your trunk. If you do the ship will sink!' To refrain from throttling his cousin Max distracted himself by scratching his arms which were covered in bug bites.

'Well, then Duffy will need to find another trunk, won't he? Another trunk just for me!' Eggy's pouting mouth drooped. The boy whom Max alluded to as *the brat* behind his back was about to cry.

'If Uncle finds out you will be in big trouble!' Max waved a finger at Eggy.

'I know, but I really don't care. It is *my* loot anyway. After all, this is our last treasure hunt, Max-i-mil-i-an! Now that father has finally returned from Constantinople. So...hurry up! Get dressed!'

'No I will not get dressed. I am not coming with you,' snapped Max, glaring at his young cousin who was finding it impossible to stand still, and continued jumping up and down on the verandah, with his small pudgy hands holding on to his travelling hat. 'And that is all there is to it!'

'Besides, I have made other plans, Eggy,' Max said with authority, looking stern, more grown-up. He did not want to confess that he had been confined to quarters, stuck on the blasted verandah until the ship sailed at noon. Eggy would laugh at him and Max did not relish being laughed at.

'Have you forgotten? Today is the day that the horse is to come down. Poseidon is coming down too...and then Iris...and... Don't you want to watch, Max?' asked Eggy, twirling around on the verandah, imagining he were Hermes about to leap into the air. 'It will be great fun!'

'What?' Max cried, sounding shocked. 'What did you say, Eggy?'

'Don't you know *Stupid!* Father said Selene's horse is coming down this morning!'

Max tugged on his pyjama bottoms. He paled beneath his tan.

'Evliya told me Selene's horse is coming down today. It's coming home with us on the boat. Don't you want to watch the awesome sight? The plunder, Max?'

Eggy twitched, anxious to flee, as Hermes would have done had he been there.

'No!' exclaimed Max, although his words were lost on the sirocco, the hot sultry wind blowing in from the Sahara.

The young messenger had taken flight, bellowing pillowcases and all. Hermes was in a hurry. The treasure hunt was about to begin.

Every morning, after breakfast, Eggy and his chums rode up to the Acropolis on their donkeys in search of treasure. All the small bits of marble (loot) that the boys found they gave to Evliya's father, or sold on to English tourists – those desperate for a souvenir, as everyone back home adored all things Greek. Eggy did not understand the first thing about money and chose not to sell his loot, so he stashed his cache in his trunk under his bed. The treasure hunt had gone on for months, so you can well imagine Eggy's trunk was so unbelievably heavy it was debatable whether the porters would be able to lift it on to the back of the camel to take down to the ship.

Eggy's loot had reached such enormous proportions that the marbles were overflowing on to the floor of his bedroom. The cellar was full of stuff. He bragged about his hidden treasure when they were alone in the garden. In fact, Eggy bragged about everything. On the odd occasion when Max had been bullied into taking part in this thieving escapade he rarely, if ever, discovered anything of interest. Max did not believe that it was proper to sell the loot on to tourists, nor did he think it was right that anyone, including his uncle, be allowed to take the loot home. He had no good reason for feeling this way. He thought it was wrong, that was all.

While Max debated all these things he stood leaning over the railing. However, Eggy's sudden revelation regarding Selene's horse kept interrupting his thoughts. The fact that the statues were being removed from the Parthenon's east pediment filled him with horror. And, he couldn't do a thing about it. Because he was stuck on the verandah.

'Bugger!'

Suddenly, he caught sight of Murgatroyd lumbering across the lawn on his small chubby legs with the remains of a wilted lettuce leaf dangling from the corner of his soft, fleshy mouth. Max wondered whether the tortoise enjoyed his habitat confined within his four stone walls, or if he should return it to the beach? But the tortoise was in no mood for frivolities. The Greek tortoise was obviously reluctant to entertain the newly arriving English tourists gathering on the lawn judging by the way he lumbered off, on his short, leathery legs into the shade of a gnarled olive tree, with his small crinkly head tucked neatly inside his armoured shell – a portable fortress of sorts.

He recalled the day that the young tortoise had come into his life, while bathing in the sea at Piraeus.

'Nikolaos!' Max shouted, standing on the shore, as he peered at a group of rough-looking Greek sponge divers gathering on the beach. 'What are the sponge divers doing to the tortoise?'

'I don't know, Menelaos,' Nikolaos said flatly while he splashed about wildly, enjoying his swim in the crystal-clear blue sea.

'The water is so refreshing, Menelaos, why are you not coming in?'

By this time Max had fled. He was halfway along the shore. He was a little apprehensive at first, uncertain of approaching the sponge divers dragging their nets out of the sea – nets filled with soggy yellow sponges. The men looked a rowdy lot. But his eyesight was very good, so he did not really need to go closer. Until...

'Nikolaos!' Max screamed loudly while standing on the sand that was burning the soles of his feet. 'Come quick!'

Max stood pointing his finger at a young tortoise tied to an iron spike stuck into the sand.

'Look...Nikolaos...look! The poor creature...what are they doing to it?'

Nikolaos emerged, naked, from the shimmering, silvery sea and wrapping a towel around his waist ran along the shore towards his friend.

Max stood nervously wringing his hands.

'Niko, we must dooo...something!'

'What?' quizzed Nikolaos eying the sponge divers standing huddled near a roasting-spit.

'Do you take me for a fool?'

'If we challenge those bloody Turks,' said he, cursing like an Englishman, 'we will end up roasting on the spit!'

Max wasn't listening. He was not to be deterred and he kept on walking towards the tortoise about to be roasted alive in the flames.

'Bugger off!' shot a sponge diver, glaring at Max as he approached the ugly scene. 'Go away kid!'

'None of your business!' shouted another.

'We sell the shell to tourists. Like you Englishmen!'

Max ignored the sponge divers standing around the blazing fire, dripping in seawater. He put his hand in his pocket. What was the going price for a singed tortoise? He hadn't the foggiest idea, but a few drachmas was all he had to lose.

'Here!' Max threw the coins down in the sand, in front of the sponge divers, trying to distract the bullies from committing murder on the beach.

The sponge divers went for it. They crouched on the beach, sifting through the sand.

Max lunged. He grabbed hold of the young tortoise that was tied to the spike, lying upside down on the beach with his soft, fleshy legs akimbo, and his small wrinkly head being singed by the fire. Max yanked hard on the spike. Unable to free the tortoise, he was forced to drag the tortoise, spike and all, with him along the beach. When they were out of harm's way he picked up the tortoise and raced as fast as he could go towards the shelter of the pier. It was then the creature poked his head out of his shell.

Were those really tears seeping out of the corners of the tortoise's eyes?

'You damn English fool,' Nikolaos screeched while running along the beach beside his friend. 'We will be roasted alive if we don't get out of here!'

'I don't care!' Max said as he stomped off in a huff. Although he couldn't help wondering who was more relieved, him or the tortoise, as it had looked at him in such an odd way that Max was convinced the tortoise had smiled.

'What do you want to do with your prize?' asked Nikolaos, teasingly, while standing naked on the beach. 'Do tortoises make good soup? Like turtles?'

'Stop making fun of me. Tortoises are inedible, you fool!'

'You are the fool!'

CHAPTER TWELVE

'The tortoise is coming home with us,' Max said in huffy tones. 'I have no intention of leaving the tortoise behind.'

And, because he always meant what he said, he proceeded to wrap up the tortoise gently in his wet towel that was lying on the beach, suddenly feeling the need to keep him safe.

'Menelaos, you are an ass! Your uncle will think you are crazy... mad!'

Max was not to be deterred. He was strong willed. He rushed towards Mopsus tethered to an olive tree by the pier and quickly placed the tortoise inside a large pannier tied to the back of his nimble-footed donkey – whose benevolence had become awe-inspiring during the long, hot summer.

After Nikolaos dried himself with a towel, climbed into his short trousers and loose-fitting white cotton shirt that all the Greek sculptors wore, they set off, heading in the direction of Nikolaos' house. Max had been invited for dinner. He could not wait. Nikolaos' mother was a fabulous cook. He loved moussaka and souvlaki and keftedes – yummy meatballs. He was drooling, just thinking of baklava, the Balkan-type pastry filled with chopped nuts and soaked with honey.

—GR ဆ—

Max was starving. He needed his breakfast. But he was concerned that Nikolaos would be waiting for him on the south porch of the Parthenon to say their last farewells. He needed to get a message to Nikolaos. He paced angrily back and forth on the verandah. What on earth could he do?

Nikolaos lived above his father's stone-carving shop at Kantharos, Piraeus' main harbour. Max had tried his hand at stone-carving on several occasions, although he found carving stone extremely difficult. What he adored most of all, however, was an invitation to dinner to experience the pleasure of partaking of Mama's excellent cooking – a combination of Latin, Greek, Albanian and Turkish all rolled into one – for Mama was from Milan. During the summer Max had been introduced to all sorts of interesting food. And most of all, Max enjoyed eating with his fingers.

But Max had discovered something even more revealing about life over the workshop, other than taramasalata, and that was that although Nikolaos' family lived in terribly cramped quarters that reminded him of a hayloft, his family appeared to be extremely happy. Nikolaos greeted his parents with such warmth and affection every time they met that Max was, well, dumbfounded. Max remained confused, asking himself the same question many times over the summer: did material possessions bring happiness? Because the way in which Nikolaos' family behaved, it meant that quite the opposite was true, because Nikolaos' family were the happiest people that he had ever come across. If this were true, then why was his uncle so obsessed with material wealth or the acquisition of Classical antiquities in particular – if, in fact – material things did not bring happiness? It was a puzzle, thought Max, suddenly recalling Nikolaos' mother singing operatic arias in the small cramped kitchen while she was making dinner. He was reminded of those happy times at dinner, while seated around the small table, everyone was laughing gayly and teasing each other. Even more extraordinary was that everyone nibbled food from each other's plates. Max had never witnessed such behaviour at the dinner table, although it was not offensive in any way.

His thoughts returned to Murgatroyd on the lawn.

Needless to say, Murgatroyd had become the star attraction at the villa. Appropriately named Murgatroyd because of the unbelievably strong resemblance to his tutor, even without the pince-nez, enormous ears and unruly hairs sprouting out of the ends of his nostrils.

Max dreaded the thought of leaving the tortoise at the villa. He had even debated taking Murgatroyd on board his uncle's East Indiaman that afternoon. Would becoming a castaway appeal to Murgatroyd? That is, whether Max could somehow manage to drill air-holes in the lid of his trunk. As Max sat on the verandah contemplating the whereabouts of a drill, he eyed a small stone glistening in the bright sun.

Amongst a vast collection of seashells clumped together on the floor lay his small cache of stones that he had discovered while roaming the Acropolis (before being banished!), The stones were ever so smooth in texture and milky-white in colour. One of the stones was a small hand. He couldn't imagine who it had belonged to because it was much too small for any of the colossal statues in the Parthenon. Another was a chunk of marble with lumpy bits on the top that looked like allegorical figures of some sort. Another stone was an exact replica of a right foot, so heavy, in fact, that he needed both hands to lift it. His imagination had run wild when he discovered the foot hidden in the rubble – thinking that because the foot was so enormous, it must have belonged to a statue in the Parthenon. Could it have fallen off during a violent storm or better still, perhaps it belonged to Athena herself, which would have been truly amazing.

The foot was about three times the size of his uncle's. Enormous really. His 'find' had seemed so insignificant at the time of discovery that he never bothered asking the archaeologists working on 'Lord Quimby's Dig' about its provenance.

All the marbles had a translucent quality, and as Max looked closely at the stones in the bright sunlight he noticed pink and blue veins running through the marbles, exactly like the veins in his own hand and foot. Had the foot been endowed with toenails, it would have looked just like a human foot. Then suddenly, Max glimpsed the faint outline of several Greek letters carved on the inside of the big toe. The letters were almost invisible to the naked eye. 'Crikey!' His uncle's magnifying glass would be perfect here, thought Max, as he traced the letters with his fingers, knowing how to decipher the Greek letters: ΝΙΚΟΔΗΜΟΣ.

Little did he know that 2000 years had passed since anyone had got that close to the sculptor who had carved the foot. Max felt as though he was touching a part of the sculptor's soul. The marble was cool to touch, reminding him of the lovely sensation of his aunt Vrai Viviette's soft cheek against his skin, when she had kissed him goodbye in London.

He had been undecided about taking the stones home with him. Why was his conscience niggling him? Max thought the stones belonged to the Hellenic people. Was he wrong to think that? He wasn't sure what to do. Perhaps he should ask his uncle. His uncle had a warehouse full of loot. He was about to remove the statue of Selene's horse. So, what did that tell him? Max remained confused. However, he decided to take his collection home with him, and hide the loot under his smalls in the bottom of his trunk. He picked up the small marble hand and, leaning over the banister, examined the stone more closely in the dazzling sunlight, trying with all his might to imagine who it belonged to, and thankful he had managed to keep the marble out of harm's way. Until...

Sir Archibald Lushington, the sole occupant of the room downstairs, banged the shutters open. The noise startled Max and his precious marble went flying off the verandah, dropping into the rain barrel down below on the lawn.

Max stifled a cry. His hand flew to his mouth as he stood peering over the railing watching ripples form in the rain barrel. He glimpsed the freckled, sun-burned, badly-blistered, bald head of the Curator of the Museum of Classical Antiquities, Sir Archibald Lushington – an exceedingly rotund figure swathed in an eau de Nil silk dressing gown, puffing on the chewed end of an enormous Dutch cigar. The plopping sound had sent the Curator scurrying to the scene, peering down into the *blasted* rain barrel. Max cowered into the shade of a bougainvillea overhanging the verandah. He did not wish to be seen by Sir Archibald Lushington. He did not wish to speak to the man. Not now. Not ever. Not after last night's fiasco. He had no intention of apologising. The dreadful scene returned with a vengeance and stayed there like the chronic indigestion his uncle suffered constantly.

Max and Eggy were racing each other down the hall towards the front door, anxious to escape after yet another boring dinner when the children present were not allowed to speak – to play hide-and-seek in the garden. Eggy, as usual, had run on ahead. But, as Max whizzed past the smoking room he heard his uncle's London agent's deep melodic voice. However, this time, it wasn't so melodic.

'Take away *everything*. Do you hear me? Take everything!'

'Please explain what you mean by *everything*?'

'I mean exactly what I said, gentlemen. Every last piece of marble that you can get your hands on. Have it removed as quickly as possible.'

'Bloody hell, Hamilton!' Don Giovanni Battista Belisario, his uncle's clerk of works, pounded his fists on the table. 'We can't do that!'

'Oh yes we can,' replied Mr Dashiell Hamilton with absolute authority, as though he were speaking from the Throne Room in Buckingham Palace.

Max stopped dead in his tracks, peeped through the thin crack in the door to glimpse Sir Archibald Lushington seated in a wing-back chair in front of the window and his uncle's clerk of works leaning on a small spindly-legged, green-baize-covered games table, with his hunched back to the door. The *not-so-dashing* Mr Dashiell Hamilton stood in front of the open window with his arms folded behind his back in military fashion. Like Admiral Nelson would have done. The gentlemen were so engrossed in conversation that the silent witness hiding behind the door went undetected.

'The man is an idiot!' The Don cried.

'Here, here!' Sir Archibald Lushington added in agreement from his comfortable upholstered wing-back chair. 'I heartily agree.'

'What may I ask, constitutes everything?' The Don asked.

'His Lordship has his eye on the Erechtheion.'

'What do you mean? He's already removed one of the maidens. Does he want to take the rest of the girls?'

'No. He means the temple...all of it.'

'What? He's mad!' Don Battista's arms were waving.

'He also fancies the Monument of Lysicrates.'

'Well, it's a damn sight easier to pinch than the bloody Erechtheion,' boomed Sir Archibald Lushington, choking on cigar smoke.

'There's more...the Temple of Athena Nike is to go. Vrai Viviette has taken a fancy to the columns. She imagines Ionic columns are more feminine and wants two or three of the columns for her boudoir in St James's Square.'

'You can't be serious.'

'Oh yes I am.'

'Have you told her how enormous the columns are?'

'Have you ever tried talking to the wall?'

The Curator sighed heavily, no doubt feeling pinched in his chair. 'God help us!'

'Has the Disdar agreed to this?'

Mr Dashiell Hamilton shrugged. 'More or less, Milord; we agreed to the terms yesterday. He wants the money tomorrow at noon. I have paid so much money to the Disdar in the last three weeks that I feel as though we own the damn Acropolis – everything!'

Mr Dashiell Hamilton was becoming indignant. His healthy glow from the Aegean sun paled in the fug of stale cigar smoke. He appeared nervous. His moustache drooped at the edges.

'His Lordship is sailing for England at noon tomorrow. He will be taking the boys with him. I know that you had planned to accompany Lord Quimby on his voyage, Sir Archibald, although I feel that it's best for you to remain here in Athens with Don Battista and myself. His Lordship will need all of us to keep things moving. There is far too much at stake now. His Lordship, or should I say his wife, has invested a fortune in these blasted stones and Quimby insists on taking as much loot home as possible.'

'I don't like it, Hamilton.' Don Battista looked grim.

'Too bad!'

Sir Archibald Lushington squirmed in his chair. He combed his hair, no longer there, obviously a habit of old. He scratched his bald head, picking the scabs.

'I have packed all my things,' said Sir Archibald. 'I have been ready to escape this hell-hole for bloody weeks.'

'Then you had better start unpacking your things,' growled Lord Quimby's London agent, looking more like a Bengal tiger about to devour his prey than an English gentleman partaking of his vintage port.

Sir Archibald Lushington sighed. He got the message.

'Now, there's more bad news. Quimby is not leaving here until the hold of the East Indiaman is full. After much wrangling, Captain Light has agreed to wait. Why, the bastard – he mistook me for the Ali Pasha! The money I greased his palm with was a bloody king's ransom! Yet the good captain was not a happy man. He had to remove one of the main beams to accommodate the enormous statue of the caryatid. It was either cut up the ship or saw the statue in half. Quimby would not be pleased. Now he wants another caryatid for either side of the grand foyer in the house at St James's Square. The damn thing should make great ballast!'

'Ha. Ha. Ha!'

'By the time the ship sails there will be enough loot in the hold to sink the blasted ship.'

'Lord Quimby has rocks in his head!'

'Ha. Ha. Ha!' Laughter engulfed the room.

'He has an almighty nerve asking us to help him raid the Acropolis!'

'He is asking the impossible!' shot Sir Archibald Lushington. 'I think it's ludicrous to expect to have anything more removed from the Parthenon. The metopes are difficult enough!'

Sir Archibald Lushington stood up. He paced back and forth, mopping his brow. He looked as though he was about to expire from the suffocating heat, which was definitely a possibility, since the gentlemen were kitted out in full evening dress.

145

CHAPTER TWELVE

Max wondered why English gentlemen insisted on retaining their English-style clothing while travelling abroad, on the Grand Tour, whether the Continent or the Near East. His uncle was guilty of this, thought Max to himself, as he listened more intently, having completely forgotten about Eggy.

Max could only imagine the misery, having to conform to such ludicrous dress requirements in such intense heat. The near strangulation of it all – with a silk cravat wound tightly around his neck, thick cotton shirt with rows of frills, no less, then stuffed into a heavily embossed silk waistcoat, embroidered with bright coloured foxes, for heaven's sake – so exceedingly out of place in the Near East, and white stockings rolled over his calves. It was enough to provoke heatstroke. To top it off, the men were wearing thick, velvet tailcoats and buckled patent leather pumps. Why, it was pure theatre, thought Max, as a brief intermission followed.

Fortunately, Max remained hidden. He kept up his vigil, with his cheek pressed to the door, listening, fearful of entering.

'Hamilton, with all due respect, it is pure madness to think that we will be able to remove any more marbles by noon tomorrow. You have no idea the trouble we have had trying to get one metope down from the blasted frieze of the Parthenon.'

'Here, here!' said Mr Dashiell Hamilton, breathing snuff into his nose from an ivory box he had extracted from his pocket.

Don Battista said, 'Deed you tell His Lordship about the saws that are stuck in the metope? Heee's not a pretty sight. The frieze looks dreadful. We need more equipment and longer saws.'

'Still, we must proceed at once, whatever the cost.' Mr Dashiell Hamilton emptied his glass.

'We can ill afford another disaster,' said Sir Archibald Lushington.

146

'Lushington, what should we do?' Mr Dashiell Hamilton asked, shooting his cuffs.

'I think the statues in the east and west pediments will be much easier to remove. Forget the metopes for now. Forget the frieze. Let's start with the statue of Athena tomorrow morning. We can begin at first light, at dawn.'

'Capital. Capital idea!' Mr Dashiell Hamilton looked pleased. 'His Lordship doesn't give a toss to what lengths we go to get the job done. We will have to use whatever force there is available. Cannon balls if need be. It wouldn't be the first time someone blasted a hole in the temple, tried to blow the Parthenon to bits.'

'Keep your voice down, Hamilton!' urged Sir Archibald Lushington. 'Someone might hear you!'

'Does it matter? The bloody Greek peasants don't give a damn about their marbles. Neither do the Turks or the Whirling Dervishes!'

Mr Dashiell Hamilton clicked his heels, boosting his height. He strode towards the games table and, as he banged his hands down, spat, 'Even more to the point, Lord Quimby insists on having the marbles delivered in time for Christmas. So, he shall have them. Let us remind ourselves, gentlemen, that we must not disappoint. It seems that Lady Quimby has been hounding him for months, wanting large statues for the foyer; does it matter that the statues aren't Roman for Christ sake. She will never know the difference! We must keep the good woman happy or...'

'Meaning?'

'Meaning, Her Ladyship will stop payment of funds!'

'That means no more money for wages.'

'That's correct.'

'We have no choice, gentlemen.'

'The Disdar is extremely unwell. This could be to our advantage. He no longer gives a damn about the stones. He could die at any moment.'

'Let's hope that he doesn't. Not until we get our marbles.'

'Did you tell Lord Quimby that you paid the Disdar one thousand, five hundred piastres for the metope laying on bedrock in a million and one pieces? I expect Quimby will be furious when he finds out.'

'No, I most certainly did not!' Mr Dashiell Hamilton said. 'He hasn't a bloody clue what he's spent money on. Now, the Disdar is demanding even greater sums. He wants two thousand for Selene's horse and five thousand for each of the statues from the east and west pediments. He thinks he's offering us a bargain price for Athena at a mere five thousand piastres! Highway robbery, that's what it is!'

'When you consider what's left of the statue. He'd want more if she had her head!'

'He wants the money by noon, tomorrow!'

Sir Archibald Lushington puffed smoke curls in the air. He kept clearing his throat. 'Athena seems reluctant to part with her marbles.'

'Reluctant or not, Lord Quimby is determined to have them – all of them – every single last one. What he doesn't know is that I have my eye on the Erechtheion. Why, the temple is a perfect summer house for the garden. Don't you think? I will make the Disdar an offer once Quimby leaves for London. The Temple of Athena Nike I imagine as a romantic folly set in the rolling hills. Imagine the sheer delight standing next to the ha-ha at the house in Wiltshire.

'So, gentlemen, have we agreed to take the whole bloody lot?'

'Why not!'

'We will require the entire British Naval Fleet to assist us.'

'Tomorrow morning at dawn we start by taking Athena, before the Turkish bastards change their minds and ban us...again!'

Max broke rank. He stormed into the smoking room, screaming at the top of his lungs. 'No. No. No!'

He ran towards Mr Dashiell Hamilton and punching him in the chest cried, 'Not Athena, Mr Dashiell Hamilton, you cannot take Athena...otherwise...the...marbles...' He was sobbing and shouting. 'The statues...are enchanted! Those that are left behind will start wailing and...sobbing...the marbles...will carry on something frightful!'

'Maximilian!' Mr Dashiell Hamilton grabbed hold of Max's failing arms and held on tight. 'Please control yourself!'

Max faced his uncle's London agent head on, while his other opponents stood dumbfounded.

'Sir, you cannot take Athena down from the Parthenon.' Max was crying. 'Do you hear me? She will never stop screaming!'

'What the devil are you talking about?' Mr Dashiell Hamilton spat, horrified. 'Have you gone mad, Maximilian?'

'It is plunder, Mr Hamilton! Plunder!' Max wailed.

Max pulled away from his captor's grasp. He swung around and glared at his enemy. 'And, you, Sir Archibald. I have seen you on your hands and knees crawling all over the Acropolis scrounging for loot.'

Sir Archibald paled.

'How could you!' Max shouted, pointing his finger at Sir Archibald Lushington. 'How could you do such a beastly thing?'

Amidst all the commotion, Lord Quimby entered.

'Maximilian!' Lord Quimby rushed towards his nephew. 'What the devil is going on here?'

Lord Quimby glared at his nephew.

'Have you been eavesdropping young man?' asked Lord Quimby, who had heard more than he let on. 'Have you, Maximilian?'

'It is extremely rude to listen to other people's conversations,' said Lord Quimby, frowning, his deeply furrowed brow deepening.

'Uncle, do you have any idea what has been going on behind your back during your absence? If not, I shall be most happy to enlighten you. Uncle, these three gentlemen are in cahoots with each other. And have been for the last three weeks. I have seen what has been going on, Uncle, with my own eyes, while you were away in Constantinople.'

'Maximilian. Please,' Lord Quimby said in a stern voice Max recognised immediately. 'Hold your tongue, young man.'

Sir Archibald Lushington waddled towards Max who was sobbing in front of the window. He was terribly red in the face and spoke in a croaky voice, 'Who do you think you are young man, making such defamatory remarks against your elders?'

Sir Archibald Lushington, dripping in sweat, pawed madly at an obscure orifice inside his tailcoat for an enormous silk handkerchief. While mopping his face, his neck and his hands he bellowed, 'I am extremely disappointed in you, Maximilian.'

'How dare you say such things!' exclaimed Mr Dashiell Hamilton while nervously running his hands through his thick wavy hair. 'How dare you, Maximilian!'

'With all due respect Mr Hamilton, Sir, I believe that you are a thief.'

'Uncle, are you aware that Sir Archibald is robbing you of valuable artifacts, right under your nose.' It was then Max glimpsed his uncle's nose and thought it was vanishing at an alarming rate.

'Maximilian! How dare you accuse me of being a thief!' cried the Curator of the Museum of Classical Antiquities, who by this time had obviously had enough. In fact he was so irate that he rushed out of the smoking room in a terrible huff...leaving a trail of stinking cigar smoke.

'And how dare you accuse *me* of being a thief, young man!' Mr Dashiell Hamilton echoed as he strode angrily towards Maximilian, about to strike him, which he had never done before. 'The nerve!'

Lord Quimby looked as though he might explode, or implode – or both – and grabbing Max's arms, pinching his skin, said: 'You will apologise to Mr Hamilton, now, young man!'

Silence.

'Did you hear me, Maximilian?' Lord Quimby said, squeezing tight, shaking Max until his teeth rattled.

'No. I will not apologise, because what I said is the truth.'

'Oh yes you will!'

'Oh no I will not.'

Max refused to back down. He was shaking like a palm leaf.

'Don Battista is in on it too, although I am not sure as to the extent.'

'Such insolence, Max!' Lord Quimby's London agent shook his head in disbelief as he hastened out of the room.

'Your behaviour is disgraceful. I am most annoyed.' Don Battista walked out of the room, slamming the door. His voice could be heard out in the hallway, 'Really, such insolence from one so young!'

'You are a disgrace to this family!' Lord Quimby barked, in a controlled, angry voice. 'Go...to...your...room...at once!'

Max hung his head low. He stared down at his sturdy English shoes wishing he could evaporate. Disappear beneath the floorboards.

'I will deal with you later,' Lord Quimby said.

'First thing in the morning, after breakfast, you will make your apologies to Sir Archibald and to Mr Hamilton. After that you will ride over to Don Battista's house and make your apologies. Then you are to return to the villa and stay in your room until we set sail at noon. 'Do I make myself clear, Maximilian?'

'Yes Sir.'

'There is one more thing. You will not be allowed to leave your room this evening, under any condition.'

'Do you understand, Maximilian?'

'Yes Sir,' said Max, in a small voice he hardly recognised himself… while rushing out of the room, and thinking perhaps he was still just a boy after all.

Chapter Thirteen
Reflections from the Verandah

Max returned to his small room on the third floor of Mrs Logotheti's rambling villa and slammed the door. He sat down on the edge of his small bed. But not for long. Not when the verandah awaited. Thank heavens he had not been banished from the verandah. And he found himself on the said verandah early the next morning, after falling asleep, curled up on the floor. He had waited for hours, yet his uncle had not come up to his room to scold him further. This did little to relieve his guilty conscience. He tried to imagine what his punishment might be, as it had yet to be decided. Was it to be ten lashings? Tarred and feathered? Or a thoroughly good spanking? Surely not. Uncle was a man of enlightenment. He did not believe in thrashing children, and he had never yet laid a hand on Max. This might change after last night's fiasco in the smoking room. Granted, he had acted abominably, although he could not have done otherwise he thought to his quivering self, while squinting in the bright sunshine. Last night's debacle returned like a ravaging centaur and throttled him. Perhaps he had misunderstood – come to the wrong conclusion? Perhaps the metopes needed to be taken down for repair. That made sense. Had the marbles been accidentally installed in the wrong order when the Parthenon had been constructed in the fifth century and needed to be put right? The removal of the moon goddess's horses' heads, though, the most beloved marbles of all, was a puzzle. Perhaps dear sweet Aunt Vrai Viviette had decided to rescue the statues – for posterity – like the caryatid. This was completely understandable. Anyone would thrill to have the head of Selene's horse sitting on a plinth in their music room. Although the fate of Kore was even more of a mystery as she was much too large for the salons at the house in St James's Square. No. None of his assumptions were right, thought Max, tugging on the buttons of his pyjamas.

The solution was to write a letter to Aunt Vrai Viviette, post-haste. She would know exactly what to do. She knew what to do about everything. He wrote to her every day. But by time the post bag arrived in England he might well be standing on the front doorstep, which wouldn't really be any good at all. Max groaned. His aunt was not the kind of woman to interfere in her husband's business, so that idea went flying off the verandah.

A full explanation from his uncle was what Max really needed. Although he doubted he would get one. Not now, after last night's fiasco. The goings-on behind the grandiose facade of 'Lord Quimby's Dig' faded with the terrible realisation that the boat was about to sail at noon.

What blasted bad luck.

Like everyone else, he had been banned from the Acropolis until three weeks ago. This wasn't the end of the world. Yesterday, he had been banished from the Parthenon, placed under house arrest. Banishment was one thing. But house arrest was pure torture and confined to quarters was the final blow, and all because of foolish blunders on his part. Life was just one blunder after another, Max thought to his utterly wretched self, as the morning sun blazed a trail of burnished gold across Athens' blue sky.

Blunders had reached epidemic proportions. Virtually everyone Max knew was guilty of making a mistake of sorts. But Don Giovanni Battista Belisario, his uncle's clerk of works who had recruited moulders, or *formatori*, especially from Italy to make plaster-of-Paris moulds of the Parthenon's marble sculptures, was also guilty of making several blunders in the last three weeks, and Max had had the misfortune to glimpse these take place, first hand.

Work on 'Lord Quimby's Dig' had come to a complete stop on the Acropolis six weeks ago. Lord Quimby's men were banned from any further excavation work on the Acropolis, and were not allowed to resume work until his uncle returned from Constantinople with the much-needed firman. Which he did, late yesterday afternoon.

The landscape painters weren't allowed to make detailed drawings or architectural drawings, as requested by Lord Quimby. The makers of casts were not allowed to make plaster casts of the Parthenon's magnificent metopes, the Parthenon's marble frieze, the marble statues or any of the antiquities on the Acropolis – the casts of statues that Max's uncle fancied for his house under refurbishment in St James's Square.

Reflecting back, Max imagined something untoward going on, upon Mr Dashiell Hamilton's return from London, because 'Lord Quimby's Dig' suddenly resumed in earnest. But it appeared to Max to be the wrong kind of earnestness.

Max massaged his temples. However, no matter how hard Max rubbed his throbbing head he could not erase the despair he endured the day before, as the metopes were brutally *gouged* out of the Parthenon's frieze.

He was unable to stop the monstrous deed.

Max curled up his legs and hugged his knees. His thoughts drifted back to the day the ban had been lifted. Of course, he had been ecstatic – to be allowed to enter the Acropolis, freely, roam the dusty well-trodden paths of the Agora barefoot, to finish his pencil drawings of his beloved Parthenon was pure heaven. However, he soon realised that the removal of the ban made not the slightest difference to him, as he had neither the five sovereigns to bribe the Turkish guards to allow him access to the Acropolis, nor the loaf of sugar, coffee or Ouzo the *lazy sods* demanded. The Acropolis, being a Turkish garrison, was controlled by the Turkish military.

Of course, Eggy didn't have a problem. He didn't need money. His closest chum was the youngest son of the Disdar who allowed the boys free access to the Acropolis, and also the Parthenon. Unfortunately, Max seemed unable to procure the required articles of bribery and had been forced to resort to alternate means. Max's housemaster at Harrow on the Hill, Mr Twelvetrees, would have been proud of Max's resourcefulness, his canny wit, as he had found a way to do his sketches without having to resort to anything untoward. He had managed to procure – the absolute – the most perfect – most divine lookout spot in all Athens – on the Hill of the Pnyx – right opposite the Parthenon.

It was perfect in every way. However, it was there, on the Hill of the Pnyx, that Max first glimpsed subtle changes taking place on the Acropolis. Every morning, after a hastily eaten breakfast, Max rode his donkey through the village and along the narrow winding path to the Hill of the Pnyx. And it was there, while sitting on a rock, putting the finishing touches to his sketches, that Max caught sight of his uncle's workmen eagerly returning, en masse, to work on the Parthenon.

At first, Max didn't pay much attention to the renewed activities taking place on the Acropolis. Scaffolding had been erected on all four sides of the Parthenon long before he had come to Athens. Alarm bells didn't start to ring until he noticed scaffolding being extended yet further along the south-east corner. Max, quite rightly, assumed that the *formatori* had been given special permission to return to the site, to resume their making moulds of the frieze. How wrong could he be.

Fascinated, is how he had felt, while standing amidst the rubble of the Parthenon, as the *formatori* made enormous plaster-of-Paris moulds of the colossal, larger-than-life marble sculptures in the east and west pediments. Athena and Poseidon and the charioteer's horse came swiftly to mind. Once the moulds were constructed, they were filled with plaster and left to dry, which did not take long in the scorching hot midday sun. Once the casts were removed from their moulds, the statues were polished. From a distance the casts looked exactly the same as the real thing. Well, not quite. Max called the casts 'fakes', which they were, of course. At first glance, it was nigh impossible to discern the fakes from the originals. However, he felt the casts lacked something. He wasn't sure exactly what it was, but they were dull, lacklustre, lifeless, sad. That was it – they were without a soul. Once the fakes had been polished the statues were packed in straw, placed in enormous wooden crates, then put in an ox-cart to Piraeus, four and a half miles away. The crates were stored in one of his uncle's enormous warehouses, until shipped to England, where his uncle, Mr Dashiell Hamilton and the Curator of the Museum of

Classical Antiquities, Sir Archibald Lushington, believed the casts of all the great works of the ancients would benefit the fine arts and the architects in Britain.

As the week progressed, however, Max noticed something was up because the moulders weren't really doing any moulding. Nor were the cast-makers making casts. Max knew this for a fact, because Nikolaos' father and older brother, Alexios, had both been fired as they could not do their job, which was dismantle the Parthenon.

As time wore on and the temperature soared, Mopsus and Max nodded off in the shade of a huge pine tree. Max didn't really know how long they snoozed as he didn't have a timepiece to check the hour. However, he awoke – to Mopsus nuzzling his pockets, on the snoop for a sweetmeat – to see all sorts of tackle being hoisted on to the scaffolding. When he glimpsed enormous toothy saws being hoisted on to the scaffolding, he grabbed his telescope, always close at hand, and pressing the spyglass tightly to his eye. He quickly scanned the Parthenon.

'Holy Mother!'

Tocsin bells tolled at the sight of Monsieur's huge ox-cart parked directly underneath the metopes. This could only mean one thing.

Something was definitely up.

With the telescope glued to his right eye, Max glimpsed a group of gentlemen in tall silk hats and elegant frock coats gathering at the base of the Parthenon. At first, he was unsure who the gentlemen in question were as the men had their backs towards him. Then one gentleman turned around and...

'Mopsus! Look – it's the Disdar!' cried Max, as though Mopsus knew exactly who the Disdar was. Other men turned around. Standing next to the Disdar was his son, Evliya. Mr Dashiell Hamilton was there too. This was not unusual, as he was his uncle's agent. It wasn't unusual to see Sir Archibald Lushington snooping around the south porch either, because he spent most days doing just that, thought Max, as he pressed his spyglass so hard against his eye that it hurt. He glimpsed more and more gentlemen arriving on the east porch. Why were these 'worthiest of men', as his uncle so rightly alluded to his team, huddled together, staring up at the metopes? Exactly the same metopes that Max had been sketching for the last three weeks.

What on earth are the men doing, Mopsus?

Don Giovanni Battista Belisario's arrival on the steps of the Parthenon wasn't a concern either, as the Latin, when he wasn't firing orders at his men, could be found sitting beneath his sun umbrella with his two mangy hounds, Dido and Aeneas, snoozing at his side, while he made detailed architectural drawings of the Parthenon.

However, Max kept up his vigil, glimpsing Mr Dashiell Hamilton rushing up the steps as though he were Pericles, for heaven's sake, about to address the Senate. This wasn't unusual either, as he was, after all, the man in charge while his uncle was away in Constantinople. Mr Dashiell Hamilton kept pointing at the metopes directly overhead, but Max could not hear a single word being said, as he was too far away.

Meanwhile the activity on the scaffolding was heating up. It looked to Max like the *formatori* were attempting to dismantle the entire building. The workmen were wielding hammers and chisels and crowbars with such force that huge chunks of marble came loose and were falling down on to the scaffolding. Don Giovanni scrambled up on to the scaffolding. There were so many men clamouring up on to it, bashing away at the metopes, that Max lost count. He was unsure, exactly, what the men were trying to do. And he could not believe what his right eye was telling him so he tried his left eye... just to make sure. It was becoming more and more obvious that the *formatori* were trying to remove the metopes from the Parthenon's frieze, although they were having such difficulty releasing the huge marble slabs that they had had to resort to using a saw to slice through the back.

Then – the saw snapped.

In the background he could see workmen bashing at the metopes with pickaxes and crowbars, in a frenzied attempt to pry the enormous marble slabs from the Parthenon's frieze blocks, the very foundation of the Athena's sacred temple. Max glimpsed Don Giovanni Battista Belisario waving one half of a broken saw in his hand. The other half of this most gruesome article of mass destruction was protruding from behind the Lapith boy's head.

Max's knees buckled.

'*Oh my God!*' Max jumped up and down, crushing his pencils and crayons spilling on the ground. The saw had got stuck in the Lapith boy's head and it was left there...on the side of the Parthenon...for all of Athens to see.

Max could feel the hair on his head bristle. His heart raced. It beat so fast that he felt it thumping right through his shirt. And he imagined it bursting as he waved his arms frantically in the stupifyingly hot air, shouting:

'Stop Stop!'

Not that it mattered. No one could hear Max shouting above the noise and the clatter. No one would listen anyway. Max glimpsed the gentlemen in long black frock coats and top hats leaving the scene. All except one. The Disdar. He was covered from head to toe in marble dust, standing hunched over the pieces of shattered metope scattered on the ground, his broad shoulders drooping downwards. He stood very still, as though transfixed, staring up at the metope, then down at the chunks of marble, a pile of rubble on the ground.

Max had to act. He absailed on to Mopsus' back and together they rode towards the Parthenon as fast as the donkey could go, which wasn't really very fast.

'Go Mopsus, go!' Max shouted, as he dug his heels into the donkey's ribs. Mopsus sensed the tension within Max and for the first time *ever*, coaxing wasn't needed to spur him on. En route Max's thoughts raced. It was obvious, was it not, that the Parthenon did not want to release the metopes from the frieze, their rightful place in antiquity? Anyone with half a brain could see that. It certainly was clear to Max, as he rode frantically towards the scene.

His best friend had told him all about the legend of the stone-carver who had carved the metopes. The twelve-year-old boy named Menelaus. Max found this astonishing, trying to imagine carving the stone, because he was exactly the same age as the sculptor. According to the Greek legend, the young sculptor was a genius, with a brilliant career ahead of him, only he fell from the scaffolding, and plunged to his death. Mysteriously, his body was never found. Menelaus remained a hero to the people of Athens. Therefore, it was a very bad decision, on the part of his uncle's team – whoever made it – to remove these two particular metopes, because they had become a memorial to the sculptor who had not only been a brilliant stone-carver, but who had also lost his life.

Mr Dashiell Hamilton had told Max that the metopes had survived every kind of plunder known to man – even earthquakes – until now, thought Max, as he drew near the base of the Parthenon. Mr Dashiell Hamilton shouted at him:

CHAPTER THIRTEEN

'Please...Maximilian...go away...please!'

'Why, Sir?' Max's small voice radiated in the suffocating heat as he brought the donkey to a halt at the base of the Parthenon, which didn't require much effort.

'Do not come any closer, Maximilian. Please. It is much too dangerous. Go away, Maximilian!'

Mr Dashiell Hamilton's voice sounded fierce as he shouted from the steps.

Max ignored the warning. He felt sweat trickling down inside of his shirt as he shouted above the hideous sound of the chisels and hammers breaking the marble apart.

'What are you doing to the metopes? Please tell me, Mr Hamilton. Then I will go away.'

Mr Dashiell Hamilton raced down the steep marble steps.

'You are not allowed to come any further, Maximilian.'

'Why not, Sir?'

'Because I said so. Do not come anywhere near the Parthenon. If you come here again with that vile donkey of yours I will have both of you incarcerated in the Tower of The Winds!'

Max cringed.

'Return to the villa at once. You are not to leave the house until further notice!'

Mr Dashiell Hamilton shouted, as the background noise was deafening: 'Now, off you go!'

Max stared hard at the so-called *dashing* Mr Dashiell Hamilton and for the very first time realised that the one person whom he had adored for most of his life was no longer dashing, had suddenly lost all of his charm. In fact, he no longer resembled the man Max had come to know and love. Max glimpsed something untoward on his

162

handsome face, something that he had never seen before – almost sinister. Although it wasn't until many years later that Max realised he had looked upon the face of a man who was evil.

Meanwhile, Mopsus was causing an awful ruckus. He was hee-hawing so unbelievably loudly that the donkey drowned out the sound of the workmen trying with all their might to destroy his beloved Parthenon. Despite the noise, all Max could think about was being incarcerated in the Tower of The Winds – the most appalling place in Athens. He did not relish being imprisoned there – it was not the kind of premises he fancied spending his last day in Athens. It was impossible to rescue the Parthenon from a jail cell.

However, Max, being his stubborn, obstinate self, slid from Mopsus' back and rushed up the steps towards Mr Dashiell Hamilton, who signalled to the Turkish guards standing nearby. The guards ran down the steps and grabbing Max by his arms and legs, threw him on to the back of his donkey. One of the guards smacked Mopsus' rump and the donkey set off, although it was the ice-cold gun pressed to his neck, which caused Max to tremble all the way to the villa.

Max felt confused by what had happened. If his uncle had been there, none of this ugly business would have happened. After all, it was his uncle's life-long ambition to preserve the antiquities of ancient Greece, not destroy them. That was the reason for hiring the *formatori* in the first place, was it not? To capture the beauty of the Parthenon, and, in particular, the marble sculptures that remained in situ on the Acropolis.

Lord Quimby's eloquent words rang in Max's throbbing head. 'Now, boys, listen to me,' he had said, while waiting for the ship to set sail from Constantinople. 'The main reason for our visit to Athens is so you can experience, first hand, the glories of ancient

Greece. As you know it has been my utmost desire to contribute to the fine arts of England, to make exact copies of Greek antiquities, especially those remaining marbles of the Parthenon. The drawings, moulds and casts that have been made will be a tremendous benefit to the fine arts and to the students of architecture. London will one day become the new Athens!' Lord Quimby had paused before adding, briefly, 'for the benefit of the civilised world'. Did this mean Greece was uncivilised? Max refrained from asking. It would not have been proper.

It was too early to go down for breakfast. He was loath to return to his room, as it was so early and he did not wish to wake anyone else in the house. Max sprang to his feet. He leaned over the banister, allowing his thoughts to drift back to the very beginning of March, at Harrow on the Hill. Max had never intended to be in Athens at all. Summer holidays were spent in France, at his aunt's summer home in Provence, or in London. However, as the house in St James's Square was being refurbished and was *no place for the boys* as Aunt Vrai Viviette wisely concluded, his uncle decided to take the boys out of school for a year, to accompany him on a Grand Tour of the Near East. As a Director of the East India Company, Lord Quimby travelled to all parts of the globe. This allowed him to indulge his passion as an avid collector of Greek and Roman antiquities, procured while travelling the world. Lord Quimby imagined this was an ideal opportunity to further the boys' education in the Classics, leaving his wife to cope with overseeing the refurbishment of the house.

The boys had spent several weeks touring the Levant, although the weather had been so unbearably hot that everyone had suffered from heatstroke. Max had the added misfortune of suffering abysmally from seasickness every time the blasted ship set sail. The ship didn't even need to leave port before his tummy turned and he spent the entire voyage, in his hammock, with his head upside down in a bucket. Eggy, on the other hand, suffered from nothing except homesickness, although he whinged and whined a lot. Especially when they travelled overland on an all-day excursion. Sharing a wooden saddle with Eggy was bloody torture. Absolute bloody torture. Max had only just recovered from the agonies of a blistered backside after their last escapade to Cape Sunium and it was an experience he did not wish to repeat. Although he did have time to carve his initials on one of the marble columns of the temple of Poseidon.

The voyage from Constantinople had been long and arduous and to alleviate his seasickness he imagined being Homer's nimble-witted Odysseus, making his ultimate odyssey, returning home to Ithaca. But the moment the East Indiaman set sail the adventure began, and epic poetry it was not. A pirate ship forced the *Ars Amatoria*, a small, single-deck frigate of thirty-eight guns, into a skirmish and if it hadn't been for the wit of good Captain Cookson and the skilful seamen pounding the pirate ship with cannon balls, they would have all perished. High seas and strong Boreas winds blowing from Thrace made crossing the Sea of Marmara a terrifying experience, although Max was unaware of the storm, with his head in the bucket. However, the *Ars Amatoria* proved a worthy ship and got everyone safely through the Dardanelles.

A three-day stop-over at Sestos had been a puzzling one. His uncle had insisted on docking at Hellespont, and leaving the boys behind on the ship. Lord Quimby and Mr Dashiell Hamilton set off on a trek, on mules, only to return with a wagonload of enormous wooden crates. Max recalled standing on the deck as crates were loaded into the ship's hold, without knowing what was inside. Mr

Dashiell Hamilton never said. Neither did his uncle. Max didn't think it was his place to ask. Eggy could not have cared less.

At noon, they were about to return home to England. The voyage, crossing the English Channel, filled Max with horror. He was convinced seasickness would be the death of him. However, seasickness wasn't the main cause of his woes. No. It was his cousin, eight-year-old George Egbert, who was, without doubt, the most precocious child in all Christendom. Why his aunt had allowed Eggy to come on such a long arduous journey was a complete mystery. Why his cousin insisted on being called Eggy was an even greater one. Eggy's nickname irked Max. In fact, everything Eggy did Max found extremely irksome. Jealousy was to blame. Eggy had everything. Max did not.

Max sighed, running his hands through his thick brown hair that would be cut as soon as the ship docked in Southampton Max empathised with Homer's nimble-witted Odysseus, as he believed that he had also been on an epic journey for the last seven years. Forced to leave his boyhood home, without knowing when he would ever return. No longer knowing where home was, exactly.

He vaguely recalled playing hide-and-seek in the garden. A grand house set amidst a truly awesome display of topiary. He recalled hiding behind the hedge, but he could not remember who he was hiding from. Not that it mattered. His memory had played a cruel trick. His childhood memories had all been swept away. He could no longer recall what his parents looked like. Yes, life could be terribly unfair, thought Max as his thoughts returned to last night's fiasco after dinner.

He found it extraordinary that the three highly esteemed gentlemen were in cahoots with each other. He had known for some time that the Curator of the Museum of Classical Antiquities – that bloody ravaging saboteur with the sun-blistered bald head and worst foul-smelling breath imaginable – had been busily stuffing marbles into enormous canvas bags, aided by his army of Turkish slaves, unable to comprehend why Don Giovanni Battista Belisario or Mr Dashiell Hamilton had not tried to stop him. At the time he imagined that the marbles belonged to his uncle. Now, he knew the answer.

Max realised he had witnessed the worst kind of plunder known to man. According to his uncle, Sir Archibald Lushington was a highly respected member of his team. After all, he was the Curator of the Museum of Classical Antiquities in London, an honoured Trustee of Cambridge University, a Fellow of the Royal Society and an elite member of the Society of Dilettanti. Baffled is how Max felt as he had watched this thieving rogue plunder his uncle's 'Dig', gradually realising Sir Archibald Lushington was a downright thief, intent on bagging as much loot as possible, right from under his uncle's nose. Whether his uncle's nose happened to be in Constantinople at the time was immaterial. And baffled is how Max remained until last night. Furthermore, he had secretly observed Sir Arthur Lushington at work, for the last three weeks, hiding in the shadows of the Parthenon's colossal colonnade, as this horrid little man foraged through loose stones on his hands and knees, like a bloodhound sniffing for blood.

One morning, en route to his art lesson, he observed Sir Archibald Lushington doing a deal with the Turkish guards, when a large bag of sovereigns brought forth enormous sacks of loot, which were then hurriedly loaded on to the backs of donkeys. At that time, he didn't know where on earth Sir Archibald was hoarding his loot, without his uncle knowing a thing about it.

CHAPTER THIRTEEN

Sir Archibald Lushington was an expert in his field, and extremely knowledgeable in classical antiquities, Greco-Romano antiquities in particular. He worked on 'Lord Quimby's Dig' as a consultant for Classical antiquities. However, this wasn't altogether true because Max had overheard Sir Archibald Lushington shouting orders at his slaves to 'take away all the stones they could find' and 'to make it snappy!'

It wasn't only the Acropolis where the *fraudsters* had been hard at work. Apparently, the entire Parthenon was 'Up for Sale'.

Max imagined Sir Archibald Lushington had an ally. But not two! Now he knew who the accomplices in this skulduggery were, but he was unsure what to do about it.

Being a Harrovian proved invaluable in his quest to discover the truth. He had studied many famous archaeologists at school and knew that the men were devoted chroniclers who travelled the world excavating lost civilisations – ancient worlds that no longer existed – the ancient Chinese Dynasties, Egyptians, ancient Greeks, Romans and Mesopotamians. What he didn't know – which was a terrible oversight on behalf of his schoolmaster – was whether these great men who studied the ancient world were allowed to bag the loot, as it were, to keep their finds. If they were, did this mean that, if Max felt so inclined, he could help himself to whatever he fancied? Let's say, a few bricks from the Pyramids or a whopping great section of the Great Wall of China? Just imagine: the English pinched Leonardo da Vinci's *Last Supper*, the greatest work of art in the Western world. How would the Milanese people feel about that? What about the Pantheon or the Colosseum in Rome? Two of the most iconic buildings in the Latin world. What if the English 'had a go' at either one of these famous buildings? It was a puzzling question indeed, and one that had nagged him for the last fortnight, thought Max, rubbing his temples.

In other words, could he, or his uncle, or anyone else for that matter, dismantle St Paul's Cathedral, the Vatican in Rome, Notre Dame Cathedral in Paris, or the entire Parthenon – and take it home, bit by bit, if he chose to? Especially if it were on behalf of the British people back home?

Was he wrong to conclude that any or all of the antiquities that were found on the Acropolis or anywhere else in Greece for that matter, belonged to the Hellenic people? It was a great privilege and also lots of fun to search for rare artifacts, to draw, to paint or to excavate the Parthenon, like his uncle's men. Or so he thought until last night. To take the marbles home, seemed wrong, but what did he know? After all he was only a boy. Max was haunted by a host of confusing thoughts, that whirled round in his head as he sat peeking over the balcony.

How would Sir Archibald Lushington feel, for example, if the Greeks suddenly arrived in London with their loot-bags and their saws and their chisels and their ugly crowbars and began chipping away at the Tower of London? Or worse…took a sudden fancy to His Majesty's Crown Jewels, in the Tower of London, and, as the British people looked on, without so much as a whimper, pinched His Majesty's precious jewels, including the King's magnificent coronation crown – the finest in all the world? It was impossible to imagine King George at the next state banquet or the Opening of Parliament without his crown.

Supposing the Greeks had stuffed their sacks with loot fit to bursting and returned to Athens – and in a final act of defiance – shoved it in your face sort of thing – had the audacity to display the objects of plunder in a shed – as the Acropolis was without suitable facilities – for the entire world to view? Or, worse, deliberately hacked off a diamond or two, then sold the precious gems on to tourists.

Max did not believe for one moment that either the Curator of the Museum of Classical Antiquities, of which his uncle was a Trustee, or the King of England would like it one bit. And assuming, let's say, this horrid piece of fiction ever took place – the Greeks plundered the Tower of London – the British would not hesitate for one moment to declare war on Greece. Lord Horatio Nelson, the Admiral of the British Fleet, plus the entire British Navy would sail forthwith, arrive at Piraeus in battleships, of which there were many, and refuse to depart Athens' famous port until His Majesty's Crown Jewels were safely stowed on board Lord Nelson's flagship.

There was another issue Max had found bothersome. Sir Archibald Lushington boasted of his finds in the garden, every afternoon, while high tea was being served. He would have during high tea, however, the gracious Lady Soames invariably 'held the floor', as his uncle commented when someone refused to stop talking.

While Mrs Logotheti's scrumptious daughters served Lady Soames and her family cups of steaming Earl Grey tea, in delicate fine English bone china, outside on the lawn, Sir Archibald Lushington came strutting through some hidden aperture in the crumbling stone wall, with his convoy of Turkish slave boys in tow. This created a flutter of excitement among the ladies, genteel English damsels sweltering in the hot sun, while twirling large sun-brollies, balancing tea cups on their knee.

Invariably, Max sat in the dwindling shade, beneath a large coconut palm, not entirely in hiding, but close to it, as the distractions were all too much for him, with Mrs Logotheti's stunningly beautiful daughters there and all. The afternoons he reserved for sketching. Only, more often than not, he found it impossible to keep his mind on his work as his ears were melting or his brain sizzling in the suffocating heat.

Yesterday, the charade had been the absolute worst as Max had watched Sir Archibald Lushington waddle across the lawn with such aplomb that the ladies were forced to stop nibbling their cucumber sandwiches. Tea cups floated in mid-air. Max was convinced that the curator and his slaves purposely sprinkled themselves with marble dust before entering the garden, just for effect, as the curator flopped down on to a stone bench directly in front of Max and brushed his good self off – in slow-motion, of course. The gentleman in question must have been sweltering in the stupefying heat by the visible stains seeping through his linen jacket. However, with a flourish of nervous excitement, he proceeded to remove his enormous canvas sack flung over his shoulder and untied it. The curator's round puffy face was scarlet. The top of his bald head was so badly sun-burned that last Christmas's roast goose came swiftly to mind.

Pure drama then unfolded.

English tourists gathered round as Sir Archibald Lushington and his slaves proceeded to open their enormous canvas sacks and very gingerly withdrew several small marble heads...then...torsos... then...several limbs...then a hand...then half a marble head... and...a foot.

Max nearly fainted.

Even the tourists were taken aback when the Lapith boy's severed head rolled about on the grass, finally coming to rest beside his broken, mutilated marble torso. In fact, everyone present gasped. So life-like were the marbles, that the ladies' English complexions paled.

CHAPTER THIRTEEN

Sir Archibald Lushington enthused, gleefully, through thick sun-blistered lips. 'What an absolute glorious find. Lord Quimby will be delighted, I'm sure, as will *our* museum in London!'

The sight of the Lapith's marble body lying in pieces on the lawn brought on such nausea that Max ran behind the garden wall and vomited. He was a little shaky afterwards and sat down on the scorched grass, haunted by his absolute best friend's poignant words, while riding their donkeys near the Hill of the Pynx, where they often met for lunch.

Tears brimmed over as Nikolaos had revealed that 'many of the Parthenon's ancient artifacts had had their noses brutally hacked off by zealous tourists, and not only by the local Turks'. The English were also to blame. Nikolaos had caught many a British sailor hacking noses off the marble statues after too much Ouzo, and he had tried to intervene but the seamen had pulled their swords. Nikolaos, unarmed, didn't have a chance. He walked away, with hatred in his belly. Why didn't the Greeks rise up? Nikolaos couldn't imagine why not; he would be the first to join up – stop the plunder of Athena's sacred temple.

Max's thoughts were interrupted by Sir Archibald Lushington's lah-di-dah accent expounding:

'Of course, these precious stones will be a tremendous asset for our Museum of Classical Antiquities.'

There was only one way the curator of the museum could have got his sweaty paws on the marbles and that was by bribing the men who had committed the dirty deed. The *formatori*. Was it any wonder Max disliked the man so intensely?

Max pushed his nasty thoughts from his mind, prompted by the goings-on below in the garden. He didn't dare make a sound. As he sat on the verandah feeling like a first former about to be given the strap, he glimpsed the abbot from the Capuchin Monastery next door open the gate and stride through the yawning orifice in the stone wall. This wasn't an uncommon occurrence. However, the oddity was that the abbot was pushing a large barrow across the lawn towards the rain barrel, the exact same barrel containing his precious marble. Max didn't dare blink as the abbot proceeded to roll up his sleeves, exposing his fat, fleshy arms, and plunged them into the rain barrel, very gingerly withdrawing the hand and then a foot.

'Holy Mother!' Max clapped his hand over his mouth, searching madly for an alternate choice of expletive.

The abbot glanced over his shoulder. He took a quick look round before hastily placing the marble in a sack inside the barrow. Then, in went the arm and out came another chunk of marble. This procedure continued until the sack had been stuffed with marbles. He then made a wide U-turn on the lawn. Sir Archibald Lushington hailed the abbot and rushed to greet him; as he drew near he leaned over and whispered in the abbot's ear. Then the abbot whispered in the curator's ear.

The drama continued. Sir Archibald Lushington withdrew a small chamois pouch from his dressing-gown pocket and counted numerous gold sovereigns into the abbot's fleshy palm. The abbot bowed, as abbots do, then he fled, post-haste, wheeling his heavy barrow through the gate, and sought the sanctity and the safety of the Capuchin Monastery.

Max glimpsed Sir Archibald Lushington fast-pacing it across the lawn and cowered back into the shadows of the bougainvillea. He despised cowardice. He wanted to cry out *thief* but his words were lost to the sanctity of the inviolable silence.

Plate X: 'A Tortured Soul'

The fragmented head and torso of a Lapith rolls out of Sir Archibald Lushington's loot bag on to the lawn of the villa where Max and his uncle are staying in Athens, much to the horror of the guests.

The two sections of the Lapith eventually show up at the Louvre in Paris in the twenty-first century causing havoc!

He had finally seen the light. The Curator of the Museum of Classical Antiquities was bribing the abbot, who, in turn, stashed the curator's loot in the crypt. Marbles that had been stolen from the Acropolis, the Parthenon, his uncle, or was it, perhaps, the Greeks themselves? He could not decide which. Talk about *hot* property.

What should he do? His uncle might think he had lost his wits.

He did wonder, however, why he felt so sad. Why mourn the loss of a lump of old stone? A marble that he had found buried amidst the rubble of the Parthenon? Stones that were of no earthly value to anyone...

It was then Max glanced down.

'Blast!' He was still in his pyjamas. This sudden realisation catapulted him from the verandah. Max stopped dead. His bare feet were sticking to the floorboards like glue. He stood perfectly still. He shuddered. He imagined that he heard a woman weeping, sobbing and moaning most piteously. The sound grew louder and louder, reaching a horrifying pitch. The crones in Shakespeare's *Macbeth* sprang to his mind, and he half-expected to glimpse a bunch of them coming rushing down the hall towards him. However, the hall was empty, so he hurried back outside, on to the verandah, and peeped over the railing.

There was no one there.

But, of course, there couldn't possibly be, because there were no old crones at the villa. And there most certainly were not any old women of any description lodging at the Capuchin Monastery. He thought he was hallucinating and once again blamed the heat. How odd, thought Max to himself; listening to the sotto voce utterance floating in on the Eurus and rushing inside, he failed to hear his uncle's clerk of works mangy old nag galloping up the drive. All Max could think about was that someone was in deep distress, and he had to find the source.

House arrest be damned!

What was the absolute worst that could happen to him? Max debated: hung by the neck from the mainsail of the East Indiaman until dead, incarcerated in the Tower of the Winds, buried alive in the crypt next door, or locked in the hold of the ship until they reached Southampton. He was beyond caring.

He was invincible.

Odysseus would not have done otherwise. His pyjamas went flying. He spied his satchel containing his sketchbooks and pencils on a chair beside the door, ready when needed. He donned the short trousers he had shortened himself, one leg longer than the other. He put on his baggy white shirt, like the Greek sculptors wore, the shirt he'd traded for a bag of cakes oozing nuts and lashings of honey. Then his not-so-white, badly nibbled straw hat Mopsus chewed for the duration of the summer, and fled with his satchel tucked under his arm.

Max raced down the hall. The old Greek peasant's words came racing back. Of course. He had heard the lament.

This could only mean one thing. The Parthenon's marbles were being ravaged! He had to get to the stable and fast. Max may only have been twelve years of age, but he was totally convinced that he could rescue the Parthenon marbles. Could he make it to the Parthenon and back before noon? Mopsus would decide, as the donkey, being his stubborn self, more often than not refused to come out of the stable.

Chapter Fourteen
Blunders Abound

Don Giovanni Battista Belisario hissed at the Curator: 'The saw... heee...snapped...just like that!'

'Whatever do you mean?' Sir Archibald Lushington asked, impatiently, while anxiously patting imaginary strands of hair no longer there, that hadn't been there for quite some time.

'Theee saw is too short! Heee's impossible to cut through the metopeee,' cried the dishevelled little man, dressed in a crumpled linen frock coat, soggy white shirt with dark yellow stains on the collar and cuffs, and a filthy cravat splayed at his neck. He was becoming more and more agitated.

'Theee one we have heee stuck in the mar...ple!'

Sweat dripped from Don Giovanni Battista Belisario's lined leathery face as he puffed at the Curator of the Museum of Classical Antiquities in pidgin English.

'All theee saws are broken...Sir Archibald...and...weee need new ones at least fourteen feet in length. Like this!' Don Giovanni Battista's thick arms reached out, nearly touching the walls.

'Without heee saws weee not able to cut through the damn frieze! We not able to extract any more of the metopes Lord Quimby wants.'

'Dearie me!' Sir Archibald Lushington rubbed his flabby chin. He glanced at the ceiling, then down at the pattern in the Turkish rug. It was obvious that he had been summoned before changing out of the ubiquitous silk dressing gown and matching slippers. 'Whatever shall we do?' *'Mama Mia!'* Don Giovanni wailed. 'Do?'

'You must do something!'

As Lord Quimby's clerk of works shouted and screamed, streaming rivulets of sweat trickled down his cheeks, dripping on to the rug. And, throwing his hands up in the air – as Latins do when feeling passionate – continued to rant.

'You must contact the Museum of Classical Antiquities at once... because without adequate saws it impossible to remove the stones. The metopes heee stay put!'

'Why not try the monastery next door?' Sir Archibald's bushy eyebrows were twitching, a sign of excitement.

'The abbot must have a hoard of useful and sundry items in his garden shed,' offered Sir Archibald Lushington, wringing his sweaty hands. Was the Curator suffering from nerves, perhaps?

Don Giovanni Battista Belisario thought about this for a moment.

'That is a good idea! I try there.'

The Curator nodded. He looked relieved. He tugged impatiently on the tie of his dressing gown. He looked uncomfortable as he asked: 'What about the statues in the pediments? The statues of Athena and Poseidon and Hermes and the horses?'

'I no do. I fed up doing this dirty work. By the way, there is one more thing.' Don Giovanni was mopping his entire head by this time.

'What seems to be the problem?' Sir Archibald was wringing his hands again.

'It has nothing to do with the saws or the plunder. A plunder that makes meee sick,' cried the aged Neapolitan in hastily plundered English. 'It is my money!'

'You tell Lord Quimby I want to see him, now!' Don Giovanni Battista Belisario spat, as he chomped angrily on the chewed-end of his cigar, dangling out of the corner of his mouth.

'Lord Quimby is sleeping. He is not to be disturbed.'

'Wake him up!' cried Don Battista. 'Now!'

'I will do no such thing.'

'Oh yes you will!' Don Battista walked up to Sir Archibald and grabbing his arms, spat in his face, with the worst garlic-laden breath. He shouted: 'I want my money 'Heee...not...pay...meee...my wage... now...I quit!'

'Quit?' boomed Sir Archibald. 'You cannot quit! Not now!'

'I go back to Naples on heee next boat!'

'Don't be a damn fool, Don Giovanni. Napoleon's troops are gaining force as we speak.'

Sir Archibald looked grey, as he stood pinned against the wall, watching The Don's cigar bobbing up and down.

'The statues must come down today. Do you hear me? Today!' the Curator of the Museum of Classical Antiquities demanded. 'When the statues come down you will be paid. No statues, no pay. It's as simple as that! If you need more men to get the job done quickly, may I suggest you try Piraeus? Round up the Greek sailors roaming the quay. Make them an offer they can't refuse!'

Don Battista shouted, 'I do no more!' His cigar fell from his mouth, rolled on to the floor.

'You pay me now or else!' His voice was so low and so gravelly he sounded like a Mafioso. You tell Lord Quimby he owes meee three years' wages. Understand meee, Sir Archibald?

Lord Quimby not pay, he lose his damn head! Like the marbles!'

Chapter Fifteen
The Plunder

When the shrill screeching sound resumed again at dawn the next morning, the Athenians wept openly in the street. Young children sobbed and covered their ears with their small hands, begging their mothers to stop the noise. Old Greek peasant women hid their tear-stained faces in their aprons, unable to bear witness to the gruesome scene unfolding before their very eyes, as Lord Quimby's workmen slogged in a near frenzy to remove the metopes and marble statues from the gable-ends of the Parthenon. Anyone attempting to intervene would be shot by the Turkish guards. Those that had tried to stop the plunder lay dead in the street.

The horrific sounds echoing within the ancient walled city of Athens that morning should have brought great shame to Lord Quimby, but, sadly, they did not. The hideous noise, created from bashing crowbars, pounding hammers and grating chisels, should have niggled His Lordship's conscience, but it did not. In fact, the sounds of plunder had quite the opposite effect on this highly esteemed, refined, enlightened English gentleman; this honourable man of noble birth, exemplifying great taste. Pure, sweet jubilation is what Lord Quimby experienced as the sound of the plunder continued, and he had no good reason to be empathetic towards the people of Athens.

Why on earth should he?

After all, Lord Quimby imagined that he had done the Greeks a great favour by rescuing their marbles from further destruction. Good gracious mercy! Imagine – if he hadn't had the foresight or the wit, to say nothing of the wherewithal, to prevent further destruction of the Acropolis' marbles by invading infidels! The answer was to remove every last chunk of stone from the Acropolis and ship the loot home to England, where the marbles would be kept safe. In years to come, the people of Greece would pay homage to his good self, for having the prowess and the means to prevent further plunder of their citadel in being blown up by cannon fire. He even fantasised continuously about a magnificent larger-than-life marble statue of himself, erected at the gates of the Parthenon, as a commemorative for his long-standing contribution to the Hellenic people.

Although he admitted, while lounging on his sumptuous bed in his suite of rooms located in a separate wing of Mrs Logotheti's rambling villa, scanning a vast compendium of letters awaiting upon his return from Constantinople, that the loud sonorous sounds emanating from the region of the Acropolis were beginning to grate on his nerves. He was still suffering the after-effects of his arduous sea voyage from Constantinople, which had left him feeling out-of-sorts and weary.

Although, he admitted, as he repositioned himself on his ample bed, amidst a sea of overstuffed cushions, that in many respects the irritating noise – the loud grating sound of saws slicing through the Parthenon's marble frieze – brought an enormous sense of relief to his benevolent self. This meant that *great* progress was being made, after three demanding years fraught with every conceivable difficulty known to man. From the procurement of several, rather hefty loans from Coutts, using collateral that *really* belonged to his wife; to say nothing of the lies, convincing dear, darling Vrai Viviette to part with a huge chunk of her inheritance; to the bothersome and on-going need for further borrowing his wife knew even less about to fund the expedition. To the hideous sums, wages to pay the *formatori*, the lazy bastards; to the thousands of pounds he had spent to bribe the Ottomans – it was – well – *crippling*.

With so much on his mind was it any wonder the irritating background noise was beginning to grate on his nerves? After all, he had extremely important business matters to contend with. Lord Quimby briefly scanned a three-page letter to his wife. Lord Quimby's soft, callus-free hands (that had never done a day's worth of manual labour in their life) gripped the pages, as he lounged on the cushions, sighed loudly, air gushing from his lungs. He crossed his legs – which he thought were much too short – and wriggled his toes. A young Albanian servant boy sat on a small stool in the corner of the room, and pulled a long string, attached to a fan, circulating the stifling hot sultry air above his master's head. The boy sat there for hours, without respite from his arduous chore, nor was it expected.

Lord Quimby's countenance brightened as he scanned the pages of his letter confirming that, after being harassed by his darling wife for years, he could finally put her mind to rest. The Roman busts to fill the empty niches he had promised Vrai Viviette for their refurbished Sculpture Gallery would arrive in time for Christmas. His darling wife would be thrilled. The architect in charge of the refurbishment, the highly acclaimed Signor Bellini, should be too.

The shipment was en route from Naples. He wondered what his wife would think of the Greek marbles. The metopes and the statues of Athena and Poseidon she knew nothing about, but it mattered not. He would explain everything when he arrived home. Then, he had a brilliant thought.

Why not take Hermes? And Iris and the charioteer? Oh my God, Vrai Viviette would die for the charioteer's horse – it was a masterpiece.

Enormous slabs of the Parthenon's interior frieze of the cella had been stowed in the ship; with any luck twelve metopes were being removed that morning. Would Kore go in the foyer of their Palladian-style house, he wondered. Lord Quimby read his own elaborate scrawl.

'My darling, there is so much to choose. I am convinced you will be thrilled with the archaic relics from the ancient past. I have included eight bas-reliefs. One in particular may be of interest, perfect for the gaping hole over the mantle.'

He had added a postscript.

The four Ionic columns from the Temple of Athena Nike that you requested will simply be divine in your boudoir, my darling, as the columns will add such grandeur to your suite.

Whether the marbles would be suitable was another matter, as his wife was famous for changing her mind. She was also extremely fussy. If the marbles were not to her liking she could dispose of the stones, donate the marbles to the Museum of Classical Antiquities in London or give them away. Pagaille House was also a consideration. This put Lord Quimby's mind to rest.

Lord Quimby clapped his hands and a small ensemble entered. He clapped his hands again and the string quartet that had come with him from London, seated themselves on pouffes on the floor and warmed up. As the insufferable background noise had become so invasive he needed something cheerful to distract his thoughts. Nonetheless, His Lordship's mood remained euphoric. After being entertained royally by the Grand Vizier, the Sultan, and the Pashas for the last six weeks he wished to maintain the illusion as long as possible. Could anyone blame him?

Upon his return, he demanded sweetmeats be on hand at all times, his suite of rooms infused with incense, fresh orchids placed on his pillow at night, silver cutlery replaced with gold, and the procurement of a hookah installed in his room for his own enjoyment. Thoughts of the Levant provoked such bliss that Lord Quimby imagined recovering from his stressful voyage in no time.

Lord Quimby's suite was located as far away as possible from the boys' rooms. He preferred it that way, he thought, while puffing on his hubble-bubble, lounging on his bed, and snug in his pelisse – a coat trimmed with ermine – a robe the Grand Vizier had bestowed on him in return for His Lordship's extreme generosity.

The Arabian Nights came swiftly to mind upon entering Lord Quimby's bedchamber because his exquisitely bolstered bed had been tented to the ceiling in pleated yellow silk, and on the counterpane lay a vast array of embroidered cushions with exotic images of the Far East in vibrant colours. Lord Quimby had been thrilled with the décor, which was so reminiscent of the East. With hindsight, *Ali Baba and the Forty Thieves* would have been a more accurate description.

As soft music filled the air, Lord Quimby clapped his hands thrice. The signal brought forth a servant girl, who magically appeared from behind a curtain. She bowed towards Lord Quimby, then sped silently across the room towards her master and proceeded to serve him a cup of strong Turkish coffee from a highly embossed silver pot on a heavily engraved silver tray. However, as she leaned over and poured the coffee her gown parted, exposing just enough taught flesh, causing the debauched, lecherous lord to quiver. Lord Quimby remained infatuated with his servant girl or rather what lay beneath her gown.

No wonder he spent so much time here.

Lord Quimby simply adored the Far East. Lord Quimby's loins ached. He was overcome, imagining what pleasure waited beneath the veil of his belly dancer, bought for a few piastres from Piraeus – or was it Corinth?

Yes, he had to admit, life in the East could not possibly get better. He was living his dream and had been for the last ten years of his life. His warehouses were bulging with imported goods from the East, and Greek and Roman antiquities he had picked up along the way. Soon, the Parthenon would be stripped of its marbles. The Erechtheion was next on his list of acquisitions. If he got there first… There were rumours flying that someone had their eye on the temple. There was always a chance the marbles could be pinched by the bloody French bastards. Then his thoughts returned to the Erechtheion and he gushed:

'Upon my word! The size of the ship needed for transporting the stones is mind-boggling!'

Thank God he had enough funds to bribe Captain Light to fill the ship's hold. Did it matter that the ship had to be ripped apart to accommodate the caryatid from the Erechtheion? Apparently not.

With any luck, his import/export business with the East would show signs of finally paying dividends; as long as the war with France didn't disrupt the transportation of goods. He had to keep the money flowing. His wife was expected to deliver a bouncing baby in four months' time. He could not recall being in England five months ago. Not that it mattered. A woman's confinement was her business.

In the meantime Lord Quimby was free to pursue his passion: the procurement of Classical antiquities. Things were well under way. Once his 'Dig' had been completed his grand house in St James's Square would be the envy of the art world – the Sculpture Gallery, a splendid showpiece of Greco-Roman marbles. The truth was his desire for antiquities had yet to be satiated. He was obsessed.

Imagine when my collection goes on view in London.

After all, London was where the statues truly belonged. Despite all the sangfroid he realised he could not have managed without his good friend, Dashiell Hamilton, his most trustworthy companion. He had also travelled the East long enough to know that the illiterate sods, the Turks and the Greeks and whoever else happened to be in Athens, no longer cared about their heritage. The Ottomans sold their children if the price was right, or their wives. Therefore, the safest place was England.

Nevertheless, Lord Quimby had a problem. He worried constantly about the state of his nose. When he glimpsed his reflection in the looking glass, it wasn't his visage – it was his misspent youth reflected back. He blamed its condition as the result of a rare type of leprous infection that caused his nose to disappear at an altogether alarming rate. Nights spent languishing in Parisian brothels and the prostitutes he had used to satisfy his lust haunted him, and he had had to resort to dabbing mercury on his nose when the excruciating pain became intolerable, like it did now.

He clapped his hands. His servant girl reappeared. He pointed to his nose and she padded towards a bureau, extracted the medicine bottle, walked over to where Lord Quimby sat on the ample bed and dabbed his bleeding nose with mercury. His Lordship cringed, as the ordeal caused him much pain. What he needed was a balloon of brandy to dull the pain and reaching over, poured the brandy from a decanter sitting on a small table beside the bed, as he did not wish to disturb the servant dabbing his nose, or the quartet playing his favourite Johann Sebastian Bach violin concerto, with the added accompaniment of an Albanian strumming softly on a rebeck.

Could Lord Quimby be forgiven for such hubris? Of course not. Society expected it of him. He was, after all, a great lord, a member of the landed gentry. His mother expected great things of him, as her eldest son – her favourite – had drowned in the swimming pool at Oxford. To make matters worse, his father had died tragically from palsy earlier in the same year. Then, of course, there was Lord Quimby's much younger wife. Vrai Viviette insisted on spending money on trivial nonsensical things such as solid gold knobs for her Sculpture Gallery, Limoges tea services that had never seen daylight and Sèvres vases and vintage champagne imported from Rheims. His wife had a penchant for expensive clothes and spent a fortune on shoes. How on earth she could do such a thing, when his needs came first?

Lord Quimby represented the very nucleus of the British Establishment. He was also a man of immense inherited wealth, after his marriage to his aristocratic French wife. Although their vast reserves of cash were dwindling faster than he cared to admit. This last expedition had taken a considerable chunk of his money and most of his wife's inheritance, yet he refused to admit it, and after three long years pursuing his dream, he had had to resort to mortgaging the Shambles, his ancestral home in Scotland, in order to secure yet another enormous loan from Coutts, just to keep afloat, offset his expenses, the bloody great ransoms the Turks were demanding for every chunk of marble he fancied from the Parthenon.

Lord Quimby was land rich. Eight generations of Quimbys had been lords of Sutherland, Perthshire and Fife and his family had remained on the King's Privy List ever since. He had inherited great swathes of land in Hampshire, a 20 000-acre shooting estate in Scotland, a silver mine in the Colonies, Pagaille House in Perthshire, a summer house on the French Riviera, and, of course, the Palladian pile in St James's Square, which was costing him the earth to refurbish.

George Henry Montague Perceval had attended all the right schools: Harrow, Eton and Cambridge. After graduating *cum laude* in Classics at King's College, Cambridge, a brief stint in the Navy followed, as was expected, as a commissioned officer, of course. His commission did not last long, as he did not relish the idea of being murdered by some ghastly infidel in a foreign country, or rotting in a filthy prison, so he invested heavily in the East India Company, importing and exporting goods the British Navy depended on, to and from the Far East. He never looked back. At the age of thirty he had inherited a seat in the House of Lords. He was expected to turn up when the House was in session – say a few words. He rarely did so – only on the odd occasion when he happened to be in London, before Parliament recessed for the summer. This political position topped a curriculum vitae that the average English male would have found, quite frankly, nauseating. Lord Quimby could not have cared less about the average English male, as, God forbid, he should ever encounter the lower orders, excluding, of course, the slave girls who appeared on demand – as all women should.

His lust for the Classics began in his first year at Harrow on the Hill. He blamed the Romans. He had fallen in love with all things

Roman while learning how to recite Latin verse, or rather Latin love elegies, especially from Ovid's *Metamorphoses*, which became the fodder for his sexually frustrated mind while growing up in the shadows of his Scottish Presbyterian grandparents. He had even named his hounds, the bitches, Helen, Penelope and Dido.

The Classical world pulled Lord Quimby in – big time. However, it wasn't until the ancient Greeks gripped his imagination at Cambridge that his obsession really took hold, and George Henry Montague Perceval had quite literally *obsessed* about the Classical world ever since. Olympia awaited.

Lord Quimby exemplified great taste. He imagined that he had more taste in his little toe than most people could ever have. He envisioned himself the perfect role model for young men aspiring to become highly enlightened individuals like himself, especially in Greek philosophy, art, drama and architecture. An appreciation of beauty was essential. Classical beauty he deemed bordering on the divine. The ancient Greeks sought truth and beauty in their daily life and he took this to heart – it became an ideal – just short of idol worship. Lord Quimby doubted his lust for all things Classical would ever end. He *had* to have the marbles.

The fact that his house in London was being especially designed to accommodate all the Greco-Roman antiquities he could plunder, or better, the fact that his darling wife had suddenly acquired a penchant for all things Classical, or secretly lusted after the male-body-beautiful in Pentelic stone, or the male-body-beautiful of his London agent, which he was unaware of at the time, encouraged the massive exodus of Greek and Roman antiquities vanishing en masse from the land of the Hellenic people. However, his thoughts were interrupted by a servant who was ushering his London agent into the room.

'Ah Hamilton!' greeted Lord Quimby hopping out of bed, grabbing his agents' arm, pumping it up and down. 'Have you seen the Disdar?'

'Yes, Milord,' said Mr Dashiell Hamilton, as he held on to His Lordship's hand.

'Good God!' Lord Quimby exclaimed. 'Come in and close the door. What a frightful noise!'

'Hellish!'

'I tell you it is pure hell...listening to this racket all day.'

His Lordship clapped his hands. The string quartet stopped playing. Another clap of his hands brought his servant girl from behind a swagged curtain with a tray of drinks. She glided towards her master, her bare feet barely touching the floor, with her slim, elegant hands holding the tray, while muttering illegibly in Arabic as she served coupes of champagne.

Meanwhile, Mr Dashiell Hamilton eyed the money bags piled high on His Lordship's desk in front of the window.

'I can see you have been true to your word, Milord.' His singularly handsome face broke into a half-smile.

'What you see my dear fellow,' said Lord Quimby, puffed up, pounding his chest, 'is evidence that Coutts has finally agreed to increase my loan.' He purposely left out that they had also agreed to bump up his overdraft.

'Thank God!' The breath gushed out of Mr Dashiell Hamilton, obviously relieved.

'In bloody time, Hamilton...in bloody time!'

'The *voidvode* will no doubt be pleased.' Mr Dashiell Hamilton appeared nonchalant as he calculated the number of chamois bags. He had never felt more elated in his life, although he refrained from showing it. Lord Quimby was unaware that he was financing his London agent's own private scheme.

'There are 1500 Turkish piastres in each bag, Hamilton.'

'So there's no need to count the damn stuff.'

'Of course not.' Lord Quimby lowered his voice: 'These are the funds that you asked for. Now, we can continue on with the plunder!'

'Is there enough here for the captain? What about the wages? Is there enough to pay the men?'

'Let them wait!' Lord Quimby roared. 'Hamilton, my dear fellow, once the statues are down we will pay them. There is just enough. How much longer I will be able to finance my expedition is another matter entirely!'

Mr Hamilton twitched nervously, shot his cuffs.

'It's a toss-up, Hamilton, whether my fortune or my nose will vanish first!'

Loud, boisterous guffaws followed.

'Vrai Viviette will be thrilled with the marbles, I'm sure. Let's hope she is pleased with the Ionic columns, although I expect it will be an absolute bloody nightmare getting them down from the temple!'

Mr Dashiell Hamilton reddened, and appeared ill at ease. He glanced at his timepiece, nervously snapping the lid.

'Well!' exclaimed Mr Dashiell Hamilton. 'We must not keep the Disdar waiting. Not if you want your statues by the time the ship sails at noon. Therefore, I must take my leave at once, Milord!'

Mr Dashiell Hamilton throttled the bags by the neck and tucked them inside the fine leather satchel that he had brought along just for the occasion. He appeared to be in great haste, as he bowed towards His Lordship, then bounded out of the room, where he found his camel waiting. Was he feeling guilty about something?

After his London agent had taken leave, Lord Quimby retired to his writing desk. An urgent letter was required post-haste, to pacify his Maltese bankers who were getting nervous, as funds had been withdrawn from Lord Quimby's current account faster than funds were put into it. Needless to say, his bankers were not privy to the outrageous amounts of cash needed to bribe the Ottomans. Of course, Lord Quimby loathed avarice of any kind. His Lordship hadn't a clue how to deal with the arrears on his accounts so he chose to ignore them. He then hurriedly signed and sealed the letter to his wife with a signet befitting the Ali Pasha.

After sealing the letter Lord Quimby realised that the din going on since dawn had ceased, and walking to the window, flung open the shutters with more gusto than he imagined befitted a proper English gentleman. He peered out, although he was unable to see the Parthenon from his room.

Not to worry. As soon as Hamilton had done the deal, work would resume, he was sure. Hamilton never let him down.

Hamilton was a godsend. He trusted him implicitly. What on earth would he do without his London agent? The man had enough piastres tucked inside his satchel to pacify the Ottoman Empire and the Sublime Porte. Once Hamilton had done the deal his worries would be over, temporarily. He could help himself to all the marbles he fancied. Although he vowed not to leave Athens without this last hoard. Before the bloody Greek peasants revolted...

Chapter Sixteen
Max Escapes

He could hear Mopsus braying long before he reached the stable. The noise was so embarrassingly loud, Max, red-faced, could only nod at the stable boy as he thrust the donkey's frayed bridle in his hand and then ran off.

'Calm down!' Max stroked the donkey's mangy coat. He knew he was in trouble by the donkey's lopsided ears. 'What on earth is the matter with you this morning? You'll wake everyone in the house, Mopsus!'

Max believed the donkey understood his every word and he spoke to Mopsus as though he did understand.

'Now, listen to me, Mopsus,' said Max, firmly, while patting the donkey's nose, 'we are going on a very important mission this morning. So that means that there is to be no doddling along!'

But he was finding it difficult to get a word in edgeways, in between the donkey's ear-splitting brays. Mopsus had a mind of his own. He continued to bare his long yellowed teeth, which was a sign that his nimble-witted friend was terribly upset, bored, hot or something else, unique to the animal kingdom, unknown to the likes of man. The braying did not stop, however, until Mopsus nosed Max's pocket, on the snoop for Turkish Delight – the much-needed bribery to entice the donkey out of his stable. Just like the Turks who guarded the Acropolis, thought Max, grinning to himself.

'Come on Mopsus!' Max begged, cajoling the donkey through the stable door. 'Hurry up!'

Mopsus was having none of it. He was being his stubborn self. Max had to empty his pockets of sweets in order to persuade the reluctant donkey out of the stable which was located to the rear of the villa.

Grabbing hold of the donkey's withers Max hopped on, and they rode down the narrow lane at the back of the villa, between the rows of neatly tended cottages. As they rounded a sharp bend, however, they met a large fleet of camels lumbering past with their humpbacks laden with baggage. Max recognised his trunk. The cameleers were thrashing the rumps of the huge beasts with switches, or *kurbashes*. Max imagined this only antagonised the camels even more because as the camels waddled down the street, they hissed and spat at Mopsus something awful. The sight of his luggage being taken down to the ship tended to exacerbate Max's bad mood, and he dug his heels in, wanting the donkey to go faster towards the Propylaea, the colossal marble gates leading up to the Parthenon. The ride should have taken twenty minutes; however, Mopsus was a happy wanderer and Max had to fight to keep him from nibbling on the long grass, and chomping on young pine branches, as they continued on the familiar well-trodden path.

As they approached the Propylaea, Max glimpsed the flower sellers with their large baskets clustered together on the marble steps. Every morning the girls from the village sold garlands of flowers to those wishing to make an offering at the shrine of the goddess, Athena Parthenos.

'Menelaos!' Daphne called to him, using his ancient Greek name, which annoyed him terribly. She was the only girl at the villa who spoke Greek. However, he was delighted to see Daphne running down the steps with garlands of flowers in her hands.

Daphne never let on that she adored this English boy, with his long legs, tousled dark brown hair, freckles on his nose and large ears. Yet it was his swagger that had captured her attention that very first day, when strolling the Agora. She had met *her Englishman*, with his himation draped over his shoulder, sitting on a stone, nursing his sore feet. Menelaos was English, yet he behaved like one of them; he even walked like she imagined Pheidias or Pericles would have done, she thought. It was almost as though Menelaos belonged in Athens, although she would never have divulged this to him, ever.

'Hello!' Max smiled at Daphne, who was in his opinion, the most beautiful creature he had ever set eyes on.

'How are you, Menelaos?'

'I am very well,' replied Max, a little shy in her company. They rarely spoke, even at the villa. He didn't want to explain the reason for his mission: to discover for himself what was happening on the Acropolis.

As he slid down off Mopsus' back, Daphne tossed a garland of flowers around Max's neck and suddenly the hot, dust-filled air was filled with the fragrance of violets and narcissi, and white jasmine, which he loved most of all. The air was so hot his nostrils hurt when he inhaled. Then she tossed another garland of flowers, this time around Mopsus' neck. It was obvious that she adored Mopsus too.

Plate XI: Mopsus – Max's beloved donkey, named after a Lapith who fought the centaurs. According to ancient Greek mythology, Mopsus was a seer and one of the Argonauts.

Daphne flashed her dark eyes at Max as she asked, 'Are you going to make more sketches of the Parthenon today, Menelaos?'

'Yes,' replied Max. 'I need to finish my drawings.' He didn't tell her that now that his uncle had returned from Constantinople, he was leaving Athens at noon.

'See you back at the villa,' Daphne said, smiled brightly, then threw her arms around Mopsus hugging his neck. 'See you soon, Mopsus!'

Max rode Mopsus along the dusty path, up the steep incline. Once they had reached the rocky outcrop of the Acropolis he tethered Mopsus to a lone pine tree.

Max waved his finger at the donkey, scolding, 'Now, there's to be no nibbling your bridle or wandering away. Do you hear me, Mopsus?'

'That's a good boy.' Max kissed Mopsus on his forehead, between his ears, which donkeys love, of course.

Max raced up the steep, marble steps leading to the Parthenon. It took some time as there were so many steps. He didn't know what to expect; the Parthenon was so enormous that it was impossible to discern whether or not anything untoward was happening on the west side of Athena's shrine. The colossal structure never failed to impress, mainly because the ancient ruin was a truly awe-inspiring sight. Max did not see or hear anything untoward and hastened towards the porch suddenly feeling *all powerful* – a member of a Hellenic tribe – an ancient Athenian nobleman. The Parthenon exemplified such power that he was swept away by it. The enormity of it completely overwhelmed him, and he was forever humbled by its presence.

There was hardly a breath of air that morning, it was so suffocatingly hot. The heat was so intense it appeared to be rising from the bedrock. It shimmered around the base of the Parthenon, like a mirage, he thought, while gazing through the rows of columns lining the colonnade, bringing a mystical quality to the ancient temple of Athena. Max stopped for a moment, wiping the sweat that streamed down his face, praying for a light breeze, as heatstroke was always a threat. As he mopped his brow he caught sight of the statues holding up the temple of the Erechtheion with their heads. The statues looked sad. No doubt missing their sister, the caryatid he had affectionately named Helen. He was thrilled that she was coming home with him in the ship but, he had to admit, he felt sad for her sisters, believing that the five statues left standing would miss her terribly.

There wasn't a sound. Max imagined that he had heard the lament above the plaintive sound of the olive branches rustling in Athena's sacred olive tree as he carried on, heading towards the east porch, leaping over massive chunks of marble, the Parthenon's once imposing entablature. Then...

He caught sight of Mr Dashiell Hamilton pacing back and forth on the steps.

Max hit the ground. The marble felt cold on his belly. It soothed his elbows. It soothed his knees. The stone felt cold on his cheek as he lay face down on a giant slab of broken marble lying on the bedrock. He didn't move a muscle, fearful of being discovered. He remained that way for some time...until a great walloping thud broke the silence.

Max screamed, 'An earthquake! An earthquake!' and pulled his straw hat down over his ears. When the ground beneath him started to shake he shouted, 'Oh my God, Athena help me!' believing he would surely die.

Terrified, he held his breath waiting to be swallowed up by the earth and did not start breathing again until the rumbling stopped. When the Acropolis quit trembling he very slowly raised his head, peeped out from under his hat through a cloud of swirling marble dust.

'Holy Mother!' Max cried. 'What on earth?'

Max jumped to his feet, at first feeling wobbly on them, then when he thought it was safe, he made his way slowly around the corner of the Parthenon. Long twisted ropes and lanyards were dangling from the Parthenon's frieze like deadly pythons about to strike. He shuddered. His legs turned to jelly. Eyes don't lie. Neither do ears. Every blow of the hammers and crowbars echoing in the hot, sultry air caused Max to cringe. Then, he spotted Don Giovanni Battista Belisario's umbrella bobbing up and down on the scaffolding. He was shouting orders at workmen bashing away at the base of the frieze.

Nikolaos' words echoed in his head. He was in tears as he told Max about the deliberate and frenzied attempts by the French to dismantle the Parthenon, bit by bit, piece by piece, saying that if the Turks allowed this terrible plunder to continue there would be nothing left of their temple. Now, his uncle's men were doing exactly the same thing.

When the enormous dust cloud cleared Max glimpsed the gaping hole in the frieze where the metope of the Lapith boy fighting the centaur had been. The reason he knew this was because the metope was exactly the same as the one he had finished drawing yesterday. Max hid behind a broken column toppled over on the ground; he curled his legs up, hugging his skinned knees. He bowed his head, covering his face with his hands, imagining he heard a loud wailing sound, as though someone was sobbing uncontrollably – yet there was no one there.

Then he remembered he had an apology to make to Don Battista before the ship sailed. If he had the time he would visit the old Greek peasant, ask him whether he had heard the lament that morning.

Chapter Seventeen
The Lament

'*Maladire!*' cursed the aged Neapolitan, with his grizzled head poking through the open window. '*Non me ne importa un fico!*'

'*Mama Mia!*' Don Giovanni Battista Belisario cried, becoming more enraged, 'Will the moaning never stop?'

The exasperated Neapolitan pounded his clenched fists on the open windowsill. Lord Quimby's clerk of works had not slept all night. In fact, he hadn't slept through the night for months, which only added to his misery. His rheumatism was so painful he could hardly move. And, Lord Quimby had neglected to send the medicine he had asked for to relieve the dreadful pain in his legs.

The diatribe with the well continued until Don Giovanni Battista Belisario could stand no more, and grabbing a paint pot nearby, tossed it out the window, splattering Rubens' Blue over everything within splattering distance – a corpus of drawings, brushes and jugs of varnish, and stacks of letters which sat on a small table next to the window. Letters he had received from Lord Quimby over the years demanding the impossible. On the top of the pile was the last letter to His Lordship requesting more capital as Lord Quimby's bankers in Malta had stopped payment on the last payment of funds.

Sadly, the flying paint pot did not alleviate the screeching sound coming from deep inside the well, and when Don Battista realised this he stormed out of the house, heading towards the well, tugging angrily on the cord of his Florentine robe, and shouting at the well, as though it understood:

'Arresto Arresto!'

He trampled overgrown bushes in his Florentine slippers.

'Stop! Stop!'

However, Don Battista could not stop the mournful sound that was so loud, he was convinced he was going crazy. When the wailing didn't stop he rushed back inside his house, slammed the door, and sallied forth towards a cupboard where he kept a bottle of brandy. Guzzling, Don Giovanni Battista Belisario slumped on the floor. He loathed Athens. Summers were hellish. The heat in Athens was much worse than Naples. He had endured much hardship in the three years he had worked for Lord Quimby, as nothing had been forthcoming vis-à-vis his promised wages. And his sweet young wife who had accompanied him to Athens got so fed up she had run off with a Greek sailor. Don Battista gradually passed out, only to be wakened from his stupor by the sound of someone banging loudly on the door.

'Maladire!' Don Battista cursed as he scrambled to his feet. When he stood up he had to grab hold of a chair, as his legs were so painful he could hardly walk. However, he could not have been more surprised when he swung open the door to glimpse Lord Quimby's young nephew and his donkey standing before him.

'Enter. Enter!' Don Battista growled as he grabbed his hounds by the collar. 'Quiet Narcissus, quiet Echo!'

Max tethered Mopsus to a post then hurried inside.

'What do you want?'

'I have come to apologise, Sir, for my behaviour last night. I am sorry. It was very rude of me to accuse you of being a thief.'

Don Battista ignored Max as he ushered him in.

Max didn't know what to expect. He had never been inside Don Battista's house, which comprised of one large room, resembling an artist's studio. Marbles lay everywhere. Several metopes were leaning against the wall and chunks of stone lay scattered on the floor. The room overflowed with art supplies, and reeked of linseed oil, stale spicy garlic sausage and body odour. Several broken easels leaned topsy-turvy against the wall and a large desk was piled high with sketches, and watercolours of the Parthenon drawn from every conceivable angle. Watercolour paint and powder had been spilled on the desk and the floor, and Max knocked over a box of oil paint trying to wade through the junk.

'I'm going mad!' cried Don Battista, who had forgotten the reason for Max's visit. 'The noise in the well is driving me crazy!'

'What noise?' asked Max, a bit miffed.

'The noise coming from inside my well, you idiot!'

'You mean your well makes a noise?'

'It's not the well, silly boy! It's something at the bottom of the well.' Don Battista stamped his small foot on the rug, shouting, 'Come outside. Here, come with me!' He pulled Max by the hand. 'You hear for yourself!'

Max followed Don Battista outside and, sure enough, as they walked towards the well Max could hear a loud moaning sound.

'Holy Mother, Don Battista!' Max cried, as he stood beside him, listening to the pitiful wailing sound coming from inside the well.

'It's awful. I heard exactly the same sound this morning, while I was standing on the verandah.'

'What you are talking about?' His uncle's clerk of works asked, burping loudly. 'That is impossible!'

'You talk nonsense!' shouted Don Battista, rushing back inside the house. 'You go now, Maximilian. Go – get out of here!'

'I came to apologise, Sir...for my behaviour last night.'

'I don't give a damn about your behaviour. All I care about is stopping the noise. In fact, I have decided to fill the well with rubble from the Acropolis, bits of marble, whatever rubble I can find!'

'No! Don't do that, Don Battista! Don't put marble in the well!'

'Why not?'

'Marble isn't good for the drinking water.' It was the first thing that came into his head. He couldn't think of anything else to say.

'You crazy!' Don Battista shooed Max out of the house.

Max ran out of the door of the house, convinced that there was a marble in the well and it was not very happy. Max needed to get the stone out of the well, and fast. But he didn't have time. The ship was about to set sail, was it not?

—◌◯◯◌—

'Diomedes,' Max called out as he glimpsed the old Greek peasant standing alone in his small garden, huddled close to his precious olive tree, the only tree left in his patch.

'What happened to your house?' Max cried in total disbelief as he ran towards his friend with both arms flying wildly about in the air, dumbstruck by the scene.

205

Diomedes was slow to speak. 'My house is gone, Menelaus. Gone! My home was demolished by your uncle's workmen. The barbarians have destroyed my home, and my garden.'

'What?' Max could not believe his eyes. 'Why?'

'Looking for marbles,' replied the old Greek, hanging his head, staring at his bare feet covered in dust.

'Where are you going to live?'

'The garden shed.' Diomedes lifted his arm, pointing towards the shed, not much more than a shelter with a tin roof.

'Don Giovanni Battista Belisario and his army of men arrived last week, bearing crowbars, picks and shovels, and began to dig in the garden, removing all my precious olive trees.' He wept as he related his story. 'The men dug up all my olive trees. When they found nothing they started digging up my vines. When the vineyard had been demolished, Menelaus, the men demolished my house!'

'Don Battista doesn't care about my welfare. When he left this morning, left me standing, weeping at an enormous hole in the ground, he said, "That will do nicely". So happy was he when he caught sight of the shed – all that's left of my home!'

It did not take long to destroy a home, the old peasant's cottage, which was nothing more than a shack that fell over every time the wind blew.

'It doesn't matter,' said the old Greek, with his arm wrapped firmly around his olive tree. 'For the last week I have watched Lord Quimby's men digging down to the bedrock, in their search for the Parthenon's marbles, to no avail!' He laughed. 'Athena, the goddess, is not giving away her marbles from her temple without a fight!'

Max smiled. He liked that idea.

'I have been living within the shadow of the Parthenon for over eighty years, and I have witnessed many things, but never have I seen such greed. My home has been destroyed, ravaged by iconoclasts with an obsession for a souvenir of the Classical world. Unaware that one day their lust will become self-defeating. Athena is a canny goddess, Menelaus. She is immortal. Athena is impossible to defeat.

'It has been a long hot summer, you will agree, without much respite from the deadly heat. Attica is prone to drought, and for many years I have watched my small grapes wither and die on the vines. My tiny crops have turned to dust. The plague, the scourge of this region, is always a threat, caused from the putrid miasma arising from the bog.'

Max listened, intently, translating Greek into English.

'We suffer from political oppression, under Ottoman rule, that has continued for so long, it no longer matters. My family has survived hundreds of years of political oppression, famine, earthquakes, droughts, plague, acts of God, but you know something, Menelaus? I cannot cope with what is happening to my beloved Greece – your uncle has an obsession with our marbles!'

'I know, I know!' Max howled, at the top of his lungs, agreeing with every word the old Greek was saying.

'Sadly, as long as your uncle is allowed to plunder the Acropolis – because plunder it is – as long as the Ottoman Empire and the Sultans ruling us are bribed, there is nothing on the face of Attica that I or you or anyone else in Hellas can do about it.

'I pray every day that the plunder will stop. And when I heard the mournful sounds this morning, I wept and continued to do so as I watched my cottage being torn down.

'I would happily forfeit my life,' cried Diomedes, wiping tears from his eyes, 'if I thought it would stop the plunder of our beloved temple, because the destruction of the Parthenon is a hundred times worse than the destruction of my cottage.

'The plunder committed by Lord Quimby is a monstrous deed – a sacrilege!'

Diomedes was very angry.

'The loud noise drives me mad. Every blow of the chisel cuts deeper into my soul.'

'Did you not try to stop the men?' asked Max becoming angry too.

'Yes, Menelaus. As I watched my life being destroyed, my small cottage demolished, I tried to intervene,' said he, while hugging the tree, 'although I was warned, I would be imprisoned in the Tower of the Winds, Menelaus. It was as simple as that. Athena would not like that. It would be silly to spend my final days rotting in prison. I am a lyric poet. Perhaps a few lines from a poem would not go amiss, as poetry has a way of cleansing the soul.'

Chapter Eighteen
The Dirty Deed

Lord Quimby looked pleased. Hot, mind you, but pleased. His Lordship sat perched on his Turkish saddle, reining in his Arabian steed – a gift from the Ali Pasha upon his departure from Constantinople – watching the action since dawn, that proved to be more entertaining than any West End play. As the drama on the Acropolis unfolded, fine particles of marble dust swirled and eddied in the suffocatingly hot air, and he quickly brushed the fine white powder from the sleeve of his coat. However, when dust from the marble got stuck in his hair and his eyelashes, making it difficult to see, his annoyance surfaced and he cursed aloud. All whilst directing his full attention towards the Greek sailors his clerk of works had hired that morning from the quay, allowing his men to continue on with the plunder.

As the colossal statue of Poseidon was being lowered down from the gable end of the Parthenon, the 9th Lord Quimby could barely contain his excitement. Within seconds another huge chunk of antiquity would be his! Euphoria like no other surged through this honourable gentleman's clotting veins, as he watched lengths of cordage being tightened around the statue, as though Poseidon were being strangled to death. The statue of Athena was next on his list of acquisitions. Meanwhile, the activity taking place on the ground was stupendous as Lord Quimby caught sight of another metope of a centaur abducting a young filly – his absolute favourite – being dragged along the ground en route to the ship. Perhaps it had something to do with the girl's exposed left breast or the beguiling way the drapery folded over the soft orb of female flesh that captured his attention; he refused to admit that he was in anyway lecherous or licentious by nature. But he could not wait to touch the stone, feel the sculpture's firm, young breasts, he thought, as sweat dripped down, gathering in rivulets on his upper lip. He didn't give a damn that the statues of Poseidon or Athena or any of the metopes had remained in situ for over 2000 years, or that these beautiful works of art had survived every plunder known to man. Until now, that is.

Lord Quimby appeared to gloat. Visions of grandeur flashed through his sizzled brain while sweltering in the stupifyingly hot sun. What bloody great treasures the marbles will be when they arrive in London, he thought, while entertaining the idea of placing the marbles on show or opening the Sculpture Gallery to a select few. As more and more lanyards were thrown over the architrave, Lord Quimby mused over his remarkable achievement. He was convinced that he could sell off residual stones if need be, to bump up his decidedly diminishing coffers. He could name his price. The British Government would pay, gladly. This was a triumphant moment indeed, thought His Lordship, as he sat bolt upright in his saddle. Hadn't he spent a lifetime making himself appear taller?

The gloating continued as he craned his neck, unable to look away for a second. After all, he was rescuing the marbles from the bloody barbarians – the Turks, the French, Latins and Greek peasants – was he not? So great was his zeal, that he plotted how he could rescue all of the antiquities in Attica. And as he mopped his sweating brow with his monogrammed handkerchief fluttering in the limpid breeze, he set about contriving a myriad of ways of obtaining *all* of the loot.

'Use the crowbars!' shouted Lord Quimby as he shifted in his saddle, straining his neck swathed in multitudinous folds of sweaty sodden linen.

'Use the longer saw!' he shouted, as the sailors, striped to the waist, struggled to pry the statue of Athena free.

'Use any damn thing you can find, Don Belisario! Just get the blasted marbles down without breakage...this time!'

'We need more men. We need more men up here!' The hunchback Neapolitan stood leaning on the scaffolding, sucking madly on his unlit clay pipe, clutching on to his tattered brolly. 'Now!'

Don Belisario shouted orders at the sailors he had recruited at dawn at Piraeus to get the job done quickly.

While an anxious Lord Quimby yelled above the clanging of crowbars and clamour of chisels, 'Hurry up Belisario! For Christ's sake, hurry up!'

'Sheee's giving us lots of trouble!' shouted the Neapolitan, ranting at Lord Quimby. 'Sheee's not coming down as easily as weee expect.'

Rivulets of salty sweat dripped from the end of Lord Quimby's vanishing nose while he cursed, 'Bloody hell! I am not leaving Athens without the statues of Athena and Poseidon on board.

'While you are at it, take all that you can. Take down every blasted one of the sculptures. A few pieces of the architrave and the pediment will not go amiss either. Good doorstops!'

'Lord Q, Don Belisario, I don't think I can stand much more of this blasted heat!'

The whinging Lord Quimby was beginning to grate on Belisario's nerves. The heat was so intense he could hardly breathe. He could die. However, his problems were much more troublesome. If he didn't complete the job he would not be paid what he was owed – the equivalent of three years' wages.

'Do you have a problem?' His Lordship shot as his sweating bottom slithered back and forth in his saddle.

There was no reply from the ugly little man sweltering in the heat. Tired and hunched the ageing Neapolitan glared wildly at the statue of Athena as the men tried to free it. He stood to one side shielding his weather-beaten face with his tattered brolly, hiding his concern. The Greeks were unable to release the statues without removing the surrounding marble facade and he had no idea what to do about it.

Don Belisario felt ill as the sailors chiselled through the stone. The hunchback winced. Deep down he knew that what he was doing to the Parthenon was a crime. But damn it, he *had* to continue. He needed money. He could not return home to Naples either, as he would be shot.

'Damn! What's the hold up?' Lord Quimby unbuttoned his crumpled waistcoat, exposing soggy wet linen. 'The ship sails at sunset and these blasted statues had better be in the hold or it's your job on the line!'

The Neapolitan was becoming a damn embarrassment, thought Lord Quimby, as the men hacked through the architrave with crowbars and saws. Lord Quimby, in a huff, dug his heels into the rump of glistening horseflesh and galloped down the southern slope into the shade of the Acropolis. He fanned his face in a feeble attempt to cool himself.

Lord Quimby gazed up at the frieze, counting the broken lintels between the triglyphs – ugly gaping holes left in the marble. An old hag came to mind, with rows of broken teeth. 'Not to worry,' chuffed Lord Quimby, the ruin, meaning the Parthenon, was dying a slow death anyway. In fact, all of Athens was drowning in dull despotism and moral decay so it was crucial that he rescue the loot. If the Turkish guards didn't sell the loot to English tourists, they extracted the lime from the marble for building material. His workforce had ground enormous blocks of marble, without so much as a thought of what was being done. They had also dug down to the bedrock, searching for marbles, but nothing of value was ever found for darling Vrai Viviette to display in the Great Hall, something to excite half the British Establishment while strutting into dinner.

Lord Quimby considered himself to be a true Classicist in every sense of the word. He had travelled the Near East offering elaborate sums of money for Greco-Roman artifacts.

Euphoria like no other swept over him as he watched the colossal statue of Poseidon lowered to the ground. And so puffed up was he while watching this hideous operation that he thumped wildly on his chest, like a gorilla feasting on bananas.

Yes. 'Lord Quimby's Dig' was going according to plan. He needed to congratulate his clerk of works, and he dug his boots into the flanks of his steed and galloped up the slope towards the site. The sun was so exceedingly bright that he had to place his hand over his eyes. What he witnessed, however, did not please him.

'Belisario?' Lord Quimby's demanding guttural voice rang out, breaking through the blazing wall of heat. 'What in blazes is going on?'

Beyond the huge marble colonnade the Greek sailors were scurrying down rope ladders, racing from the site, as though they were being chased by the devil.

'Did you give the men permission to abandon the site?'

Don Belisario said nothing. He threw up his hands in total despair.

The sailors were racing down the south-east slope of the Acropolis, while Don Belisario stood beneath the badly butchered architrave of the Parthenon. The sky overhead looked black even though it was only mid-afternoon.

Lord Quimby could barely hear his clerk of works hushed octave. 'It's the lament, Milord, the *lament!*'

'What?'

'The lament, Sir. The Greeks heard the mournful wailing sound of the marbles weeping, Milord. They are frightened. They are terrified. They quit. The men are refusing to come back!'

'Bloody hell,' roared Lord Quimby. 'Tell the sailors to return or else they will not receive their wages!'

'They don't care about their wages!'

Lord Quimby pulled his gun from its holster – he wasn't being exposed to the incursions of robbers and wandering tribesmen.

'Tell the sailors that I will shoot dead anyone who does not return to work. Do you understand?'

Don Belisario paled like a corpse. Desolate, he called to the men. Lord Quimby had turned into a madman, an evil man. The Don was sorry that he had ever agreed to do his dirty deed.

Chapter Nineteen
Maximilian Has a Dream

As his head was about to be split open with an axe, Max awakened, screaming. Suffering inconceivable pain, he writhed about wildly in his bed, imagining that he was being savagely and brutally bludgeoned to death. It was that last horrific blow to his head that had finally roused Max from his dream.

Max continued to scream, while fending off the vision of the grimacing centaurs, the savage beasts desperately trying to kill him. He cried and moaned most piteously, consumed by the terrible plight of the Lapiths raging on in his mind. Because, in his dream, Max *had* become the young Lapith boy locked in mortal combat with his evil foe – the gruesome centaurs, the half-man half-beasts with their hoary beards and bulging eyes, monsters attempting to smash his head open with an axe.

His dream had been so real, so life-like, that Max truly believed that the fatal blow to his head had actually been brandished and that he lay dying. His dream had been so powerful he found it impossible to think otherwise. While blinded by this terrible illusion he reached up, and held his throbbing head with hands he imagined were no longer there. He could *feel* the jagged bone biting through his wounded flesh, he could *feel* his blood gushing from his severed head, he could *touch* the gaping wound in his scalp, he could *feel* the searing pain as it shot through every fibre of his being.

He imagined that his right hand had been hacked off with one fateful blow. He imagined that both his legs were brutally hacked off above the knee, and that his left arm was gone. And, so were both his feet. The butchers had reduced his lithe young body to a shattered mass of badly mutilated stumps of barbed and broken bits of white marble.

By the time Max had struggled free of his captors' grip and escaped the savage wrath of the mighty centaurs, he had awakened fully from his dream. However, doesn't it seem a bit odd, dear reader, that the gut-wrenching sobs emanating through the whitewashed walls of the villa went unheard? His young cousin who slept in the next room failed to hear Max screaming. As did Duffy, the boys' aged tutor, who slept in a small bedroom down the hall. The Albanian servants who spent the night curled up on thin floor-mats right outside his room in the hallway, didn't hear a sound. Even the lodgers, of whom there were many, failed to hear the shrill ululations echoing from within Mrs Logotheti's rambling villa.

During the night Max's attic room had become a torture-chamber for its ravaged occupant, who, in one last frenzied attempt to relinquish his dream, relieved the (imaginary) pain in his arms and legs, and began clawing at the bedclothes tucked in tightly around his bed with arms like stumps of torn, mutilated flesh. After much thrashing and flailing, the weary prisoner managed to free himself of his torturous shroud, and lay on his bed in the dark, gasping and moaning most piteously.

Until Aurora, the goddess of the dawn, winked at the sun god Helios driving his golden chariot across the clear azure sky. The bright sun rose above the villa, peeped through Max's open window forcing him to open his eyes, wide. He didn't dare look down at his body – what he imagined was left of it – and consumed in an agonising paralysis, he stared unblinkingly at the ceiling. However, Max did not really *see* the ceiling. What he imagined was much worse – a chasm of cold, hard, nullifying fear reflecting back at him, pressing down harder and harder on to his body. The force was so great that he had difficulty breathing until a little owl hooted outside his window. The sound was a familiar one. The two owlets, Thomas and Tommy, had been roosting in the pine tree all summer. However, the moment proved to be an iconic one, as the owlets swooped down from their solitary perch and landed on the open windowsill. Athena's archaic symbol of wisdom had something important on its mind, because one of the young owls refused to budge. It sat perched on the sill hooting and bobbing its head continuously until Max looked its way. In a knowing response, the small owl blinked its huge black eyes several times. Then nodded its small feathered head, as if to say:

'Don't worry. You will be all right now.'

Then, a sudden gust of wind caught the owlet by surprise and the mythical bird took flight, disappearing, as if by magic, into the dawn's early light. Had the small owl's enchanted, plaintive call empowered Max in some strange way? Provided the inner strength he so very badly needed to face his debilitating fear head-on? Because, as the owl soared above the trees, into the heavens, Max suddenly sat bolt upright on his small bed and looked down...

Surely...his...eyes...were...deceiving him?

Plate XII: Metope of a Lapith carved by Menelaos. This is also the metope Max watches being 'plundered' by his uncle, causing him to experience horrifying nightmares that last a lifetime. The metope remains on display in the Quimby Gallery to this day.

'My legs!' Max shouted as he looked down, gaped at his small calloused feet protruding out of the ends of his crumpled Egyptian cotton pyjamas. Squirming on his bed he cried out:

'My legs!'

So shocked was he by the sight of his legs he was reluctant to move or bend down and touch his toes and he sat on his bed looking totally and utterly dumbfounded.

He thrust up the sleeves of his cotton pyjamas expecting to find broken stumps, but to his utter amazement, his arms were dangling out of the sleeves.

'My arms...my arms...! Holy Mother...I still have my arms!' Max was finding it impossible to believe that he still had both his arms – and that both his hands had not been hacked off by the gruesome centaurs.

Dazed, while staring through the murky dawn, Max sat on his bed, snug against the wall in the corner of his small room, convinced that he had experienced the worst nightmare of his life. But the room failed in every way to resemble a battlefield. It was neither littered with splintered bones, blood, guts or gore, nor were his badly mutilated, severed arms and legs piled on the floor. He was unable to comprehend *why* his blood wasn't splattered on the walls, on the bed, soaking through the lumpy, straw mattress, and seeping through the crumpled bedlinen.

He doubted his ability to ever glimpse a metope without being reminded of his nightmare. It made him squeamish. In his dream the Lapiths had come to life – so great was his empathy for the battered clumps of ruinous stone, those marble statues of mortals and immortal gods and goddesses that seemed...well...almost...human.

Max scanned his small attic overflowing with a summer's accumulation of junk – his yawning trunk unpacked by servants, as their return voyage home had been cancelled until further notice. His uncle wanted all of the marbles removed from the Parthenon. Was it any wonder he had a nightmare?

It had all been a dream. One horrific nightmare.

But just to make sure that his body hadn't, in fact, been chopped up into little pieces, he dangled his long, skinny legs, that were getting longer by the day, legs he thought much too long and altogether much too skinny, over the side of the bed, and began wriggling his toes, luxuriating in the feel of the deep Turkish carpet underfoot. Pure joy surged through every fibre of his being.

He wasn't made of stone after all.

No, Max was *not* the one being mutilated, nor was he being savaged by centaurs, although he strongly believed that he had become the young Lapith boy in his dream, exactly the same metope that he had witnessed being removed from the Parthenon.

Meanwhile, so relieved was Max at finding himself in one piece, he virtually leapt out of bed. His dream had shaken him badly and he felt a bit wobbly on his feet. But he remained unconvinced that he wasn't made of stone and – this is the unbelievable part – Max ripped open his cotton pyjama top, splaying the buttons, searching for signs of bruising on his shoulders, chest and stomach. *Nothing!* His imaginary dream-world had tricked him. There wasn't a single mark on his body. So great was his imaginary suffering, that Max truly believed that he had been brutally tortured. But he had proof – otherwise why did his entire body hurt? Why could he feel excruciating pains in his legs? And as he rubbed his throbbing head trying to ease the pain, he felt as though it had been *his* flesh and *his* bone that was being hacked to pieces, torn from the marble flesh of the same Lapith boy that he had watched being – either deliberately or maliciously, it was impossible to tell – gouged out of a metope with a crowbar yesterday afternoon. The carved figure was so unbelievably life-like that it was as though the Lapith's body was being ripped apart. Was it any wonder Max felt such empathy towards the metopes, the marble figures carved in the enormous marble slabs, being removed on the south side of the Parthenon's magnificent marble frieze? And as he walked outside on to the verandah, he was plagued by one question:

Was it possible for marble statues to have souls – a sort of spirit within? Because the effect the dream had had on Maximilian Henry Perceval had been truly astonishing.

Chapter Twenty
The Treasure Hunt

Youthful arrogance prevented the boys from hearing the lament early the next morning. They could not have cared less about the fate of the metopes or the marble statues of those unfortunate gods and goddesses ripped out of the belly of the Parthenon. All they cared about was searching for more loot.

That morning Eggy had raced on ahead of Evliya and the other members of the group gathering at the base of the Acropolis. He had climbed on to an enormous marble column toppled over on the ground and stood teetering back and forth with his pudgy hands held over his big blue eyes in visor-like fashion, scanning the pile of rubble newly scattered on the ground. He was Hermes. He wore cut-off nankeen trousers, straw hat, two linen pillowcases billowing out behind him in the breeze and winged sandals on his feet.

Eggy waved his chubby arms, shouting as eight-year-old boys shout. 'Come on chaps... Let's go and search for more loot!'

'I'm coming!' Sébastien Fauvel leapt over a broken capital. 'Papa wants all the loot we can find!'

Sébastien's father was a French diplomat. He was also an avid collector of Greek and Roman antiquities and had sold many of the marbles to the Louvre in Paris. The boys really enjoyed visiting Sébastien's palatial villa in Corinth that was bursting with treasures found on the Acropolis. They poked fun at the marble heads – Monsieur Fauvel called *busts* – with defaced noses, ugly grimacing faces, marble curls and bulging eyes. The boys spent hours peering inside elegant glass cases containing bits of broken Grecian pottery with naked men and women painted on the side, and marble ears and toes and thumbs that had been deliberately hacked off the statues of the Parthenon. The boys dreamed of having as much loot as Sébastien's parents.

'I'm coming too!' Gio, short for Giovanni, was the nephew of Lord Quimby's clerk of works, Don Giovanni Battista Belisario. He was the youngest member of the group. He tagged along because he liked to be seen with the older boys; however, he was too young to hunt for loot and spent most of the time perched on broken columns, sucking his thumb. Gio was always telling the other boys how important Eggy's father was because he had come to Athens to rescue the marbles.

The boys thought rescuing the marbles was a capital idea; however, they failed to understand why the statues had to be shipped all the way to England when Florence or Rome was much closer. The boys agreed that it was none of their business. Did it matter that English tourists wanted a souvenir to take home, to boast about to their friends? The boys did not care, no, not one bit. They dreamed of owning a house full of statues of naked women, young goddesses with slender arms, smooth rounded bottoms and firm creamy white breasts.

The next two members to arrive were Gunther and Friedrich who came rushing along the winding path looking like Vikings about to conqueror the Anglo-Saxons, with their blond hair blowing in the breeze, and their bright blue eyes scanning the mighty Parthenon that loomed before them. Gunther and Friedrich spoke very little English. But language wasn't an issue.

As the boys charged up the steep incline, making their way towards the steps leading up to the Parthenon, with their empty sacks flung over their backs, the sound of their young voices suddenly came to a full stop.

The boys screamed.

A loud thunder was heard in the distance as an enormous block of stone crashed down from the opposite side of the Parthenon. The noise was so terrifying and so loud that the boys ran back down the hill, huddled together like rugby players in a scrum, too frightened to move. Shaking and crying hysterically the boys held on to each other, while shattered marble exploded and powdery marble dust clouded the air.

'Let's go and see what happened!' cried Evliya, the first person to free himself from the scrum, and leading the other boys, set off, racing up the hill towards the scene with his bright red fez falling from his head and his white silk pantaloons billowing out around his long skinny legs. Meanwhile, Gio, who had been hiding behind a massive, toppled, fluted column, was so frightened he was afraid to move and began to cry, tears streaming down his small crumpled face, splashing on to the stone, the bedrock of the Acropolis.

Max looked as shattered as the stone as he stared up at the gaping hole in the Parthenon's frieze.

When he heard Gio sobbing, Max shouted out, 'Don't cry, Gio, it's all right!' and ran to comfort Gio by lifting the little boy up in his arms. 'Don't cry, Gio!'

'I want to go home...Max...I want to go home.'

Nikolaos, who was also standing nearby, was so distraught he was becoming hysterical.

'The metope...the...metope!' cried Nikolaos, sobbing. This was all he was able to say. 'The metope! The metope!' Nikolaos refused to go anywhere near the shattered stone.

'Calm down, Nikolaos!' cried Max, as he rushed towards his friend with Gio in his arms, grabbing hold of his flailing arms, and trying to comfort him. 'Calm down!'

'I can't calm down, Menelaus. The metopes were carved by my ancestors!'

'Bloody hell!' Max swore. He sounded just like his uncle.

'I can't stay here. I can't stay here a moment longer!' Nikolaos fled down the hill with tears streaming down his face.

'Nikolaos, are you mad?' Evliya asked, rubbing marble dust from his eyes.

Impudence showed on the Turk's smudged face as he watched Nikolaos racing down the dusty path, and wrinkling his nose hissed, 'Imagine weeping for a lump of old stone!'

For the second time in less than a minute Max swore under his breath, 'Bloody hell!', which had to be something of a record.

Then, Evliya shot, 'Come on lads, let's go. There will be lots of loot now.'

By the time the boys had reached the summit, the show was over. Lord Quimby's men had all vanished, leaving a massive grave of shattered stone in their wake. The marble chunks that had fallen from the frieze were either too large or too jagged to put in their loot bags. However, not far from where the pile of rubble lay, a large clump of stone had been unearthed during the crash. All the boys ran towards the stones and crouching down on their hands and knees, began foraging on the ground, squabbling among themselves over the best pieces.

'The loot belongs to me!' Eggy pulled on the stones, trying to grab the largest chunk of marble out of Evliya's hands.

'No it doesn't! The marble belongs to me! The loot belongs to my father!' Evliya shouted. 'So you can't have it!'

'I don't care about you or your fathers!' Gunther shouted, holding himself erect, adding to his height. 'I am taking the stones home with me. I am German! We look after our treasures. We are a proud race', and pointing to the gaping hole in the frieze shouted, 'The German Chancellor would not allow this terrible atrocity to happen to our beautiful buildings in Munich!'

'Copenhagen is the safest place in the world!' Lars said. 'So I take my stones home!'

'Let's fill our bags!' offered Eggy, rubbing the dust from his face.

'*No!*' Max waved his finger at the boys. 'The stones do not belong to us!' Max glared hard at the boys. His words tumbling out of his mouth before he even realised what he was saying. 'We cannot take the loot home because the loot belongs here in Athens. The stones belong to the Greek people.'

'Who are you to tell us what to do?' Evliya said huffily, with his hands placed defiantly on his hips.

Max picked up a small chunk of stone and while blowing away the white powdery dust, ran his fingers along the raised surface, trying to imagine what the carved figures meant.

Meanwhile, Sébastien had rushed forward with a small chunk of stone in his hands. 'I have an idea – Papa will know what to do. He will take all the stones we can find as he wants to donate the marbles to the Louvre in Paris.'

Max did not like the sound of this. 'I have a better idea,' enthused Max, as he flung his satchel from his shoulder. 'Let's each take a small piece of stone. Only one – understand – as a keepsake.'

'That's a capital idea!' chimed the boys in unison.

Max slid his chosen chunk of stone inside his goat-skin bag, unknowingly brushing away 2000 of years of dust from the precious stone. He felt extremely protective of the marble. He wanted to keep it safe, which was silly when he thought about it later.

And so, the boys filled their loot bags. However, no sooner had Max placed his stone in his bag than the irritating sound of the ship's bell rang in the distance. The East Indiaman was preparing to set sail.

'Come on, Eggy,' said Max, walking down the steps towards the gate. 'That's enough loot.'

Friederich had something he wanted to say and he ran towards Max, shouting, 'This place is a dump, Maximilian, so it doesn't matter what we take. Father said that we can take as much loot as we want. Who will know the difference? The peasants don't care. See those folk standing over there? They don't care either because tourists will buy all the loot we can find!'

'You mean those tourists standing by the gate?' Evliya piped up. 'They have so much money they pay my father hundreds of piastres for one piece of stone. Noses are a favourite!'

Evliya stood looking towards the Erechtheion. The Turkish guards were standing by Athena's sacred olive tree selling bits of stone. 'Let's see how much we can get for our treasure!'

Max stayed behind, clutching his satchel tightly under his arm. He didn't really want to join in. As Evliya rushed past he turned around and with his loot bag high above his head, laughed and shouted, 'You...foreigners...you don't know nothing...we Turks... we smart people...we get rich selling loot to foreigners. Don't you know...Maximilian...no one cares about old rocks. So, why should you...why should you?'

Chapter Twenty-One
St James's Square, London

The highly acclaimed architect, Signor Alberto Bellini, experienced such untold elation as he flung open the door of his makeshift office in the nether regions of the newly refurbished Palladian-style house in St James's Square, that he burst into song. He had good reason to rejoice.

After all, hadn't he achieved the impossible?

Such untold elation wasn't uncommon for one of Latin descent and he allowed himself to be swept away, evoking such passion within him that La Scala came swiftly to mind. This melodious outburst was due to the fact that, goodness knows how, after many failed attempts, he had finally managed to complete the last tour of inspection of Lord and Lady Quimby's Palladian-style house, and, as unbelievable as it seemed, his client, the formidable Lady Quimby, was *pleased*. But for how much longer? Signor Bellini did not know, nor intended to remain in residence long enough to find out, as he planned to make good his escape immediately after clearing his desk.

Signor was a man of great passion. His solo, *bel canto* performance from Mozart's *Don Giovanni* made his eyes water, as it filled the damp, dark, musty air of his makeshift office with joyful song. His office, an antechamber of little consequence located on the ground floor of the east wing of the house, had been a cloak-room used by the late 8th Lord Quimby; however, after his death some years ago, the room was no longer in use.

He had waited for this day for years, he thought, as he peeled off his long green dust-jacket, and flung it in the bin, relieved to be disposing of that which had hung on his back for the last five years. Then, Signor Bellini began in earnest to clear his draughting table, piled high with architectural drawings and elevations of the west wing, that had been redesigned so many times he had lost count. The new additions included the Sculpture Gallery, especially built to house Lord Quimby's burgeoning collection of Classical sculptures collected over the years, three petite salons, the Music Room (large enough in which to play a round of golf), and a boudoir of staggering proportions on the first floor, as Her Ladyship had taken a sudden fancy to Ionic columns – the reason for which will be explained in due course.

Signor Bellini stuffed his drawings inside his fine Italian-made leather case – the drawings were returning home with him to Padua in a fortnight. The mere thought of his beloved Padua brought forth a libretto worthy of such fortissimo that tiny cracks appeared in the freshly plastered ceiling. However, his rendition of Mozart's *Figaro* ended abruptly on a half-note when Luigi bounded through the open door.

It was Luigi's last day on the job and Signor Bellini was sad to see him go. Like all apprentices from the Eternal City, he was neatly dressed in dark-blue overalls, loose-fitting white shirt and black beret, leaning *à droit* on a mass of glossy jet-black curls. The added flourish of a bright red neckerchief tied in a enormous bow gave the aspiring young artist the *esprit de corps* of his profession. Luigi could not have resembled Rembrandt more if he had tried – even with the splattered Rubens's Blue paint smeared on the elbows of his shirt, and smudges on the end of his nose.

'Signor Bellini!' Luigi cried, while gasping for breath. 'Signor Bellini...Lady Quimby said...to come *adesso!*'

The paintbrushes Luigi was holding on to wobbled, dripped on to the parquet floor, as he stood on the threshold, stammering, 'Lady Quimby...says...that you...are to come to the Sculpture...Gallery...at once, Signor.'

'Sorry, Signor,' said Luigi as he glanced down at the puddle on the floor, embarrassed. 'Lady Quimby...said...something...else... Sir...I could not understand.' Luigi's English wasn't very good.

Luigi could have been speaking Hungarian. It made no difference. Signor Bellini got the message, and in a great huff rushed out of his makeshift office. And in tandem they hastened through the labyrinth of back halls while Signor Bellini cursed in his mother tongue, which in English went something like:

'That frightful woman, what could she possibly want of me now?'

It was a considerable distance to the Sculpture Gallery, as you can well imagine, dear reader, as the house was of gargantuan proportions – similar in size to London's Guildhall. Luigi knew the way and the young lad rushed on ahead of Signor Bellini, opening and closing numerous sets of French doors leading from the North Tribune to the Sculpture Gallery. He was careful not to leave fingerprints on the inlaid with Venetian glass, solid-gold doorknobs in the shape of dolphins Her Ladyship had especially imported from France. It took more than five minutes to reach the Great Hall, that boasted a fabulous collection of antique statues in Roman-style niches, freshly painted murals of bucolic Italianate landscapes and a stunning fresco ceiling.

An army of porters were busy hanging huge gilt-edged portraits of the Quimby dynasty on crimson silk-lined walls – an endless task, thought Senor Bellini to himself – as they hurried on towards the Sculpture Gallery, whizzed past the restored marble statues of Lucius Antonius draped in a toga and wearing sandals on his feet, and Lucius Verus on the other side of the Tribune in the same costume. Andrea di Pietro della Gondola, or Palladio as he was more commonly known, would be pleased, Signor was convinced, as he spied the elaborately carved grotesques, griffins and lions grinning from every corner, halls lined with *trompe l'œil* pilasters and gilded Corinthian columns reaching the ceiling. He finally arrived at the North Tribune, the apex, an elegant *tour de force* of Palladian architecture, the cruciform hall.

The Sculpture Gallery had become the centre of Lady Quimby's imaginary world, thought the highly acclaimed architect, as he padded silently across the black and white harlequin marble floor, in his handmade patent leather boots – made-to-order from Milan – to greet his client.

'Where on earth have you been?' Lady Quimby demanded icily, waving a letter under his nose, impatiently tapping her elegantly shod foot on the black and white marble floor. 'You know how I loathe being kept waiting!'

'Forgive me, Milady,' Signor Bellini replied, humbly, as he reached for Lady Quimby's outstretched hand, feeling more like a puppy being scolded for puddling on the floor than a world-famous architect. 'I came as fast as I could, Milady.'

'Well, not fast enough. May I remind you, Signor, that you have not been released from my employ just yet!'

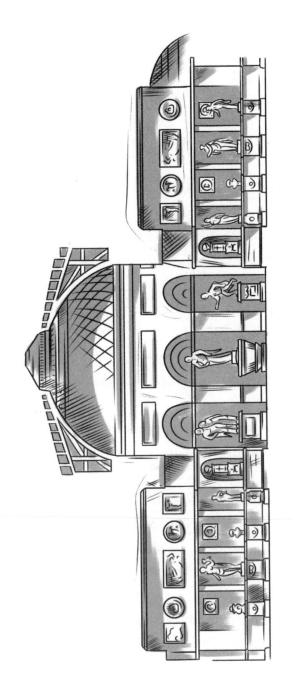

Plate XIII: Senor Belini's interior elevation of the Sculpture Gallery, designed especially for Lord and Lady Quimby's private collection of Parthenon statues. The statues were taken by Lord Quimby for display in his palatial town house in St James's Square, London.

233

Signor Bellini glanced the other way...hid his disdain.

'I received a letter from Custom House in the morning post wishing to advise that the marbles we have been waiting for have finally arrived and are being delivered this morning!'

'That's wonderful, Milady,' replied the Latin in a humble voice. As he turned he ran his small elegant hands over the stone, felt for imperfections in the scagliola pilasters on either side of the double doors leading to the Sculpture Gallery.

'Yes, it is wonderful, Signor Bellini, and to think that the marbles will be here for Christmas after all!' Lady Quimby scanned the letter. 'We are to expect twelve crates, exactly the right number of busts.'

'This is good news, Milady,' Signor Bellini enthused forcing a smile. He didn't really give a florin about her damn marbles, although he never let on.

'It's not good – it is wonderful news!' Lady Quimby gushed.

'However, I need your assistance, as I have not a clue where to place the busts!'

Lady Quimby scanned the empty niches lining the walls of the Sculpture Gallery that had remained void for more years than she cared to admit.

Signor Bellini was in no mood for trivia. He was most anxious to take his leave as a potential client awaited. The constant sound of Lady Quimby's high-pitched voice drove him mad, as the Sculpture Gallery was without fixtures and furnishings, with nothing to absorb the sound.

Lady Quimby trod back and forth on the highly polished marble, waving her velvet-clad arms trimmed in ermine. 'I haven't much time. The coach is waiting to take me back to the house in Kent. However, I cannot decide where the marbles should go. Which bust should go where, Signor Bellini. I was hoping you had made a diagram showing where the Roman busts should go.'

'Have you failed to do so, Signor?' asked she, huffily.

Signor Bellini scratched his head. Then he pointed towards the first niche, 'Now let me think. I believe Julius Caesar came first and... then...'

'Good, Signor Bellini. Who should go in the second niche?'

'Alexander the Great!'

'Good. Who should go...here...in the third niche...'

Lady Quimby hastened on without taking a breath.

'Let me see. I believe Bacchus, Lord Quimby's favourite, was to come next and then Neptune.'

'What do you think, Milady?' asked Signor Bellini, shrugging. Did it matter? She would change her mind anyway.

Lady Quimby viewed the yawning niches with disdain or fondness – or both – it was impossible to ascertain. 'I am not sure.'

'Perhaps...Augustus...and...Marcus...Aurelius...should he not come next?'

Signor Bellini walked away. He couldn't stand another minute. He didn't quite know what to do with himself as he hovered in the Sculpture Gallery, waiting for the marbles to arrive, watching what was going on.

Artists were tidying up. Scaffolding was coming down. Ladders were folded up. Canvas shrouds, used to protect the marble floors, were being folded up, after repainting the ceiling for the sixth time. And the *formatori* he had especially recruited from Milan looked pleased, no doubt relieved, after five long years on the job, to be done with the materials used to make plaster-of-Paris mouldings and ornate frescoes.

Lady Quimby, oblivious of the goings-on around her and blue with cold, stood waiting beside an empty plinth, scribbling on the back of the letter from Custom House with a small gilt-topped pencil.

'The Sculpture Gallery will be *so* evocative of the "spirit of the ancients"' enthused Lady Quimby, smiling brightly, her fine alabaster skin drawn taut over high cheekbones, as though she herself were made of marble.

'It's so reminiscent of the Palladian style, Milady!'

'I totally agree, Signor.' Once the marbles are placed in situ,' said Lady Quimby as she removed her kid-glove, ran her bare hand over the carved marble fluting, caressing the colossal Corinthian columns lining the colonnade.

'Rococo, Gothic, Picturesque bore me silly,' Lady Quimby chided as she glimpsed the long row of colossal columns lining the colonnade, rising twenty-five feet above her head; columns that had arrived in the first shipment of marbles from Naples.

'Why, Signor, I feel dizzy just looking up!' Her Ladyship was forced to lean against a column to steady herself. 'I am so glad I changed my mind and chose the Corinthian columns. Of course, I have Mr Dashiell Hamilton to thank for developing a taste for all things Palladian!'

Sweat gathered on Signor Bellini's brow, which was difficult to imagine as he was also shivering as the temperature was close to freezing in the Sculpture Gallery. He was forced to rub his hands together to keep warm. As he did so, he could not help thinking Lady Quimby was without doubt the most difficult client imaginable. He had tried to make allowances, as the baby's death was a terrible blow to Her Ladyship. Nonetheless, she remained insufferable. For the simple reason she was forever changing her mind, from the colour of the marble to the style of doorknobs. From the length of the finials to the thickness of the plinths – forcing the Latin to the brink. And, in the last year, as the house was nearing completion, she had suddenly taken a fancy to all things Greek. Signor Bellini had had to put his foot down, as the English say. He had threatened to quit. Lord Quimby's London agent had obviously influenced Her Ladyship, as her attitude towards all things Greek increased with each of Lord Quimby's London agent's visits, which seemed more frequent of late.

While Signor Bellini waited he secretly eyed his creation – the finest example of Palladian in London. Stunning frescoes lined the rotunda, painted with bucolic murals of allegorical Italianate landscapes and picturesque scenes of Roman ruins. Rising above this illusive, lofty space was a magnificent coffered dome similar in style to the Pantheon in Rome. He scanned the ceiling where cherubs, gods and goddesses frolicked playfully on fluffy white clouds, while surreal, mythical creatures from Roman legends peered down from the sky. Murals covered the walls. Scenes of the Classical world overwhelmed the senses. A labyrinth of marble anterooms led off the Sculpture Gallery, salons large enough in which to play tennis, lined with *trompe l'œil* pilasters and colossal Corinthian columns from a ruin in Rome.

'To think,' cried Lady Quimby, as her pinched expression changed from piqued to ecstatic in a matter of seconds, 'that the marbles will be here by the time the boys come home from Harrow on the Hill.'

'Eggy will be delighted I'm sure,' said Signor Bellini, spying the door, ready to bolt at the first opportunity. He wasn't so sure about young Maximilian.

'Eggy has dreamed of having a Sculpture Gallery ever since he returned from Athens last autumn.'

However, all mention of the boys soon vanished as an extremely large man was ushered into the Sculpture Gallery by a porter delivering furniture, as the servants had not yet returned to the house.

'Good mornin', Ma'am,' boomed the man, smiling through thick, leathery lips and yellowed teeth as he nodded, nervously wringing his large gloved hands. 'I am from Custom House.'

The man came from within the sound of Bow Bells, the East End of London, which seemed to annoy Lady Quimby terribly as her right shoulder visibly twitched on every syllable.

'Mr Snodgrass, Ma'am, at your service.' As he introduced himself he tugged on the flaps of his long leather apron. 'If you prefer, you may call me Bob.'

Lady Quimby flinched. She could not contemplate using the name 'Bob'.

'Upon my word!' exclaimed the man, obviously overwhelmed by the sight of the lavish fresco ceiling. 'I doubt ever havin' the privilege of seein' anything quite so beautiful, Ma'am!'

The man from Custom House stood admiring the lofty scenes from above, while several carters dressed in the garb of their trade – long leather aprons, enormous leather gloves reaching to the elbow and jackboots – wheeled in small wooden crates on barrows.

Lady Quimby's countenance, rarely relieved of a smile, brightened considerably, as she guessed that the crates were exactly the right size to contain the long-awaited marble busts.

'As you know, Ma'am, we've been 'ere before, with deliveries from Custom House.'

'That is correct,' replied Lady Quimby as twelve crates were deposited on to the floor of the Sculpture Gallery.

The man from Custom House acted as though he himself had just taken possession of the house in St James's Square, thought Lady Quimby, stiffening, as Mr Snodgrass strode across the huge expanse of empty space, thumping loudly on the marble. It took some time to reach her side. When he did, he peeled off his cap, exposing a receding hairline of tufts of carrot-red hair and a deeply furrowed brow – a ploughed field that rose up and down when he spoke – which she found most distracting. However, the body odour coming from him was just as off-putting.

'Sorry for the delay, Ma'am. But, you see, Ma'am, we had a delivery to make to the Duchess's house in Park Lane and we had to call for extra wagons as the crates were so large – enormous. We had no end of trouble loading and unloading the crates. They were right awkward, they were.'

As Lady Quimby impatiently waited for the man from Custom House to finish his story, she eyed the twelve crates. However, as anxious as she was to view the contents it was suddenly put on hold when an army of about twelve men proceeded to wheel in an enormous wooden crate on a metal platform. In fact, the crate was so large she could not possibly imagine its contents. It was large enough to hold a baby elephant.

'Good gracious! What on earth?' cried Lady Quimby as she viewed the wooden crate being unloaded in the centre of the floor.

'The crate contains a giant statue,' replied Mr Snodgrass as his ample body sagged, like a giant panda cornered in London Zoo, and he perused the Bills of Lading in his right paw and flapped his apron with his other paw. 'It's the statue of Poseidon plus all his body parts, Ma'am,' puffed Mr Snodgrass while he signalled to his lackeys.

'Poseidon?' Lady Quimby inquired anxiously, as the toe-tapping resumed at a much faster pace. 'I don't need any more statues. There is no mention of statues in this letter from Custom House.'

'The crate has your name on the lid, Ma'am. So that must mean that the crate belongs to you. Or perhaps this is another batch of crates, Ma'am.'

'What are you saying, Mr Snodgrass?'

The man from Custom House sucked through the gaps in his missing teeth.

'Please allow me to explain, Ma'am.' More apron flapping. 'There is an attachment. According to my notes, the shipment you were expecting went missing...shall we say...I'm sorry...Ma'am...but.... [gulp]...we have been informed that the Naval ship sank and the twelve crates you were expecting are sadly, Ma'am, shall we say, at the bottom of the Bay of Naples!'

'Goodness gracious mercy!' Collapsing, Lady Quimby gripped hold of a nearby plinth to steady herself. 'Whatever shall I do? Lord Quimby will be furious when he finds out about this!'

Mr Snodgrass's bushy eyebrows twitched nervously – the ploughed field rose to meet the red, tufted thatch. To give the man his due, he immediately sensed his client's distress.

'Don't you worry, Ma'am. The crates are in the process of being salvaged, according to my note at the bottom of the document.'

Lady Quimby looked at Mr Snodgrass with a blank expression on her face. It was obvious that she had not heard a word he had said.

'I am sad to say these 'ere crates, Ma'am, aren't the ones you was expectin'. They can't be 'cause they didn't come from Naples. These came from Piraeus, although I must say it was some time ago – 12 October to be exact.'

'I'm sure these crates contain what you've been waiting for, Ma'am,' said Mr Snodgrass, waving his leather glove, indicating to his men to continue with the delivery.

Lady Quimby hadn't a clue where Piraeus was although she never let on, and having regained her composure, she relinquished her plinth. She hastened towards the crate and glimpsed the Customs' labels written on the top. 'Goodness me,' said Lady Quimby, peering through her pince-nez at the label. 'This has Athens, Greece, stamped on the lid. If what you are saying is correct, that the twelve crates I was expecting are now at the bottom of the sea, then what is inside these ones?'

Mr Snodgrass tugged on his whiskers. 'Allow me to explain. The shipment came with strict instructions, stating that the crates were not to be released until the contents had been examined by the gentleman who had shipped the goods. He arrived at Custom House on 15 December and, might I add, it took over a week to check the contents as there were so many crates. I am the only other person who knows the contents, as I was asked not to divulge what lay inside.' Mr Snodgrass's eyes rolled upwards, recalling the pound notes he had received for keeping mum. 'I must say, Ma'am, it was a mighty strange request.

'I assisted the gentleman as he divided the crates between your good self, himself and Sir Archibald Lushington, the Curator of the Museum of Classical Antiquities. We delivered the remaining crates to the Duchess's house, Delphi House, c/o Lady Marianne Wortly, early this morning, as I said before. It took us all morning as the crates were so enormous, so heavy and difficult to manage, that we could only load one crate at a time. That's why we were late. However, Mr Dashiell Hamilton very kindly paid all the charges. He paid for delivery to your address and to have the goods released from bond, which I might add, cost a small fortune. So, you haven't a thing to worry your pretty little head about, Ma'am.'

Lady Quimby's jaw dropped. 'Did you say Mr Dashiell Hamilton?'
'Yes, Ma'am.'

Lady Quimby stiffened as she snatched the document from Mr Snodgrass's hand, then snapped officiously, 'Let me see the Bill of Lading. I see! Mr Dashiell Hamilton paid the duty on the entire shipment, yet he only took delivery of half of it. Sir Archibald and myself got the rest.'

The man from Custom House nodded. 'That is correct, Ma'am.'
'Thank you.'

An uncomfortable silence followed.

Nothing more was said.

Finally, 'Might I add, Ma'am, we had to call for another six wagons. And another twelve men, as the crates are so heavy, so large. However, the lads would be mighty pleased to open the crates for you, 'cause the boxes are right heavy, Ma'am.'

'Please do,' said Lady Quimby, muttering, 'If he calls me Ma'am one more time I will scream.'

Everyone in the Sculpture Gallery gathered round as the first crate, which Lady Quimby imagined containing a Roman bust, was prised open. Artists, plasterers, apprentice sculptors, even the sweepers leaning on their broom handles, looked on fascinated, while the men slashed the ropes with their pocket knives. Using crowbars dangling from their blue overalls they prised open the lids, releasing a foul stench into the cold draughty air. The smell of wet, mouldy straw filled the Sculpture Gallery and in a matter of minutes the pristine marble lay strewn with discarded packing material.

Lady Quimby, being extremely sensitive to evil-smelling odours of any kind, held a silk handkerchief tightly to her pinched nostrils and walked closer to the wooden crate.

She looked hopeful as the lid was prised off and glimpsing the yawning plinth imagined soon it would be filled. She breathed: 'It's the marble bust of Caesar! I know it is, Signor Bellini!'

However, when opened, a large, marble head lay packed in layers of mouldy straw. Horrified, after the object was removed, Lady Quimby cried, 'Why, it's not a Roman Emperor at all! It's the most revolting *thing* that I have ever seen!'

'*Mama Mia!*' Signor Bellini exclaimed, as he peeped inside the crate. His olive skin rarely changed colour; however, on this occasion his visage turned scarlet, offering, 'It's definitely not Roman!'

'I can see that, Signor!' Lady Quimby shot.

'It's the head of a woman!' Signor Bellini exclaimed, as he put his hands on the bust. 'The head of a goddess, perhaps,' said he, as she has a crested helmet, with up-turned cheek pieces. 'I can see a faint outline of a Sphinx. Sadly, the head has suffered great damage, no doubt ravaged by time, the elements.' He looked a little closer. 'Her nose has been deliberately defaced, hacked off by infidels or barbarians I expect, centuries ago. This is a rare object, Milady.'

'I'm not entirely sure, Milady, although it could be Roman, Hadrianic!' added Signor Bellini while studying the marble in greater detail.

'I don't care whether its Romanian or Ethiopian, Signor. Nor do I care how rare it is, Signor. Please, take *it* out of here at once.'

'Yes, Milady,' replied Signor Bellini. 'What do you wish me to do with the head, Milady?'

'Bury it in the garden!' Lady Quimby howled.

'Do you wish to see inside another crate, Milady,' asked Signor Bellini wanting to move matters along.

'Of course!' retorted Lady Quimby, anxiously.

However, when the lid came off an enormous marble head was revealed with a curly beard and bulging eyes.

'What on earth!' Lady Quimby huffed, as she peered into the crate. 'It's not a Roman Emperor! It's a hideous monster!'

'It is Poseidon, as the name has been written on the lid,' said Signor Bellini, while glimpsing the vast and expanding array of crates paraded into the gallery, unloaded on the floor.

'Let's see inside the next crate,' offered Signor Bellini, remaining optimistic.

The men from Custom House took some time to prise the lid off, as the lid was the size of a flatbed wagon used to deliver coal. However, the contents were met with the same despair.

'Good grief!' Her Ladyship blushed profusely, as she glimpsed inside the open crate, gazed upon the statue's genitalia carved in stone. She drew back, hid her face with her small elegant hands, unable to comprehend. 'Where on earth is his toga?' As the marble sculpture was of a reclining nude figure, 'It's shocking!'

'There has been a dreadful mistake,' offered Signor Bellini, as he scanned a vast and sundry assortment of broken marble statues packed around the marble statue – like broken angels buried in straw.

Yet the crates kept coming, wheeled into the Sculpture Gallery. The next wooden crate was so extremely long and narrow that six men and four trolleys were required to move the crate into the Sculpture Gallery.

'I can't imagine what lies inside!' Lady Quimby held her breath like a small child, as the badly damaged lid was prised off. The contents lay hidden, wrapped in a white cotton shroud, as though the object lay in a coffin, awaiting its burial.

Lady Quimby watched the men very gently draw back the shroud, and she glimpsed the face of...

'Good Lord!' Lady Quimby screeched as the face of Kore was revealed. She clutched her throat, gasping for breath, and backed away, imagining a fit coming on.

'Signor Bellini, what on earth is *that?*'

'It is a marble caryatid, Milady,' whispered Signor Bellini as he held Her Ladyship's arm, fearful of her fainting. Assuming she was unaware what a caryatid was he hastened:

'I recognised her immediately. She is the famous marble statue of a young damsel, one of six sisters, young maidens with baskets on their heads holding up the Temple of Erechtheion in Athens. She is very beautiful, Milady, and an extremely important piece of antiquity from ancient Greece, an important artifact indeed. I can't imagine why it was removed from the temple, although Lord Quimby must have had good reason for doing so.'

Meanwhile, the men had taken it upon themselves to remove the shroud from the statue. The statue had had a profound effect on the men in some strange way, and although the marble statue was enormous, extremely heavy, they handled her gently, as though it was real. A reverent silence filled the air. The artists had tears in their eyes. It was astonishing, the powerful effect the statue had on everyone in the Sculpture Gallery.

Lady Quimby paled, her countenance as ghostly as the shroud.

'What should we do with the statue?' Signor Bellini asked.

'Roll the thing in a carpet,' said Lady Quimby, 'there are several rugs in the hall. Have it taken upstairs to the attic. Out of my sight. I can't imagine having that thing anywhere near the Sculpture Gallery!'

'The statue is so enormous I don't think it will fit in the attic. The statue is so heavy it will take a hundred men to left it!'

'What do you suggest, Signor?'

Signor shook his head.

'Well, you had better hire the men!'

Despite all the fuss about the caryatid, wooden crates continued to be wheeled into the Sculpture Gallery, lids peeled off, one by one.

'Please. I can't take any more,' Lady Quimby said, as she sped past another crate, 'I do not wish to see the contents of any more crates.' A crate was packed with Persian slippers, copper and brass candlesticks, incense burners, trinkets, beads, cushions, and a camel-saddle that, as it was being unwrapped, released a mass of insects crawling out of the leather on to the marble – insects that had come all the way from Greece.

Signor Bellini asked for one last crate to be opened. It was roughly sixteen feet in length and two feet in width.

'Finally!' Signor Bellini exclaimed as straw fell away from the marble. 'The chimney piece of Aesculapius has arrived, Milady. Come and see! Please – the gaping hole in the wall in the Grand Foyer will be filled!'

Sadly, it was not the long-awaited chimney-piece.

'That's not what I asked for!' Signor Bellini boomed as he crouched down, examined the marble carving more clearly. 'This is a metope of a Lapith fighting a centaur.'

'How disgusting!' Lady Quimby took a quick glance then turned her head away. She failed to see the beauty in the flabby centaur with a missing leg and grisly head grappling a young woman with her breast exposed. 'It's obscene!'

'There are fifteen crates exactly the same,' said Mr Snodgrass, rubbing his ample chin, 'They are being kept in storage at Custom House, as the wagon wasn't large enough to hold all the crates. Mr Dashiell Hamilton took ten crates exactly the same and twenty-five went to Sir Archibald Lushington.'

'Thank you,' said Signor Bellini, who felt the need to change the subject and hastened: 'Do you wish to have the metope installed over a mantlepiece, Milady?'

'Absolutely not!' Lady Quimby snapped. 'Take all these things away immediately!'

'Where do you wish the marbles to go, Milady?'

'I haven't the foggiest idea 'Try the coach house!'

'Yes, Milady.'

'What would you like done with the one remaining unopened crate?' Signor Bellini asked, hovering, glimpsing the names of the statues written on the lid. 'Do you wish to see the contents? There is a statue of Hermes, a charioteer, a horse, horses' heads, why the list goes on and on...'

Lady Quimby was at her wits' end.

'Take all the crates out of here immediately!'

'Yes, Milady.'

'Have the crates stowed in the garden, until I decide what on earth to do with them!'

'There is always the house in Scotland, Milady.'

'Excellent idea, Signor Bellini!' exclaimed Lady Quimby tapping her toe, numb with cold.

'Have the crates sent to the Shambles at once. The Scots, the heathens, might like them. Now let me see. The dairy hasn't been used for donkey's years. Neither has the piggery or the cow-shed. The

247

Plate XIV: Charged with divine sexuality, the god of wine Dionysos (minus his cup) caused Lady Quimby to swoon when the enormous wooden crate was opened at the house in St James Square, London.

ice-house is a perfect place to store stuff of no earthly good, no use to anyone.'

The toe-tapping resumed in earnest. 'The gardens need smartening up. The gardeners can use the marble slabs for filler for the retaining walls...as I can't possibly imagine what else to do with so many.' Her voice was trailing off.

'Yes, Milady,' said Signor Bellini, as he hurried out of the Sculpture Gallery with sudden renewed vigour, more than he had experienced all morning, firing orders at the men from Custom House on the location of the gardens.

'Whatever shall I do?' said Lady Quimby quietly to herself as the last crate finally went wheeling past. Lady Quimby grimaced as she glimpsed the empty row of niches, failing to hear light footsteps.

'Gracious mercy!' Lady Quimby uttered softly to herself. 'Whatever was my husband thinking of!'

'It no longer matters. You won't have to worry my darling!'

Mr Dashiell Hamilton had crept silently into the Sculpture Gallery unbeknown to Lady Quimby and while gathering his mistress in his loving arms breathed, 'My angel. My darling. Quimby won't be coming home for Christmas!'

He kissed Vrai Viviette passionately, 'And to take your mind off all this unpleasantness my angel, we have a box at the opera tonight!'

—◌◌ ◌◌—

The wind tore violently at Signor Bellini's cloak. He didn't mind in the least. The wind was nothing compared to the seismic encounter he had experienced that morning while burying the bust in the potager. His top hat went flying as he hurried along Piccadilly towards Delphi

House, hopping over the muck from the horses while en route to the Duchess's grand house overlooking Hyde Park Corner. Signor Bellini knew exactly where to find the house, as he frequented Mr Poots' Apothecary Shoppe regularly, located in Old Park Lane behind her grand mansion. Lady Marianne Wortly lived in the grandest house in Mayfair, he thought to himself, as he reflected on the Duchess's letter, with the most unusual request.

Would Signor be so kind as to construct a large shed in the back garden to house highly important artifacts that her dear friend, Mr Dashiell Hamilton, had collected during his tour of the Levant, Near East.

Signor Bellini refused. Her request had been an insult to his profession. A joiner could build a shed. Was her grand mansion not large enough to house a few artifacts? However, the mention of Mr Dashiell Hamilton raised his curiosity, and, as he sped past Mr Poots's Apothecary Shoppe, sure enough, he glimpsed enormous wooden crates stacked high on the back lawn. The same crates that the man from Custom House had made reference to that morning. The wooden crates, of which there were many, were exactly the same size and shape as Her Ladyship had had forcibly removed from her house in St James's Square. Needless to say, he resolved to discover for himself what was inside the crates, and as he raced up the steps leading into the grand house he concluded that London must be fast becoming the 'New Athens' because there were more marbles in London than either Athens or Rome.

Plate XV: Athena's shield originally carved by Nikodimos and his team of sculptors in his humble workshop in Piraeus in fifth century BC.

A small section was discovered by Max in 1802 and became a treasured keepsake. However he had no idea that it was an integral part of Athena's shield or belonged to the Parthenon.

251

Part Three
London, Approximately
Ten Years Later

Chapter Twenty-Two
The Spirit of the Ancients

The attic had gone cold. The meagre coal fire had turned to ash in the grate. A fierce north wind played havoc with the ill-fitting windows, rattling the mullions of Mr Poots's Apothecary Shoppe in Old Park Lane. Torrential rain had poured down for weeks and overflowed in the gutters, sluicing off the roof. Sometime during the night the weary draughtsman had fallen asleep at his desk, only to be awakened at dawn by a loud bang. Maximilian Henry Perceval awoke with a start to find himself slouched over his drawings and Murgatroyd staring at him out of the corner of one eye.

'Crikey. Was that you, Murgatroyd?'

The tortoise shrugged his leathery head. He was used to being teased. Max stared bleary-eyed at the tortoise full of the joys of spring, after awakening from hibernation a fortnight ago, and a sure sign of warmer weather to come.

'Lucky sod!' Max fancied a long slumber, six months at least.

He had often wondered whether he had done right by bringing Murgatroyd home with him to England. After all, Murgatroyd was a Greek tortoise and perhaps the *Testudo graeca* missed his homeland.

Plate XVI: 'Murgatroyd'
This is the *Testudo graeca* that Max rescued from being roasted alive on the beach at Piraeus. However, two hundred years later, it is the tortoise's carapace that holds the dirty secrets bringing the Quimby dynasty to its knees.

Perhaps he was secretly pining for the hot sandy beaches at Piraeus, the warm 'wine-dark' seas of the Mediterranean, without the sponge divers, of course. Perhaps the tortoise, who had doubled in size, longed for female companionship, a beguiling young creature to cosy up to, as he himself fancied some fetching young thing to snuggle close to on cold dark winter's nights in London.

'Enough of this nonsense!' exclaimed Max squinting through the dim light, unable to decipher the hands on the mantle clock. He had developed eye strain over the years while working on detailed architectural drawings in the light of a single candle. He began searching madly through his drawings piled on his desk and suspecting the tortoise of theft blathered:

'Murgatroyd! What on earth have you done with my spectacles?'

Of course, his spectacles lay buried under his drawings, and as he put them on he glanced at his gold timepiece sitting on a pile of textbooks.

'Good lord, Murgatroyd. Look at the time!'

Max had slept late. It was half-past six. Classes began at the Royal Academy in three hours' time.

'Fancy breakfast?'

Murgatroyd blinked as he burrowed deep in his sand box, stowed beneath Max's desk. There was no reply from the ravenous tortoise, who sat munching greedily on an apple core – all that remained of last night's supper. Max expected the tortoise to reply, convinced that one day Murgatroyd would say something profound – he looked so wise.

Another loud bang sent Max rushing towards the window. All was quiet below in the lane. He returned to his desk. In his haste, however, he accidentally knocked over the stool and, as he righted *the damn thing*, the aspiring architect caught his sleeve on the lid of the inkwell and it went flying, causing a great drama to ensue that morning above Mr Poots's Apothecary Shoppe in Old Park Lane.

'Blast!' Max cursed as Indian ink splattered his drawings. Drawings he had laboured over for weeks. A host of invectives echoed in the small attic in a frantic attempt to mop the thick globs seeping through the layers of fine vellum. It was no use. His drawings were ruined. The most important in his collection.

'What in blazes am I going to do now, Murgatroyd?'

Murgatroyd did not answer, nor was the deployment of cunning rhetoric on offer. He noticed every time he cursed or swore, which was more often than not of late, Murgatroyd's round bald head shot out of its stronghold and the tortoise glared at him. Scolding him. Obviously, a reprimand was in order, and Max still a sixth former.

'Not that it matters any more, old bean.'

Max grim-faced stared at Murgatroyd. 'It no longer matters about my drawings or anything else. My life is ruined!'

Despairing, Max slumped down on to the three-legged stool. The same stool he had fallen asleep on. He shook his tousled head ruefully, banging his clenched fists angrily on his desk. Murgatroyd shrank back inside his shell, upset by Max's ranting.

He wished he had never entered the *damn* competition, held every year at the Academy. The prize: the Royal Academy's Gold Medal for Architecture. It was open to all graduating students at the Royal Academy, of which he was one, after five tedious years cudgelling his brains. He had been confident entering the competition, convinced his drawings were worthy of the prize. He had dreamed of, finally, becoming a commissioned architect, travelling throughout Greece and Asia Minor on a drawing expedition, sketching the statues and buildings of the Classical past, the ancients.

Max had never stopped longing to return to Athens, to watch the sun rise over the Parthenon, Athena Parthenos' ancient temple. The thought of wandering aimlessly along the dusty paths of the Agora made his toes itch. Riding his donkey amidst the ruins of the Acropolis made everything itch. He dreamed of swimming naked in the sea, at Piraeus, like he had done, when he had been twelve years of age, still just a boy. For years he had dreamed of sharing a wine-skin with his absolute best friend, Nikolaos, with whom he had lost touch. Now, the chance of ever having a reunion with his friend was gone. As were spending lazy afternoons lounging in the shade of a palm tree, sleeping naked on the verandah of Mrs Logotheti's rambling, Turkish-style villa, listening to the haunting sound of the owls hooting in the pine trees...

He missed Mopsus most of all. He loved the donkey more than he had ever loved anything in his life: his ridiculous antics for a start, his lopsided ears that twitched unmercifully especially when on the snoop for a sweet. Turkish Delight was his favourite. He missed his hee-haws that woke every living creature on the eastern slope of the Acropolis and the softness of his shaggy coat against his skin. Donkeys were part of Greek culture, symbolic of ancient times.

Never, once, had he stopped dreaming of returning to Athens, to Attica, the land of myths and legends, of Cyclopes and lotus-eaters, of immortals and mortals, and marble statues of Greek gods and goddesses and eponymous heroes. Lunch in London failed miserably in comparison, unlike lunching in the Plaka in Athens, perched on the steps of the Parthenon, basking in glorious sunlight, while nibbling chunks of fresh feta cheese, ripe olives and juicy fresh figs, picked that morning from the tree – and with Daphne, the girl of his dreams. What had become of the ravishing creature with the glossy, jet-black hair and the sweetest, most beguiling smile in the world? What had become of Kore, the enchanting statue of Helen? What had become of the metopes and the statues his uncle had taken down from the Parthenon during that last week in Athens? He must ask his uncle now that he had returned from that ghastly prisoner-of-war camp in Toulon, although he loathed the thought of going to the house in St James's Square. Eggy's tragic death didn't help the widening chasm between his uncle and himself.

The thought of never glimpsing the Parthenon again caused such deep, emotional pain, he failed to see how he was going to cope with life, and his future, and slumping over with his arms resting on his knees, he caught sight of Murgatroyd tucked up inside his shell. Max had tried to imagine lumbering through life with a cumbersome great shell on his back. The weight alone was enough to overwhelm. Actually, in many ways, the tortoise was half-animal, half-stone, his shell, equivalent to a stone fortress. That meant, in many respects, Murgatroyd was made of stone. Images of stone brought the Parthenon racing to mind and hovered there, as he had spent the last ten years of his life drawing a building made of stone. Therefore, could there be more to stone than he imagined? Perhaps there were elements within him, within the stone itself, that were similar to the tortoise? Did this explain his deep sensitivity towards the Parthenon marbles? Did this explain the reason for his belief that there was a life-force in the marble? Possibly…

Suddenly the tortoise winked at Max, as he had acquired the odd habit of late of winking out of the corner of his right eye whenever Max took himself too seriously. Of course, Max smiled. However, the winking was so reminiscent of his headmaster at Harrow-on-the-Hill that Max was frankly astonished.

Max's thoughts returned to the Academy and the competition, stipulating the entrant provide a portfolio of drawings, a selection of their choice, but from each of five categories.

Max didn't even have to think about his selection. There could be none other than the Parthenon itself. And he had worked through the night for weeks, making detailed pen and ink drawings of the Parthenon's west pediment from memory. He glimpsed his ruined drawings shrivelling on his desk from the black Indian ink. The drawings were unacceptable for presentation.

There was so much controversy raging about the fate of the marbles that he had included two drawings of the metopes; however, the drawings were ruined by one flailing swoop of his *blasted* arm.

Now, his dream of winning the prize was gone. He could feel the life-force deep within slowly draining away, imagined dying in the attic above Mr Poots's Apothecary Shoppe in Old Park Lane.

What was the use of living anyway?

However, even in his deep despair he continued to ask himself the same question: the whereabouts of the Parthenon marbles. It had been revealed only last week that the Parthenon had been plundered beyond all recognition. A student at the Academy had received a letter from his father, a naval officer in the British Fleet. Apparently, upon a recent visit to Athens, he found the Parthenon in a perilous state. Of course, this devastating news evoked such debate among the students at the Academy that the fate of the marbles was on everyone's mind.

Max needed to see the devastation for himself. He found it utterly impossible to imagine that almost all the enormous statues were gone. Max stretched his memory as far back as it would go. After they had left Athens, ten years ago, had his uncle's workforce that remained behind removed the remaining statues?

What had had become of Mr Dashiell Hamilton's share of the loot? Sir Archibald Lushington had no qualms about displaying his share of the loot at the Museum of Classical Antiquities. He knew this to be true, as he had spent hours there sketching detailed drawings of marbles. The little hand in particular. He had left Athens before being able to rescue the small hand from the abbot. A hand was one thing. The colossal statues from the east and west pediments were something else. The puzzle about the whereabouts of the marbles ended abruptly when another enormous crash resounded outside, and Max leapt to his feet, ran to the window, just short of three strides, threw open the sash and peered out as a gruff voice shouted down below:

'Hurry up men 'cause this bleedin' crate weighs a tonne!'

Max leaned out the window. He craned his neck, glimpsed the goings-on in the walled garden next door.

'Good heavens!' he cried, as enormous wooden crates were being unloaded from a delivery wagon. 'What on earth has the Duchess bought now?'

Max leaned out the window as far as possible without falling, watching the delivery men stacking several enormous wooden crates on the lawn. The crates were so unbelievably large that he could not imagine what the contents might be. Then, without further ado, Max pulled his head inside the window and slammed it shut.

He dithered. He couldn't really bang on the Duchess's front door. Inquire as to the contents of the crates that she had taken delivery of that morning. No more than he could inquire as to the contents of

262

her house. It was none of his business, he thought, returning to his desk.

Always foppishly dressed, Max shrugged inside his long velvet robe, a rather futile attempt to keep warm. Thank God he was in possession of his long, quilted robe, a present from dear, sweet Aunt Vrai Viviette, that last Christmas prior to her running off with Mr Dashiell Hamilton to America, that is. His velvet robe was worn for comfort as well as warmth, as several and sundry layers of clothing were urgently needed to prevent chilblains and frost-bitten toes. A white shirt was worn beneath his sumptuous robe, washed and ironed by his good self, as his lodgings came without laundry facilities. He kept his neck warm by winding it in layers of immaculate white stock, tied tightly in a bow, as the draughts blowing through the cracks in the mullions, howling under the ill-fitting door were, shall we say, on the gusty side. His Nankeen breeches, buttoned tight at the knee and his highly polished boots were an essential part of his ensemble, without which he would have surly perished in his humble lodgings.

Desolate, and shivering from cold, Max flung himself down on his small cot snug in the corner of the room, and pulled his greatcoat over his shoulders, a hand-me-down from a friend while studying at Cambridge.

England had to be the most miserable place on earth during the long winter months.

No wonder he longed to return to Greece, he thought, desperate for a smoke – something to calm his nerves. His clay pipe rested on a small chunk of stone right beside the bed, and he tapped the bowl lightly on the marble to loosen the tobacco, then striking a match lit up. As he puffed on his pipe his eye lingered on the obscure chunk of marble he had kept safe in his possession for the last ten years.

He studied the marble in the dawn's early light, running his hand over the gorgon's head, the badly worn figures of the Amazons. He had often wondered whether the chunk of stone was in any way connected to the Parthenon, but that's about as far as the wondering got, as it no longer mattered. The marble made an excellent stand for his pipe.

The aromatic tobacco was calming and he leaned back against the cold wall watching smoke curls drift towards the ceiling, which wasn't really very far because it was so low.

What on earth am I going to do?

Years of billowing pipe smoke had yellowed the ceiling, the walls papered with sketches of ancient Greece, every last ruin on the Acropolis, representing five years of hard slog. Architectural renderings and cartoons he had designed himself, anatomical drawings taken from real-life models, rich allegorical landscape drawings and sketches of Athens, and drawings of the colossal larger-than-life statues from the Parthenon's west pediment − the one he knew best. His entire collection of drawings curling at the edges had been pinned helter-skelter on the sloping, gable-end of the ceiling.

Max puffed on his pipe. The hands on the clock reminded him he was still an apprentice draughtsman, expected at the Royal Academy. What was the point of going to class? He didn't want to be an architect any more. He didn't want to do anything any more except sulk. Oh, for the privacy of the third-floor verandah in Mrs Logotheti's rambling villa!

His maudlin thoughts grabbed him and held tight. He decided that he wasn't going back to the Academy. What about his future? Without a profession, how would he survive? Employment as a labourer, a carter, shovelling coal, or mucking out stables or piggeries for a living, earning a paltry wage had no appeal whatsoever. The thought of barely enough funds for pipe tobacco or a pint at the local Star and Garter propelled him from his bed.

Max eyed his collection of ink-splattered drawings with contempt. His life was wasted. Without question, thought he, grimly, and tossed his drawings in the grate. Perfect for lighting the fire.

It was time to tidy up. He placed his textbooks neatly on the shelves above his desk, the shelves groaning with memorabilia of his life, his stay in Greece and his more recent past. Two ancient Athenian skulls, the finds of an archaeological dig in Troy on one terribly hot summer's day; a phial of hemlock he'd won playing whist at the Royal Academy; a badly constructed plaster cast of his left hand, a souvenir from his first term in the Plaster Room at the Academy; a rather motley collection of stuffed owls he had fancied, after he had rescued the collection from a rubbish bin while strolling along the Cam one early morning at Cambridge.

Max tossed bits of stale bread and cheese at Murgatroyd who was lumbering towards him on his chubby legs, becoming larger by the day. He scanned his humble lodgings. Home. The house in St James's Square had remained closed up, except for the back kitchen, where Duffy lived, while his uncle lay rotting in some ghastly prisoner-of-war camp in France and his aunt and Eggy now lived in America with Mr Dashiell Hamilton. He had been invited to go; however, he politely declined. Imagine sailing to America? Seasickness would kill him off before the ship left port.

However, one day, he planned to reclaim his boyhood home in Scotland, a derelict pile that had been boarded up since the tragic death of his parents. He dreamed of redesigning the house himself, converting the original house into pure Greek Revival, with enormous fluted Doric columns, a huge marble frieze, and metopes and pediments. Like the Parthenon in Greece. Pagaille House was enormous by any standards. Perfect.

His thoughts drifted back to Athens and the old Greek peasant's words came to mind. He compared losing his boyhood home to the Greeks losing their marbles. He wanted his house back. Therefore, he understood why the Greeks wanted Athena's temple back. The marbles were part of their heritage. He had great empathy for the people of Greece because he himself had been stripped of his heritage, his family home. Therefore, he knew all about the sadness that came with losing one's treasures. Sadly, those that had never suffered from this kind of loss had no idea how it felt. Because you don't realise how precious things actually are until they are taken away. He had lost his home and it hurt and it never stopped hurting. Even after fourteen years. He was determined to get his house back. The Greek people felt the same way – Athena wanted her temple back. Perhaps he could help in some way.

His lodgings represented home. He had never experienced the luxury of feeling at home anywhere in England, certainly not St James's Square. After being sent down from Cambridge during the first term for writing pamphlets on the plight of the lower orders, he had had a bloody great row with his uncle, who happened to be in London at the time, and Max had been told in no uncertain terms not to expect an allowance and to stay out of the house until he managed to do something useful with his life. Acceptance at the Royal Academy was deemed 'useless' by his uncle; however, it was fulfilling his dream to return to Greece, study the buildings of the ancients. However, that idea had just gone by the by.

But something twigged.

Suddenly, Max lunged at Murgatroyd. He gathered the frisky tortoise in his arms, kissed him smack on the nose, a wet nose at that, then he raced down the stairs and out of the shop with his greatcoat slung over his shoulder. Murgatroyd was pleased to be out in the open air. Max understood this to be true, as the tortoise *looked* pleased – he even smiled at Max. He had lived with Murgatroyd long enough to recognise a smiling tortoise when he saw one.

'Hello!' Tommy, the apothecary's young son, ran towards Max as soon as he saw him. 'How is Murgatroyd?'

Tommy was always happy to see the tortoise, as the boy loved feeding him carrots, bits of fruit and scraps from Mrs Poots's kitchen.

'We are both quite well, thank you Tommy,' said Max, as he placed Murgatroyd down gently on the wet grass in the back garden. 'Would you like to look after Murgatroyd for me, Tommy, as I have an important errand to attend to this morning.'

'Oh Yes, Sir!' replied Tommy, hopping up and down on the wet grass. 'We like to chat.'

'Thank you again, Tommy,' said Max as he hurried through the gate behind the shop. He had a long walk ahead. The house in St James's Square was some distance, although, hopefully, his mission would not be in vain.

Chapter Twenty-Three
The Daemon of Worthy Men

'Hurry up, Duffy!' Lord Quimby blared at his aged manservant, sounding like a ferocious wildebeest, although he was a considerable distance from the Kalahari Desert or a stampeding herd of antelopes. 'Try another blasted crate!'

'Yes, Milord,' replied Duffy, hastily nailing shut the crate. 'Which one, Milord, as there are so many?'

'That one!' boomed the irate lord, pointing towards a crate in the centre of the Sculpture Gallery. 'Over there!'

Lord Quimby glowered angrily at the rows of wooden crates strewn with mouldy straw reeking of putrid seawater, lining the North Tribune. The crates had been salvaged from the bottom of the Bay of Naples, an exercise that had cost him the earth. This outrageous sum did not include the bill from Custom House, which brought the total to a staggering £7000.

'Milord!' Duffy shouted from the opposite side of the Sculpture Gallery, 'the marble is not what you imagine. Why, it's another section of the Parthenon's frieze.'

'Blast!' Lord Quimby cursed loudly.

'That makes twelve sections of frieze, Milord, and twenty metopes.'

'Bloody hell,' cursed Lord Quimby slumping down on to a massive marble slab; an inscribed stele that he had prided himself on rescuing from a village in the Dardanelles years ago, because the villagers credited the stele with miraculous powers and used to roll the sick on it in the hope of a cure. Perhaps he should roll himself on the stele, although he doubted it would cure him – nothing would bring his nose back.

'I'll try that one,' said Duffy, pointing towards a crate at the end of the hall, 'That crate, Milord, looks the right shape for the horse's head.'

'Well hurry up, Duffy, the coach is waiting!'

Duffy was tiring of Lord Quimby's continual tirade, shouting orders at him as he had all morning, and quickly prised open yet another enormous wooden crate, which wasn't difficult as the wood was rotting through. He dug down beneath the straw...

'Milord!' Duffy exclaimed from the hall, 'it's the horse – Selene's horse! The statue we have been searching for!'

'Bravo!' Lord Quimby, ecstatic, clapped his hands like an excited child.

'Now, nail the crate shut.'

'Yes, Milord.'

'The horse's head is to be delivered post-haste to the house in Scotland. No, better still, I will take the marble with me to Scotland. I shall have it placed on a plinth in the Music Room!'

'Shall I open any more crates, Milord?' asked Duffy, becoming more and more agitated, while waving a crowbar at the mountain of unopened wooden crates lining the North Tribune.

'No, Duffy. Thank you. I have no wish to see any more.' Lord Quimby blasted at his aged manservant. 'I have had enough!'

'Yes, Milord,' Duffy's tired voice echoed in the sombre light of the Sculpture Gallery. His Lordship had become a bitter man since his son had died, and impossible to serve. The sooner he left for Scotland the better, thought Duffy, exhausted.

'What is to be done with the sixty slabs of the Parthenon frieze, Milord, and the metopes and the statues?'

'I haven't the foggiest idea, Duffy. And, quite frankly, I no longer care. I don't give a toss about the blasted Parthenon frieze.' Then rubbing his forehead, shot, 'I can't understand what on earth I was thinking about having the frieze removed in the first place. I will need a museum to display all of the damn stuff!'

'How many metopes were salvaged?' Lord Quimby asked, snug in his pelisse, the same fur-trimmed robe that the Ali Pasha had presented him with on his journey to the Levant years ago, after he had successfully bribed every Grand Turk in Constantinople; allowing him to plunder *all* the temples on the Acropolis.

'Last count, Milord,' replied Duffy, tugging on his stockings, his chilblains bothering him, 'eighteen. There appears to be some discrepancy in the number of metopes, Milord. There were twenty-three metopes in all, according to the Bill of Lading from Custom House.'

'Perhaps our most trustworthy friend, Mr Dashiell Hamilton, absconded with my marbles Duffy...as well as my wife...the bitch!'

Duffy cleared his throat. He stared at the putty in the elaborate frescoed ceiling.

'Thank you, Duffy, that will be all,' said Lord Quimby as he rubbed his painfully sore and bleeding nose, reminded not for the first time of the Parthenon's defaced marble sculptures. The ironies in life, he thought bitterly, were truly astonishing, while comparing his vanishing nose to the statues with their noses hacked off.

Lord Quimby remained seated on the stele that rested on an enormous marble sarcophagus; dare we say yet another plundered treasure from the Near East. He briefly scanned the appalling mess that lay before him as the Sculpture Gallery was overflowing with mouldy straw from the enormous wooden crates that had been delivered that morning from Custom House. He shook his head ruefully, suddenly realising that he hadn't a clue what marbles lay inside the crates. Loot. That was all he knew. Loot.

Not that it mattered.

The ship's manifest had been lost ten years earlier after the ship sank to the bottom of the sea while en route to London. Mr Dashiell Hamilton had managed to salvage all the marbles he could, although it had taken three years and a considerable chunk of his wife's cash to complete the job. The marbles had remained at Custom House, waiting to be claimed by his good self upon his return home a fortnight ago, after being released from prison in Toulon. As the marbles had been held in bond for nearly eight years and no one had claimed them, Customs House had taken it upon themselves to dispose of the statues, as an auction house deemed the marbles worthless. Custom House were considering sending the marbles to the dump. However, a housebuilder offered to remove the stone from bond free of charge, intending to use the loot for landfill. Lord Quimby had arrived home in the nick of time. However, the exorbitant sum required to release the marbles from bond had all but crippled him financially. He paid the bill, albeit begrudgingly. His appetite had been satiated. He no longer wished to glimpse the marbles ever again. Or be reminded of his insane expedition to Athens.

Lord Quimby slumped forward on the marble stele. He realised that he was a broken man, in every sense of the word. Because it wasn't only the acquisition of the *blasted* marbles that had broken him.

Lord Quimby found himself incapable of holding back his tears as he pawed his pelisse pocket through bleary eyes, extracting a crumpled missive, received a week ago from Admiralty House, informing him that his son, George Egbert, had perished from plague while crossing the English Channel. Eggy had to be buried at sea. Lord Quimby sobbed openly, haunted by the ghastly vision of Eggy's body being hastily wrapped in a shroud and dumped overboard. His son's bloated corpse bobbing about in the English Channel while being ravaged by seagulls.

It was an understatement to say His Lordship was bereft. He was grief-stricken. He no longer gave a damn about the marbles. Or that his wife had run off with his London agent. All he wanted was his son back. But that was never going to happen.

Lord Quimby's privileged life in all its faded glory had come crashing down – paradoxically – exactly like the metopes he had plundered from the Parthenon.

His Lordship had lost his enormous family fortune, all of his inherited wealth. Vanished within the last thirteen years. Every penny of his wife's inheritance had been wasted, although he was loath to admit it, and now he had sacrificed his beloved son, Eggy, as Eggy had been on his way home from Athens, after overseeing the last delivery of marbles. He had also lost another son, a stillborn child, although he questioned the father; his health, equating to the majority of his nose, rheumatism, contracted while imprisoned in a ghastly prisoner-of-war camp for the past six years; and if this compendium of woes weren't enough to put any good man down, Lord Quimby had returned to London to find his preposterously grand Palladian-style house in St James's Square – that he had spent several fortunes on refurbishing – empty, except for Duffy who lived in virtual isolation, holed up in the back kitchen.

The shock of finding his wife gone had been horrendous. The fact that she had run off with that swine, Mr Dashiell Hamilton, was a disgrace. Diabolical. Lord Quimby vowed that if Hamilton ever had the nerve to show his face in London town ever again, he might find himself fighting a duel. The bloodthirsty French were not the only ones capable of lopping off a head.

His Lordship had decided to close the house, and retire permanently to the house in Scotland. He could no longer abide the house in St James's Square. The Shambles was the perfect place to watch his extremities wither and die as his hands and feet had also been affected by the leprous disease. The Shambles was perfect, was it not? A demesne befitting his tortured self.

'Ha, ha, ha!' Lord Quimby suddenly laughed hysterically. 'Why – The Shambles and I are both in the same shambolic state!'

His Lordship grimaced. He had failed to comprehend that he had a problem of such magnitude that everything else paled in comparison and it was this: what on earth to do with the marbles that reached the ceiling of the blasted Sculpture Gallery?

Lord Quimby's stomach turned. The sight of the marbles made him retch. What on earth had prompted him to raid the Parthenon in the first place? He hadn't the foggiest idea, he thought miserably, as he struggled to his feet, shuffled wearily through the debris, passing by the marble busts of Julius Caesar, Alexander the Great, Bacchus, Neptune, Augustus and Marcus Aurelius, woebegone statues in their faded niches containing Vrai Viviette's much sought after busts of Roman worthies.

'What a farce!'

The busts she had longed for had finally arrived, yet his wife had fled, and now, she would never see them.

Lord Quimby quickened his pace. The coach was waiting. He could not escape his wretched fate fast enough. He never wished to set foot in the house ever again.

If he had the funds he would send the marbles back to whence they came – to Athens. As the marbles had brought nothing but grief, Athena was to blame. The Greek goddess had it in for him, without a doubt.

Duffy could orchestrate the disposal of the marbles. Whether the Museum of Classical Antiquities in London agreed to pay the hefty sum of £35 000 he so desperately needed to console Coutts was the question. Lord Quimby continued on, shuffling through the labyrinth of empty halls until he caught sight of a man walking towards him in the shadows and, thinking that he was the carter from Custom House returning for some absurd reason, roared in a hostile voice. 'Take away as much as you wish. Whatever you so desire – I don't want any of it!'

'What is it that you no longer want?' asked Max, emerging from the shadows.

'Oh, it's only you!' Lord Quimby squinted through the vapour of damp air, swirling marble dust. 'What the devil do you want?'

'Good morning, Uncle.'

'Good? What's good about it, Maximilian? This house is in mourning or have you failed to remember?'

Max ignored his uncle's sarcastic tone as he glimpsed wooden crates lining the halls, while debating the possibility of a house being in mourning. 'What's inside the crates, Uncle?'

'Nothing...nothing that would be of interest to you, young man,' snapped Lord Quimby hotly.

'What brings you here?' asked Lord Quimby. 'Need more money?'

'No, Uncle,' replied Max flatly, struggling to control the rage that welled up from within. Why couldn't he find his voice? Max ran his hands over the crates stacked to the ceiling next to him. He glowered hard at his uncle. After all, he had waited for ten years for this moment. He *knew* that the crates contained the marbles. He *knew* that his uncle had plundered the Parthenon. He *knew* that his uncle had taken everything he could get his hands on from the Acropolis. He knew that he had ravaged Kore. He knew that all of the colossal figures were there in the Sculpture Gallery...he just knew it.

Lord Quimby squeezed past Max, continued on down the hall in the gloom, while Max followed behind like one of his hounds.

'Have you forgotten how to shave, Maximilian?' snapped Lord Quimby, irked by his nephew's presence, unable to abide the sight of him now Eggy was gone. 'Cut your hair?'

Max said not a word – silence his only defence.

'Doesn't Mr Poots's Apothecary Shoppe sell shaving cream?' chided Lord Quimby, 'Finding difficulty in keeping yourself well groomed, Maximilian?'

Max rubbed his stubbly chin, more than a week's worth of hairy growth. Everything else about his person was immaculate.

'Forgive my appearance, Uncle. I did not expect to find you up at such an early hour. I came to see Duffy. Do you know where he is?'

'I am not a footman, Maximilian!'

'I am sorry to be such a bother. Forgive me. I am in a dreadful hurry. I wanted to ask Duffy if he knew the whereabouts of my trunk, the one I took to Athens.' Max regretted coming to the house. He was twelve years old again. However, it was Duffy himself who came to his rescue.

'Hello, Duffy,' said Max, smiling brightly.

'Hello, Maximilian.' Duffy poked his head out from behind a door. 'How are you?' As he spoke he eyed Max up and down.

'Quite well, thank you, Duffy.' Max smiled at Duffy, as the old manservant had become a true friend over the years.

'You are too thin, Maximilian.' Duffy squinted at Max. 'Don't you eat the pork pies I send or do you feed them to Murgatroyd?'

The thought of Murgatroyd munching on pork pies brought a broad smile to Max's handsome face, a smile that quite literally lit up the dark, dingy hall. Laughter filled the damp air. 'Yes, Duffy. How on earth did you guess? Of course, I share all my pies with Murgatroyd!'

'Keep your voice down!' Lord Quimby snarled, failing to see the humour.

'Do you know where my trunk is, Duffy, the one I took to Greece?'

'Try the attic.'

'What attic?' Max hastened, as there were at least half a dozen attics in the house.

'The attic over the summer kitchen,' replied Duffy.

Lord Quimby kept touching the hole in his face where his nose had been, as the disgusting, weeping orifice had started to bleed again.

'Thank you, Duffy,' said Max. 'I will only be a short while. I am expected at the Academy in an hour's time.

Before setting off in the direction of the summer kitchen, Max grabbed Duffy by the hand and pumping it up and down whispered, 'Thank you, Duffy – Murgatroyd and I so enjoy the weekly hamper from Paxton and Whitfield. Without the pies we would surely perish. So, please, please, you mustn't stop sending the hamper. Especially the fruit tarts, because they are Murgatroyd's favourite!'

Duffy winked at Max, then he retreated.

Max walked along beside his uncle, whispering under his breath, 'Blimey. It wasn't only the marble statues who lost their noses!'

The gods could be a revengeful lot. Soon, his uncle wouldn't have any nose at all. In fact, he thought his uncle no longer resembled his former self, whatever self that might be, as his uncle had always been an aloof, cold, enigmatic figure. Not unlike Narcissus, mused Max as he rushed past the marble bust snug in its niche, as the resemblance was truly astonishing.

A muddle of dimly lit passageways waited.

'This house is so large, Uncle, one needs a chaise to get about!'

'Don't be impudent!' boomed Lord Quimby.

Max, in a devilish mood, asked as they carried on, 'Why on earth did you do it?'

'Do what?' asked the disgruntled lord.

'Whatever possessed you to convert this magnificent house into a museum of Classical antiquities? If you fancied an Italianate lifestyle why not buy a villa in Verona, Milan or Rome?' Max let rip. 'The thought of living in a house filled with marble statues fills me with horror. I might lose my wits surrounded by imaginary figures lampooning in idyllic surroundings, glaring at me from every salon. Marble statues are meant to be outdoors, Uncle, in the open air, not kept inside without sunlight. Marbles need to breathe!' He was going in for the kill. 'Like the statues that you had taken down from the gable-ends of the Parthenon.'

Did Auntie really want all this, Uncle?' asked Max as they strode past another Roman-style mural painted with voluptuous young maidens in light repose.

'What possessed you to rebuild this perfectly fine London house, then proceed to fill it with marble statues, adding false perspectives, tripods and fire-breathing she-goats, murals and bogeys with lions' heads and serpents' tails grinning at us from the corner of every room?'

The answer failed to materialise as Lord Quimby threw open the next portal they came to and striding through, slammed the door in Max's face.

Enraged, Max continued on until he came to a narrow flight of stairs leading up to the attic on the fourth floor. A wasteland of junk, generations of detritus from the Quimby dynasty greeted him.

Like all aspiring draughtsmen, Max had developed a keen eye for detail and spotted his trunk on top of a large wooden tea-chest in the far corner. Cobwebs dangled from the rafters, tickling his nose, a poignant reminder of the passage of time. Max lunged at his trunk, brushing away the dust, revealing numerous air-holes in the lid, ventilation for Murgatroyd's journey home to London. He threw open the lid...

All of Athens came rushing back. Vivid images of honey-coloured ruinous stone. Max rubbed his eyes unable to erase the image of the Parthenon from his mind.

Inside his trunk were his Egyptian cotton pyjamas, neatly folded and smelling of must and mildew and salt-sea air. Beneath his pyjamas lay his treasures. All that remained of his holiday in

Greece. His crumpled straw hat, nibbled round the edges by none other than Mopsus, of course. Max prayed to Athena to protect his nimble-witted friend from harm as he wandered the dusty paths of the Agora. Although he doubted Mopsus were alive after ten long years. His baggy white shirt lay neatly folded beside the nibbled hat, although the shirt could no longer be described as either white or large. Had his shirt shrunk as it seemed to be so much smaller? His short trousers he had shortened himself lay underneath his shirt. Max slid his hand inside the small pocket and sand from the beach and three piastres fell on to his lap.

However, Max, anxious about his drawings, dug down deeper inside his trunk, until he came to a tin box with a young Greek girl playing a flute painted on the lid. It was filled with lead pencils with chewed ends, broken crayons, worn pen-nibs, bits of charcoal, powder for paints, and icing sugar, and all that remained of some Turkish Delight, Mopsus' favourite. A goat-skin bag lay hidden beneath the tin. Max reached in, and untied the string revealing a pair of leather sandals that had hardly been worn, and smelt, well, like Greece.

Max's satchel was at the bottom of his trunk and when he tore it open his drawings were there, exactly as he remembered. The sketches of the metopes were perfect. He didn't have time to look through his sketchbooks as he feared being late for class. However, as he was placing all of his treasures neatly back inside his trunk he spotted a white towel in the corner with something lumpy hiding inside. It was the towel that he had wrapped Murgatroyd in, the day he had rescued the tortoise from being roasted alive on the beach at Piraeus.

Max sat back down on the floor and unwrapped the towel very slowly, not knowing what to expect, or what keepsake lay wrapped inside. Max fumbled in his coat pocket for his spectacles, studied the large clump of stone in great detail, tracing the outline of Athena's aegis with his fingers. The allegorical figure was of Phobos, representing fear. Max understood this, as he had been studying the ancient Greeks at the Royal Academy for years. Suddenly, that scorching, hot summer's day on the Acropolis came racing back. What had become of the other chunks of stone that the boys had bagged that day in Athens? The memory of Evliya shouting at him silenced his questions:

'You foreigners...you...don't...know anything do you? We...Turks...we...smart...people...we...control the stupid Greek peasants. We...get...rich...selling loot to you foreigners... Don't you know... no one cares about old stones...so why should you...so why should you...so why should you!'

The shrill, irritating sound of Evliya's voice kept repeating over and over again in his mind, as though it were yesterday. The sound made him angry and he tried to silence the Turk's voice by quickly wrapping the chunk of stone in the towel and placing it back in his trunk. He slammed the lid, hard this time. Tears streamed down his face and pinged on the lid as he grabbed his satchel, sped towards the back stairs.

Max had been completely taken aback by his reaction to what lay inside his trunk. All of Athens had come rushing back that morning. The contents of his trunk were really nothing more than a lot of old junk, nothing of real value. Yet what a powerhouse of emotion his boyhood treasures had evoked within him. Others may think the contents worthless junk; however, to Max his treasures meant the world − more than money, more than grand houses. The happiest days of his life lay tucked away inside his trunk and images of the Parthenon flooded back. Could the same not be said about the Parthenon? To those less enlightened, the Parthenon was nothing more than a pile of ruinous stone. To others, like himself, the Parthenon was an iconic building and every chunk of stone a treasure, symbolic of the very life-blood of the people.

Was he, in fact, also weeping for the Parthenon? In his mind, he realised he had personified the Parthenon. Athena's temple had become a salient being. He imagined that if it were possible for the marbles to weep, to shed blood, the stones would have done so when his uncle ravaged the Parthenon. Blood would have oozed out of the pink-veined marble, splashed on to the pious, iconoclastic heads of the butchers who dared to call themselves enlightened, the barbarians who had the audacity to remove the metopes and the frieze and almost all of the colossal statues in the east and west pediments. When his uncle ravished Kore, ripped her from the temple of the Erechtheion, 'like Niobe' the caryatid would have wept 'her desolation in stone', and as the statue was being hauled away, her 'expression of so great a soul was beyond the force of mere nature.'

Max was determined to return to the house the next day to collect his truck. He vowed to keep his treasures safe, always. After all, his keepsakes represented what he imagined to be the very essence of his soul.

While Max had been reacquainting himself with his boyhood, the rain had stopped and glorious sunlight streamed through the dormer windows high in the eaves of the grand house in St James's Square. He was in such a hurry to be on his way he accidentally tripped over a rolled-up carpet blocking his path.

'Damn!' Max cursed loudly as he lay sprawled on the floor, rubbing his shins. As he did so, however, he suddenly became aware that not only had the carpet been rolled, which rugs from Turkey *never* are, but that something extremely hard lay inside the carpet and being curious by nature, tried to unroll it. It was so heavy he was finding it difficult, and impatient as always, Max gave up and peeped into the end of it...

'Blimey!' Max tapped the stone. He knew a marble when he saw one and he tugged madly at the carpet until enough had been removed to reveal...

'Kore!' Tucked inside was the statue of Kore! Helen! The maiden he had fancied so long ago, with the basket on her head. Max clawed back the carpet until he could see her face and cried: 'I have got to get you out of here, Kore!'

Max slumped down on to the rolled-up statue. What on earth was the caryatid doing in the attic? Max could not possibly imagine. He ran towards the stairs, shouting at the top of his lungs:

'Uncle, why have you kept Kore imprisoned in the attic all these years? And wrapped in a Turkish rug no less! You could have at least used a Greek rug. We need to get Kore out of the attic. She needs to be out in the garden, in the open air where she belongs!'

Max rushed down the hall towards the Sculpture Gallery, only to find it empty. His uncle had gone. Lord Quimby was on his way to the Shambles. Max stood in the gloom staring at the enormous crates lining the hall. He knew the ugly truth. What his uncle had done to the Parthenon was a crime, yet Max felt as though he were the only person alive who knew it.

Chapter Twenty-Four
The Profit of Noble Struggles

He was late. *Damn.* Max cursed aloud as he rushed through the main entrance of the Royal Academy Schools at New Somerset House, just off the Strand, and hastened up the grand stairs leading to the classroom on the first floor, with his portfolio tucked under his arm. The musty odour of wet plaster, linseed oil and paint permeated the stuffy air, the very ether of the building, the fabric itself, he thought, treading softly on the marble, not wishing to make a sound, having acquired great respect for the Royal Academy in the last five years.

There was a certain sanctity and reverence about the place he compared to hallowed ground, and it raised his spirits. Most days, just being there, cocooned within its walls, instilled a measure of confidence within him, although it certainly was not confidence Max experienced as he rushed down the hall towards the Plaster Room. It was total and utter despair. A fortnight had passed since he had learned the truth about the fate of the Parthenon marbles yet he could not confess it to anyone. Honour was part of being a gentleman. The Quimby dynasty would fall apart like the Parthenon if he revealed all.

Max carried on down the long hall, passing by enormous richly-gilded paintings of important dignitaries of the Royal Academy that hung on the walls. Enormous plaster casts of Apollo Belvedere, Laocoon, the Belvedere Torso and Hercules to name a few – some of the greatest works of antiquity – were interspersed with elegantly carved marble busts of Greek philosophers and Roman Emperors with marble curls and straggly beards, sitting smugly on ebony pedestals and fluted marble plinths. Max nodded at Plato and Socrates, Euripides, Pheidias, his alter ego, the greatest architect of all, and Pericles, wearing his famous helmet on his elongated head. He winked at 'Old Squill Head', a habit of late. He wondered whether the two great men knew what had become of the Parthenon. Although Max wasn't convinced that they didn't already know about the hastily chiselled plunder that had been orchestrated by his uncle. Those Greeks were a canny lot.

—◌ ◌—

The students were drawing lots for their places when Max entered the room. The noise and tumult was ear-splitting. The students were either playing leapfrog over their box seats or pelting each other with bits of modelling clay and crusts of stale bread and because he was late, Max had to settle for a box seat at the very back of the classroom, which wasn't an issue, because he invariably sat apart from the other students. He preferred it that way.

The noise and tumult ceased while Max was placing his portfolio of drawings on the easel in front of him. Then a massive wood-panelled door flew open and the Keeper and Deputy Librarian, Mr George Michael-John, ushered the panel of judges into the room – those who had been invited to judge the students' work. Sir Archibald Lushington happened to be among the esteemed group. He was now the Director of the Museum of Classical Antiquities in London and a highly esteemed trustee of the Society of Dilettanti. Other members of the group included Mrs Siddons, the famous actress, a number of highly acclaimed artists, the President of the Society of Antiquities and the President of the Royal Academy, Benjamin West.

Sadly, he hadn't an ally among the lot, thought Max nervously shuffling his drawings, twitching on his box seat. And to take his mind off himself, as the distinguished panel of judges proceeded to make their way slowly around the classroom he sat scanning the clutter – plaster-of-Paris casts of Roman busts, bits of Greek frieze, fragments of marble statuary, a plaster foot, a hand, half of a head and a broken torso, casts of body parts he had spent the first year of his tuition learning how to copy.

Sir Archibald Lushington's presence was quite disturbing for Max as he had not had the displeasure of meeting the *thief* since that fateful day in Athens when the marbles rolled out of his canvas sack on to the lawn at Mrs Logotheti's villa. Max cringed. He wondered what had become of the marbles Sir Archibald had bribed the abbot to keep hidden in the crypt, although many were on display in the Museum of Classical Antiquities. He had spent days sketching *his* hand. The small delicate marble hand that had fallen into the rain barrel. The marble hand with Nikodimos carved in the stone, the marble that he hadn't been able to retrieve before sailing home. His daydream, however, was suddenly interrupted. The judges were coming his way.

Max sat fussing needlessly over his drawings placed neatly on the easel he had been nervously straddling for the last hour. The judges were getting closer, until coming to a halt in front of his work.

Max cowed back on his box seat as the judges thumbed through his drawings of the Parthenon, one by one. No one looked pleased. Displeased was more like it. He might as well have sketched the Freemason's' Hall and Tavern at the end of the road, he thought to himself. After what seemed like an eternity the judges departed, pouncing on the poor bastard seated next to him.

Once the judges had finished making their round they took their seats. Then the President of the Royal Academy strode up to the podium. His familiar voice echoed in the musty, dimly lit hall:

'My lords, ladies, gentlemen, distinguished guests and students, it is a great pleasure to welcome you to the Royal Academy!'

A round of light applause followed.

'Thank you.'

Max could not sit still. He fidgeted with the buttons on his frock coat. He tugged on his coat sleeves. He ran his hands through his thick mane. He scratched his hairy chin. His very life depended on winning the prize. All he could think about was returning to Athens, visiting his beloved Parthenon. His weary self had thought of nothing else. He longed to visit the Acropolis. Ride Mopsus. Roam the Acropolis in his bare feet, with his best friend Nikolaos. He dreamed constantly of his beautiful Daphne – the reason he bought frivolous bunches of violets at Covent Garden every Saturday.

'It gives me great pleasure to welcome our distinguished guest speaker, the Director of the Museum of Classical Antiquities in London, the Honourable Sir Archibald Lushington.'

A robust round of applause followed. However, there was one in the audience who refrained. Yes, dear reader, it was the student sitting on the rough wooden box seat at the very back of the Plaster Room.

Sir Archibald Lushington waddled towards the podium. Disgusted, Max turned his head away. He had to swallow hard to prevent bile rising in his throat, finding it impossible to be in the same room with the man.

'My Lords, ladies, gentlemen, distinguished guests, students of the Royal Academy, allow me to begin by saying how deeply honoured I am to be invited here today.'

The Director of the Museum of Classical Antiquities was a great deal more rotund than the last time he had seen him, although his personal habits hadn't altered, not one bit, thought Max, as he spied Sir Archibald push imaginary strands of hair back on his bald head. Max chuckled to himself. Perhaps he had never had hair.

'On behalf of the Museum of Classical Antiquities may I say how extremely excited I am to be able to announce that in the last fortnight we have been able to enhance our collection at the museum. Due to the great benevolence of one of our patrons, we have had the extreme good fortune of extending our collection of classical Greek antiquities, especially the marbles excavated from the Acropolis in Athens, bringing the Hellenic world closer to home, home to England, where the stones belong!'

'Here, here!' everyone in the classroom cheered.

'Please, allow me to continue. As many of you know the Parthenon in Athens is the greatest example of architecture the Western world has ever seen and, thanks to the generosity of our patron, who wishes to remain anonymous, we now have on display six metopes from the Parthenon frieze. We strongly believe that this collection will benefit all our students, give you a better opportunity to study the Classical world, increase your knowledge in ornamental draughtsmanship. Thank you.'

Thunderous applause followed as Sir Archibald Lushington bowed, sat down in his chair, his ample flesh hanging over the seat.

Then the President of the Society of Antiquities walked up to an easel at the front of the classroom and grabbing a pointer directed it towards a rendering of the Parthenon. He said:

'Take this excellent rendering of the Parthenon's west pediment, for example, as the temple of Athena Parthenos has enormous historical and archaeological significance. The building is of utmost importance to the arts in Britain today. It is our hope that England will become another Athens. As you know Edinburgh is fast becoming the Athens of the North. The ruins of the ancient past have withstood the test of time, and, now that we have rescued the marbles from further destruction in Greece, they shall no doubt continue to do so, for an eternity.'

Mr George Michael-John was so enthusiastic his voice rose to a high pitched squeak. Evidence he could hardly contain his enthusiasm for all things Greek. Then he walked back to the podium.

Max could not believe his ears. Since his visit to the house in St James's Square to collect his trunk a fortnight ago his uncle had, unbeknown to him, donated six metopes to the Museum of Classical Antiquities in London. What happened to the rest of the marbles? Max's mind drifted, he only half-listened... 'I have chosen a few words from *Reflections on the Paintings and Sculpture of the Greeks* by Johann Winckelmann: "To the Greek climate we owe the production of *taste*."'

Max's mind wandered...

'"There is but one way for the moderns to become great, and perhaps unequalled; I mean by imitating the ancients."'

Imitating? More like plundering the ancients, thought Max becoming irate.

'"Truth springs from the feelings of the heart. What shadow of it therefore can the modern artist hope for, by relying upon a vile model, whose soul is either too base to feel, or stupid to express the passions, the sentiment his object claims."'

Max had a few words to say about truth.

'"These they raised above the reach of mortality, according to the superior model of some ideal nature."'

Max could not breathe. What did the man know about ideal nature?

'"Soaring above the senses... "'

Soaring above theft, thought Max, bitterly, as the blood rushed to his head. The people of Greece had their temple plundered. It was not the time to read poetry.

Then Max watched the President of the Society of Dilettanti as he came forward. He was holding a large manila envelope in one hand and a blue velvet box containing the King's Medal in the other. He smiled brightly at the audience. It was the first smile Max had witnessed all day.

'Now, the moment that you have all been waiting anxiously for has finally arrived,' said he, while glancing down at the name written on the envelope.

'The judges have made their decision. Therefore, it gives me great please to announce the winner of the King's Medal for Architecture is Mr Maximilian Henry Perceval.

'The prize had been awarded to Mr Perceval, not only because of his exceptional talent as a draughtsman but also for his ability and his foresight for capturing history in the making. I refer to Mr Perceval's exceptional drawings of the Parthenon, as many of the precious marble statues are no longer in situ. Therefore, we are highly indebted to Mr Perceval for this. On behalf of the Royal Academy I am extremely proud to present the King's Medal to Mr Perceval and ask that he come forward to receive his prize. At the end of term he will be travelling to Athens to draw the ruins of ancient Greece.'

Students thumped on their box seats. Everyone gave a victorious round of applause as Max made his way slowly towards the podium. His dream had finally come true and he whispered:

'Athena, Murgatroyd and I are coming home!'

Part Four
2008/2009

Chapter Twenty-Five
The Legend Continues

Max had fallen asleep at his desk only to waken with a start, finding himself slumped over his laptop and his iPhone pinging. 'Damn!' cursed the Classics scholar when he glanced bleary-eyed at his phone. His tutorial was in an hour's time and he hadn't completed one single translation. He could barely understand the Latin version for Christ's sake. Why on earth had he chosen to read the Classics? He must have been out of his head when he chose to read Greek. It was a dead language. He should have stuck with a living language. Latin was easy compared to Greek in hexameter verse.

No one spoke Greek anyway Not even the Greeks.

Max rubbed his eyes, scanning Ovid's words reflecting on the page.

'He fell in love with an empty hope, a shadow mistaken for substance...'

Max flipped through the pages.

'Those beautiful lips would implore a kiss, as he bent forward the pool would always betray him. He plunges his arms in the water to clasp that ivory neck and finds himself clutching at no one.

He knows not what he is seeing, the sight still fires him with passion.

His eyes are deceived, but the strange illusion excites his senses.

Trusting fool, how futile to woo a fleeting phantom.

You'll never grasp it. Turn away and your love will have vanished.

The shape now haunting your sight is only a wraith...'

However, the Latin poet wasn't the only haunting as an enormous shadow loomed in the open doorway of Max's digs on the third floor of King's College, Cambridge.

'Don't go back to sleep, old man,' boomed a deep male voice, 'just wanted to enlighten you and share a few facts about modern Greece that I gleaned on YouTube last night.'

Harry's unshaven face glimmered in the shadows, 'Did you know that,' asked Harry, smirking, 'the Greeks have more sex on the beach than any other nationality?'

'So?' Max, blushing, glanced bleary eyed from his laptop.

'So – this has to be the best reason ever to visit Greece!' exclaimed Harry. 'I have a few more delicious facts for consideration, such as, Greece is the most sexually active country in the world. And prostitution is legalised. What more does a man need in life? I'm considering doing my Masters in Athens!'

'Is that all you think about, Harry?' asked Max, while staring at his best mate blocking the doorway, with his enormous paw clutching the door frame.

'What really brings you here? Scrounging for a clean T-shirt?'

'Yah...you could say that.'

'Can't you afford to buy a T-shirt, Harry?'

There was no response from Harry who padded silently around Max's room, opening cupboards, peeking inside the wardrobe in a terry bathrobe that barely touched his knees, as he had had the same bathrobe since fifth form.

'Got it!' Harry waved his prize in the air, signalling to his mate, whom he'd known for the last fifteen years. 'I'm gone, old man. Want to meet at the pub for some cheap fizz after tutorials?'

'Sounds good to me!'

Halfway out the door Harry turned, breathed before he slammed the door, 'Max, you lucky sod, you're all sorted when it comes to shagging on the beach – you have Helen!'

Max glowed red.

'God...what...a...babe!'

Max remained seated at his desk, scanning his emails. There was one from the babe, Helen, a short greeting from his grandfather and several from his mother.

His grandfather, Opa, lived alone at Vanderhoofen Castle, in Germany, a few miles east of Berlin. Max simply adored Opa. He loved to visit the castle, especially at Christmas, when it resembled the castle in Disneyland, Paris, with thick globs of snow piled on the high-pitched roof and long skinny icicles dangling from the eaves which crashed down in the middle of the night, frightening the life out of him.

There were three emails from his mother who lived in the south of France. When she wasn't sending him texts she sent him silly cards or care-packages with biscuits wrapped in cheap cotton T-shirts, as though he were still boarding at Harrow on the Hill. Of course, madeleines were his favourite although French pastries didn't last as Harry invariably scoffed the lot.

CHAPTER TWENTY-FIVE

For years Max had begged his mother, who lived at La Redousse, a belle époque villa in the south of France, to return home to England. To no avail. All because five years ago she had converted the potting shed in the garden into a donkey sanctuary and every stray donkey within a tail-wag of the back gate was taken in. The beasts had taken priority over *his* life. In fact, he wouldn't be surprised if donkeys had taken up permanent residence inside the house. His mother was nuts about baudet du Poitou donkeys with fuzzy ears and shaggy coats. And she had named the last three donkeys she had rescued: Chaos, Rhetoric and Satire. Rhett, Scarlet and Marilyn would have been more apropos. However, this absurd bit of whimsy was the direct result of his mother developing a passion for ancient Greek philosophy and he had only himself to blame, as he was forever rambling on about the ancient Greeks.

Upon mature reflection, his mother's affection for four-legged beasts was a saving grace, as they were a distraction from the two-legged beasts. Another man or in particular another husband was not what his mother needed, and he threatened to disown her if she ever married again.

His mother had moved permanently to the house on the French Riviera after his father's tragic death and she had never returned to the house in St James' Square. Thoughts of his mother made him feel terribly sad. He was a coward when it came to emotional pain.

Max snapped his laptop shut, tucking it under his arm. Heartsick, he got up from his desk and striding across the room flung himself on his bed. He hugged his bear Scruffy all over again. He had celebrated his twenty-third birthday last week. Too old for bears, you say. Not so. Scruffy had been his trusty companion since birth. Scruffy had also been at Harrow on the Hill for ten years and suffered the effects of ruinous tumble-drys at Cambridge; he was beginning to show his age. Scruffy's right ear had gone missing in first form, his head wobbled back and forth something frightfully, his right eye, sadly, had been gouged out in a pillow fight in prep school, and his stuffing was forever coming out of his left paw. Consequently, stitching-up was always needed. Matron at Harrow on the Hill had been happy to do the stitching, as she had rescued hundreds of bears during her tenure, although this was never divulged to anyone, especially those on the outside world.

To most Scruffy was just that, scruffy. A worthless, inanimate object, a clump of static, inert matter – a furry bag stuffed with cotton wool. However, a metamorphosis of sorts had taken place over the years. Scruffy had gained iconic status in his lifetime as a bear. Mainly, because Scruffy provided comfort when Max desperately needed it. Scruffy never let him down either. Not like his fellow man, Scruffy was always there for him. The bear even had a 'reserve seat' in Max's rucksack, as he and Scruffy had travelled the world together. On long-haul flights, Scruffy was invaluable as he made a great pillow. Max, suddenly in need of companionship, checked his emails. He opened his laptop. There were several emails from Helen, with attachments. Max snuggled down beneath his duvet.

Dearest Menelaus, (She always called him Menelaus even though she knew his name was Maximilian.)

How are you my love?

I have so much to tell you, Menelaus. The New Acropolis Museum is complete. The building is quite simply magnificent. Wait till you see it for yourself. All open space. It's a wonderful environment in which to work, as it allows one's imagination to soar beyond the confines of steel and glass towards the Parthenon itself. I can see the Acropolis from my desk. Pericles would be impressed with our new museum. The brilliant architects have combined the old with the new, the splendour of ancient Greece with the modern world.

My love, my work continues to be difficult, as so many of the marbles are missing. There are ugly, gaping holes, Menelaus, where the sculptures should be. We are so frustrated knowing that the marbles are elsewhere in the world. Remember Nikolaos? He has spent weeks trying to re-create the missing section of Poseidon's torso, without success. It is impossible to imitate the geniuses who carved the stone so long ago. We have the front section of Poseidon's torso here in Athens but we do not have the back section. As you know, Menelaus, the section we so desperately need of Poseidon is in your museum.

Athena remains a challenge - we still can't find her head. How goes our latest caper? Managed to pinch it yet? Also, many sections of her aegis are of special significance. One section is in Copenhagen, one in France, one in Germany and one in Britain. The chunks of marble have allegorical figures carved in the stone. I have enclosed a PDF with a diagram. A section of Athena's shield with the gorgon's head is also missing.

As Max read on, he sensed her despair.

Sadly, so many of the statues are in your museum. You cannot possibly imagine the hostility we harbour because of this. We despair at the sight of ugly great globs of plaster-of-Paris; dummies we call the lumps of clay we are forced to use in place of the original statues. I am begging you, my love, which as you know is difficult for a Greek, please ask your uncle to send us the section of Athena's upper torso in time for the official opening.

If this is a problem ask him to please send Kore. At one time we were prepared to sacrifice our beautiful maiden, Kore, the caryatid from the temple of the Erechtheion, for a marble from Athena's temple. However, when I mentioned this to the headmistress of the primary school, which is situated in the shadow of the museum, she said the children were most upset. They begged her not to allow this monstrous deed to take place. Kore is like a sister to these children. They draw pictures of her and put them on the wall. She is loved most of all, although the head of Selene's horse comes a close second, especially with the young boys at the school. They pray to Athena every morning during assembly that Kore will come home one day The sooner the better. If your uncle needs convincing we will invite him to the school next time he is over visiting Father. Let him ask the children how they feel about the Parthenon marbles locked up inside your museum. The children believe Kore cannot breathe. She is sad and alone. They also believe that one day the statue of a young maiden from Carye's, will return to her rightful home and no one can ever change their minds.

Menelaus, my dearest love, we have talked about this so much in the last year. Your uncle must understand that it is impossible to finish our displays without the marbles. The Parthenon marbles belong to us. The stones belong to our nation. You must explain to Lord Quimby that he would be a hero if he sent the marbles back to Greece. We will honour him by

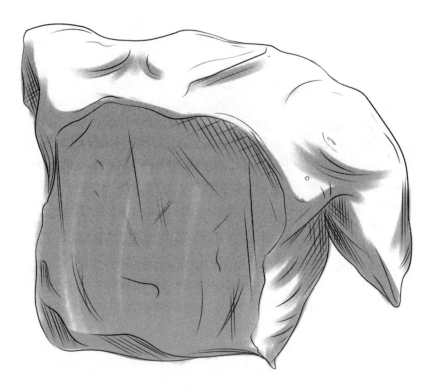

Plate XVII: Torso of Poseidon

This was the section of Poseidon's torso that Helen desperately wanted to remove from the Museum of Classical Antiquities. However, Lord Quimby, the director, refused to cooperate. The missing fragment is in the Acropolis Museum in Athens.

erecting a marble statue of him in the foyer of the New Acropolis Museum. He would like that, would he not? Your uncle must be able to recall the famous actress, Melina Mercouri, when she became Cultural Minister of the Greek Government and she declared to the world's media that the Parthenon represented the 'the soul of Greece'. With the destruction of the Parthenon came the destruction of the soul of the Greek people, just when the country was about to be liberated from the Turkish yoke.

We like to think that the British are kind, generous people, with high morals. Like your Queen. she is an honourable lady. Not only is she a queen she is also a woman. Athena was a woman. A goddess The Queen also understands what it means to be British. Do you think she would sympathise with us, and convince the trustees of the Museum of Classical Antiquities to part with one of the marbles - allow us to be Greek?

Greece is in moral and political decay. My beloved Athens is in a shambolic state and getting worse every day. The city should be razed to the ground and we should start afresh. Our buildings are in disrepair. Rubbish overflows in the streets. People are out of work. The ancient Greeks would be horrified. Foreigners must think that we no longer care. Perhaps they are right. We have so little self-respect left as a nation, as so much has been destroyed or plundered or lost over the hundreds of years of foreign occupation.

Ask your uncle this question. Please? As British allies did we not do our part during the Second World War? Did we not fight to keep the Nazis at bay? We were heroes because of our great national strength, our refusal to give in to the enemy. I think that we Hellenes have contributed to the welfare of all.

Remember when we were together in London last Easter? You showed me so many buildings with Doric columns and friezes adorning palatial mansion houses. Everywhere you look there is evidence of the golden age of Greece. Even the British Museum and the Bank of England have Grecian facades. Has the Western world not benefited from these glory days of ancient Greece?

My darling, can your uncle not find it in his benevolent British heart to send at least one marble back to Greece - on the first aeroplane flying east? Any airline will do, I'm sure. Remind your uncle that the Olympic Games are coming soon to your country. A good source of revenue for London, yes?

You know, Menelaus, we can do nothing about the past. We are not blaming anyone. Every nation on earth has been plundered. Greece is no different. We have learned to forgive. We have even learned to live with the Turks. We all have skeletons in our cupboards. The past is no longer the issue. However, sadly, the Parthenon has become a monument to our barbaric past and no longer a symbol of victory. As it was and as it should be.

What should we do? What can we do? Start a revolution? I would give everything I own, my life, my love, if it would bring the marbles home.

On a happier note, I hope that you and Harry have decided to come to my birthday party. I would love to see Harry again, too. We could all go sailing in the Gulf of Corinth, visit Patmos, have tea with the monks. Piraeus is so over-crowded during the summer months. Glitzy yachts remind me how superficial my life has become. Father's new yacht is embarrassing. He has lost touch with reality. 'Kallisti' is the largest yacht in the marina in Piraeus. Such ostentatious wealth disturbs me greatly.

Captain Balonos will take us anywhere we wish to go. Would you like to go swimming again with the enormous Greek tortoises in the shallow waters at Hydra? Crete is a wonderful place to stop over for a picnic. Please tell Harry that I have booked a stateroom for him on the yacht. But you, my love, are bunking in with me.

Athens is so much worse since you were here last year. So, you must prepare yourself. Life for most Athenians has become exceedingly difficult. Graffiti is everywhere. Athens is crumbling down around us. Yet we remain optimistic. Thank goodness Father has a few euros in his bank otherwise we would struggle to survive as most of the country does. If he gave all his money away it would not be enough. The corruption continues to erode at the very heart of our democratic society, although I no longer believe it is democratic our politicians need to act. However, they seem the most corrupt of all. It's like being controlled by the Mob... the Mafia.

Father is so excited about celebrating my birthday on his new yacht. So, please come, my love, as I desperately need your company. Father's choice of female companionship irritates me to such an extent that I spend most of my time in my stateroom, trying to avoid the bimbos flaunting their skimpily-clad bodies before him - after his money. His latest squeeze is younger than I am! Father should be ashamed of himself, but sadly he is not. He has lost his soul. Avarice bought it. All Father cares about is money; how to make it and how to spend it. And, most of all, how to avoid paying tax.

Just say yes, Menelaos.

All my love, always,

Helen xxxx

PS Good luck with our latest caper. The fact that the statue of Athena is without her right foot bothers me most of all. We need Athena's aegis. If you find any of it...send it...COD.

—CR ED—

Metaphorically speaking, the Parthenon marbles were much like Scruffy. Inanimate objects – nothing but clumps of ruinous stone. No earthly good to anyone, or so one might think. Yet how far from the truth could one get. The stones meant more to the Greeks than one could possibly imagine. More valuable than diamonds or gold.

Perhaps it was time to hasten back to the time of the ancients, embrace their sentiments for sentient beings, things that we, in the modern world, deem worthless, because science and reason has destroyed our ability to embrace the elusive in life, the intangible. If we can't fathom it, it does not exist.

Max had never thought about the Parthenon in that light before, although at that moment the Parthenon got shoved aside. He had been momentarily caught up in daydreams. His imagination soared far beyond the analytical and the conceptual thinkings of Cambridge, coming to rest on the Greek island of Patmos. Max hungered for his Helen. In his eyes, she was his Greek goddess. His Helen of Troy. She had captured his heart when they had first met in Athens two years ago. Helen had grace, charm, wit and eternal beauty; what more could a man want?

'Bugger!'

How he longed to hold his true love tenderly in his arms, feel her slender body close to him. Be swept away by her scent, the sensation of her soft delicate skin against his. However, his wild, amorous thoughts were put on hold. Michaelmas Term ended in a fortnight and he had an essay to write, and, as he ruminated deep within about this sadly neglected fact, he leapt out of bed, tugging madly on his worn boxers with faded red lips printed everywhere, giving 'frayed around the edges' new meaning entirely. He narrowly avoided stepping on his laptop in his haste, rummaged madly in the bin, desperate for something to chew on, to keep his wicked, licentious thoughts at bay. A stale jellybaby, a rogue KitKat, a Mars Bar, anything, really, would do, thought he, as he scrounged through the bin until Maximilian Henry Charles Perceval, the Marquis of Haddington, the next in line to the Quimby dynasty, came upon a half-eaten tub of Pot Noodles which he devoured in one gulp. However, as Max leaned against the wall staring blindly at the plastic pot, a line from Shelley's 'a sphere of tortured matter', sprang to mind. Had he himself not become a sphere of tortured matter and was becoming more and more tortured every day? His life at Cambridge was about to crash, due to his appalling grades, because he was hopelessly in love and couldn't think of anything other than Helen. His allowance was gone. He was also convinced that his brain was shrinking, due to copious G and Ts and/or pints of his favourite lager consumed nightly in the pub. Thus, the crash site was fast becoming a bomb site. Disappearing beneath the floorboards of King's College suddenly had appeal. Would Quantum Mechanics allow him to evaporate in the foggy Cambridgeshire air or should he drown himself in the Cam?

A long weekend was coming up. Last year Max had been invited to Scotland. This year he'd received another invite; however, he declined graciously. The thought of spending the weekend with his friend Tarang Ajmera, feeling like the lowest member of the Indian caste system was too much. His friend's obscenely wealthy parents from Jaipur owned an enormous deer stalking estate in the Scottish Highlands. The rain drizzled down continually. There was one consolation: caseloads of booze were delivered to the castle every day, by helicopter, no less – Hendrick's and tonic flowed non-stop. He must remember to take cucumber the next time he visited. The booze did soothe his ego, the Delhi belly or whatever ailment one might encounter while ensconced in the enormous baronial pile playing mah-jong.

Unlike most of his chums at Cambridge who had access to zillions, Max struggled to make ends meet. He could not afford to travel back and forth to the French Riviera on a whim. But half-term was a breeze in comparison to Christmas holidays, which proved to be a complete and utter nightmare. Hopefully, an invite from Opa would be forthcoming; however, his options were limited.

One year his uncle invited him to spend Christmas at his cottage in the Cotswolds with his rather *chummy* chums. He went. How could he refuse when his uncle had paid his school fees? It was a bloody disaster from start to finish. His uncle's latest boy-beautiful – whom Max thought utterly repulsive – Wayne was there. The boy, who was not much older than Max, swanned around the house in a pinny for heaven's sake. The last time he had visited his uncle's cottage was with his parents. Needless to say family ghosts had raided the place. Phantoms lurked in the garden, the kitchen, his wardrobe, shower cubicle, even the loo. He couldn't escape fast enough and left, spending the rest of the holiday sulking, drinking pints of warm beer in the local pub while daydreaming of making mad, passionate love to Helen.

Harry didn't suffer bouts of holiday fatigue. What he did suffer with was his mother. Much to Harry's chagrin, his mama had remarried – for the third time, which was difficult to imagine given her young age. Harry and his mother were from California. When Max and Harry had been at Harrow, Max had secretly nicknamed his mama, 'Lulu from La La Land' and it had stuck. Lulu had been a *Vogue* fashion model until she got her claws into old Jonesie-boy. She was a stunner, no question. Whenever he had the privilege of being in the company of Harry's luscious mother he was reduced to stuttering, or was it stammering? He never knew the difference. Distracted, shall we say, by her heavenly charms; being a breast man and all, or was it legs? He could not decide. Breasts that looked as though they would pop out of whatever flimsy see-though top Lulu was squeezed into at the time, which wasn't much of anything, really. But, as luscious as Lulu was, her appearance did not make up for the fact that Harry and his mama did not communicate nor could he abide his new step-father. Although as poor ol' Harry was already on his third father his displeasure, Max felt, was justified. The problem was Lulu from La La Land was extremely demanding of her husband's time, leaving Harry out in the cold, as it were. Mama was also rather flighty, a bit silly; however, she wasn't a stupid girl as she had married well. She also had a Southern drawl, having attended a girl's finishing school in the 'Deep South'. Max completely understood why his best mate found it impossible to take anything his mother said seriously, with an American accent that reduced him to sniggering.

Nevertheless, it turned out that Harry was a rather clever chap. Top grades, top athlete, great fun, best mate. He was also twice the size, which really rattled Max, who felt scrawny in comparison. Harry's arms were thrice the size of his. Even without a stitch on Harry resembled an American fullback with the tackle. He virtually swamped everyone, including his mother, as she had to be a size zero. However, Lulu had yet to accept the fact that Harry had grown up, because she still called Harry 'her baby' or 'my darling boy'; this really got up his nose, and it drove him to the edge. There wasn't a thing he could do or say about his mother's choice of endearments, or her inability to choose the right husband. Heaven forbid Harry should ever express his feelings. His stepfather didn't have any and his mama just plain ignored him. The only *thing* Mr Rupert Longfield-Jones understood was money, or more precisely, the acquisition of barrows full of American greenbacks, as he had made one hell of a lot of it in a short space of time. There seemed to be no end of the dosh, as 'Honey' was a wealthy hedge-fund manager with a brass-plate in London, around the corner from the house in St James' Square and a head office on Wall Street in downtown Manhattan. The fact that he took a chopper to work really impressed Max, as he deemed this simple means of transport perfect sense.

There was an even more unbelievable side to Lulu and it was this: Lulu from La La Land always wore jewels. Max had known the woman for fifteen years and in all that time he had *never* once glimpsed that famous bosom without rocks. Whether she was at Cambridge standing shivering on the sidelines freezing to death watching Harry play rugby, or helicopter skiing at the poshest ski resorts, like Davos or Klosters. Harry, being a good lad, had felt sorry for him one Christmas and invited him to go skiing at Davos, and since then, the word sloshed had taken on a whole new meaning. He could not recall one sober moment (this was prior to Cambridge). He had been brain dead for two weeks. Everyone was sloshed. It was a total piss-up from start to finish. Max had had to resort to taking gobs of pain killers every night to relieve the nausea. Is that all zillionaires did for heaven's sake?

Returning once again to Lulu: she was always dripping in sparkly baubles. Diamonds were obviously her favourite. Max had asked Harry about his mama's rocks one night while slumped on the floor in Davos, after copious gin-fizzes, and Harry explained that mama's jewels meant more to her than anything else in the world. Obviously Max imagined Lulu wearing diamonds while shopping in Palm Beach or flaunting her emeralds on the beach in Miami. What about the bath?

Lulu's birthday was coming. This invariably meant a champagne party at Annabel's. He was expected to take a gift. Did Lulu know the difference between Hermes head scarves and a fake from Pound Stretcher? He rubbed his stubbly chin. He couldn't afford posh perfume either. Max dithered. Would Lulu know the difference between Chanel No. 5 or some god-awful stuff from the local chemist? Sickly smelling eau de cologne in fake plastic bottles, reeking of lavender or lily of the valley that reminded Max of the wrinkly old dears he sat next to on London buses, jolting over Putney Bridge, whenever he had been to visit his chums. Thank God that wasn't often, although Putney was up and coming. Suddenly he had a cerebral moment... lip-gloss...that was it! Lulu from La La Land must go through one hell of a lot of the lippy-stuff because she layered it on so thickly that it came off on the rim of her champagne glass...so...lip-gloss it was.

Another niggling woe surfaced: his overdraft was all used up. To his eternal dismay and that of his bank manager, Max was always living beyond his means. To add to his mountain of woes a paper on Shelley was due in a week's time and he hadn't even started the bloody thing.

Agitated, Max kept snapping the elastic waistband of his boxers. Helen's words echoed in his mind. Athena's aegis in particular. The first part of their *caper* had already been executed. He sent a brief text to Pippa wanting an update as he trailed back and forth in his room. What he needed was a cup of tea. He plugged in the kettle, searched for a rogue teabag. Somewhere in the inner recesses of his nimble-witted brain he recalled seeing a piece of stone with an allegorical figure carved on the top. Was it Phobos? He couldn't remember.

Max scratched his head. Dandruff flaked on the floor as he poured boiling water into the cup. He was becoming more and more exasperated until the light went on. Of course! The house in London.

It was a five-minute walk to the train station.

He forgot his tea. He flung open the door of his wardrobe, scattering empty beer bottles on the floor. A rancid smell greeted his nostrils. A fug – a heady mixture of stale lager, a week's supply of fusty boxers, jockstraps minus the straps, all a bit whiffy, he thought, while muttering aloud to himself.

'Max, old man, you really ought to do something about the God-awful smell in this wardrobe!'

Although he was convinced the disgusting odour kept the moths at bay, not that it mattered, as the moth-holes in his T-shirts added character, a certain *je ne sais quoi*.

Max was the nephew of the latest Lord Quimby, of the infamous Quimby dynasty. He sent a text to his uncle, although he could always be contacted at the Museum of Classical Antiquities. If he planned it right, he could scrounge a free lunch out of the old sod while picking up the key to the house in St James's Square. The house was empty as Matilda, the housekeeper, who lived over the coach house, always seemed to be on holiday in Spain.

Fifteen years had passed by since Max had lived at 42 St James's Square. On that same day his boyhood ended. Another crash site. He only returned when invited to do so by his uncle.

Shortly after moving to France his mother remarried. Again – for the third time. (Did everyone on the planet marry three times?) To her fitness instructor, no less. Max had been gutted at the time – meaning literally going beyond devastated. He flatly refused to attend the wedding. The simple truth that he had not even been invited to the damn thing was not the issue.

So, his mother lived permanently in France and he boarded at Harrow on the Hill prep school from the young age of eight. This gut-wrenching ordeal had near-crippling side effects, resulting in his desire to isolate himself, defiantly, from the outside world. He eventually closeted himself up in the sprawling, self-reflective surroundings of Cambridge, while searching in a near frenzy through the musty tomes of the ancient Greek and Roman philosophers; demanding answers to life's woes. He had spent years searching the musty tomes in the Classics Department at Harrow, and then Cambridge. The ancient Greek and Roman lyric poets had provided him with a few answers as he shared their belief that philosophy's fundamental purpose had to be the pursuit of truth. Max got some comfort from this, although his problem was he was always asking himself *why*. Why was he always questioning the meaning of life or the existence of his soul? Whether he was in possession of a soul was another matter. The other nagging questions plaguing him were about death. He wasn't absolutely sure whether he believed in death since you are unaware of it when it happens, how do you know when you are dead? He wasn't actually sure if he were alive either, because the only time he ever felt truly *alive* was when he was with Helen. The rest of the time he felt dead. Many people he knew didn't seem to be really alive, either; not as he imagined full-on life. Most people existed, that was all. Hence, his conviction that he had never really and truly lived.

He may not have found the answers but he was still searching. Elysian Fields was not what he was looking for. He wanted to know how to cope with life – tragedy in particular. Hence, the debate with the ancients continued: why did his father have to die, the one man whom he adored more than any other in the entire world and whose face he could no longer recall? This, he thought, equated to two tragedies. Why did he still feel abandoned by his mother even though she was always telling him how much she loved him? If she loved him so much, why not return to England? Why did he feel like a ward of his uncle even though he was twenty-three years of age? Why didn't he have a happy family life, with a mum and a dad and siblings? Why did he feel all alone in the world whenever he wasn't with Helen? Why did he have such long scrawny arms? Why did he have freckles all over his face when there wasn't much sun in England? Why weren't his teeth straight? Why did he have such foppish hair?

Why wasn't he cool? Why wasn't he a jock? Why couldn't he drink twenty pints of lager without passing out? Why couldn't he be happy without Helen?

Religion had failed him. Monotheism wasn't his bag either. If the truth be told, while reading ancient Greek and Roman legends as a small boy, he had developed a closer affinity with paganism. Max desperately needed to get inside the heads of the ancient lyric poets. The Greek philosophers had a few pithy sayings; however, fluent Greek could prove beneficial. The Romantic poets had a good line or two. Shelley in particular wasn't afraid to delve deep into the meaning of life.

He was haunted by his past. Even now, the pain of his father's sudden death was still raw; which was exacerbated by his mother's idiotic marriages. If the truth be told, Max had great difficulty dealing with all the fallout. He barely coped with life at times. He had a huge chip on his shoulder the size of a bloody boulder. Who wouldn't?

Insufferable is how he had become even to his own self. And lately something else had begun to niggle. He was without a *raison d'être*. His life didn't *really* have a purpose. Cambridge had given his life meaning for the last four years; however, after Cambridge, then what? He didn't have any direction. He couldn't fill the void in his life. Who cared? He could vanish and no one would notice. Who actually cared whether he lived or died? His mother didn't care, otherwise she would have come home. She preferred the company of donkeys. Helen cared. But how much? He didn't know. He couldn't really open up to his friends, not even Harry. His mates might think he was suffering from depression. He wasn't. His life was totally void of meaning. That was all. There was a difference. He couldn't seem to rid himself of the pain and the anger that he had accumulated since childhood. Fencing had taught him how to put his pain and fear behind him. He also joined the Drama Club, and, on stage, he forgot his pain. Although the pain and the sorrow he witnessed in the real world made no sense.

A symposium was the answer. Imagine, engaging in rhetoric with the ancient Greeks. Imagine sitting outside on the lawn, sipping copious Pimms, engaging in lengthy debates on the meaning of 'The unexamined life is not worth living'. Perhaps he should try going barefoot. Roaming the streets of Cambridge without shoes might provoke an insight or two; however, England was so abysmally cold and damp at the moment his toes might freeze. Not a good idea.

Max imagined the world had gone mad. Animal cruelty was a good example of this. He found it impossible to sit through animal documentaries on TV, as he became so enraged he shouted and screamed at the screen. Cruelty towards animals was a crime. He dreamed of saving every endangered species, especially the rhinos and the elephants and the pandas. Every single creature man was bent on destruction. Whenever he saw a photo of a rhino with its horn sawn off he wept. His soul bled. He wanted to shoot the buggers who had committed such an evil deed. Why was this brutality against innocent animals, the world's most beautiful creatures, allowed to continue in the twenty-first century? In the so-called civilised world, which Max concluded wasn't civilised at all? Man's inhumanity towards man and animals reduced the human race to total and utter barbarianism. No wonder the Greeks despised barbarians. Max despaired as he combed his hair with his hands. Another of the 'whys' was: why on earth were there still barbarians two and a half millennia after the Greeks had rid this evil of the world?

That is why Ovid was his man. In *Metamorphoses* Ovid explained it quite simply, when in Book One, *The Creation,* he referred to the world as one enormous seething mass of chaos, which it was, of course, in the beginning. Ovid went on to say that the world was a dreadful place comprising evil, chaos and turmoil, then man entered the frame, tried to create order out of chaos. Ovid said that man's 'brutality is true to their origin'. Therefore, Max concluded that human beings were not really good folk. In fact, they were and still are a rather nasty bunch, which meant humans have a really bad side, a brutality, as it were, and unless man controlled this brutality, it reared its ugly head. Brutality exists deep within all of us and we are incapable of ridding ourselves of this brutality, even after sixty million years. So, chaos is here to stay. Max shook his head. Adam and Eve weren't to blame after all. It was just how the world was in the beginning.

So, Ovid had the answer.

One day Max hoped to make a difference. He wanted to do his bit, rid the world of chaos. He knew not how or when, but he wanted to contribute to making the world a better place. Shouldn't everyone that has ever lived have done the same? Thanked the gods for having lived?

He loved life. Life itself. Every cosmic layer. Every blade of grass. Every handful of dust. He loved every wild animal and every pebble on the beach, every block of stone holding King's College, Cambridge, together. He loved the sound of barn owls hooting outside his window at night, and he loved Scruffy, his bear, nothing more than a bag of cotton wool with one floppy ear. He loved every marble statue in the garden at La Redousse, especially Nirvana. He adored the glorious red sunsets he glimpsed from his window and gentle snowflakes floating through the frosty air at Opa's castle in Germany.

He loved Iris' rainbows. The way she painted the sky after a storm had to be a great wonder of the natural world. He adored sitting curled up on the sofa in front of a roaring log fire reading from Horace or Homer. However, he loved to travel most of all – experience life for himself. Travel reminded him of Greece and his thoughts swiftly returned to Helen and his love for her. He had fallen in love with Athens because of Helen, whom he had met on an archaeological dig in Greece during his second year at Cambridge. They had spent their days and nights together, roaming the Plaka and had made love in the shadows of the Parthenon, in the light of the most enormous full moon that he had ever seen; as though Selene herself was blessing them. Helen adored 'her beloved Parthenon' and her passion had woven its magic on Max too; the most iconic structure in the world had magically sealed their fate and their love.

Helen had a cause that gave her life meaning. Real meaning. Max longed for such a cause, yet it had not been forthcoming. He refused to become maudlin and shifted his thoughts. He could not predict the future. One thing was for sure – he absolutely had to find the section of Athena's aegis Helen so badly needed to finish the display at the museum. This meant only one thing: he was being forced to confront his demons – head on – and return to the house in St James's Square.

Chapter Twenty-Six
Francesca's Dilemma at La Redousse

'Xavier! Where is the damn house?' Monsieur, the junk dealer from Marseilles, growled impatiently at his mate, as he drove his battered Citroën at breakneck speed along the bleached and craggy stretch of coastline towards La Redousse, a belle époque villa set high on a cliff near Menton on the French Riviera.

'*Voilà Voilà*!' Xavier pointed to the gap in the long row of cypress tress. '*Voilà*!'

The junk dealer from Marseilles kept his hand on the clutch, ready to shift into low gear at a moment's notice. He was in a desperate hurry. He needed to clinch the deal before Madame changed her mind. The lady on the other end of his mobile phone that morning was most anxious to sell several marble statues in her garden and Monsieur could not wait to get his greasy paws on another piece of garden statuary as American tourists were in town. The Riviera had its charm even in late autumn. The New Yorkers bought marble statues by the boat-load to take back home to the 'States' to tart up their palatial mansions in the Hamptons or bungalows in West Palm Beach. Tomorrow was the antiques market in Marseilles and if the

Plate XVIII: The statue of Athena.

statues were half decent he could sell them for a hefty profit, as long as his wife didn't fancy the statues for their small balcony. Françoise had nagged him all summer for something *très belle* to hold flowers, as terracotta pots swamped the terrace. It was a difficult decision, whether to keep himself or his wife happy. He enjoyed buying his mates a round in the Minerva Bar in the old market town. These thoughts whizzed round and round inside Monsieur's bald head as he took his sabot off the accelerator, slowed the van down until it purred, made a sharp left turn past the hedge, and swerved up the drive. His old Citroën bumped and thumped along the dusty track, past enormous citrus groves and fruit orchards, towards La Redousse until coming to a screeching halt at the front of the imposing belle époch villa with rambling porticoes and a crumbling facade.

Xavier threw open the door of the van and leapt out. Monsieur took a moment longer. He needed to check his cash and flipped through the wad of euros in his pocket. Monsieur liked cash. When he was satisfied he had enough money he flung open the door on his side, and jumped out, banging it shut. One day soon, he imagined the door falling off its hinges. However, this was the least of his worries, he thought, as he and his mate strode towards the front door of the villa, with all the confidence befitting two junk dealers from Marseilles.

Xavier pulled the bell. As the two men waited on the threshold for someone to answer the door, the driver of the van stood back from the door, but as he did so, carved words in the stone facade above the lintel caught his eye. He had no idea what the words meant as he could not understand Latin.

'Multa renascentur quae jam cecideree'

CHAPTER TWENTY-SIX

'Many words will be reborn that have already been lost.'

—ର ଯ—

Francesca could not stop shivering as she stood on the crumbling stone steps at the bottom of her much loved garden, gazing from afar at the enchanted marble bust of Minerva for the last time. Her shivering fit continued although it wasn't the sudden drop in temperature or from the blast of cold air blowing down from the Alps. No, it was more ethereal than that, something deep within had provoked her sombre mood, she thought, as light rain splashed on to the marble bust, snug in its niche at the top end of the balustrade, the Roman goddess's resting place for years. It looked even more shattered in the grey light.

Francesca was beginning to regret her decision to part with the marble bust. However, it was too late now to change her mind as the junk dealer from Marseilles was to arrive at any moment to make her an offer. To give her *cash*, to be more precise. The statue was the first to go. One of many Italianate sculptures in the garden she was forced to sell, as she had been teetering on the edge of a financial meltdown for months and could no longer squeeze a penny out of her overdraft. A week ago all her credit cards had been cancelled, even her American Express. And, yesterday her current account had been made null and void.

It got worse.

The roof was desperately in need of repointing, in lead – more costly than gold. The boiler, constantly on the blink, needed replacing or she would freeze to death next winter. She was desperately in need of a new winter coat as she had used her old coat to wrap the newborn donkey in. Her Ferragamo shoes were run down at the heel, heaven forbid, and holes had appeared in the soles. However, there was an even greater tragedy looming. The drinks cabinet needed topping up. This she deemed totally unacceptable.

Francesca burst into tears. What on earth was wrong with her? Annoyed, she brushed away her tears. Perhaps she was overlooking one salient fact. By parting with the statue, she was also parting with something precious, a family heirloom. Minerva was Max's favourite, and, without it, the garden would never be the same again. Max would be furious when he found out what she had done.

What fun they had had designing the Italianate garden. Max had thought his find equated to the most awesome archaeological find ever when he had come upon the head while digging potatoes in the potager next to the potting shed, at the house in St James's Square. When she moved permanently to the Riviera she brought it with her. She could not possibly leave Minerva behind in the potting shed, as the goddess had become part of the family.

Max had been captivated by the Roman statue and over the years developed a passion for all things Roman. Thereafter, summer hols were spent scouring the markets in Nice for marble statuary. Max was so keyed up about reading Classics that they decided to create a garden based on the Classical ruins of ancient Rome. Gradually the Greek legends replaced the Roman legends. Odysseus had become Max's hero when he was at Harrow and he loved to recite verses from Homer's *Odyssey* while lounging on the lawn.

Max had developed a love of the Classical world. Now, however, that was all about to change, thought Francesca, as she rushed along the narrow winding path through the colonnade, a sculptural mass of ancient Doric, Ionic and Corinthian, unable to escape the haunting, dark eyes following her at every turn. Why hadn't she ever had the bust appraised? Its provenance, though, was of no importance. Max was convinced that the bust was Roman and insisted on calling her Minerva because of her eternal beauty. All too fleeting happy memories of Max ended as she drew nearer, the goddess's deep-set dark eyes peered at her with such intensity that she was forced to look away. In exactly the same way the young tawny owl had, thought she, reminded of the bird peering through her kitchen window early one morning. A rare occasion indeed for such an elusive creature, thought Francesca, shivering, as she waited for the junk man to arrive.

It was not the time to be sentimental.

The garden was a glorious muddle of urns, marble columns, arches, portico shards, sarcophagi and statues. She had asked herself once more: why have such affinity for chunks of ruinous stone? Was it really a reflection of her life, one that had been in ruins for a very long time? Perhaps the ancient marbles were a sad reminder of her misfortune, as a single parent for most of Max's life, since her bitter, acrimonious divorce from her third husband. Divorces had played a significant part in destroying her life. Her first husband, her *Cherie*, had been a French aristocrat, an absolute darling, who she discovered, while walking into their bedroom one night at their grand chateau in Burgundy, preferred the company of younger men. Then, Charles, her second husband and Max's father, younger brother of the 12th Lord Quimby, had died in a tragic car crash while speeding along the Grande Corniche after too much champers. She had been driving. The guilt she experienced after his death had been paralysing. So, what did she do? She rushed headlong into another man's arms, married her third husband, her 'hunky fitness instructor', which had also ended in divorce, ten times more bitter and acrimonious than the first. The brute had fled the country without paying her a penny of the money she had lent him to start his fitness clubs. Bereft of her life-savings and her heart broken, she soldiered on. Divorce had cost her dearly: the loss of her new Mercedes, her family's precious works of art, originals for heaven's sake, a set of twelve Chippendale chairs, and the family silver – all gone, to pay the legal fees. Last summer she had emptied her safety deposit box at the *banque* in Monaco, and auctioned what remained of her jewellery. Lushington's had been called in. She had no choice. The damn roof leaked.

Fortunately, La Redousse had been bequeathed to her by her late husband. However, there wasn't a penny to provide for maintenance, and she really struggled to keep the house up to scratch. She could barely make ends meet. Nevertheless, she carried on as best she could, sold fresh herbs from her potager at the flower market in Nice, wrote articles, books that never got published.

As a freelance journalist she was always submitting pieces to *Tatler*; however, the glossy mag had flatly rejected her article for the last issue. She had attempted, without much success, to revoke Friedrich Nietzsche's argument that *Was mich nicht umbringt macht mich stärker* was wrong.

She believed this was *nonsense*. A fallacy of the worst kind, as his saying led the reader to believe that failure made one stronger. Francesca was living proof that quite the opposite was true, because every time she suffered a blow – whether a disastrous marriage, yet another humiliating rejection letter in the post, her herb garden failed to produce healthy aromatic plants three years running, resulting in financial ruin, or she was forced to sell her son's beloved marble statue – her life was made worse. Much worse.

Therefore, she concluded, quite rightly, that she wasn't made stronger by loss – years fraught with struggle and grief. She was made weaker and becoming weaker by the day, without sufficient funds to lead a happy, fulfilled life. Every time life smacked her on her arse she was made weaker and she wasn't sure how much more she could withstand before crumbling like the stone column toppled over on the ground in front of her.

Tatler always failed to be impressed by her work.

Back to the loss thing: take the loss of possessions; keeping in mind that material things are just that, material, inanimate objects, for the time being. At some stage in one's life material things morph into one's precious possessions, treasures, family heirlooms, and gradually over the years reflect the very essence of a person's life-story, a person's character, their inner soul. She imagined Minerva to be a perfect example of this because once the statue was removed from the garden something precious would be lost for ever. Max had great affection for the stone. He would miss Minerva terribly if she suddenly disappeared from her plinth. A very wise sage said that every time a person touched an object they left part of their soul embedded in it. Francesca worked backwards with this highly enlightened thought, concluding that this meant that not only her son's soul and her soul had become embedded in the stone but also those of all the persons who had ever touched the stone, including the sculptor who had originally carved the marble thousands of years earlier in Rome. It was an interesting theory. Perhaps this explained her affection for Minerva, a chunk of chiselled stone that had been empowered by its past. She had never thought about material things in that way before.

So, Francesca had to conclude that one's possessions gradually became a reflection of one's soul. Like La Redousse. The house was fast becoming utilitarian, cold, lifeless, dull, boring, moribund.

At one time La Redousse had been a treasure trove of soul-stuff; now it was a shell of its former self. An empty tortoise shell sprang to mind. Then for what ever reason, the Parthenon came to mind. Why had she burst into tears when she had first glimpsed the Parthenon in exactly the same way as she had done now? At the time she was unable to understand why. She had felt rather silly standing in blazing hot sun, on the rock face of the Acropolis, gazing up at the lofty structure, awestruck, nothing more than a pile of crumbling rock, an ancient Greek ruin. Why did the Parthenon wield such power over her, power that came from within the very stone itself? Stone that begged to be touched. The marble was so cool to touch, just like her skin. She smiled to herself, recalling how touching the stone had magically empowered her in some way. At the time she had noticed that the man standing next to her must have felt the same way, because he couldn't stop stroking the fluted column toppled over on the bedrock. She had received comfort from touching the stone, which, thought Francesca, a temple ought to do.

Although, upon reflection, had her emotional outburst something to do with loss? Had she experienced, at a subconscious level, the tragic loss the Greek people had suffered for thousands of years, and continued to do so? Or was her tragic loss reflecting back at her? Perhaps a little of both, thought Francesca, as she reached out and gently touched the head of the Roman goddess.

However, she had to admit that she believed the marbles in the garden possessed a 'spirit within', a *genius loci* of their own, which she realised was really stretching her imagination. Inanimate objects

Plate XIX: Example of an aegis worn by Athena showing a gorgon's head. The aegis is immortal, ageless and protects the allegorical figures, phobos (fear), eris (strife), alke (strength) and Ioke (pursuit).

326

were just that. Stones were stones and nothing more. Yet, she had begun to think differently about the marbles of late and, often, while standing alone among the statues, she had found herself talking to the stones, engaging in rhetoric if you please, debating the meaning of her existence. Bedlam awaited no doubt. Max was forever asking her opinion about the fate of the Quimby Marbles. Her reply was always the same: that she was convinced that the statues longed to return home, after being forced to live in exile for thousands of years. Of course, she had Minerva to thank, because without her, she wouldn't have given the marble statues a second thought.

That glorious autumnal day sprang to mind when Max had discovered the bust buried beneath a thick layer of moss in the garden at the house in St James's Square. At first, they imagined it was a huge boulder; however, Max continued to dig, unearthing the marble bust, ravaged by time, earth, wind and rain. At the time they had tried to imagine why the bust had been buried in the garden; however, she never thought any more about it. It was a worthless object, otherwise why on earth would anyone bury it in the garden? They adored Minerva and that's all that mattered.

Was she betraying Minerva by booting her out of the garden, selling the statue to the junk dealer from Marseilles? Francesca debated as she shrugged deeper inside her jacket, a relic from her past life in England.

She tried to imagine. Heaven forbid, some brash American tourist, without an iota of taste or appreciation of the Classical world, bought Minerva for a pittance at the antique market in Marseilles, shipped her to Las Vegas or Hollywood or some ghastly place, where taste meant the flavour of a Big Mac, and displayed her in the bath. Or what if Minerva were badly abused, which wasn't impossible to imagine, given the perilous state she was in, and someone hacked off what little remained of her once aquiline nose? Or, worse, kept her imprisoned in a dank, dark cellar without realising marble statues needed to breathe? They needed to be kept outdoors in the open air, because that is where statues belonged. Marble statues were designed for open spaces. What if her owner mocked her stunning, natural beauty by placing pots of petunias on her noble head? These thoughts provoked such dismay she became frantic. But it was too late to change her mind. She could hear the van thundering up the drive, glimpsed the cloud of dust as she walked around the corner of the house.

—◌ ◌—

'*Bonjour, Monsieur,*' said Francesca as a matched pair of men in blue overalls walked towards her.

'*Bonjour, Madame,*' breathed the junk dealer in his husky voice furred from too many cigarettes. 'I am Monsieur Benoît and this is Xavier.' He introduced himself and his mate, while peering at his potential client from under his black beret pulled down over his eye, chewing the butt end of a broken pencil.

'We have come to see the statues.'

'Follow me,' said Francesca flatly, leading the way, unable to keep the angst from her voice. She needed to get this ghastly business over and done with as quickly as possible.

'The first marble sculpture I wish to sell is in the parterre garden at top of the stairs.'

The junk dealers were so enthusiastic they ran on ahead. When they reached the site exclamations of delight filled the cold, damp air. Rain had turned to sleet. However, nothing put the dealers off.

'*Oh là là!*' chimed the junk dealers in unison.

'*Elle est très belle!*'

The junk dealers enthused while rubbing their wet grubby hands all over the statue's delicate face.

This really annoyed Francesca. Minerva deserved respect.

'How much do you want?' asked the junk dealer from Marseilles as he peered closely at the marble, smacking his lips.

Francesca didn't know what to say. She wondered, however, what the ancient Greek comic-poets would have had to say about the drama unfolding in the garden, worthy of a Greek tragedy. Who knew, thought Francesca as she hovered between two crumbling Doric columns, waiting for the smelly junk dealer from Marseilles to offer her an absolute fortune.

As the junk dealer licked his pencil, Lady Francesca Perceval wondered why she continued to think like a Classicist even though she had never studied the Classics. Max had a lot to do with it. Her thoughts returned to the present when Xavier snapped the buckles on his blue overalls.

She waited.

She found it difficult to breathe, as rain poured down, splattered on the crumbling stone. Her life flashed before her. Suddenly, she wanted rid of the bust. Such despairing thoughts prompted:

'Well? Monsieur,' she huffed, as she stood with her hands on her hips, 'what is your best offer?'

'Twenty-five euros is my final offer.'

Francesca couldn't recall a first offer.

'It's the best I can do, Madame.'

'At that price, I might as well give it away,' snapped Francesca, her beautiful face shadowed in grey light. It wasn't only the sky that looked piqued.

The junk dealer tugged on his beret, scratched his bald head.

'Well, now, let me think,' he puffed, he didn't want to lose the sale after coming all that way, besides the garden was full of junk he could sell for a tidy sum.

'I offer you a better price, Madame,' said he, smiling brightly. 'Twenty-eight euros. If it makes you any happier...then...I already have a buyer.'

Francesca smiled. Contemplating her empty larder...yawning drinks cabinet...faux fur coat...lead for the roof...

'You see, Madame, my wife has been nagging me to find her something nice for our balcony, something chic, *très parisienne.*'

Francesca briefly considered her options. There weren't any. Becoming impatient to move out of the garden she hastened, offering her hand, 'That's fine, you have a deal.'

How long did it take to destroy a dream, ten years of work?

The junk dealer shook her hand while his sidekick spotted a trolley leaning against the garden shed and in a matter of minutes Minerva had been hastily removed from her plinth, wheeled out of the garden with more gusto than was necessary. Francesca followed along behind watching Minerva's head wobbling back and forth something frightfully, looking as though she had just been guillotined in the Jardin des Tuileries at the height of the French Revolution. Francesca looked away. Minerva was not going to forgive her.

However, as he whizzed past Francesca, the junk dealer enthused, 'My wife will be thrilled. She always wanted something *très belle* for her prize-wining petunias, prize-winning geraniums!' Francesca's worst nightmare had been realised. However, it was too late. They had shaken hands. She could not get the junk dealers from Marseilles out of the garden fast enough.

'Thank you for coming, Monsieur,' she said, as he wheeled the trolley along the path at the side of the house, into the drive.

Francesca stood back watching Minerva being hoisted into the Back of the beaten-up van.

Then, Monsieur withdrew his wad, counted the euros. However, he stopped counting when she screeched:

'Monsieur. Stop! I have changed my mind!'

'What?'

'*Pardonnez moi!*' the junk dealers from Marseilles shouted in unison. 'You have changed your mind? You mean we've come all this way for nothing?'

'I am so sorry,' said Francesca, her hands clutching her face.

'The nerve!' spat Xavier, glaring at Francesca as if she had lost her wits, which she probably had.

A lot of swearing in French followed as the two men climbed inside the back of the Citroën and withdrew the marble bust, then rolled it out of the vehicle on to the trolley. Then jumped into the van and slammed the door.

Francesca stood in the drive, listening to the motor revving. Petrol fumes clogged the air, as the empty van thundered down the drive. She watched the van disappear from view.

'You fool!' Berating herself had become a habit of late and not an endearing one at that.

However, she was all alone so it did not matter. She glimpsed Minerva on the trolley. Francesca could tell that the goddess was upset with her, she could see it reflected in her deep dark eyes.

Suddenly she had had enough and picking up a flower pot nearby flung it at the statue.

The flower pot smashed against the bust, fell to the ground. Then, Francesca realised what she had done.

'Minerva I am so sorry!' Francesca sobbed.

The statue was only a clump of ruinous stone, so why on earth should she apologise? To feel empathy towards the bust was nonsense, pure and simple, thought Francesca as she grabbed hold

of the wooden handles and in a frenzy pushed the trolley down the path in a great huff. Minerva was being returned to her plinth.

How fickle! She had nearly sold Minerva for the measly sum of twenty-eight quid. Well, euros. And as she hurried down the narrow path with Minerva wobbling back and forth on the trolley Francesca suddenly realised that she might not know the value of the marble, but she was definitely worth more than twenty-eight euros. Minerva was a classy lady. She had Classical features. She must have had a helmet at one time because she had cheek-pieces. She had been very beautiful in her day. There was something else about Minerva that was unique. She had a sexy, pouting mouth. Francesca produced a deep, throaty, sexy laugh. The sculptor must have been quite the lad to have given his statue such enormous sensual appeal, lasting for thousands of years.

'*Wow!*'

Besides, she had been daft to think the sale of the marble was enough to solve her pending financial woes. Twenty-eight euros was not going to pay for her roof to be mended. It wouldn't buy her a warm coat either. Lushington's... Tomorrow she would text the auction house in London. If she decided to sell Minerva she might as well find her a good home.

After Francesca had safely restored Minerva to her plinth, she returned the trolley to the shed. As she closed the door she suddenly felt as though someone was watching, and turning around, heard a young barn owl hooting in the long row of lofty pines above her head. She hooted back, always sympathetic with the natural world. But she couldn't help thinking how odd that was since owls rarely appeared at that time of day. After that she thought nothing more about her brief interlude with Athena's sacred owl as she hurried down the lane towards the postbox.

Of course, the postbox was overflowing with junk mail. She flicked through the bills, disappointed there wasn't a letter from Max, although she had received a postcard from the Louvre in Paris, hastily written by her dear friend Jean-Pierre, whom she had befriended while studing at the Sorbonne.

She scanned briefly:

Dear Francesca,

I have quit my job at the Louvre, due to the most extraordinary circumstances...all will be revealed. Looking forward to our rendezvous on Friday...

What could have possibly caused Jean-Pierre to quit his job? He had worked at the Louvre for twenty-five years. She would soon find out, thought Francesca, as she tucked the postcard inside her back pocket, and hurried towards the stables. The donkeys needed to be feed, and the stables needed mucking out.

Chapter Twenty-Seven
The Haunting at the Louvre

There wasn't a sound in the museum that night, not a murmur, as the janitor pushed his dust-mop back and forth across the wooden parquet floor. Jean-Pierre kept his head down. He didn't dare look up, fearful of being spooked yet again.

With great trepidation Jean-Pierre continued pushing his dust-mop back and forth, whizzing around the bases of the enormous marble plinths, as it was his responsibility to keep all of the colossal marble statues in the Department of Greek, Roman and Etruscan Antiquities clean and free of dust. Jean-Pierre had been a janitor at the Louvre for the last twenty-five years and he knew every nook and cranny of the museum.

When he came to a display case, one of many in the gallery, he very gingerly removed the key from his back pocket and unlocked the display case containing three small chunks of marble from South Metope XVI from the Parthenon in Athens, precious artifacts from ancient Greece. When nothing untoward happened he sighed, breathing heavily.

'So far so good!'

Every night, for the last fortnight, whenever Jean-Pierre went anywhere near the display case something strange bordering on the macabre happened in the Antiquities Department and he did not like it. No – not one bit.

Until recently he had loved his job. He had even asked to work the night-shift so he could be alone with the larger-than-life marble statues of Greek gods and goddesses. He was passionate about the Classical world and had visited the Pantheon in Rome and the Parthenon in Athens many times over the years. In fact, when he had applied for the janitorial position at the Louvre he specifically asked to work in the Department of Greek, Roman and Etruscan Antiquities just to be close to the marble sculptures and he had kept his position at the Louvre ever since. He had been happy at work until a fortnight ago when the Director of the Greek Antiquities Department had insisted on a reshuffle, resulting in an entirely new collection of *objets d'art* being moved up from the basement to enhance the department's existing collection.

Jean-Pierre readied his duster, as though preparing for battle, as he reached into the display case and very quickly dusted the fragments of stone. A tortured soul if ever there was one, he thought to himself, as the expression on the Lapith's face was pitiful indeed.

The next case contained small chunks of Athena's aegis with an allegorical figure of Eris carved in the marble. Another chunk had a section of a gorgon's head carved in the stone. Beside it was printed: 'The figure of Eris represented strife in the ancient world.' When he had given the stones the once-over with his duster he returned the marbles to their rightful place on the green baize and closed the lid. When nothing untoward happened Jean-Pierre backed away, greatly relieved, and stood leaning heavily on his mop handle, and started breathing again.

All was quiet in the museum that night; the security guards were nowhere in sight as Jean-Pierre carried on with his cleaning, whizzing past the enormous section of the metopes of the Parthenon frieze that had also come up from the basement. This time, however, as soon as he started to dust the marble torso of the Lapith boy, he heard the most God-awful sound.

'*Mon Dieu!*' Jean-Pierre froze. The blood-curdling noise sounded like a young boy screaming in terrible pain. He slammed the lid down hard not wanting whatever lurked inside to escape and becoming alarmed, he drew back from the display case as though it were on fire.

Jean-Pierre was terrified. He couldn't say a word to his boss, as he would think he was demented and have him locked away in an asylum. Although at that very minute he was so distraught he contemplated quitting his job. Jean-Pierre imagined that he was hallucinating as he continued with his dusting, and was so distressed he finished his shift early, convinced he was going mad. He didn't sleep when he went to bed that night, unable to comprehend what had taken place in the gallery. The dreadful noise reminded him of mourners wailing at an Irish wake.

The next night the same thing happened. However, this time he was ready to confront whatever demons lurked inside the display case, and as soon as he came on duty he walked straight towards it, opened it, and removed the Lapith's head and his torso, placing the marbles on the floor. When the mournful sound stopped he assumed that whatever haunted the marbles had been set free. Jean-Pierre strongly believed that ancient stones held many secrets, that the marbles had a spirit deep within the stone itself. He should know; after all, he knew the marble statues better than anyone else in the world. He spent nearly every night with the statues and he strongly believed that they wanted to get out of the Louvre, to be set free.

Jean-Pierre pondered all these things as he debated what to do about the haunting at the Louvre. He decided to ask the Director to change his shift, perhaps move him to the gallery of Roman Antiquities. Then another incident occurred, confirming his belief that the Greek marbles were enchanted. The following week Jean-Pierre had been dusting the frieze, the newly installed marble panel on the east wall of the gallery and exactly the same thing happened. But this time the noise was so disturbing he cut short his shift, feigning a sore head, which was definitely the case by the time he left work that night, and he refused to do any more dusting. He had considered taking a leave of absence, to visit his dear friend Francesca who lived in the south of France. Would she think he was mad if he told her about the haunting at the Louvre?

Chapter Twenty-Eight
The Marbles are Stolen

'The marbles!' Pippa slammed the phone down. 'Oh my God!' exclaimed the bouncy blonde as she jumped up from her desk, racing out the door of the Director's office.

'Sir!' Pippa rushed down the hall, hoping to catch the Director of the Museum of Classical Antiquities before he left the building.

'Lord Q!' Pippa called to her boss as she leaned over the banister at the top of the stairs. 'The marbles!'

'What about the marbles?' Lord Quimby demanded, impatiently, coming to a halt halfway down the stairs.

'A marble has been stolen!' Pippa whispered, trying to sound shocked, which was rather difficult under the circumstances.

'Good lord!' The Director of the Museum sounded as though he had the wind knocked out of him. 'Bloody hell!' he cursed under his breath.

'I have just had a call from Mr Holloway in the Quimby Gallery, Sir,' said Pippa, with her long, elegant hands pressed to her cheeks, a fake shade of crimson, her long blonde hair falling demurely over her twinset and tight cashmere-clad bosom. 'Mr Pickles discovered the theft when he came on duty this morning. Apparently, Athena's right foot has been stolen!'

'Could it not have gone missing?' asked Lord Quimby.

'The case wasn't broken into, Sir.'

'How odd!' Lord Quimby frowned.

'Mr Pickles said that the display case was found open, Sir.'

'Unlocked?'

'Yes, Sir.'

'Who on earth would want Athena's right foot?'

'I can't imagine, Sir.' Perspiration had broken out on Pippa's nose. She appeared nervous and tugged on her hair.

'Neither can I, Pippa.' 'Thank God the marble wasn't one of ours. The foot came from Lushington's as part of Sir Archibald's collection. Don't tell Lushington's for heaven's sake!'

'No, Sir.'

'Thank you, Pippa,' said the highly acclaimed Director of the Museum of Classical Antiquities, as he padded silently down the stairs in his sturdy bespoke Lobb brogues.

'Bloody hell!' Lord Quimby swore as he carried on down the steps. 'I can't believe it!'

The Director of the Museum was deeply concerned although his anxiety did not in any way reflect on his face. He was on his way to meet with Holloway, the Curator of the Greek and Roman Antiquities Department, concerning another matter, so he would shortly be getting all the details. It looked like an inside job as there was no sign of a break-in. Lord Quimby was reluctant to involve the police. Imagine the publicity! What would the bloody Greeks do if they discovered one of the Parthenon marbles had gone missing? However, the police needed to be called in to investigate at some point if the museum was not capable of solving the mysterious disappearance of the marble itself.

Not to worry.

He thought it most odd as he headed towards the exit. They had never had a theft, *ever,* in the history of the museum.

Never mind, he thought as he glanced at his watch, all will shortly be revealed. He had an hour before meeting his nephew at one o'clock. He had invited Max to join him for a light lunch in the Rotunda, although, upon reflection, he wished he had cancelled the damn thing. He had received several text messages from Max, wanting the keys to the house in St James's Square. He said something about a trunk in the attic.

Max was becoming a nuisance thought Lord Quimby, as he left the west wing of the building, where the main offices were, and walked across the forecourt enjoying the fresh air. He was only *too* aware of his nephew's woes because every time Max came up to London he either begged for lunch or wished to debate the ongoing fate of the Quimby Marbles. At the moment, he deemed the latter inappropriate lunch conversation. He wasn't in the mood to discuss the reunification of the Quimby Marbles to Greece, nor was he feeling charitable. Lunch conversation revolved around the same old thing – Max's mother's financial affairs. Francesca was his late brother's wife, his sister-in-law. *Dreadful woman.* Thank God the *bitch* resided permanently in the south of France. The last he'd heard she was writing a column for some trashy magazine. Max had mentioned something about a book on growing herbs getting published the last time they met. How many times had he heard that over the last twenty years? Francesca's problem was she hadn't a clue how to earn real money. In fact, she could barely manage to support herself. Charles had made a bad decision when he married Francesca. Bloody fool. He hadn't married for money. Francesca failed to make enough money as a journalist to support herself and her son. And, unfortunately, Max's inheritance from his father didn't click in until he was twenty-five. Wise move on behalf of the trustees. However, the trustees had named him as Max's guardian. He paid for Max's school fees, which he deemed reasonable; after all Max had had a place at Harrow and Cambridge even before he was born.

Lord Quimby had agreed to meet his nephew in the Quimby Gallery beside Max's favourite marble, Selene's horse. Whenever he had brought Max to the museum as a little boy he made a beeline for the horse's head. Of course, it was a favourite Quimby Marble, beloved by all. People came from all over the world just to see it. The moon goddess's head was a fantastic drawing card for the museum thought Lord Quimby, as he strode towards the grand entrance leading into the museum. The caryatid was also a favourite, as were all the marbles from Greece. His great-grandfather had been a man of vision. The Quimby Marbles contributed to making the museum the greatest in the world.

No one would have ever guessed that the Director of the Museum of Classical Antiquities was suffering from duress as he strode through the massive double doors into the foyer. He held his head aloof, his bearing ramrod straight. Every step he took was deliberate. Heaven forbid he should put a foot wrong. Four years at Sandhurst had left their mark, amazing after thirty odd years. Strutting through the hallowed halls at Cambridge in his hat and gown had also added a layer of veneer. The 12th Lord Quimby, James Henry Perceval, exuded all of the qualities befitting a true English gentleman; after all, *class* was something you were born with and Lord Q definitely had class.

Such refinement. Such panache. Such breeding.

However, there was a catch. Wealth wasn't the only commodity required to get one through the portcullis. One needed to be a member of that elitist of English clubs, a member of the Landed Gentry, if one had not been blessed, born an aristocrat that is.

The Quimbys had padded through the oak-panelled corridors of power for centuries. Snug or was it smug within the cosseted, nigh impossible to penetrate marble fortress, that penultimate layer of the British Establishment. When you arrived, you were there for life.

This *savoir faire* of Britishness reflected in every fibre of Lord Quimby's being, from the starch in his collar to the turn of his cuff, gold sleeve-links included; and from the gold signet ring always on show, even in the bath, to the pattern and colour of his fine woollen socks. From the cut of his coat to the way he held his knife and fork. And as Lord Quimby hastened towards the gallery he did so with all the impeccable, imperial calmness with which he had lived his privileged life. The tourists crowding the Quimby Gallery that morning could not have imagined a serious crime had taken place in the Greek and Roman Antiquities Department and that the Director of the Museum hadn't a clue how to deal with it.

'It was nothing to worry about,' Lord Quimby said, muttering aloud to himself, as he entered the Quimby Gallery as though he were the sole proprietor of the Panhellenic world; it boasted a Classical facade with a host of pedimental figures carved in marble above the doors and massive Corinthian columns on either side of the entrance. So reminiscent of the mighty Parthenon in Greece, he mused as he strode through the portal with eyes gazing upwards. Lord Quimby despised snobbery of any kind. Yet he kept his steel-blue eyes focused towards the ceiling, well above the common masses, ignoring the security guards and not acknowledging the staff, as the Director was most anxious to escape the Asians, Eurasians, Indians, Americans and a large party from Greece, all anxious to view the marbles.

At the end of the gallery was the Curator of the Classical Greek and Roman Antiquities Department standing in front of the display case, with his hands folded, surrounded by an army of security guards. Holloway looked awful – drawn, pinched around the mouth and what little hair remained was sticking up, as though he had been scratching his head.

Lord Quimby glared at the Curator as if to say, this is your fault. How on earth could he let this happen?

Holloway shrugged. He bit his lip, as though he were a naughty schoolboy.

Lord Quimby turned his head, embarrassed by Mr Holloway's lack of finesse – waving his hands in the air, as though he were flagging a bus. The Curator's complexion matched the marble, unlike his own flushed countenance, after engaging in blood sports in the Home Counties three days running.

Lord Quimby, irritated by Holloway's antics, glanced down, brushed an invisible speck of lint from the sleeve of his finely woven Savile Row coat – albeit a well-preserved version of its former self or was it his father's? He could not recall, after so many years hanging in the same wardrobe, smelling of vintage port and stale Cuban cigars. The Director of the Museum simply could not abide a thing out of place. As Lord Quimby or Lord Q as everyone called him (even Her Royal Highness) had an eye for detail. In fact, Lord Quimby secretly prided himself in knowing the whereabouts of every single artifact in the Classical Greek and Roman Antiquities Department; therefore, there was no need to fuss about the sudden disappearance of Athena's foot. The stone would show up eventually. There was so much stuff in the basement that Holloway could find something else to fill the display case. He doubted Athena's foot would be of interest to the general public. Did it really matter? The tourists wanted to see the larger-than-life marbles, the bigger the better.

However, Lord Quimby *knew* his marbles. His great-great-grandfather had bequeathed the marbles to the museum in the nineteenth century. What an honourable thing to do. He could have kept the marbles all to himself. Lord Q thought for a moment. His mind raced. There were probably a few marbles around somewhere, there must be, although he hadn't the slightest idea where. Not that it mattered. The basement of the museum was jam-packed with marbles, a lot of clutter, really.

Lord Q also prided himself on being a true Classicist. He had boarded at Harrow, of course; didn't all Quimby males? He had received a PhD from Cambridge in History of Art, a doctorate in Greek and Roman studies from Oxford and an Honorary Degree from St Andrews University, because of his family's huge contribution to the Classical antiquities of ancient Greece, after he had written a paper, 'The Return to Order'.

'What's happened here?' Lord Quimby said stiffly.

'That's what we are trying to discern, Sir,' replied the Curator, repressing a shudder, depressed by the dullness and the greyness of the gallery. Had the Curator failed to recall that the Greek statues had been created for the open air and should be exhibited outside? How could a man of his expertise fail to remember such an important detail?

'It's Athena's right foot, Sir!'

'Where the hell is her left foot?'

Holloway rubbed his jaw. His fingers were raw from chewing his nails. 'I don't know, Sir. I can't understand it, Milord, as there is no sign of a break-in.'

'I can see that!' Lord Quimby snapped.

'The other puzzle is: why not take everything in the case? Why steal Athena's right foot? You can see the outline of the foot in the faded green baize, Sir.'

'Find something to put in its place, Holloway.'

'What do you suggest Lord Q?'

'You choose...for God's sake, Holloway. Anything you wish. There are enough marbles in the basement to fill the entire museum threefold!'

'Yes, Milord.'

'If the thief returns tomorrow morning,' said Mr Pickles, standing nearby, 'there won't be any marbles left in the Quimby Gallery.'

'Any thoughts who you think the thief is?' Lord Quimby asked.

'I don't know, Sir,' replied the security guard, crossing his arms, squinting down his nose, obviously in deep contemplation. 'But whoever it is has a great affection for Athena!'

Holloway said, 'It's an inside job, for sure, because the thief either picked the lock or had a key, otherwise the glass would have been smashed.'

Everyone standing round nodded.

'Let us keep this to ourselves,' said Lord Quimby, quietly, 'for the time being, anyway. We really don't need any more publicity at the moment. The Hellenic Society will be arriving at two o'clock sharp, holding a demonstration inside the Quimby Gallery about the fate of the marbles. The Minister of Culture for Greece is in London, and has been on the phone twice this morning, requesting another

345

interview, as the Greeks want their marbles back in time for the grand opening of the New Acropolis Museum. We wouldn't want the Hellenic people to know that we've lost their precious marbles would we, after being the guardian of their marbles for hundreds of years? The marbles no longer belong to the Greek people anyway. So, its hush hush. Understand?'

'Whose are they, Sir?' asked Mr Pickles, 'The Quimby Marbles, I mean. We all know the marbles were pinched from Athens!'

'That makes the stones "Hot Property" if you ask me,' interjected the Head of Security.

'Um Um!' Lord Quimby glanced at his watch, 'So sorry, gentlemen, forgive me, I really must dash.'

'Lord Q, there is another matter. The security guards on night shift are refusing to guard the caryatid and we have had to cordon off the gallery. In fact, two guards have quit. The guards think that something odd is going on. We have a major problem here, Sir.'

'You sort it out, Holloway; after all, it's your department!'

'I'm meeting my nephew, Max, for lunch,' Lord Quimby was mumbling. 'I hope he doesn't keep me waiting.'

'Max? Why, he has been here for hours!' Holloway enthused, smiling for the first time that morning, or was it days? 'I saw him wandering through the halls when I came into the building. It must have been about eight o'clock.'

Lord Quimby walked away. He didn't listen to what the man was saying. He could not have cared less. His thoughts were elsewhere. Until today the fate of the Greek marbles was secure within the bosom of the British Establishment, snug inside the Museum of Classical Antiquities, exactly where they should be. Now, he wasn't so sure, even though he had the entire British Establishment behind him.

Lord Quimby could see Max standing in front of the horse's head. He appeared to be having a word with the statue because he was standing looking directly at the horse, waving his finger.

'Uncle!' enthused Max, as he held out his hand, offering up one of his famous smiles that stretched the full length of the gallery. 'I was just having a word with my favourite marble, as I'm planning to help it escape out of this mouldy old place!'

'Honestly, Maximilian,' quipped Lord Quimby, taking his nephew's large hand in his own, pumping it up and down. 'Talking to stones, are we, really?'

'Yes, Uncle, I was. I was asking Selene's horse when it wanted to go home, to Athens where it belongs. In fact, I was about to ask you the same thing. Don't you think it's time you sent Selene's horse home to Athens?'

'No, Maximilian,' said Lord Quimby, ignoring his nephew's comments. 'Selene's horse is a major attraction. Although, I do question your sanity, as talking to stones makes me wonder.'

'Well, the statue needed someone to talk to it, don't you agree, Uncle? An enlightened conversation would not go amiss.'

When there was no response from the Director of the Museum Max asked, 'I haven't caught you at a bad time, have I?'

Max sensed something was wrong. His uncle seemed to be distracted, which wasn't that unusual when he came to think about it.

'No. No. Of course not, dear boy,' replied Lord Quimby, as though Max was still eight years old.

'Are the statues giving you trouble, Uncle? Causing a fuss? Wanting to escape? I can't blame them, as it's such a dreary place, depressing actually.'

347

'Must you, Max?'

Max and his uncle made their way slowly through the gallery, as they always did.

'The marbles look dreadfully unhappy, mournful, somewhat sad, don't you think, Uncle,' said Max, rubbing it in. 'I can tell, even though they don't have heads. Take Iris, for example. Imagine how happy Iris would look with her head!'

'Exactly my boy!' enthused Lord Quimby, 'I have been hounding the museum in Athens to send Iris' head to us for years!'

Max shot back, 'Haven't you got it wrong, Uncle? Shouldn't you be sending Iris' torso over to the museum in Athens...after all, she belongs to the Greeks not to us.'

'Hardly!' Lord Quimby laughed nervously. He did not appreciate Max's humour. A reply was not forthcoming. Max was used to his behaviour, as he used silence to put people off.

'A girl needs her head, Uncle, Athena needs her arms and legs and foot!'

Max felt the tension between them building in the stale musty, air-conditioned atmosphere. He could feel the tension emitting through the fabric of his uncle's bespoke pinstriped suit as he scanned the metopes at either end of the gallery, the enormous frieze, fifty-six slabs in all, running along the walls, inside-out of course. He glimpsed the enormous chunks of marble standing on plinths, like body parts, cadavers from a car crash. Those statues with faces looked glum, desolate – rather forlorn. Max wanted to shout at the top of his lungs, *These statues belong in Greece, in the New Acropolis Museum in Athens!*'

Helen's words screamed inside his head. There was no point in broaching the subject, he had argued with the man every time they met about the return of the marbles to Greece and his uncle had a quick retort waiting every time. Something to do with the trustees and 'the power vested in them'; what does the garble mean? He had no idea but didn't think it made much sense. But what did he know? Max could not stand there a moment longer without becoming enraged and he snapped, while extracting the drawing of the west pediment from his pocket.

'Uncle,' said Max, thrusting Helen's sketch in his face. 'Have you ever seen any of these pieces of marble outlined in the drawing?'

Lord Quimby glanced at the drawing. 'No, I can't say that I have.'

'How could they disappear off the face of the earth?'

'I haven't a clue, Max!'

'What happened to Athena's right foot?'

'Who cares, Max?' said Lord Quimby as he bowed his head, unable to look his nephew in the eye.

'Helen thinks that the pieces of Athena's aegis are here in the museum. She also believes that the statues missing from the pediments are here somewhere in the UK. She doesn't know where but she suspects they might be hiding in someone's cellar. This is because the statues went missing at the same time as great-great-great-grandfather took the marbles down from the Parthenon. Hermes' head is a good example. We have his torso but what happened to his head, that which he had the day he was removed from the Parthenon. The examples go on and on. Have you ever seen Athena's head or Poseidon's head, Uncle, or chunks of Athena's aegis?'

'Of course not!'

Suddenly the stroll came to a full stop, as did the conversation, the silence biting into the air, thick with deception, lies, avarice...

Max couldn't stand another minute.

'Do you have the keys to the house? I haven't much time. I'm catching the train back to Cambridge as soon as I'm finished at the house.'

Why couldn't he call his uncle by name? Uncle Jimmy. Uncle James, Uncle Jamie, perhaps? Nothing sounded right, had the proper ring to it somehow. As his uncle searched his pockets for the house keys Max asked:

'Would you like to know something really amazing about the horse's head, Uncle?'

There was no response.

'I'll tell you anyway. Helen told me that a young slave carved the horse's head. A girl – imagine! Can you believe it? It's extraordinary!'

'Don't be daft!' retorted Lord Quimby, as his eyebrows inched upwards towards the ceiling.

'I'm not daft!' cried Max. 'According to the Greeks Selene's horse was carved by a young slave girl. Her name was Syrinx. She was named after a famous water nymph, as she had been found by the water's edge by a brilliant stone-carver, Nikodimos. Whom I might add carved several of the statues in the Quimby Gallery.'

'That is the most preposterous story I have ever heard,' spat Lord Quimby, pursing his lips, obviously annoyed.

'I have lots more legends. Would you care to hear another legend... Uncle...about the metopes?'

'No, I most certainly would not,' replied the extremely disgruntled lord.

Max was not being put off and stood pointing to the metope on the far wall. 'See that metope, Uncle, of the centaur dragging off the young girl? Well that metope was carved by a sculptor without thumbs?'

'Maximilian! Really! How on earth could a sculptor carve marble without thumbs? Why, it would be impossible!'

'Well, it's a true story, Uncle,' said Max, as he held his shoulders back, straining his jacket that he had outgrown a few years back. 'Greek legends always contain a smidgen of truth. Would you not agree, Uncle?'

No response.

'Don't you think its about time we sent all the metopes and the marble statues back to Athens? Where they rightfully belong?'

'No, I most certainly do not!' spat Lord Quimby, holding out the house keys. 'Really Maximilian, I'm beginning to wonder whether Helen is the right sort of girl for you. She shouldn't be telling you such nonsense. Imagine the reaction from the public if this sort of rubbish got out. The press would have a field day!'

Max stared at the statues. Truth stared back. Truth was a strange thing, he thought angrily, repeating Keats famous line: '"Beauty is truth, truth beauty, that is all ye know on earth, and all ye need to know." Do you recall this line from "Ode on a Grecian Urn"?'

'Of course, Max.'

Max knew Helen was telling the truth. He believed the stories surrounding the stone-carvers, he thought they were fascinating and he wanted to know more.

'I am sorry, Max,' said Lord Quimby, apologetically. 'I shan't have time for lunch. Something has come up. Here...take the keys.'

Lord Quimby handed Max the keys to the house in St James's Square. 'As I said in my text, Matilda is in Spain. The house is empty. If you choose to stay over, you will find your room ready for you. When you leave, please leave the keys under the Grecian urn by the coach house.'

'Yes, Uncle,' said Max stuffing the keys inside his coat pocket.

'Well, then, I *shan't* keep you,' said Max, as he picked up his backpack leaning against the marble plinth of Selene's horse. 'Thank you. I promise not to make a mess. Like the last time...'

'Yes...um...um...fine...' Lord Quimby was mumbling again as he glanced at his watch for the hundredth time. 'There are tins of lager in the fridge...they've been there for ages.'

'Thank you, Uncle,' said Max, as he tugged on the collar of his jacket, which was without doubt the rattiest Barbour in all Christendom. He had debated bequeathing his Barbour jacket to the Quimby Gallery. But he couldn't bear to part with it. Not just yet. It was a relic from his days at Harrow and he loved it.

'Good heavens!' Lord Quimby exclaimed, as he watched Max struggling with his backpack. 'What on earth have you got in there, gold bricks? It's so heavy-looking, Maximilian!'

'Textbooks,' added Max in a flash, 'exams coming up. Sometimes the train is late.'

'How did you manage to get past security?' asked Lord Quimby, rubbing his chinless chin.

'Uncle, really! The security guards have known me since birth!'

'Yes, I guess you are right,' said Lord Quimby, waving a dismissive hand, as though he were letting the dog out.

'Goodbye, Maximilian.'

'Goodbye, Uncle.'

Max was left standing in the Quimby Gallery trying not to smirk. As he did so he watched his uncle stride towards the exit, thinking his uncle was the perfect man for the job. He was, after all, a man of great taste, moral rectitude, as they say (whoever they were), and his uncle certainly had integrity. He knew right from wrong. Integrity was one of three words engraved in Latin on the Quimby coat-of-arms. In fact, integrity was so deeply woven into the moral fabric of Lord Quimby's English soul that it was impossible for him to think otherwise. However, his uncle's integrity was about to be tested. When he discovered what a terrible caper had been committed right under his aquiline nose.

Why, it was positively shocking.

—◌◍—

Max had one last visit to make before he left the museum. It was impossible not to without having a private word with Kore. As you can imagine, the conversation was similar in content to the one he had had with the horse's head.

For whatever reason, the statue of Kore stood in an anteroom. Why this was, Max was unsure, although there must have been a good reason for doing so. By this time Max's backpack was weighing him down but he carried on nonetheless. As he approached the chamber he noticed that it had been cordoned off. A security guard was sitting on a stool nearby and he asked:

'Pardon me, Sir,' said Max, 'I would very much like to view the caryatid.' He didn't want to add, 'and have a conversation with the statue', as he might be taken away in a straitjacket.

'And I see that the statue has been cordoned off for some reason. Why is that?'

Max could see no earthly reason for not being allowed into see Kore. 'How do I arrange to get access?'

'I'm sorry, Sir,' said the guard, flatly. 'No one is allowed in to see the caryatid.'

'Why not?' asked Max.

The guard squirmed on his stool. 'The security guards have refused to guard the statue and I for one have also refused!'

'What on earth are you talking about?' demanded Max, impatiently.

'There's something spooky going on in there at night!' The security guard shuddered.

'Spooky? What do you mean?'

There's a ghost in the chamber.'

'A ghost!' exclaimed Max. Max didn't know what to think. Although one thing was for sure, his pack was getting heavier by the minute.

Meanwhile, people were gathering by the cordoned off anteroom, peering over the rope, trying to see Kore.

'The gallery is closed, folks!' said the guard.

'Closed? The gallery can't be closed. We've come all the way from Athens to see our Kore!' exclaimed a man holding on to his wife's hand.

Max stood back and listened.

'How can you turn us away?' cried the wife standing beside the man. 'Kore belongs to us!'

'Can't you make allowances?' Max asked the security guard.

'We have come all the way from Athens to see our beloved marble statue and we are not allowed through the cordon!'

'This is disgraceful!' shouted Max. If you wanted to be heard you had to shout. It's what one had to do every so often in life. In fact, he shouted so loud all the people in the Quimby Gallery gathered round.

'I am truly sorry!' cried Max. 'Kore belongs to you!' He was furious. 'One day the statue of your beloved Kore will be returned to Greece – I intend to make sure of it!'

Everyone in the gallery gathered close to Max. The family from Greece held on to Max's hands as they clung together.

Max refrained from revealing his identity, ashamed to be a Quimby for the first time in his life.

'We believe we will never see Kore again,' said the woman with obvious resignation.

'Believe me, it will happen!' said Max, as he shook the lady's hand, then walked away from the anteroom. Not only weighed down by what lay hidden inside his backpack, but also by the terrible injustice that had been going on for two hundred years.

He turned and walked away. For the first time in his life he understood what it meant to have a cause that was bigger than himself, something worth fighting for. Suddenly, his life had meaning. He resolved to do everything in his power to help the Greek people get their marbles back. After all, it was only right that he, a Quimby, should be responsible for returning the marbles, as it was a Quimby who had plundered the stones in the first place. He could no longer bear to see the right stifled by the wrong.

The Museum of Classical Antiquities had a lot to answer for, thought Max, as he caught a half-a-glimpse of Kore, one of the most exquisite marbles in the world, standing alone and forlorn in her prison. Because that is what it was – a prison cell. 'Kore looks as though she were in exile,' he whispered to himself, with absolute conviction.

'Do not despair, Kore. Soon you will be set free. I am going to get you out of this drab, dismal place. The schoolchildren in Athens are waiting for your return!'

Chapter Twenty-Nine
Max Meets Murgatroyd the Tortoise

The bus ride from the Museum of Classical Antiquities took for ever. The rush-hour traffic clogged every artery. The London bus crawled along Piccadilly at a snail's pace until coming to a wrenching halt directly in front of Fortnum & Mason. It would have been faster to walk, Max thought, and if it hadn't been pouring with rain, he would have. Max leapt off the bus, greeted by the deluge and gale-force winds, and within seconds he was soaked through to the skin, as the wax had worn off his jacket years ago. He didn't have far to go to St James's Square.

It took every ounce of strength not to turn and run when he caught sight of the house silhouetted against a dull grey sky; an enormous brooding monster on the opposite side of the square. Every blasted time was the same upon returning to the house, once his boyhood home.

Every damn time.

Grief tugged unmercifully at his heart, grief that should have faded long ago. What was wrong with him? He couldn't still be grieving for his father, his childhood, his mother, a boyhood that got cut short through no fault of his own? Whatever the reason there wasn't a blasted thing he could do about it.

Max rushed up the steps, and shoved the key in the lock. The years slipped away. He was eight years old again. He flung open the massive oak door painted in shiny black enamel, of course. It sported a magnificent brass lion's head doorknocker that he could tell had recently been polished as he caught a whiff of Brasso in the damp air. Max walked into the house where he had spent the happiest years of his childhood.

Don't be bitter. Harry keeps telling you bitterness is a useless emotion.

Max flicked on the overhead light, illuminating the magnificent interior of one of the most important collections of art in London – an aesthete's dream.

Ghosts of the past rushed out to greet him, and grab him by the throat. Max shied away. *Coward...* He shivered. The house was colder inside than out. Typical. Max had no wish to linger and he hurried down the hall, leaving wet footprints on the cherry-red carpet. There were several enormous grand salons on his right and the Sculpture Gallery running the full length of the house on his left. Max ignored both. He was a coward, remember. He wished he had worn blinkers. Nevertheless, he continued on towards the back of the house. En route, he stopped briefly at the foot of the grand circular staircase. He could not bring himself to venture upstairs where his bedroom was as he had no wish to revisit his lost childhood.

Enormous gilt-edged portraits of the Quimby dynasty lined the silk-covered walls of the stairwell. Marble statues filled every apse, niche and plinth. Colossal Corinthian marble columns reached twenty-five feet above his head. So many imposing portraits of the Quimby family hung on the walls one could not fail to be impressed as the 'National Gallery' continued up three flights of stairs. The portraits had hung on the walls for centuries and would do so until the walls fell down, because the trustees of the 9th Lord Quimby's estate had a say over everything in the house. Even the positioning of the family portraits of long-dead souls who mysteriously came to life in the flickering light of a mammoth chandelier, dripping in Italian Murano crystal.

The magnificent full-length portrait of the 9th Lord Quimby – Max's great-great-great-grandfather, the epitome of bloodstock and lineage – held court at the top of the stairs. However, the painting was totally out of character for an English portrait as George Henry Montague Perceval looked slightly too relaxed, seated at a games table, with his long legs stretched out in front and two Russian wolfhounds snoozing at his feet. The lofty Parthenon loomed largely in the background and numerous marble slabs and a metope leaned against the garden wall. He recognised the metope of the Lapiths fighting the grisly centaurs; it was exactly the same metope that hung in the Quimby Gallery.

Something prompted Max into taking a closer look and he raced up the stairs. This time he looked at the portrait from an entirely different perspective, after all one of his Cambridge Mods was Greek and Roman architecture. He had also been to Athens many times and he had seen the Parthenon for himself. Many items in the foreground looked familiar; however, there were many he did not remember. A rather noble looking bust of a Greek god with leonine curls and a broken nose sat propped against an overstuffed hassock. Why couldn't he recall it? Or the bust of Hermes who sat on a marble plinth – he would recognise Hermes anywhere because of his youthful expression and his winged hat. Why weren't the busts in the Quimby Gallery? What had become of Hermes' head?

Beside Lord Quimby's portrait hung a painting of vivacious Vrai Viviette standing in her garden at La Redousse, (the same house his mother lived in). Vrai Viviette appeared a kindly woman with an agreeable countenance and a noble bearing, unlike the petulant fury reflecting on the faces of the women standing beside her with funny hairdos. Obviously, it wasn't fashionable at the time to smile, thought Max while scowling at the grand ladies dressed in their outrageous frocks. Max had seen enough. He ran back down the stairs, stopping briefly to examine the portrait of his great-great-grandfather's family with a title etched on a gold plaque. '10th Lord Quimby, Maximilian Henry Perceval and his family.'

Max stood back taking in the full canvas, a bucolic landscape similar to that of a Constable, without the haystack. The 10th Lord Quimby was seated on a fine-looking horse, surrounded by dogs, Cavalier King Charles Spaniels that were racing around the noble steed. Lord Quimby appeared a jolly fellow, as though he enjoyed life. The painting included two young boys primly dressed in sailor suits, who were playing with a large tortoise lumbering across the lawn. Max grinned. The enormous creature was totally incongruous although it was popular to have exotic pets at the time, just as Byron did.

Max knew the story well. The 10th Lord Quimby had been a student at the Royal Academy. When he was twenty-one he had been awarded the King's Medal for Architecture and spent the next three years in Greece drawing antiquities, ruins of the ancient world. Upon his return to England he had rebuilt the Shambles, the finest example of Greek Revival in Britain. However, young Maximilian met with tragedy as he drowned while swimming in the sea at Piraeus; his body was never found. Max shuddered. He didn't like the macabre story although he did wonder why Lord Quimby's wife had been excluded from the portrait.

At the end of the Great Hall a small, rather insignificant painting of a young woman hung above the doorframe. He did not ever recall seeing the picture, not much more than a hastily drawn sketch with a *of no importance* sort of feel to it. Max peered at the picture, staring through the lengthening shadows wondering why the young woman was deemed unworthy of a gold name plate as her name had been hastily scratched in the wood.

'Daphne' – that was all. Who was this startlingly beautiful young woman with an almost ethereal quality about her, as a penumbra of light illuminated her entire face? It was unlike anything he had ever seen before. It was startling. He wanted to know more about Daphne...

At the end of the Great Hall was the staircase leading up to the airing cupboard. When he reached the second landing he threw open the door, to be met by a gust of stale air. The cupboard was lined with shelves piled with freshly ironed linen and several pulleys hung down from the ceiling, much needed equipment when drying wet laundry on damp days. A naked light bulb dangled from the rafters like a python about to strike, Max thought, as he stared into the miasma of dust, mould, tinged with camphor, lavender, withered mice and rising damp. He knew the cupboard well as it had been his secret hiding place when feeling rather sorry for his visceral indelible self, keeping out of the way of Nanny or the servants. The airing cupboard was his shelter when he was a boy, a place to hide from the world. In the corner of the airing cupboard was the trunk.

Shit. Bugger. Damn!

The trunk was empty except for a dirty towel scrunched up in a ball and an enormous tortoise shell lying upside down in the bottom. Max slammed the lid, his memory had failed him. He sat down on the top of the trunk and hung his head, as self-pity had become a habit of late. What had happenend to the chunk of Athena's aegis? Then, something caused Max to pull on the towel, and in doing so, the small chunk of stone with the figure of Phobos carved in it fell out on to the floor.

'Helen – wait until you see *this* my love!'

Max wrapped the stone up tightly in the towel, as though it were made of gold; as he did so, however, he glanced at the tortoise shell, which suddenly reminded of his affection for endangered species. The shell had once upon a time housed a living creature. He couldn't leave the tortoise shell in the trunk, could he? If nothing else the shell would spruce up his digs, a sort of conversation piece. Harry would love it. Max gathered the tortoise shell up in his arms, as it was that big, and wanting to see more held the carapace up close to the swinging light bulb.

'Hang on a minute!'

Murgatroyd had been scratched on the underside of the shell. *'Murgatroyd! The tortoise's name was Murgatroyd? Never!'*

He could not imagine calling a tortoise Murgatroyd. He could not imagine calling a donkey Chaos either. Wait until he told his mother about Murgatroyd. She would definitely understand. However, as Max turned the shell right-side-up, a small package fell out of the hole where once the tortoise's head had been and it lay on the floor, scattering the dust and the bits of brittle sealing wax on to his jeans.

As he picked up the bundle of letters neatly tied with faded red ribbon, he noticed the seal matched his own signet ring. Max sat down on the trunk, untied the ribbon and gently flicked through the letters written in an elaborate English scrawl and addressed to 'Lady Vrai Viviette Perceval'. Further down the pile the handwriting changed dramatically. The letters were addressed to the same person although the scribe was a lot younger as a deliberate attempt had been made to make every letter perfect, just like a young scholar. The last two letters were entirely different as the scrawl had such flourish he imagined the writer was the author of an illuminated manuscript.

Max was beginning to feel the cold and he very quickly stuffed the letters inside the shell and hugging the towel and the shell tight, hurried back down the stairs. He was starving. A packet of crisps was all he'd eaten all day. While en route to the kitchen his thoughts returned to the last time he had raided a pantry. It had been three years ago, Ladies Day at Royal Ascot. After the races Max and Harry crashed a party next door. One good thing about ol' Harry was he really knew how to *pull* the girls and after copious Pimms Max felt obliged to return the favour by inviting half of St James's Square back to the house. His memory failed him completely after that – well, not quite. How could he forget standing in the pantry with this gorgeous girl, wolfing down cold baked beans and warm lager then passing out on the floor, only to wake the next morning with a vile headache and this Essex babe lying next to him with her long slender legs wrapped around him. It was none other than Pippa – his uncle's PA. He nearly died of embarrassment. He blushed just thinking about their tryst in the butler's pantry. Pippa wasn't the least offended and had since become good friends. She was his mole. Essex girls were up for anything. So, he had involved Pippa in his latest caper. Sadly, there was no Pippa or Helen to share his tin of baked beans, Max thought miserably, as he whizzed past his only companion, a cold-blooded sculpture of the ravishing Venus de Milo.

By the time Max had stuffed his face with cold baked beans, minus the toast, as he couldn't be bothered to defrost the bread from the freezer – Harrow all over again. After he tidied up the kitchen, quaffed the last can of lager in the fridge, Big Ben sounded, reminding him that the last train left Kings Cross in less than an hour and his wet clothes were still in the dryer. Max had stripped down to his T-shirt and his boxers with zero elastic and faded blue elephants. He checked the dryer in the laundry room. As his clothes were still damp he padded through the halls in his bare feet en route to the Sculpture Gallery where he had left his jacket hanging over the firescreen – which was a totally absurd thing to do without a fire.

As he approached the massive double doors leading into the Sculpture Gallery Max shuddered violently. He suddenly felt as though he were walking into a mausoleum, a burial place for dead sculptures, not dissimilar, in fact, to the way he felt in the Quimby Gallery. He had placed the tortoise shell on the mantlepiece and as he had a few minutes to spare until his socks dried he decided to have a brief scan through the letters. He was desperately in need of some entertainment to distract his thoughts, as those blasted demons had their harpy claws around his throat strangling him. Max grabbed a throw from the sofa and huddling down under the blanket started reading.

26th of April 1812

Dear Aunt Vrai Viviette,

It is with a heavy heart that I write this unhappiest of missives. As you cannot possibly imagine the destruction, desolation and despair I found waiting upon my return to my beloved Athens.

Sadly, the lofty Parthenon resembled a pile of bleached bones. Shamefully, where there were once metopes and triglyphs there are ugly, gaping holes, like an old hag without teeth. Such hastily chiselled plunder. The magnificent marble frieze has been destroyed. Almost all of the marble statues of the Greek gods and goddesses once standing in the east and west pediments are gone. Missing. To say nothing of the interior frieze on the cella.

How on earth can I begin to capture the glory of ancient Greece when there is hardly anything of her glory days left standing on the Acropolis? My heart bleeds. I cannot but weep, dear Aunt Vrai Viviette. Do we realise what we have done by plundering the mighty Parthenon? I don't think so. We haven't the faintest idea. We should be shot. We have committed a dreadful crime. I stand before the Parthenon weeping while those self-righteous boobies at home swoon over the marbles, Greek statues adorning our palaces, our stuffy drawing rooms. My soul weeps as I glimpse the empty spaces, where once the magnificent statues once stood. Where is Poseidon and Athena and Hermes and the enormous horse, and the three marble heads of Selene's horses missing from the east pediment?

Forgive me, Auntie, I can write no more, I am overcome with grief, sorrow weighs heavily upon my heart. Has uncle been released from prison? Please ask him what he knows about the marbles.

Your most loving nephew,
Maximilian

Scanning madly, Max opened the next letter in the pile.

1815

Dearest Aunt Vrai Viviette,

Amidst the shame, the chaos and the pain I am proud
to announce that my wife will be accompanying me
on my homeward journey to England. Daphne and I
were married last week, on the beautiful, enchanting
Greek island of Patmos, as she finally consented to
become my wife, after months of my persistence.
You will absolutely adore my Greek goddess as Daphne
is stunningly beautiful. She comes from the north
and her hair and features are finer, much fairer.
She will make you extremely proud dear auntie. The
benevolence of the gods continues to surprise me,
as my darling wife came to me quite by accident,
when I rescued her as she was being sewn up in a
canvas sack by Turkish officials after being wrongly
accused of a most hideous crime, and about to be
taken out to sea and thrown overboard. The thought
of such a cruel deed fills me with revulsion, as does
the plunder of the mighty Parthenon... Hopefully our
first child will be born in England....

Signed, once again,
Your humble servant,
Your loving nephew,
Maximilian

CHAPTER TWENTY-NINE

The letters fell from Max's hand onto the floor, his thoughts whirling madly round and round in his head. He chose another letter, written in much younger handwriting.

Athens, Greece
July 1802

Dearest Auntie,

How are you? I hope you are well and the refurbishment of the house is not causing you too much stress. Although I have felt nothing but distress since my last letter to you, Friday last.

Oh Dearest Auntie, I have been suffering terribly from the worst nightmares, every night, for the last week, and they are so horrific that I am frightened to go to sleep at night, fearful I will experience another horrid nightmare. In my dream, I imagine I am actually a Lapith boy about to be butchered by a grisly centaur. As this is the ugly scene I witnessed from afar, last week, as two marble metopes were being taken down from the south side of the Parthenon. When I awoke I realised that it wasn't centaurs who were being bludgeoned to death, it was workmen on Uncle's Dig. So, Auntie, you can well imagine my distress, watching Uncle's beloved Parthenon being destroyed by the formatori and, sadly, during his absence

Of course, everyone in Athens wept Do you think Uncle would mind terribly if I shot the men? Because that's exactly what I would like to do, as he is not here. Uncle has been called away to Constantinople, on business, and I don't know who to tell or what to do. I tried to intervene, however, Mr Dashiell Hamilton sent me away. You always know what to do, Auntie, so, please help stop the plunder, sort out this dreadful mess for Uncle.

Forgive me, Auntie dear, I must hurry. I do so wish to get my letter in the post-bag. I believe the British Naval cargo ship is leaving for England at noon and my donkey can't go very fast. Although you are far away, I pray that you can help.

Everything is fine. I am having an amazing time in Athens, although we are expected to leave for home very soon.

Your most loving obedient servant,
Your nephew,
Maximilian

Max could not believe what he was reading as he threw his jacket over his shoulder and clutching Murgatroyd's shell under his arm – the creature who had revealed so much to him in the last half hour – and raced out of the gallery. He could not have left the house without the shell; however, to secretly harbour affection for a long-dead tortoise called Murgatroyd was madness.

—◌ ◌—

The whistle blew. The train was pulling out of the station as Max flung himself down on the first empty seat that he came to. The bright lights of London flashed by amidst a blur of North London suburbia. His heavy backpack with its valuable contents and Murgatroyd neatly wrapped in the towel lay next to him on the seat. With any luck no one would want to sit next to him, as he was in no mood for polite conversation. Max sat with his long legs thrust under the seat in front of him, shrugging inside his damp jacket, huddling down in his seat, the vile odour reeking of a life he didn't want to get close to. Max felt sick, as the smell emitting from the loo at the back of the train was making him nauseous. His thoughts raced. He glanced at the bulky towel, chuckling to himself.

Max, old man, Harry will think you are a nutter.

His thoughts returned again and again to the house in St James's Square. It had become a shrine to the Quimby family; it no longer served a purpose other than to house the long, forgotten ghosts of the glorious past or rather relics of a vainglorious past of the Quimby dynasty. Just like the collection of marbles in the Museum of Classical Antiquities.

Max loathed the house. He never wanted to return. Houses were for families and he wasn't fortunate enough to have a family. He had relatives but that wasn't *his* family. The Shambles no longer belonged to his family either.

His thoughts drifted as he looked at the bulky towel, finding it impossible to believe what truly astonishing secrets Murgatroyd had revealed to him – secrets that one day would shock the world. Dare he reveal all? He wasn't sure, although he was absolutely convinced about one thing.

'Murgatroyd! We are going to Athens in May. It is where you and I belong', said Max to the empty shell, as though the tortoise was still alive inside his shell, understood every word. 'We all need a home, old man.'

His thoughts returned to the Quimby Marbles, representing what it meant to be British; yet for the first time in his life he couldn't have cared less about the Quimby Gallery and even less about the marbles than he could have possibly imagined. Marbles weren't just marbles. They were a force to be reckoned with. Perhaps the stones had a destiny. Perhaps the marbles wanted to go home to Athens, like Murgatroyd, thought Max gently patting the towel.

Happier childhood memories of his very first visit to Athens when he was a small boy returned. He remembered how he had stood beneath the mighty Parthenon in blazing hot sunlight, holding on to his mother's hand, telling her in no uncertain terms that Grandpa Quimby had to glue the Parthenon back together. Then he had the nerve to add as he stood with his hands on his hips, 'Every man in England should lend a hand!'

Well, thought Max, perhaps it was time for all the men in England to help stick the Parthenon back together, and it just so happened that his uncle was in possession of the glue.

Suddenly, Max felt hopeful about his future. He was deeply in love with Helen and prayed she felt the same. He couldn't wait to see her, to hold her close. He was looking forward to celebrating her birthday. He needed a special present. Helen had everything money could buy. He must look for something original…

Chapter Thirty
Man is Made of Stone

'Right. Let us begin from where we left off yesterday.' Mr Hunt sat on top of his desk, like he always did, and swung his right leg back and forth, like he always did. The leg-swinging had become a ritual that continued on throughout the lecture. Max had no idea why his Classics professor always sat on top of his desk. Perhaps he had an aversion to chairs, or the leg-swinging alleviated some of the stress incurred while trying to teach a vaguely intellectual bunch of students the Classics?

'It's time to delve deeper into the meaning of another few verses of the great Publius Ovidius Naso. What is *Deucalion and Pyrrha* really about?' Mr Hunt asked the class as he ruffled the pages of Ovid's *Metamorphoses*.

'Yes. Fletcher.'

Fletcher mumbled as he lowered his hand, 'Stones, Sir.'

'Please, speak up Fletcher. Speak up!'

'Yes, Sir.'

'What about the stones?' Mr Hunt asked, with more leg-swinging, only with much more gusto this time.

Several hands shot up.

'Yes, Ajmera.'

'The stones represent bones, Sir,' Tarang replied from the back of the lecture room, 'the bones of man, Sir.'

'Yes Ajmera. Good,' enthused Mr Hunt, as though Ajmera had just discovered an oil well outside in the playing field.

'Now, do we have an iconoclastic reader among us today with energy, verbal wit and subversive intelligence willing to read a few verses of Ovid?'

The students kept their hands lowered.

'Longfield-Jones, feeling up to it?'

'Not really, Sir.'

'Why not?'

'Trouble concentrating, Sir,' replied Longfield-Jones, rubbing his furrowed brow, pretending his head hurt. 'I have been burning the midnight oil, while debating the benefits of residing permanently in Greece on YouTube.'

'Care to enlighten us, Longfield-Jones?'

'Not really, Sir.'

Harry collapsed in a fit laughter.

'I fail to see the humour, Mr Longfield-Jones. Something worth sharing with the class? I thought not.'

Mr Hunt scanned the room. 'Perceval, how is your concentration this morning? Head bothering you? If not, perhaps you would be kind enough to read for us today. I'm sure the class will be delighted.'

'Yes, Sir.' Max rose to his feet amidst a cacophony of shuffling textbooks and nervous coughs.

'Please, continue on from where we left off yesterday, Perceval.'

Max cleared his throat, delaying the inevitable.

'They were long dumbfounded. Pyrrha was first to break the silence and voice her protest aloud. She refused to obey the goddess... Our mighty mother is Earth. I believe what is meant by her bones are stones on her body, and these we are bidden to cast behind us... stepping out boldly, scattered some stones behind their backs, as the oracle ordered. Who would believe what ensued, if it wasn't confirmed by tradition? The stones started to lose their essential hardness, slowly to soften, and then to assume a new shape. They soon grew larger and gathered a nature more gentle than stone. An outline of human form could be seen, not perfectly clear, like a rough-hewn statue partially carved from the marble and not yet properly finished. But still, the part of the stones which consisted of earth and contained some moisture was turned into flesh; the solid inflexible matter was changed into bones; and the veins of the rock into veins of blood. In a moment of time, by the will of the gods, the stones that were thrown from the hands of a man were transformed to take on the appearance of men, and women were fashioned anew from those that were thrown by a woman. And so our race is a hard one; we work by the sweat of our brow, and bear the unmistakable marks of our stony origin—'

Mr Hunt interrupted Max. 'Thank you, Perceval. Thank you. Enough for today.'

Twenty arms suddenly shot up into the air.

'Sir?' asked a girl seated in the front row. 'Does this mean we are all made of stone?'

'What do you think, Allardice?' Mr Hunt was swinging both legs, banging the front of his desk.

'I find it hard to believe,' said Allardice fiddling with strands of her long dark hair, 'that bones last as long as stones.'

'Anyone wish to debate this?' Mr Hunt asked, as he removed his spectacles, breathed hot breath on the glass, polished his spectacles on the sleeve of his gown.

'Yes, Perceval, do you have something to add?'

'Well, Sir,' said Max, 'actually, Sir, I can relate to the stone theory, in principle, because, while I was rummaging around in the house in London last weekend...' Max suddenly lost his confidence and started stuttering.

'For heaven's sake, Perceval, please continue!' Mr Hunt was inching closer and closer to the edge of his desk.

'And, well, Sir, I was sitting in the living room, which isn't really a living room but a gallery, the Sculpture Gallery to be exact, and well, Sir, as I sat on the piano stool...I noticed a small marble shaped exactly like a hand – that my father used as a paperweight – resting on a pile of sheet music. When I picked up the marble I noticed tiny pink and blue threads running through the stone, just like veins in my hand, and the marble was so smooth, it felt exactly the same as my own hand, like flesh, as I rubbed the marble.'

'Thank you, Perceval,' Mr Hunt said, 'most enlightening, most enlightening.'

Then another hand shot up.

'For heaven's sake, Hastings, what is it?'

'Sir,' said Hastings, 'marble is metamorphic. When the stone is first quarried, it is soft; however, over time – I'm not sure exactly how long – the stone gradually hardens. Hence, marble has the ability to change from one state to another.'

'Yes, Perceval, what is it?'

'I brought the paperweight with me,' enthused Max, as he extracted the small marble from inside his coat pocket and striding up to the front of the classroom, placed the small smooth stone into Mr Hunt's hand.

'Sir, I believe we came from stone...because I weigh eleven stone... stone, Sir!'

'Longfield-Jones, please do not interrupt the class.'

'Sorry, Sir!'

Lots of snickering followed. 'Perhaps we should ask the Rolling Stones what they think, Sir?'

'Please, Longfield-Jones, enough!'

'When you look closely at the marble it does look very similar to human flesh...and it's veined in blue or red...exactly the same as our veins,' said Mr Hunt, whose right leg suddenly stopped swinging. Perhaps his leg had something to say?

'We can't be made of stone!' echoed in the classroom.

Mr Hunt stood up. 'Settle down class. Settle down.'

'Mr Hunt, Sir!' said Harry, from his seat. 'As I am a cerebral man, a man of science, I prefer to think like a scientist. I need facts. Mr Smith gave a lecture last week on quantum physics or quantum theory and he said that everything in our universe is connected to everything else. This happened because of the very nature of matter, or did he say structure? He also said that everything in the universe is made up of protons, neutrons and electrons, forming the building blocks of life. So, whether it's you or me or the chair or the blackboard or the stones we are connected. All connected to each other!'

'Thank you, Longfield-Jones. Woodward, do you have something interesting to say?'

'I watched this really brainy physicist on TV last week and he talked about the meaning of the universe. He said that mountains contained a life-giving force. Well, Sir, mountains are made of rock.

So there must be a life-force inside the marble. He also said something about energy being trapped inside the rock!'

'Just like the stones in *Metamorphoses*!'

'Yes, Salvesen, you could say that,' agreed Mr Hunt, while flipping through the pages of Ovid's *Metamorphoses*.

'If we are all connected, Sir' enthused another student from the back of the room, 'no wonder we feel such an affinity with stones!'

'Just like the Quimby Marbles in the Museum of Classical Antiquities in London!' said another girl from her seat. If the physicist is right than that explains why I feel so sorry for the statues locked up inside the museum. No wonder the statues look so miserable. The statues must be screaming inside but no one can hear them. It must be terrible. What if the statues really want to be let out of the museum, Sir? Perhaps we could help, Sir?'

'Let's not get carried away, Hamilton,' said Mr Hunt.

'If we are connected to every single living thing that has ever lived, we must all be connected to the stones.'

'That is ridiculous!' said Harry.

'If you interrupt once more Longfield-Jones you will be asked to leave the classroom.'

Harry hung his head, feigning a pout.

'Sir? What about Pygmalion? In *Orpheus' Song* Pygmalion was madly in love with a marble statue – a stone, Sir!'

'Perfect example,' said Mr Hunt suddenly enjoying the debate.

'Yes, what is it?'

'It's not exactly stone,' said Coopersmith, standing up, fanning the pages of his textbook, 'however, I would like to read a passage from Ovid, Sir. The last lines of the *Creation*. "Thus clay, so lately no more than a crude and formless substance, was metamorphosed to assume the strange new figure of Man." So it makes no difference, clay or stone, does it?'

'I'm sure we all have an opinion about stones,' said Mr Hunt, as he glanced down at his watch.

'We will continue our discussion tomorrow,' said Mr Hunt as he leapt off his desk.

'Class dismissed.'

The door banged open. A lot of shuffling feet were heard echoing in the hall. Mr Hunt was still holding on to the small smooth stone. The marble hand felt wonderful to touch, just like human flesh. Even after sixty million years.

—◌ ◌—

Meanwhile, outside in the hall, Max had cornered his friend.

'Listen Harry... I need a large favour.'

'What now?' Harry moaned. 'You haven't run out of dosh again, have you?'

Max lied. 'No, damn you. Listen to me. Helen mentioned in her email that the sculptors are trying to piece together all of the statues in the west pediment. The statue of Athena is, of course, the most important statue.'

'Soooo?'

'Well...Harry...turn around for a minute...look at me. This is *très* important.'

'Ok Ok!' said Harry, sighing over and over again. 'I have rugby practice in ten minutes, so hurry up!'

'It's to do with the Shambles. I believe that there are bits of marble lying around the house. I recall last Christmas seeing a chunk of stone in the library, a doorstop. It could be the chunk of Athena's aegis that Helen is looking for. Anyway...'

'Sooooo? Hurry up Max, will you.'

'Would you text your mum ASAP and find out whether the doorstop is still propping open the door in the library. Ask her whether she has seen any Greek marbles in the library or anywhere else inside the house or even outside.'

'Do you expect Mama to know the difference between Greek marbles and breeze-blocks or paving stones?'

'Yes!'

'Oh bugger, I just realised something. The marbles don't belong to us any more, so even if there are Greek marbles in the house I can't have them, can I, Harry?'

'I don't know, Max I need to ask Mama.'

'Damn!' Max's freckles appeared to dance on his wrinkled-up nose.

Max stood combing his tousled hair with his hands. 'Do you think your parents would mind if I pinched the doorstop?'

'I haven't a clue. The house is a mess. Most of the house is being restored at the moment. There are skips everywhere. Even inside the house!'

'Perfect. Then no one will notice whether the doorstop went missing or not...would they...Harry?'

Harry began shifting his weight from one foot to the other.

'Please, Harry, just ask your mum about the blasted doorstop!'

'No.'

'Ask the maid or the chandler or the electrician, or plumber for Christ's sake? Ask the butler – he's a good man.'

'Jenkins?'

'Yes – Jenkins.'

'Listen, Max, I have an even better idea. Why not come to the house, root around for the goddamned marbles yourself. Come for the weekend.'

'Oh, thank you, Harry...thank you...all the Greek gods will thank you one day. This is the best thing that you have ever done in your morally corrupt life!'

'You know what I think, Maximilian, I think you've lost your bloody marbles!'

Chapter Thirty-One
The Head of Athena Revisited

Guillaume d'Hautpoul swerved around the hairpin bend in the road while driving his brand spanking new Porsche Carrera at breakneck speed along the perilous stretch of road, the Grande Corniche, towards La Redousse. The head of Lushington's European Sculpture and Art, Paris Division, was on his way to meet his client, the delightful Francesca. After weeks of exhaustive research, he had finally managed to identity the piece of garden statuary she desperately wanted to sell. Guillaume was no fool. He had already sussed a potential buyer, an exceedingly wealthy client from Dubai, an Arab sheikh willing to pay an extortionate amount for the bust as he wished to extend his collection of Roman artifacts in his palatial villa nearing completion in Morocco.

This was his third visit to La Redousse – the fabulous belle époque villa sitting majestically on a cliff high above Menton on the French Riviera – because of the huge and ongoing discrepancies that had ensued over the provenance of the marble. Now, thankfully, these issues had been resolved.

When the gleaming robin-egg blue Carrera suddenly zoomed around another hairpin curve, swerving sharply to the right to avoid an oncoming car, Lushington's leading expert on Classical antiquities never even flinched. He carried on, with confidence, patting his new Louis Vuitton crocodile case resting next to him on the seat, knowing that Francesca would be thrilled to know the marble bust, although badly damaged, was worth considerably more than expected. There were a few minor details that needed sorting out regarding provenance but hey, not to worry. Lushington's were able to provide Madame with a valuation they considered acceptable in the current auction market. Now all he had to do was convince his client that the reserve bid that he had in mind was acceptable.

Guillaume geared down into second. If the marble bust fetched its estimated price at Lushington's upcoming sale in London in late January, Francesca could find herself better off, with funds to repair the footpath.

A long row of cypress trees came into view. Guillaume ground the gears, sped along the dusty track, bouncing over potholes the size of craters, and thundered past olive groves that hadn't been pruned in years. His first visit to La Redousse sprang to mind. He had expected something quite grand. What a shock he had found waiting. The state of the house was appalling, however, the Italianate garden was spectacular. Guillaume came to a thundering stop in the circular drive, and hopped out of the car with his case held closely to his cashmere-clad chest. A mistral tore at his back, ruffling his jet-black hair as he rushed towards the entrance, and pulled on the bell cord.

Francesca never answered the door. Why bother? Shivering from the cold Guillaume hastened along the narrow path beside the house overgrown with brambles and wet slippery moss, made even more perilous in the descending twilight. His shoe caught the edge of a flagstone, and he tripped over the crumbling stone. Like open wounds that refused to heal, he thought ruefully, and hurried on.

It was obvious Francesca desperately needed money.

The path led to the conservtory, a 'lean-to' tacked on to the back of the villa. It was, he concluded, Francesca's favourite spot because every time he visited La Redousse, he invariably found her seated at her desk, hunched over her laptop, tapping away. She never divulged what she was writing and he thought it rude to ask.

Francesca must have heard his footsteps, because as he reached the conservatory she ran to the door, waving him inside.

'Hello, Guillaume,' enthused Francesca as she reached for his hand. 'Please. Come in. Sit down!'

'Thank you, Francesca,' replied Guillaume, thinking Francesca had to be one of the most enthusiastic people that he had ever met. Her smile virtually lit up the conservatory as she ushered him inside.

'I'm sorry that it has taken so long to get back to you, Francesca. I know how anxious you are to sell.'

'Not to worry.'

'Care for a glass of red wine?' asked Francesca, as she reached for a bottle of Bordeaux sitting amidst the clutter on her desk.

'Yes, thank you. That would be very nice.'

As Francesca poured the wine, Guillaume continued.

'Finally, I have managed to establish a value for the bust; however, we still have a few problems concerning provenance to iron out.'

Francesca frowned, revealing her concern.

'It's the lack of provenance. We, meaning Lushington's, have to be very careful when selling important works of art. We need absolute proof of provenance. Our clients demand transparency. We need to go over this issue again, do you mind?'

'No, of course not,' said Francesca as she sipped her wine, wriggling nervously in her chair.

'You mentioned that you found the bust in the garden. Approximately fifteen years ago.'

'Yes, that is correct.' Could he tell she was lying?

'In the potager,' added Francesca hastily. Did it really matter whether the garden was in London or not? Besides, this was all about survival.

'You were living here at the time. The house is in your name; therefore, we can safely say that the marble bust is part of a private collection. This is the only way we can get around this "provenance" thing.' He smiled. 'The fact that the bust was buried in the garden, rather than on display in the house, is immaterial.' Are you happy with this, Francesca?'

'Absolutely!'

'Good. I will however, require a copy of the deeds to the house, as verification that the land in which the statue was found belongs to you. If the house wasn't in your name, the owner of the property would be entitled to claim ownership of the marble. It's like oil rights!'

'I only wish to sell the bust not the damn house!' Francesca could feel her angst rising. She was angry. The mere thought of Quimby getting his greedy paws on any of the proceeds from Minerva made her squirm.

'In this business there are always complications. Now, care to hear some good news, Francesca? I have finally managed to identify the bust. It has taken some time but I can safely say that the bust

THE HEAD OF ATHENA REVISITED

is the monumental head of the Roman goddess, Venus. She is the original of a Roman Imperial sculpture from the Hadrianic Period, circa AD 130–8. According to our team of experts at Lushington's there is a copy of her in the Vatican in Rome!'

'My word,' exclaimed Francesca, brightening, 'how very grand!'

'This is good news, Francesca!' exclaimed Guillaume, who leaned a little closer, captivated by the light reflecting in his client's luxurious dark brown hair.

'Now, all we need to do is agree on a reserve bid for the bust that we both feel is acceptable to protect your investment.'

'Yes, of course,' she said quickly, 'what is the valuation you placed on the marble?'

Francesca wriggled about in her chair, crossing and uncrossing her long legs clad in skinny jeans, completing the ensemble of retro cashmere sweater and knee-high boots.

'Lushington's has,' said Guillaume, keeping his voice controlled, 'placed the value of 200 000 and 250 000 pounds sterling.'

His client did not respond. Francesca just sat there, staring at him; her haunting dark eyes penetrated deep into the inner recesses of his Franco-American soul. Eyes filled with intrigue, sadness, despair, surprise or delight – he could not tell. For a second Guillaume imagined his client passing out as she clutched the arms of the shabby wicker chair to steady herself. A chair on par with the rest of the villa. Shabby-chic came to mind. He was about to grab hold of her, which would not have been unpleasant in the least he thought.

However, Francesca revived and smiling brightly said in a flat voice, 'Really? Can the marble actually be worth that much?'

'Yes, it can.'

383

Guillaume sat on the edge of a wobbly wicker chair squeezed in between a motley collection of dead tomato plants in enormous terracotta pots and a plaster bust, a rather curious rendition of Julius Caesar eying him from a wooden plinth. Potted herbs and empty clay pots were everywhere, on the floor, the windowsills, the desk – every available space.

'Are you happy with this valuation?'

'Yes...of...course,' said Francesca.

'Good. Now, all we need to establish is a reserve bid for the marble. Shall we say, £150 000?'

'Sounds good to me,' said Francesca, sounding nonplussed.

'Good. Guillaume wasted no time in extracting the documents from his case.

Well. I guess that settles it.' Francesca hastened, after a quick glance at the documents with the familiar Lushington logo, the head of Selene's horse embossed on the letterhead. 'Where do I sign?'

'Please.' Guillaume leaned closer to his client. 'Sign here, where the x's are.'

Was it his imagination or had the faint lines around her eyes relaxed ever-so slightly? He kept reminding himself that it was none of his business; however, he failed to comprehend why this lovely woman lived in a villa that was quite literally falling down around her, with no one except a motley collection of wayward donkeys for companionship.

'Our delivery van will collect the marble next Tuesday, if that's convenient for you. The bust will be shipped directly to our Bond Street store in London.'

Francesca nodded.

'Our men will pack the bust on site, if that's OK, Francesca, in order to prevent any untoward damage to the marble. There is no need to worry.' He smiled, wanting to reassure her.

'Yes, that's absolutely fine,' Francesca replied, handing the signed document back to Guillaume.

Before he placed the documents inside his case Guillaume glanced at the signature at the bottom of the page, his deep brown eyes widening in the deepening twilight. *Lady Quimby.* He struggled to maintain his composure as he snapped the solid-gold clasp shut. Francesca was related to the *Quimbys.* He stood up, hastened towards the door of the conservatory, his tall frame blocking the last rays of a cold, watery sun. Of course! She must be Charles's widow whose brother-in-law was the Director of the Museum of Classical Antiquities in London. The Quimbys had millions. Why was his client living in such appalling circumstances?

'Thank you for coming.' Francesca, smiling, offered her small, elegant hand.

Such a firm handshake, he thought, holding her hand a moment longer than necessary.

'Thank you, Guillaume, thank you for your help.'

'Thank you, Francesca!' exclaimed Guillaume, suddenly feeling the urge to place a protective arm around her shoulders. 'Please, do not worry about a thing. We will find a good home for Minerva, or should I say Venus?'

He couldn't divulge he had a buyer. He didn't know whether she would be happy or sad, and for a brief moment imagined she might change her mind if he told her.

'I can find my way, Francesca, so there is no need to come out on such a blustery cold night.'

'Goodbye Francesca.' On the step he turned and waved.

However, something was bothering him as he hastened along the slippery path, and it wasn't the fact that his client was related to one of the most powerful families in England.

No. It wasn't that at all. He had a knack for reading people and he believed his client was reluctant to part with the marble bust, even though, he guessed, the sale would save her from pending financial ruin. He had expected Francesca to be thrilled at the price; however, it seemed that the opposite was true. Why was Lady Quimby so attached to a chunk of ruinous stone? He failed to understand his client's attachment to the marble. Then again, he failed to understand why such a beautiful woman lived alone in a villa crumbling down around her.

Chapter Thirty-Two
Rupert Longfield-Jones Meets a Goddess

Rupert Longfield-Jones strode through the revolving door of his office and headed down the Avenue of the Americas. His driver was not far behind in his Bentley; however, he much preferred to walk, ignoring the cold northerly wind howling through the wind-tunnel created by New York's mammoth skyscrapers blocking the sun, not much more than a sliver of light squashed between blocks of cold steel and concrete. When a whirlwind of grit and dirt caught him by surprise he shrugged, cursing the litter from the street as it gradually gained momentum, hitting him in the face. It only exacerbated his already black mood, one that had been building with an even greater velocity than the wind, after the Dow Jones dropped a trillion dollars at four o'clock.

Rupert Longfield-Jones was in one hell of a bad mood, made worse when his BlackBerry vibrated inside his coat pocket. He knew who it was as he withdrew his phone, glanced down at the name registered on it.

'Honey? Rupee? Honey I can't hear you...where are you?'

'Yes darling...I just left the office. I am on the street.'

Muffled wailing tones followed.

'Calm down Lulu, darling, I can't understand a word you are saying!'

'Stolen? What's been stolen?'

'Stop crying, Lulu, I can't hear you!'

An ambulance roared past, lights flashing, siren screeching.

'Lulu darling, stop screaming!'

'Your diamonds...what about your diamonds?'

'Your mother's tiara...your...Fabergé necklace...your diamond bracelet...your twenty-five diamond engagement ring from Graff... the earrings...the ones I gave you...all stolen!'

'Good lord!'

'When did this happen, Lulu?'

'What? Speak up!'

'What did you say, this afternoon?'

'The Charity Ball...you have nothing to wear to the Charity Ball tonight?'

'What? The bus just roared past. Stop crying, Lulu!'

'You can tell me all about it when I get home.'

'Lulu, stop it I can't understand you.'

He repeated everything she said. 'The police had the audacity to tell you not to panic, they will be there shortly!'

The line went dead – cut off. Rupert shook his head. Lulu without jewels was like the Queen without her corgis. They went everywhere with her. Lulu could not function without her diamonds, her stones, as he called his wife's precious jewels.

One of the most successful hedge-fund managers in New York crossed the street at the end of the second block. He hurried down the avenue, tugging irritably on his old blue-and-white-striped muffler from Harrow, dreading the long dark nights in downtown Manhattan, the blustery cold days in New York City.

He hauled himself back from the brink of despair, allowed his thoughts to soar – landing on the lawn in the backwater of Scotland. He missed the Scottish mist. He missed the rainbows. He missed the verdant green hills, the moors and the harr blowing off the North Sea, to say nothing of indulging in a fine single-malt, seated by an open fire in the Red Lion, his local drinking hole within staggering distance of the house. Yes, he thought to himself, he definitely missed the Shambles – his latest acquisition – a mouldering Greek Revival pile that had belonged to his old school chum, 'Quim'. The nickname had stuck since Harrow as the lordship thing had to go to make everyone feel equal. The Shambles had been in the Quimby family for hundreds of years. However, his brother's death duties had all but crippled 'Quim', and he, Rupert, had come to the rescue, and bought the house and enough pasture land for his wife's horses – all for a mere pittance – the price of a successful day playing the market. The Shambles, at that very moment in time, seemed a hellishly long way away, thought the new laird of the manor, as he narrowly avoided being run over in rush-hour traffic, zigzaging past anxious commuters rushing to Central Station, and adding another layer of stress to his already stressed-out life. He was on his way to Rockefeller Center to view a new collection of modern art, before leaving for London. Although Lulu needed a pacifier – three million dollars worth to be exact – before he took the chopper.

'Good evening, Sir,' greeted the receptionist, as Rupert Longfield-Jones rushed through the door of Rockefeller Center, greatly relieved to be out of the wind. 'Glad you could come on such a blustery cold night.'

'Thank you,' said Rupert, patting his mop of thick brown hair with one hand, searching through the pockets in his overcoat with the other. 'I have a catalogue here somewhere.'

'Sir?' asked a waiter standing nearby, balancing a tray of Bollinger champagne.

'Thank you,' said Rupert as he flung his coat over his shoulder, as he imagined Humphrey Bogart might have done in *Casablanca*, and with his glass in his hand joined the throng, the super-elite of downtown Manhattan.

Rupert's wife, Lulu, did not share his enthusiasm for modern art. Now that the house in Long Island had been recently done up, the Longfield-Jones's really did not need another enormous canvas to hang on their walls, since every wall in the house had been painted beige.

Thoughts of their palatial spread in the Hamptons vanished however, when he caught sight of a magnificent canvas titled, 'Caught in a Storm'. Couldn't be more appropriate, he muttered to his long-suffering cynical self. 'I will have it!'

The theft of his wife's jewels was unfortunate, somewhat disturbing, although not tragic – her affection for her jewels he thought obsessive – although it was probably her own fault, because Lulu never kept them locked in the safe.

Not to worry, he had time to pop into Graff on his way to the Wall Street Heliport where the chopper was waiting to take him to JFK. The flight to London was leaving in two hours. It didn't give him much time. How long did it take to spend several million dollars?

It wouldn't take him long to choose a bauble for Lulu as she absolutely adored diamonds; the bigger the better. Christmas was coming, as was her birthday. This year she'd hinted at yellow diamonds, although much larger stones, as if last year's weren't big enough. Last year Lulu coveted black diamonds. The year before, pink diamonds. The photographs in the newspapers of the Queen's jewels didn't help matters. Sitting on the sofa in the drawing room at the house in the Hamptons, Lulu had shoved the newspaper article in his face. How many carats were required to satisfy his wife's passion for jewels? Purchase the biggest rock in the shop – that would do the trick!'

To Rupert, yellow diamonds resembled the fake topaz that cosmetic companies used to use to jazz up their packaging, promoting cheap perfume. But what did he know about diamonds? As long as Lulu got diamonds, she would be happy...at least...for another year. What Lulu wanted Lulu got and that included everything that his newly-acquired wealth could buy. And, as he strolled past another painting while guzzling his third glass of champagne, his wife's southern drawl screamed inside his head.

'Honey? Whatever shall I do, Rupert?' she had cooed on the other end of his Blackberry, as only a gal from a South Carolina finishing school could do.

'Something with noble provenance darling!'

He could hardly hear his wife sobbing hysterically on the phone and, downing his champagne, reached for another as the waiter whizzed past.

I know I'm drinking too much but who gives a damn?

Lulu dreamed of being a princess. Americans fancied royalty like crazy. If the truth be told, Lulu had fallen in love with him because of his English accent. She loved the idea of class – and yet she didn't have any. Class was something you were born with. You either had it or you hadn't.

CHAPTER THIRTY-TWO

Rupert bought the canvas, 'Caught in a Storm'. It would be perfect for one of the enormous drawing rooms at the Shambles. He could buy every painting in the gallery and they would still barely cover the walls, there were that many. Lulu never commented on any of the works of art that he bought. All she cared about were her jewels or her damn horses. But he bought the painting anyway.

A dose of cynicism swept through his Anglo-American veins as he walked up to the reception desk, extracted his 'plastic' from inside his coat pocket and signed his name. There were enough funds in his account to buy every painting on Fifth Avenue. Although, not nearly enough to buy his wife's love. Everything in life had a price.

He'd met his present wife, a stunningly beautiful fashion model at a beach party for the rich and famous in southern California. She was his third wife. Of course he had married on the rebound after divorcing his second wife – didn't everyone? Lulu was sixteen years his junior and deep down he knew the age difference was going to be a problem, if indeed it wasn't already. Their relationship had been based on lust. Now, the lust was gone – big time – nothing would bring it back. When had he first realised his marriage wasn't going to last? Was it while sunbathing on the beach in the Bahamas? Skiing on the piste at Davos? Faking an orgasim at the George V in Paris? Did it matter that another bloody divorce was pending? Even more startling was that he no longer cared. Although, one thing was for sure; neither he nor his wife were happy any more, and yet he had only recently admitted this terrible truth to himself. He stared at the largest canvas in the collection – yet another acquisition. How much stuff was needed to make a person happy? His only happiness of late was walking his dogs on the beach on Long Island. Alone. All he *really* wanted was to be left alone.

Not a healthy sign, Old Man.

When he and his wife spent time together, all they did was argue. In hindsight, Lulu should never have moved into his flat in Manhattan's Upper East Side. Within weeks of her cluttering up the master bathroom, hogging more than her share of the walk-in closet, changing the colour of the walls to beige, nagging him constantly about absolutely everything – including the lack of vegan food in his fridge and the fact that his socks had holes in the toes – the lustre had worn off, disappearing down the drain along with the bath water. The funny thing was, and it really wasn't very funny, the more money he spent in the pursuit of happiness – whether it was a Monet, property in the Hamptons or a private jet – the less enjoyment he got in return. In other words, he wasn't getting a good return on his investment.

Something had gone terribly wrong in his personal life and he could not figure out what the hell it was. Something was missing. He had everything money could buy and yet nothing of real value. Therein lay the problem. He had chased the American Dream all his life, thinking money could buy happiness. The reality was – he had got it wrong. Life didn't work that way. Happiness, within himself, continued to evade him. He felt empty. Hollow. No matter how much he spent, he could not fill the hole in his soul and the chasm was getting larger by the day. He couldn't buy his way out. He didn't want for material things, but he kept spending anyway. Like a fool. One thing he did know – his stomach ached. Perhaps his gut was trying to tell him something, because the pain never went away.

The Longfield-Jones' world consisted of hob-nobbing with those with social mobility, the super-elite and other 'hedgies' with planet-sized egos with an extreme aptitude for making millions from speculating in the global economy; either the bond market, hedge funds and currencies. So that he had to keep spending American dollars, otherwise Uncle Sam or the English equivalent, the tax man, grabbed it.

His thoughts shifted dramatically when his mobile pinged. He scrolled through his text messages. The first message was from his stepson Harry who wanted to know whether he could use his credit card to buy his mum a pair of gloves in Hermes for her birthday. As the price was a shocking £950, he didn't know whether he should proceed with the purchase without informing his step-father, because his American Express card was over its limit.

There was a text from Lulu, demanding to know when his flight arrived at Heathrow. What time was the chopper expected? Did he remember they were to leave for the charity ball at six o'clock sharp and that their neighbours were coming along in the chopper? Neighbours who had more or less invited themselves.

'Damn!' Rupert sighed, 'damn the ball.'

Then his iPhone pinged. It was an overseas call.

'Yes, hello?' said Rupert, annoyed, his business voice clicking in.

Then the crackling stopped...

'Why, Potch You old devil! How good to hear from you. How are you?'

'Where in the blazes are you?'

'Athens? What are you doing in Athens at this time of year? What's wrong? Bored with the gorgeous blondes in the Caribbean?'

A lengthy pause followed.

'The blondes?'

Riotous laughter followed.

'Bonds. Sorry. I thought you said blondes!'

'What about your bonds?'

'Sinking?'

'Damn, Potch (resorting to Dimitri's nickname from Harrow). Hell, that's bloody awful!'

'Yeah, the market is jittery here too. Don't remind me. Lost a mitt-full today!'

Another lengthy pause.

'Would we like to meet in Athens...next year...in May? Sail the Greek Islands? What? Does it have any appeal?'

Rupert scratched his head. He didn't respond immediately.

'What, Helen's birthday, her twenty-first on the fifth of May. I don't know Potch.'

'I'm not being an old fart!'

'Great fun...what is large enough for half the population in Manhattan?'

'Sorry old man...the bloody yacht!'

'She's what?'

'Speak up Potch...we're losing contact. She's a second cousin to the Queen Mary? Gosh!'

After a few seconds Rupert said, 'No, I don't think so... *Potch.*'

'I am listening.'

'Good for business? What did you say? There is lots of money sloshing about. Greeks desperate to get their money out of the country...hedge their bets...funds.'

Rupert had trouble with the connection.

'Yes, spot on there, Lulu would just adore Kallisti...all 250 feet of her. '

Rupert's options flashed through his mind. Birthday bashes equated to a splash at Annabel's, a mammoth suite at the Ritz in Paris or Madrid or the Carillon; she loved Santorini but not at this time of year. They did the Cayman Islands last year. He had suggested a safari in South Africa which was a no-go. No bathtubs. Lulu could not possibly entertain the idea of holidaying in a place without state-of-the-art marble bathroom facilities...

'I'm not sure Potch!'

Then, after a short pause...

'You're joking? Bring who, my stepson, Harry?' Rupert asked, sounding surprised.

'Well, in that case I will ask Harry and see what he says.'

'She needs a few distractions...that bloody museum has really taken a toll on...who? Your girl...Helen.'

'Just like my 'new' old pile in Scotland', Rupert was mumbling to himself.

'What museum?'

'You can't see the marbles for the goop!'

'Potch, are you accusing us of stealing the Parthenon marbles?'

Dimitri never let him forget that he was half British.

'You don't give a damn about the marbles, Potch. If you did, you would support Helen's cause, donate a few damn euros to the museum,' snapped Rupert, angrily.

'Don't get so huffy, Potch!'

'Sorry, Potch...'

'We'll come!' said Rupert finally.

'Take care Potch.'

The mobile phone went dead.

Rupert Longfield-Jones summarised briefly. Lulu simply adored yachts, sailing the Med in particular. She adored absolutely everything that breathed zillions. Even better, Lulu looked zillions in her bikini, what little there was of it. The girl was quite simply perfection when it came to the female form. She was a stunner. However, heading towards the door he couldn't help wonder what would happen if suddenly all the money ran out. If he lost all his wealth. He didn't need to wonder for long. He knew the answer. His marriage would end. The pain in his gut was much worse. He had just purchased a painting worth two million dollars for heaven's sake so, why on earth did he feel so *bloody* empty in the inner recesses of his weary soul? Didn't he have everything in the world, everything money could buy? His property portfolio consisted of a lavish penthouse in Manhattan, a spread in the Hamptons, an even more palatial villa in Lyford Quay in the Bahamas, a Georgian house in Belgravia in London and a mouldering pile in Scotland. Why not throw a few million at it – perhaps it would cheer him up. It was hard to believe Rupert was in his prime; most mornings he looked bloody awful. He was one of America's most lucrative hedge fund managers; more from luck than brains. Children were not part of the equation. Did the world really need another of his offspring? He thought not.

He questioned the meaning of his life as he walked through the grand foyer of Rockefeller Center towards the revolving doors, only to find himself backtracking because it was then, at that very moment, that Rupert Longfield-Jones glimpsed the face of a goddess.

Rockefeller Center vanished beneath his feet, so utterly transfixed was he by the extraordinarily beautiful face with enchanting, sorrowful dark eyes that caught his and held on tight, penetrating deeply into the dying embers of his troubled soul. He couldn't move.

He had to have her.

He could have anything he wanted in the material world.

Who was she? He didn't know, but he *had* to find out.

Rupert took a closer look. He bent over the magazine rack beside the reception desk, staring at the face on the cover of *Lushington's Auction Sale of Classical Antiquities* taking place at the Bond Street store in London on 28 January. He would be in London anyway. He took the catalogue from the magazine rack, thrusting thirty dollars into the nearby security guard's hand.

He said, his husky business-like voice softening, 'Keep the change' unable to take his eyes off the beautiful face adorning the front cover.

Rupert Longfield-Jones knew nothing whatsoever about Classical antiquities. He had a degree in English literature from Stanford University although it hadn't really done him much good. He could recite the odd verse from Shakespeare's *Hamlet* or a few lines from Milton's *Paradise Lost* when called upon at a boring dinner party. Not that any of this mattered. He was utterly captivated by the face on the cover. Without realising that one day, in the not too distant future, *that* face would become the most powerful symbol of beauty and of truth in the Western world.

Chapter Thirty-Three
The Shambles Revisited

Lulu slammed the phone down, cutting him off. She sobbed. She swore, which she was more inclined to do of late. 'Bastard...if *you* spent more time at home, this ghastly business would never have happened!'

A cacophony of heart-rending sobs following in quick succession emulated from the guest bathroom – the only bathroom in the house where the plumbing worked.

The sound of tinkling ice cubes clinking in her glass alerted Lulu to the wretched fact she needed another *Skinny Bitch* comprising 99.9% vodka, without a hint of soda.

'Jenkins!' Lulu shouted at the top of her lungs, forgetting she had fired the butler that morning, shortly after breakfast, for failing to stock the drinks cabinet with vodka. As today was Sunday there wasn't a liquor store, which the British called an off-licence, that sold vodka within twenty miles of the *god-damned* place. *'Gracious mercy!'* Lulu envisioned she might shrivel and die at the Shambles. God forbid.

'Jenkins was useless anyway, so there was no loss!'

However, there was no response. How could there be? There was not another living soul in the house as the staff were on holiday leave, due to the on-going refurbishment of the house. The guest bathroom was a mere half-mile from the butler's pantry anyway. Yes, The Shambles was so enormous that unless one had good reason to venture into a particular area of the house, one would not do so. Meaning Lulu could rage all she liked. Without an audience, however, what was the point? She sobbed anyway nonetheless.

Lulu sank deeper into the roll-top tub, reviewing her *bitch-list* which was as long as the drive. Topping the list was her stolen jewels.

Her husband came second. As mentioned, the 'bastard'.

Third, The Shambles – appropriately named, because the house was in a perilous state and had been for some time. As the house had been empty for years, the ceilings in the main drawing rooms had fallen down and had had to be ripped out. The cherry-red carpet, leading up three flights of stairs had been torn up as the plumbers were installing central heating for the very first time, which was hard to imagine in the twenty-first century. Layers of wallpaper had been stripped from the extensive halls, and electrical cables snaked along the floor, over the doors, dangling from the rafters as the electricians re-wired the entire house. The ghastly smell of rising damp made her nauseous, without heat to keep the must at bay. Making life even more impossible, the skip hire company had insisted on putting enormous skips inside the house as there was so much debris – yes, the house was that big. She had insisted on a complete refurb. The previous owner, Rupert's old Harrovian chum, hadn't a clue how to decorate the interior of his house. What Lulu had found most distasteful were the marble statues and she had rid the house of them all, with the exception of the horse's head in the Music Room as Lulu

400

absolutely adored anything with a mane or a tail. The statue had been delegated to one of the out-buildings, as she intended to tart up the rhubarb patch with the statue next spring.

Item number four on the hit list: returning to America. Three years after taking possession, the refurbishment of the house was still in progress, without an end in sight. Consequently, Lulu was desperate to escape to the sunny climate of California. Let her husband sort out the mess. Rupert, in a moment of weakness, had bailed out his friend and bought the house, fulfilling his dream of re-living the life of an English country gentleman, as he had done as a child, leaving Lulu in charge of overseeing the refurbishment.

As Lulu soaked in the tub the fifth item on the list came swiftly to mind: her life in Britain. A life she loathed to such extent that phone calls from California brought a deluge of tears streaming from her eyes. The only thing that kept her sane had been the pending arrival of Buttercup's new colt. However, Buttercup had given birth to a still-born and the death of a thoroughbred pony had brought on another flood of tears. Thankfully the bath was able to accommodate the extra deluge, as there was never sufficient hot water to fill the tub.

Having drained the bottle of Smirnoff, Lulu wallowed in her misery, returning, once again to the evening ahead. The new Armani couture gown she had chosen to wear to the charity ball at the Dorchester had cost, dare one say, the equivalent of a down-payment on a small house. She struggled to see how she could possibly endure the evening without her diamonds, as the Smith-Ballard-something-or-others, might suspect her of not having any class. Heaven forbid! Why couldn't she ever remember their neighbours' last name? Triple-barrelled names were beyond her. Double-barrelled names she could manage, as she had been a Smith-Mills prior to marriage and a Longfield-Jones after that. If she chose she could call herself Lulu Smith-Mills-Longfield-Jones! Imagine! It boggled her mind. Would the neighbours be impressed? She thought not as nothing she ever did seemed to make an impression on the Brits. There were more good reasons to sob: how to cope without her twenty-five carat diamond engagement ring. Or, say, she suddenly felt all weepy because of the theft and broke down in tears, which she was prone to do, after copious vodkas. Lastly, what on earth would she do if the bartender failed to understand how to make *Skinny Bitches?* Because, that's all she would drink after discovering that white wine made her fat.

Lulu gradually sobered up, re-filled the tub, a mere trickle of lukewarm water, then lay back with her head resting on the rolled rim of the free-standing bath, staring at the walls. She eventually stopped sobbing and for a moment completely forgot the theft of her jewels.

'Good-gracious mercy!' Lulu shouted. 'What are those things on the wall? Why – they are the most hideous things I have ever set my eyes on!'

Lulu splashed in the tub. 'Of course, when the workmen removed the wall-board the wall-plaques were revealed!'

So intrigued was she by this she raised herself out of the tub and pranced over towards the plaques, in the nude, dripping water on the floor. Lulu took a closer look.

'Gosh Quim, with all that money you would think you would have more taste!'

However, one thing was for sure, thought Lulu, as she tapped lightly on the plaque, unable to discern the composition of the material. 'Tomorrow I am having all these hideous things removed and put in the skip!' Then, she turned around, counting aloud to herself. 'Good heavens!' There were eight plaques stuck to the walls.

Suddenly, she was reminded of her very first visit to the Museum of Classical Antiquities in London, because the plastic plaques looked exactly the same as the plaques on the walls of the famous Quimby Gallery... Quim's gallery.

Shivering, Lulu towelled herself dry. Her *baby* was arriving at any moment. Harry had sent her a text explaining that they were taking the overnight train from London and then catching the train home. Harry's best friend, Maximilian, had been invited to stay for the weekend. She dithered. Where on earth was she going to put the boys? Every room in the house was a complete and utter disaster.

What were they going to eat for supper? Her cook was not on duty, and she had fired her butler. Lulu burst into tears. Things were definitely not going her way. She tipsy-toed over the bare wooden planks on the bathroom floor, en route to her dressing room where she squeezed into her skinny jeans, threw a cashmere jumper over her head, donned a pair of jewel-encrusted Jimmy Choos, then hobbled down the hall crying.

'Rupee... Honey, why aren't you here when I need you?'

Rubbing her eyes, smudging her mascara, she ran down the stairs, tripping over the electrical cables.

'We can't possibly go to the ball. Not now. Not without my diamond tiara!'

Hopefully her husband had bought something suitable in New York. Although, she doubted it, as nothing on earth could replace her jewels.

—☙ ❧—

Baudelaire's words echoed loudly in his head as Max opened the door, walked into the enormous kitchen, one of three at the Shambles. *'In a palace there is no place for intimacy.'*

403

'Hello, anyone at home?'

No answer.

Harry had explained that the staff were not in residence.

He kept his coat and hat on as the house was freezing then continued on, stepping over the mess scattered on the floor. Max was anxious to carry on with his mission. Feeling more like a thief than a house guest prowling through the labyrinth of halls with his backpack flung over his shoulder. The house resembled a war zone. He hardly recognised the place. The house had been completely gutted. There was nothing left of the original interior. Everything was gone. Max, in shocked silence walked through the halls. He was devastated.

Thankfully Harry had remained in Edinburgh to visit a girlfriend. This meant Max could snoop for the marble undeterred, as there didn't appear to be anyone in the house.

All the original wall coverings had been ripped off. He could see the bare plastered walls. Then, he caught sight of the massive mahogany doors leading into the library. The doors were open. This was a good sign, thought Max as he ran towards the only room in the house that hadn't been totally gutted.

There was the doorstop propping open the door. Just as he remembered it! He crouched on the floor, ran his finger along the faint outline of the Gorgon's head carved in the stone. He pulled Helen's drawing out of his pocket. Everything matched perfectly. He couldn't wait to text her. She would be thrilled. Max wasn't sure what to do. He needed to discuss his find with Harry. He couldn't just stuff the marble in his bag. Because the precious marble, part of Athena Parthenos' shield no longer belonged to his family. The quandary ended, however, when that famous American drawl echoed loudly in the hall.

'Max! How are you?' Lulu cried, as she hurried towards him, her eight-inch heels clicking on the floor. 'Looking for mice?'

'Oh H—e—l—l—o!' said Max, stammering, hurrying to his feet, rubbing dust from his jeans and walking towards Lulu from La La Land with his sweaty hand thrust out. 'I am very well, thank you.'

'Have you mislaid something Max?'

'I seem to have dropped my pen, Ma'am.' He couldn't really tell her the truth. That he was about to pinch her doorstep. Mrs Longfield-Jones wouldn't understand. He was really struggling.

'Your pen?'

'Um...Uh...um!' He wanted to come clean but couldn't. 'It's rather difficult to explain Mrs Longfield-Jones.'

'You look as though you were about to pinch my doorstop. Lulu giggled. 'I have had one thief in this house this week Max and I do not want another.' Mrs Longfield-Jones smiled; she adored Max. He was so charming. He had such beautiful manners.

'How are you Ma'am?' Why on earth did he have to resort to using the nauseating American vernacular.

For Christ's sake Harry, hurry up. I need rescuing.

'I was on my way to the kitchen. Know how to make pancakes, Max?' asked Lulu as she wiggled past in her tight jeans, 'because I don't.'

'You could try frozen ones, Ma'am,' replied Max trailing along behind Harry's mum, thinking, god, she looked terribly upset, as though she had been crying. Her eyes were red-rimmed with black mascara smudges on her face. He had never seen her without lip-gloss either. Something else was missing...he couldn't quite put his finger on it...

As they trudged through the debris Max asked, 'What have you done with the marble statue of Selene's horse Ma'am?' Longfield-Jones was such a mouthful. 'The statue in the Music Room I believe.'

'I got rid of it. I couldn't wait to rid the house of all those hideous things. The statue of the horse was the first to go. Not sure what to do with it, Max. I thought I might mount the head on a plinth, jazz up the potager garden. The skip hire man has offered to take the stone to the dump though.'

'Take the statue to the dump?' Max cried as he walked through the opening where the door had been. His tutors at Cambridge had taught him to speak up. Speak his mind. 'With respect, Mrs Longfield-Jones, may I suggest before sending any of the statues to the dump, you contact Lushington's, have a proper valuation done on the statues?

'The statues could have value, even though they are reproductions,' then added hastily not sure she would understand, 'reproductions of the originals, as it were.' He wasn't sure if she understood that either.

'Whatever for? Quim told us that the statues were no earthly good – junk – nothing but junk!'

'Well, I beg to differ, Ma'am.' said Max. 'People like to purchase marble statues for their gardens, tart them up. You could consider putting the statues into auction. You might be surprised to find they have value, Ma'am.'

'Value? Max, really, I very much doubt the statues are worth the trouble.'

Although, he could tell Lulu was doing her sums. She was counting on her fingers. 'Do you think the marbles would make enough at auction for a new croc Hermès bag, a Kelly bag in yellow, Max, or a Birkin bag, because if not, then I'm not in the least interested.'

Max ran his hands through his mop of dark brown hair that fell forward, irritating him. He reserved comment on the abhorrent practice of making ladies designer handbags from endangered species. Nor did he wish to argue with Harry's mother.

'You see Max, sweetie pie – there you go, looking just like Hugh Grant again – I could do with another Birkin bag!'

'Ma'am, where are the skips?' said Max, blushing, finding it difficult not to look at her bosom. 'I'd like to have a look at the marbles that came out of the house. Perhaps take one last look at the horse!'

'Have a look. By all means, Max,' replied Lulu, as she tied an apron around her tiny waist, then, looking puzzled, asked, 'Where do you think the frying pan is kept Max?'

'Where did you say the marbles were Ma'am,' hastened Max, ignoring her question.

'Have a look in the walled garden. That entire area is being demolished. All of the out-buildings are coming down to make room for more stables.'

'Thank you' said Max, and fled.

He ran outside. The chopper was circling overhead, ready to land on the lawn. Mr Longfield-Jones had arrived home. However, as Max raced along the path, he cried, 'Of course Lulu from La La Land's jewels were missing from that famous bosom.

—◌ ◌—

'Charlie?' Rupert Longfield-Jones spoke to the captain on the inter-com. 'Charlie? Can you see Lulu standing on the lawn?'

'Yes Sir,' replied Captain Strickland. 'Don't worry, Sir. I have spotted her.'

Rupert peered out of the window of the helicopter. Then he glimpsed at his Jaeger-Lecoultre Reverso. Thank god he had time for a drink or three before going to the ball. He patted the Graff box sitting on the leather seat next to him. Lulu will just love it!

Once again, Graff's had come to his rescue. He had bought the most expensive tiara in the shop. Lulu would be happy. Now, she could go to the ball, like Cinderella.

As the Agusta Westland circled, preparing to set down on the land in front of the house he got a closer look at his wife's face. She looked dreadful. Like a drowned rat with her full-length sable coat wrapped tightly around her.

Lulu rushed towards her husband as soon as he stepped out of the chopper and Rupert caught his wife in his arms, sheltered her from being caught in the down-draught from the whirling blades.

'Honey!' gushed Lulu pecking him on the cheek. 'Thank god you are home. I have been frantic. To think all my jewels are gone!'

'Calm down darling,' said Rupert, grabbing Lulu's hand. Why was it always so cold? 'Let's go inside where it will be warmer.'

'Warmer!' Lulu screamed at him. 'Warmer! Is the heat all you can think of at the time like this?'

'Relax Lulu,' said Rupert, while helping her up the steps in her ridiculous shoes into the library, the only room in the house where the walls hadn't been ripped out and the fireplace still worked.

'Relax?' Lulu was hysterical. Crying and shouting, she screamed. 'Honey! How can I relax when my jewels have been stolen? We have had a robbery in this house Rupee, right under our noses and you want me to relax!'

'For God's sake Lulu,' Rupert backed away from his wife. He had never seen her so distraught.

'Sit down darling.'

'No, I won't sit down!'

'Let me help you with your coat.'

'I'll keep it on, thank you. The damn house is freezing!'

'Shall I pour us a drink? What you need is a good stiff brandy.' They both did.

'I hate brandy!'

'Well, how about a vodka?'

'There isn't any vodka – in the drinks cupboard or anywhere else in this mess and there isn't any ice either,' sobbed Lulu, as she collapsed onto a pouffe beside the smouldering fire. 'I fired the butler this morning for forgetting to buy vodka.'

'You fired the butler?'

'Uh huh.'

'You fired Jenkins!' Rupert laughed, unwinding his muffler, preferring to keep his coat on, it was so bloody cold and damp. 'Well, I'll be damned. You fired Jenkins for failing to re-stock the drinks cabinet?'

'Yes...honey,' she mumbled through sobs.

'It's twenty five miles to the grocery store and today is Sunday!'

Rupert rubbed his jaw, as he always did when dealing with his wife. 'You know what I think darling? You were set up!'

'Set up?'

'Jenkins deliberately failed to stock the drinks cabinet. He wanted you to fire him!'

'I don't understand Rupert.'

'Our butler was the thief. By now, he'll have left the country. In fact, he's probably already done a deal with the Russians. Sorry darling, but you will never see your jewels again.'

Lulu was trembling uncontrollably.

'Would you care for a nice hot cup of tea?'

'I loathe tea!'

Rupert walked over to the drinks cupboard, and poured two very large whiskeys. He thrust one glass into his wife's trembling outstretched hand.

'Lulu, drink this.'

He sat down on the sofa and said in a calm voice, 'Now, start from the very beginning.'

'I was out riding when it happened. The theft, I mean. I had been hacking all morning. Jenkins was here. Martha came in to do the laundry but left before I did. When I returned from the stables, I went into the library, you know, my morning tipple as you say to warm me up and there wasn't any vodka in the cupboard. Jenkins was here. When I confronted him he told me that restocking the drinks cabinet wasn't part of his job description. And, that he had actually had enough. He couldn't stand working in the house with all the mess. I asked him nicely to take the car into Edinburgh to buy the vodka but he refused. So I told him he was through.

'I was so upset I ran upstairs. However, as I lay on the bed I started thinking about what jewels to wear to the ball tonight. You know how much I love to wear Mommy's Art Deco diamond tiara, you know the one, honey, the one I wore last year to the Black and White Ball. I couldn't decide whether to wear that one or the Lover's Knot tiara that daddy had had made especially for my twenty-first birthday. I couldn't make up my mind so I decided to take a look in the safe, help me decide.'

At this crucial junction in the story Lulu began sobbing hysterically. 'When I opened the door of the safe, all the velvet-lined boxes were gone. Everything was missing.'

'Had the safe been broken into?' Rupert asked. 'Sign of a break-in.'

410

Lulu sobbed. 'Honey, you know I never lock the safe. I can't be bothered locking and unlocking it all the time because I am always diving into it. I'd spend all day opening and closing it. Besides, there is no one around for twenty-five miles!'

'Lulu, do you know what this means? We will not be able to claim on our insurance.'

Lulu wiped her eyes on the sleeve of her fur coat.

'Do you have the faintest idea what your jewels are worth?'

'No.'

'The last estimate was thirty-five million pounds, perhaps more. The replacement value will be staggering!'

'The replacement value?' Lulu cried, sipping on her whiskey. 'My jewels cannot be replaced Rupert, Mommy's tiara is a family heirloom. Fabergé. It is part of a suite remember, with the earrings and bracelet to match...

'Mommy will be distraught. How am I going tell her? Grandmama's diamond engagement ring is gone too. And the pink diamond encrusted bracelet and the black diamond necklace you gave me last Christmas is also gone.' Sniffle, sniffle. 'Rupert, honey you must *do* something.'

'Yes darling.'

'It's too awful for words.' Lulu cried, choking and sobbing.

Rupert reached over, gathered his wife in his arms. 'Darling, listen to me, all I care about is you, and that you are safe and no harm has come to you.'

Lulu buried her face in his coat.

'Cheer up, my love. It's not the end of the world. Look. I bought you a little something in New York, I hope you like it.'

Rupert extracted the box from his coat pocket.

411

'Darling, this is for you. It's from your favourite jeweller!'

Lulu didn't say a word as she opened the familiar Graff box. She peeped inside, like a small child would do upon opening a birthday present. Then, she quietly shut the lid.

Lulu threw the box at Rupert, sobbing.

'I don't like it! I don't want it! It's not anything like Mommy's tiara. It's not the same! I wanted a tiara exactly like Mommy's! Take it back!'

Rupert gaped at his wife. She had turned into a monster.

'My jewels are all I have in the world, in this godforsaken country. They are all that truly mean anything to me. This house means nothing to me. My jewels are irreplaceable Rupert!'

The theatrics continued. Lulu should have studied at RADA.

'It will be impossible to replace jewels with such noble provenance – you must understand that. Unless we catch the thief which I think is most unlikely.

'I hate Scotland! I hate England! The Royals are all I care about. You know how much I loathe the rain and the fog and the damp weather. I can't stand being here without you. In fact, I'm considering returning to live California.'

'Don't be silly darling. You're upset, that's all. Shall I draw you a hot bath? You know a bath always makes you feel better.'

'I just got out of the damn bath!'

Then Lulu huffed, 'Rupee is a bath all you can suggest when my life has been turned upside down? Doesn't anything mean anything to you any more? If not, than I feel sorry for you. You are not the man I married.'

At this point in the saga Lulu gathered her coat around her and rushed out of the library, however as she fled, she stubbed her toe on the doorstop.

'Ouch! That frightful thing! Why on earth are we keeping such an ugly piece of stone in this damn house?'

Rupert watched his wife go. He hadn't seen her so upset since Buttercup's colt died.

—◌ ◌—

Lulu's dramatics exhausted him. Frankly, his demanding wife exhausted him. Rupert sat down on the pouffe in front of the dying fire, sighing loudly. He shrugged his shoulders. The fact that Lulu didn't like the tiara was soul-destroying. Five million American greenbacks worth of diamonds and the jewels weren't suitable. He downed his whiskey then walked over to the drinks cabinet and poured himself another, filling the tumbler. The single malt soothed his throat, numbed the ache in his belly. *Small pleasures...small pleasures...*

He recognised the heavy footsteps pounding down the hall.

'Hello Harry.' Rupert said flatly, using his business voice when speaking to his stepson. 'Is it really the weekend again?'

'Yep,' replied Harry, as he flung himself down on the sofa next to the fading fire, folded his arms in front of him, in a protective fashion.

'Where's mama?'

'Bathing.'

'Mama never bathes at cocktail time.' Harry started to yawn.

'She is really upset about the burglary. Let her be.'

'Yeah, all right Rupert.' Flexing his muscles. 'I don't understand Mama. It's not the end of the world, like the damn house is on fire. What's for supper?'

413

'I have no idea,' replied Rupert starchily as he punched the keys of his mobile phone. 'We are going to the ball tonight in London so you will have to fend for yourself.'

'I invited Max for the weekend. I guess I'll take him to the pub. You haven't seen Max have you Rupert? He is supposed to be here. He should have arrived hours ago.'

Rupert nodded.

'Guess I'll sit here and wait.' Harry's voice trailed off, as he reached inside his bag for a packet of crisps.

Rupert and Harry sat together in the library. Harry munched noisily on his crisps, played with his mobile phone. Rupert sighed a lot. Both tried to avoid the other. Small talk was never an option. The only distraction was the smouldering fire, although not for much longer as the fire was about to go out. Rupert stared into the bottom of his empty glass, imagining a week at the Priory wouldn't go amiss. He needed to make a call and grabbing his phone from the arm of the sofa, punched in the numbers.

'Yes. Longfield-Jones here, I'd like to place a bid of 175 000 pounds sterling on Lot # 23. Yes, in your up-coming sale, yes...in January,' he said, sounding impatient. 'Yes, that's right, the marble bust. Yes, I beg your pardon, yes, the bust of the Roman goddess, yes, I am well aware the sale is a long way off. You have my account details on file. Thank you.' The phone went dead.

'Hey Rupert!' Harry perked up. He turned on his side, resting his enormous arm on the cushion, while shoving crisps in his face. 'I didn't know you were interested in Roman statues.'

'I'm not really Harry,' said Rupert, staring at the dwindling flames, wondering where on earth the wood was kept. 'But I've taken a fancy to a marble bust that's coming up for auction in January.'

Westminster City Council

Mayfair Library

Borrowed Items 09/02/2018 13:01
XXXXXXXXXXXX3899

Item Title	Due Date
* Plunder With Intent	02/03/2018

Amount Outstanding: £0.55

* Indicates items borrowed today

Looking to fill your new
e-reader? Download e-books and
e-audiobooks for FREE at
www.westminster.gov.uk/libraries

'I don't get it. Why on earth did you have all of the marbles removed from the house if you have a desire for marble statues? '

Silence.

'It's not the same thing Harry.'

'It makes no sense at all,' said Harry rolling off the sofa. 'I'm going to the kitchen. Perhaps Max is in there. The builders haven't removed the damn fridge have they Rupert?'

As he headed towards the open door of the library, side-stepping past the doorstop, Rupert called out, 'Potch has invited you to Athens next year. It's Helen's twenty-first birthday. He wants to know if you would like to go.'

'I know. I got an email from Helen. Sounds good to me,' replied Harry as he shuffled out of the library, 'Max's a lucky man. He always gets the gorgeous babes!'

Rupert watched his stepson fade from view, wondering why on earth Harry had invited Max for a long weekend when the house was a complete and utter mess.

—◁ ▷—

It was a brisk ten-minute walk to the walled garden. He knew the way. He had played in the garden as a child and fond memories lurked in the bushes, the hedge, the topiary, even now, after so much time. The walled garden hadn't seen a gardener in years. All that remained were the remains of a fruit orchard – badly in need of a prune – surrounded by a massive display of brambles. A south-facing greenhouse attached to the garden wall was chock-a-block with junk, garden furniture and enormous terracotta pots with withered orange trees.

The number of skips in the garden was staggering. All with 'Watford Skip Hire' stamped on the side. It was a long way from Watford, but never mind, what did he know? The skips were virtually overflowing with rubble; redundant building material from the house. Max looked inside the first skip he came to. A pauper's grave for unloved marbles he thought, as he ran his hand over the smooth stone reproductions that came from Athens in the nineteenth century. There were about twenty skips in all, full of debris and broken statues. He searched through the skips. No sign of Selene's horse.

What a waste.

Max had suddenly seen enough. He turned to go. Then, he caught sight of a picture that had been tossed out. He reached into the skip, extracting the picture, trying not to cut his hand on jagged, broken glass. Of course! The picture, a magnificent, finely detailed pen and ink drawing of the Parthenon's east and west pediments had hung on the wall in the library.

'Sketched by Maximilian Henry Perceval, Athens, 1802.'

Max smashed the glass. He removed the drawing, folded it gently and stuck it inside his coat pocket. However, as he tossed the broken frame into the skip with more hostility than he could have ever imagined something else caught his eye. He had often wondered what had become of the paperback that he saw had been tossed out without a second thought. A book covered in grit, mould, sawdust. Max blew away the muck and the cobwebs, and glimpsed, *Being Shelley* by Ann Wroe. One of the most thought provoking books he had ever read on Shelley. Max shoved it in the inside pocket of his Barbour, excited about being reacquainted with an old friend. The book was just what he needed for his essay on Shelley.

Night was drawing in. He shivered, cursing the damp, dismal Scottish weather. He turned and ran, hurrying past the dairy, a huge octagonal shaped building made of stone. The demolition team had removed the door. How could he resist taking a peek inside? However, the dairy had clerestory windows which had been boarded up and Max failed to see the walls had been stripped of their blue and white tiles exposing enormous marble slabs of the Parthenon Frieze that had not seen daylight for over two hundred years.

Max hurried on until he came to a cavern overgrown with weeds and bracken. Max could not ever recall seeing the cave before and assumed the builders must have come upon it by accident, and as there were no windows in the cave, he assumed the building had been the ice-house at one time.

Curious, Max walked inside. It was like walking into a tomb. The odour was putrid, a combination of stagnant water and rotting wood. It was difficult to see, however his eyes soon adjusted and he stood peering into the murky chasm, a plethora of wooden crates, all different shapes and sizes, stacked to the dome-shaped ceiling. He couldn't imagine what lay inside and backed away, anxious to escape the foul-smelling cave.

As he turned to go he just happened to glance inside a crate resting on the floor by his feet. The crate was open and he could see a chunk of marble through the mouldy straw. What on earth was the bust doing in the cave? He crouched down to take a closer look then snapped a photo with his mobile phone, intending to send it to Helen. She would know whose head it was...

Max rushed out of the cavern. It was getting dark and he quickened his pace, rushing past the stables, the chicken coop and the cow sheds while cursing, *'Damn! My search has been in vain,'* as he stared into the piggery.

He couldn't believe his eyes. Sitting on the floor of the piggery was the marble statue of Selene's horse, the statue that had been in the Music Room, the statue he had loved so much as a child, and still did. The statue was an exact replica of the head of moon goddess's horse in the Quimby Gallery in London. His mind raced. Max threw open the iron door and walked inside, just as the marble caught the last rays of sunlight. Why had he never noticed it before? He was dumbstruck. The marble had a luminosity and depth to the stone that wasn't visible in the statue in the Quimby Gallery.

Max sat down on the statue, crossing his legs. He had to convince Harry's mother not to part with the statue. Perhaps she would sell it to him? Something else for his digs. Max sat patting the head of the horse, while the legend of Syrinx returned to haunt. He had often wondered whether the ancient Greek sculptors left their mark on the stone, like the bronze sculptors and he searched his pockets for his army knife, shining the tiny torch over every square inch of the stone; the mane, the mouth and the ears until he suddenly came upon two Greek letters carved inside the horse's nostrils; α for alpha and Ω for omega (the beginning and end of all things).

Max gave the statue an affectionate pat on its nose. He didn't know what to think. He wanted to text Helen to tell her about the doorstop but there was no mobile reception in East Lothian. Then he heard Harry calling.

'Max Max!' Harry ran towards him. 'Where on earth have you been? I've been looking everywhere for you! Want to go to the pub because I'm dying for a pint!'

'Harry. You are not going to believe this...'

'What am I not going to believe?' Harry asked.

'I'll tell you when we get to the pub!'

'We're also going to discuss where to go for Christmas.'

'I know where I'm going Harry. I need to see Opa. I have a few concerns that I need to discuss with him.'

'Don't you want to come to Davos, Max?'

'Are you kidding Harry, I'm still recovering!'

Chapter Thirty-Four
'Volledig' (The Fullness of the Void)
Axel Vervoordt

'We've spoken so much about the Quimby Marbles over Christmas Opa, but tell me, what do you *really* think the Parthenon is all about? Why all the fuss about a pile of old stones?'

'Would you like an architect's point of view or a political one?'

'Umm,' said Max running his mittens along the snow-topped hedge in the topiary garden. 'Start with the architect.'

'Do I have all day?' Opa grinned.

'Yes, Opa, you most certainly do.'

'I don't know where to start, so let me begin with energy.'

'Energy?' Max wrinkled his nose, 'energy?'

'Yes. William Blake said "Energy is Eternal Delight". He couldn't have been more right!'

'I'm not sure I understand Opa.'

'Well, allow me to explain. I bet you have never heard the theory that every building has a certain energy, an energy deep within the building itself. As you want to discuss the Parthenon, I will use it as an example, perhaps the best example in the world. I need to add, however, that the energies put out by the design structure, are ineffectual unless they are received by an instrument that is attuned to them. That instrument of course, being the sensibilities of the people who view the building, like you and I when we visit the Acropolis.'

'The Parthenon is nothing more than a ruin Opa, so does the building even in its ruinous state have energy?'

'The temples on the Acropolis, albeit the Parthenon or any other, like the Erechtheion or the Temple of Athena Nike may appear to be a ruin but they are anything but!'

Opa had stopped walking. His arms were high in the air. Max could tell he was excited. 'Furthermore, it is an insult to the Greek people to allude to any of the structures on the Acropolis as a ruin, Max, so please, I never want to hear you referring to the Parthenon as a ruin ever again.'

Max nodded. 'But, I *still* don't understand Opa.'

'It is all to do with the "'capacity to respond to design stimuli'", as it "'differs greatly with each individual'". Let us use the Parthenon. I fail to see how anyone can stand before the Parthenon without being painfully aware of the extreme sensitivity the Greek people possessed and still do in the twenty-first century. I recall being reduced to tears the first time I gazed up at the Parthenon, and I know your grandmother was too. It's the energy that the stones give off that we feel, at a subconscious level, because we cannot see this energy.

'However, some people do not feel this energy and to these poor souls the Parthenon is nothing but a pile of old stones.'

'Opa, I feel sorry for those who cannot feel this because everyone I know who has visited the Acropolis admitted that they were in awe of the mighty fortress, humbled by it.'

'Theoretically speaking, every building that had ever been built gives off a certain amount of energy, whether it's the Empire State Building in New York, the Louvre in Paris or the Vatican in Rome.'

'Why that's truly awesome Opa!' Max exclaimed, 'this puts a whole new light on the Parthenon.

'Tell me more Opa. Tell me more!'

'Well,' said Opa, 'the minute we apply a glimmer of consciousness to a mechanical gesture like the sculptors did when carving the marble, '"new impressions come into being". For consciousness rejuvenates everything, even a block of stone that anyone ever touched, even during the actual construction of the Parthenon.

'Think of it this way Max. When the stone-carvers or even those employed in restoring the Parthenon, right now, touch the marble, they are effectively empowering the stone by sending "warmth to everything that that person touches". Have you ever heard that old proverb, that when you touch an object that person leaves part of their soul behind?'

Max thought for a moment. His father's paperweight came to mind, and the tortoise shell, Murgatroyd. 'Yes, I have.'

'When we glimpse the Parthenon, we think we see marble, but, in actual fact what we feel goes way beyond the realm of consciousness. We experience all of the emotions, within our collective consciousness, of the Greek people. We feel their pain and their grief and their joy, culminating from the past two and a half thousand years. We can't really express what we feel. And, of course there are those unenlightened souls that feel absolutely nothing when they stand before the mighty Parthenon, however, it is their loss.'

'I agree with Gaston Bachelard when he said that a house, or in this case the Parthenon "is a sort of airy structure that moves about on the breath of time".'

'That is the most wonderful saying I have ever heard!'

'Can I go back to the energy thing for a moment, Opa? The reason I feel so comfortable, let's say, in the library at Cambridge, possibly has something to do with the energy within the library itself?'

'Absolutely, subconsciously the library holds deep within its walls, so much of its past history of all the students who used the library. You could say that the library has a soul. I know this sounds daft but it is true Max. We think inanimate objects are clumps of matter but they are not. Ask a physicist!' Ideas were coming fast and furiously.

'What about the castle, Opa?'

'The castle is a perfect example of this. Think of the centuries that the castle has been here and the human beings who lived within its walls!'

'It's as though the castle itself speaks to us on a subconscious level.'

'It's astonishing, really!'

'Inanimate objects will never ever be the same again,' said Max.

'Inanimate objects are not really static.' Max wanted to add his thoughts about Scruffy packed in his suitcase but decided against it – that may be stretching his grandfather's theory a little too far.

'Yes, you could say that,' Opa said, as they trudged along a path, ploughing through drifting snow towards the enormous topiary garden lined with box hedging, making their way slowly towards a marble sculpture standing on a stone plinth in the centre of the garden.

'You know Maximilian, we couldn't have happened upon a more perfect example of what we were discussing just now,' enthused Opa, waving towards the statue with his mitten.

'You remember seeing this before don't you Max?'

'Of coarse I do, Opa, although, I never liked it.'

'The statue doesn't have her head. Statues without arms and legs and heads make me feel sad.'

Max pointed towards the statue. 'She doesn't have much character, does she, without her head? In fact, she reminds me of the statue of Iris, in the Quimby Gallery. Iris must be bereft without her head. The trouble is she knows her head is in Athens, which makes her angry.

I always try to imagine how much nicer Iris would look with her head.'

'Have I ever told you that the statue is actually Greek?'

'No? Really!' Max's ears perked up under his fur earmuffs.

'The statue is the torso of a Greek goddess, Athena Parthenos, I believe. At one time the statue stood on a plinth in the garden at the Shambles.'

'Really? The Shambles?' Surprise filled Max's voice.

'Yes, that's right Max.'

More pieces of the puzzle were fitting together. He could hardly contain his excitement.

'The statue was given to us as a wedding present. All because your grandmother had an affection for it for some strange reason. The statue is from the fifth century BC. The provenance doesn't really matter. The fact that the torso has been in the Quimby family is all that's important and long may it remain.'

'Have you ever considered returning the statue to Greece, Opa?'

'Of course not Max,' said Opa, tugging on his fur-lined cap. 'It doesn't really matter any more. I think the Greeks need to sort themselves out first. Greece is a mess. Corruption is out of control. My argument is, if the Greeks can't look after themselves, then I fail

Plate XX: A bear named Scruffy – an inanimate object stuffed with cotton wool, or a more importantly, a much-love object of affection. After years of wear and tear, Scruffy becomes a treasure, much like the Parthenon statues.

to see how they can look after the Quimby Marbles if we decided to return the stones to Athens.'

'What they do with the marbles is their problem. The marbles belong to the Hellenic people, Opa.'

'Now we're getting into politics Max, and I don't like discussing political issues on an empty stomach. Let's have lunch before I drive you to the airport.'

Max was not in the mood for lunch. Although it was freezing cold Max could feel sweat trickling down inside his shirt. He had been waiting for this discussion for weeks. There was no stopping him...

'How can you live with your conscience, Opa? Knowing full well that the New Acropolis Museum in Athens will be opening next year and that the Greek people are desperate to have their marbles returned, not only from London, but Copenhagen, Munich, and Paris, and not do something? All member states of the European Union. You know all this Opa, don't you? You also have the power to do something, working with the European Parliament. What does the German Chancellor say? Don't you ever discuss this issue in Brussels? How can you sleep at night, knowing that you have a vital piece of Athena Parthenon in your garden and just ignore it?'

Max had been taught to respect his elders, especially his grandfather, however he was about to lose it.

Max didn't wait for a reply. He was engaging in rhetoric with his tutor at Cambridge and nothing on earth would stop him...

'I want to share something with you Opa. One reason I was anxious to spend Christmas with you is to share something, that, quite frankly I think you will find unbelievable!'

Max took several deep breaths.

426

'Quite by accident, I discovered marbles hidden at the Shambles. I found marble statues, metopes and sections of the Parthenon frieze that have been missing for the last two hundred years!'

Opa stopped dead, his boots crunching in the snow. His jaw dropped. He removed his spectacles, rubbing his piercing blue eyes. However, he didn't speak a word.

'Harry and I discovered a section of the colossal statue of Poseidon standing in the duck pond. We discovered metopes on the walls in the dairy and another horse's head in the piggery. This is blasphemy. An insult to the Greeks. We found crates of marbles in the cow-shed, and twelve slabs from the Parthenon Frieze mounted on the walls in the guest bathroom. Harry's mother thought they were plastic. Do you want to hear more Opa?'

Opa shook his head. His countenance reflected white as the snow.

'Let's walk back to the house Max. I'm freezing. I will reserve comment after we have had a whiskey.' Opa was shivering. He looked as though he had aged ten years in the last five minutes.

Max was shivering too, but it wasn't from cold. 'I have a line from William Blake, care to hear it Opa?'

'"The ruins of time build mansions in eternity".'

It didn't matter that his grandfather refrained from comment.

Max was angry. He resented being deliberately put off by his grandfather. Politics be damned. This wasn't a political issue, it was a moral issue. Although, he couldn't wait to text Helen. She would be over the moon to think he had discovered a piece of Athena's statue in Germany, no less.

Chapter Thirty-Five
The Auction

The hammer fell. 'Sold!' The auctioneer's refined plumy voice brought the bidding for Lot # 21 to a close. 'Sold to the lady in the front row. Paddle # 86. For the sum of £125 000.'

By late afternoon Lushington's Bond Street sale of Classical antiquities was in full swing. The saleroom jam-packed with London's discreet West End dealers representing their anonymous clients; the super-rich, uber-chic, global elite – all bidding against each other, eager to possess a chunk of Classical antiquity to enhance their residences in London, Moscow, Mumbai or Hong Kong. Needless to say the most sought-after pieces were going further afield.

Seated in the front row, amidst the burkas and the brollies and the bling, sat a wealthy Anglo-American, Rupert Longfield-Jones who appeared agitated, repeatedly stabbing at Lot # 23 in the catalogue with the gold nib of his Mont Blanc pen.

He was in a hurry. His time was valuable. He should have sent his PA along, or, made a telephone bid, but he wanted to see the goddess 'in the flesh' as it were and he wasn't disappointed. He was taking his Venus home with him.

'The next lot is the upper part of a limestone sarcophagus from the 3rd Dynasty, 380–43 BC. We have a reserve bid on the telephone of £120000. I will start the bidding at that price. Do I have 130, 130 in the room...140... 150...on the telephone...

Patience was not Rupert Longfield-Jones' greatest virtue. His driver was waiting outside to take him to Battersea Heliport. Charlie was waiting to whirl him off to the Shambles in the chopper before the weather closed in. Snow was expected. Rupert suddenly felt hot, claustrophobic. Squeezed between a lady sitting on his left – an older, ampler version of Beyoncé hiding behind enormous Chanel sunglasses, while hugging a Hermès handbag to her fur-clad bosom; the same croc Birkin bag he'd given Lulu for her birthday last year – and, an Asian man on his right, immaculate in a black-navy silk suit. Without doubt, the most expensive suit in the room. Unfortunately, the aroma of stale dim sum permeating the silk cancelled any amount of Eastern refinement the gentleman had, as the odour was rather off-putting, thought Rupert, as he juggled his paddle, iPhone, Blackberry, Lushington's catalogue and his cashmere coat folded neatly on his lap.

Meanwhile, the sale of Lot # 22 ended and Lushington's porters, sporting long black aprons and white shirts wheeled in Lot # 23, centred on a trolley draped in green baize. Rupert Longfield-Jones had been waiting for this moment for forty minutes and he had no intention of leaving the saleroom without the object of his desire.

'Lot # 23,' said the auctioneer, 'is the monumental marble head of the goddess, Venus, a Roman Imperial sculpture from the Hadrianic Period, circa AD 130–38. The bust, although somewhat damaged, is the original and comes from a private collection in France, however, the owner wishes to remain anonymous.'

'We have a reserve bid of £150 000. Let us start the bid at £160 000. Anyone in the room...do I have 160...160. Yes madam, thank you, 140...140...140 on the telephone, that's 140 thousand pounds...160.'

The bidding limped along.

Rupert Longfield-Jones' paddle shot up and down. The nonchalance of Lushington's auctioneer was beginning to irritate him; he might as well have been auctioning jellybeans for heaven's sake.

Nevertheless, the bidding for Lot # 23 continued to rise, forced up by several telephone bids and a woman seated at the end of the row, next to a marble column.

'Thank you madam, said the auctioneer, that's £200 000 for Lot #23. In the room...anyone in the room...

The bidding was as jittery as the Dow Jones on a late Friday afternoon thought Rupert, as his paddle bobbed up and down.

The lady seated in the front row by the column was forcing the price up well beyond what he imagined the bust to be worth, however, he had to have her.

Bloody fool! Rupert's inner voice screamed, as his paddle shot up in the air and stayed there.

'All done then, that's £250 000 for the gentleman seated in the front row, going once...twice...'

'Stop! Stop!' screamed a man from the back of the room.

Suddenly the auctioneer's hammer hovered in mid-air.

'Stop the sale!' The man shouted. 'Stop the sale!'

'Pardon me?' asked the auctioneer.

'Stop the sale Lot # 23 is not Hadrianic. It is not a Roman statue!' The man with a gravelly accent shouted, 'The bust is Greek, a marble bust from the Parthenon in Athens.

'The marble is the head of Athena Parthenos!' The gentleman was becoming irate and he rushed forward towards the podium where the auctioneer stood. His umbrella and catalogue falling to the floor. 'The marble has been missing for over two hundred years!'

'What on earth' boomed the auctioneer as he threw his gavel down onto the lectern, 'are you talking about?'

'Please, allow me to introduce myself. My name is Alex Kazantzakis. I am Professor of Greek Studies at the University of Athens. I am an expert in my field, and I believe the head is Pentelic marble from Greece and—'

The professor never got a chance to finish. He was interrupted by another man standing by the window.

'Well, I believe the bust is the head of a Nereid, from the monument in Xanthos, from 390–80 BC!'

'Excuse me,' said Rupert Longfield-Jones, as he stood up, his commanding voice silencing the room. 'Forgive my ignorance, or should I say my lack of expertise on Greek and Roman antiquities, however, I fail to see the problem here. Does it make any difference whether the marble head is Greek or Roman?'

'Sir, with respect,' said the visiting professor of Greek studies. 'I have spent my life searching the world for Greek marbles; the Parthenon marbles in particular. Trust me. I am able to recognise a statue of Pheidias a mile away.'

'Whether it's Pheidias' or some other Greek's, I still remain confused.'

'My flight to Miami leaves in an hour so...' The American woman at the end of the front row was on her feet, shouting in a loud voice, 'can we not just continue with the sale?'

'Here, here! Let's see where the bidding goes,' said another.

'Through the roof you fool,' said another.

'Well, what's wrong with that?' asked another man.

'The bust must be withdrawn from the sale,' said the auctioneer. 'The Parthenon marbles have become a political issue and Lushington's has no wish to become embroiled in a national debate, and one I might add that has been raging for centuries!'

People were standing up, peering over the heads of those standing in front of them, while others were rushing up to the front of the room, wanting to examine the bust. Voices rang out.

'What will happen to the marble?'

'The marble will be returned to its owner,' replied the auctioneer, shooting his cuffs and looking extremely uncomfortable.

'Who is the owner?' asked an Asian woman dressed immaculately in Channel couture. 'I'll pay whatever the owner is asking, *whatever* they want...'

'The marble belongs to us!' said the humble professor from Athens. 'The marble belongs to the people of Greece.'

'Why don't you buy it back?' said a dealer with a cockney accent, obviously from the East End of London.

'Why should we? The marble belongs to *us*. If you had your TV stolen you wouldn't expect to buy it back from the thief. Lord Quimby pinched, or should I say, plundered the Parthenon at the beginning of the nineteenth century and everything that he took, including the head of Athena should be returned to Greece!'

By this time everyone in the salesroom were clambering over their bags and their brollies and the gilt-wood chairs in order to get a closer look at the bust. They wanted to touch the head of Athena, as though she were a real goddess.

'Order!' shouted the auctioneer. 'Order!

'Please return to your seats!' The auctioneer looked a little flustered. 'Guards...call security.

Lushington's saleroom is to be cleared immediately. Lot # 23 is being removed from the sale until further notice.'

Rupert watched the bust being wheeled out of the saleroom on a trolley. His goddess was gone. But not for long. Rupert was a businessman. He intended to find out who the anonymous owner was and make a deal privately.

He walked out of the saleroom finding it impossible to believe what had taken place. Greece was in a terrible mess. The country was bankrupt. The Greeks hadn't a cent to bless themselves with, other than Potch. He wondered what he would say about the marble, although he didn't think his old chum would care too much about the Parthenon marbles. Yachts were his thing.

He was on his way back to New York. No one in New York cared about the Parthenon marbles. New Yorkers didn't even know where Athens was for heaven's sake. As the unhappy investment banker rushed out the door onto Bond Street, he couldn't help thinking about the marble head of Athena and the power she wielded. Even now, after two thousand years. It was awe-inspiring.

Chapter Thirty-Six
We Are All Greek

'*Pateras*!' Helen waved her Rolex Oyster Perpetual Date, just set in twenty-one enormous three carat diamonds, in the air for all her guests to see. 'It's gorgeous! Thank you *Pateras*. How did you guess a watch is exactly what I wanted for my birthday?'

Helen leaned across the table, hugging her father, the Tiffany box tumbling onto the deck which was littered with expensive wrapping paper, lavish bows and posh velvet boxes: Louis Vuitton, Graff, Dolce & Gabbana and Chanel to name a few. She threw her arms around her father's neck, holding him close, kissing him on the cheek. 'Thank you *Pateras*, my Rolex is the best birthday present ever!'

'You are most welcome, darling,' replied Dimitri, beaming, 'just enjoy it. There is no excuse for not knowing when the boat sails!'

Helen sat at the head of the enormous marble table opening her birthday presents while the crew replenished her guests' glasses with her favourite Dom Perignon. Not that anyone needed more champagne. Champagne had been flowing non-stop since dawn and would continue to do so until the small hours of the morning. Helen's birthday lunch had been going on for hours, which wasn't unusual;

Dimitri was an excellent host and thoroughly enjoyed entertaining, especially on board Kallisti. Because Helen's birthday was a casual affair he had chosen the sky lounge on the upper deck – one of six decks – to hold the celebration, as the view of the Parthenon across the harbour was breathtaking. Dimitri caught his lover's eye and winked. He had fallen madly in love with Badiya, a rather exotic woman from Dubai; mainly because she was extremely wealthy in her own right, which allowed Dimitri to relax in their relationship as she wasn't after his bloody money. Badiya was a royal princess, adding a touch of class to his otherwise stark, material world and he loved it. Dimitri was in a happy mood that day, as he had invited his old school chums from Harrow to join him. Dimitri sat back in his chair puffing on a Cuban cigar, listening to his guests' conversations...

'Honey?' Lulu cooed seductively from her deck chair, like she always did in the company of others. 'Don't you just love Kallisti?'

'Umm...why, yes, of course darling,' replied Rupert, gazing longingly out to sea as he leaned on the magnificent marble table, carved in the shape of the Parthenon. 'She's quite all right. Yes, she's a stunner, all forty-eight metres of her.'

'How many feet is that honey?' Lulu asked while she rummaged through her Hermès beach bag – ten thousand pounds worth of croc; lip-gloss not included.

'For heaven's sake, Lulu. Honestly!' shot Rupert, rolling his eyes behind his Ray-Bans, 'Didn't that fancy finishing school teach you anything?'

'You don't have to snap my head off honey, I only asked a simple question.'

Rupert caught the waiter's eye – who was immaculately dressed in sparkling white uniform, and pointed at his empty champagne glass like a jerk. The only way to get through the day was to keep drinking. Boredom had set in, big time – and they had only arrived yesterday.

The problem was his wife. Lulu wasn't herself and hadn't been since the butler had absconded with her baubles. Every social occasion was pure hell. Lulu complained she had nothing to wear in the diamond department. He had spent millions replacing her jewels and all had been returned to her except the largest rocks from Graff Bond Street, but Lulu was still not happy, and neither was he. This was entirely exacerbated by the fact that the insurance company refused to pay out because his wife had failed to lock the safe. He could have invested heavily in the property market in Mayfair, or Park Avenue, for all the money he had spent in the last year on diamonds. The crazy thing about the theft was that his wife blamed him. Her words rang in his ear, 'If you had been at home honey this would never have happened!'

So the theft had caused a rift the size of the San Andreas Fault and the chasm was deepening with every social engagement. Life was hell. They were constantly at each other's throats. Helen's birthday bash was no different. While he drank himself into oblivion, Lulu cosied up to Potch's guests, debating the length of their yachts, discussing the heat or inquiring about the ownership of the boats bobbing up and down in Piraeus harbour. Russian plutocrats, all of them, Rupert thought, as he watched a mammoth sailboat glide past without so much as a whisper, engines gently purring.

Booze to the rescue. Booze fixed everything, concluded Rupert as the waiter refreshed his glass. He eyed Potch's latest 'squeeze' tip-toe up the stairs and swan onto the sun deck. All Potch's babes looked the same; clones with different coloured hair. Gorgeous models, every one. Princess Badiya was no different. Right out of *Tatler* or *Vanity Fair*. Photo-shoot perfect, hiding behind enormous white designer sunglasses, a Gucci sun-visor, gold bangles up to her elbows and Greek sandals studded with precious jewels – diamonds – in your face bling. Rupert watched her stroll seductively towards the table, her kaftan catching in the gentle breeze exposing long, gazelle-like legs, slender thighs. God! What a tease, thought Rupert, recalling his much younger, less-flabby, chauvinistic self; she didn't even give him a nod. She wasn't really his type – he wasn't sure what his type was any more. However Badiya was definitely much more pleasing to look at than a thousand OTT yachts birthed in the harbour.

'Honey, your Rolex is divine!' Lulu gushed, fiddling with her phantom diamond necklace. 'I just love the diamonds around the face and the pink strap!'

'Thank you Mrs Longfield-Jones,' said Helen holding out her slim wrist. 'Now, I've no excuse for being late for work.'

'Work?' Lulu looked slightly aghast. 'Harry never told me you worked! How interesting. Where do you work Helen?'

'I work at the new Acropolis Museum over there!' replied Helen enthusiastically, pointing towards Athens. 'See, at the base of the Acropolis.'

'The Apopolis?' Lulu asked, playing with her long blonde hair, the way models do when bored or hungry, which had to be most of the time. After all, there was only one thing in Lulu's life, now her jewels were gone and that was herself. 'Where is the Apopolis?'

Everyone at the table laughed, including Badiya. 'Lulu darling, it's not the Apopolis, it's the Acropolis!'

'Where is the Acropolis, then?' quipped Lulu, pouting. 'Where is the Acropolis, Badiya?'

'You have been staring at the Acropolis all day Lulu,' shot Rupert, embarrassed by his wife's apparent lack of general knowledge. He was nibbling on a platter of freshly caught calamari, quite simply the best he had ever tasted.

'I didn't know *that* did I Rupee!' blasted Lulu, angrily at her husband. They really had been at each other's throats all day.

'What do you do at the museum?' asked Lulu, tugging the spaghetti straps of her bikini up-lifting her bosom. She was tanned to absolute perfection, like all super-rich babes.

'I am a sculptress Mrs Longfield-Jones.'

'And, might I add, a brilliant one at that!' enthused Dimitri. 'However, Athena has been giving you a real fight, hasn't she darling, because Helen hasn't been able to piece together the statue that she has been working on for the last six months!'

'Athena? Who is Athena?' Lulu asked sucking on melting ice cubes, the last of her *Skinny Bitch*. 'Is Athena one of your politicians?'

Helen giggled. So did everyone else.

Badiya said, 'Athena is a Greek goddess, right Potch? Athens is named after Athena Parthenos who was a cult figure in ancient Greece.'

'Really? That's awesome!' Lulu replied, intrigued, as she dabbed her nose with sun-screen worth more than a month's wages for the average cash-strapped Greek. 'Helen, please, I want to know more about Athena!'

'Well,' said Helen, warmth rising in her voice, 'several pieces of the original statue of Athena – that stood in the gable-end of the Parthenon – went missing, shall we say – and, I am finding it almost impossible to piece the statue together with the bits we have at the museum. My job as a sculptress is to compensate for the statue's missing parts by making plaster-of-Paris sections to fill in where the missing pieces of Athena should be.'

'Where are the missing pieces of Athena located – I mean, you know, the original pieces?' asked Lulu, jiggling her glass high in the air, indicating to the waiter to bring another.

However, their conversation was cut short.

'Excuse me, Mrs Longfield-Jones,' said Helen, jumping up. 'I can see Max and Harry coming across the harbour in the launch!'

Helen left the table. She raced down the spiral steps in her shorts, T-shirt and hand-made sandals, minus the gemstones of course. However, she met Lord Quimby coming up on deck.

'Good afternoon, Sir,' said Helen, shaking his hand, briefly, then she hurried down the stairs. She loathed the man. Her father had been to Harrow with Lord Quimby and they had remained good friends. Helen couldn't forgive her father for this, but then again, *Pateras* wasn't supporting her cause. He wasn't interested in the return of the marbles. All he cared about was sailing the Med with a string of bimbos trailing on his arm. The thought of seeing Max again, however, after nearly a year, filled her with joy. She was madly in love with *her* Englishman. Although he didn't know it, not yet, but soon he would when they were alone on the beach. She had asked Captain Balanos to take them to Patmos tomorrow, and had even arranged a very special picnic to celebrate. Did Max feel the same?

'Quim!' Exclaimed Dimitri. 'Lovely to see you. You've arrived just in time to wish my girl a happy twenty-first birthday!'

'Good to be here Potch!' said Lord Quimby, slapping Potch on the back, en route to the bar.

'Quim!' Rupert greeted his old school chum. 'Good to see you. Want your damn house back? The Shambles is all yours. Statues and all – they frighten the daylights out of me!'

Quim roared with laughter, shooting his cuffs. Imagine. French cuffs and sleeve links on a yacht. 'I left the statues for you! They make excellent company. Never argue. Never nag!'

'Don't mention nagging!' said Rupert under his breath.

'It's great to see you again,' and turning around Quim said 'Lulu! And you too, how lovely to see you my dear? Enjoying the Scottish air are we, hacking at the Shambles?'

'I am quite well,' replied Lulu through pursed lips, waiting to be kissed. 'Thank you Quim, however, let's refrain from discussing the Shambles or the drab Scottish weather. The Mediterranean sun is much more to my liking!'

'As you wish,' said Quim, kissing the air above Lulu's cheek. 'I can't believe how dreadfully hot it is,' he exclaimed, moping his brow with his polka-dot handkerchief that he had extracted from his breast pocket. 'Even in May!'

'What on earth will the heat be like in July?' asked Lord Quimby, loosening his club tie – the one with the diagonal stripes.

'Bloody hot Quim!' offered Potch, 'insufferable really!'

'Christ, Potch, Kallisti is a floating palace!' Quim enthused, while surveying the deck. 'Your yacht is large enough for a hotel!' Then, looking somewhat askance he asked, 'What if I need to escape? Where the devil do you moor your dinghy?'

'No dinghy Quim, just the launch!'

'How do you like Kallisti, Jonesie?' Quim asked. 'I bet your good wife would love a boat like Potch's for her birthday?'

'When that Scottish pile of yours is no longer a shambles I might consider something that floats but until that time comes Quim, we'll stick to taking the jitney to and from the Hamptons.'

'Waiter' said Potch, guiding his old school chum towards the bar. 'A good stiff G&T for my good friend.'

Dimitri, one of Athens' wealthiest shipping tycoons, returned to his seat at the head of the table. Dimitri was the worst dressed man on the ship. He wasn't very tall, which meant his baggy sweatpants worn with cotton T-shirt and bare feet did nothing to enhance his physique. Two thousand years had come to pass yet bare feet were still *de rigueur* in Greece.

Then Lulu asked, while pointing at his T-shirt, 'For Lord's sake Potch, 'who is that old woman on your shirt?' Lulu was squinting through her Gucci shades. 'What does it say? Greek isn't it 'cause I can't understand a word. Greek is so darn hard to read!'

Potch glanced down at his worn T-shirt smiling broadly. 'Helen gave me this shirt for my birthday this year. She had it made especially for me. Everyone who sees one wants one and now Helen has set up a business selling T-shirts at the market with Athena on the front.'

Potch added, 'Helen is always thinking of ways of spreading the word, wanting the world to know about her cause; our ill-fated marbles. Helen lives for the day when the marbles will be returned to Greece.'

'So!' asked Lulu, impatiently. 'What does it say on your T-shirt?'
'Athena Rocks!'

'This was the first of four T-shirts my daughter has designed. Another, of the Parthenon says, "The Parthenon Rocks". And, another of our beloved statue of Kore, the caryatid has the words

"Kore is Coming Home" printed beneath the statue. The last shirt to be printed is of the moon goddess' horse, and it says, "Selene's Horse – We Love You".

'I want some of those T-shirts. Several dozen each – the Californians will go crazy!'

'Place an order with Helen when she returns. She will be delighted!' exclaimed Dimitri, proudly.

'Potch?' asked Lulu. 'Badiya was very kindly explaining about the Parthenon...have I got that right...the Pantheon?'

'The Pantheon is in Rome darling,' snapped Rupert.

'Must you interrupt honey?' shot Lulu. 'Anyway, Athena is a Greek goddess. Harry would say Athena is cool. And, I agree!'

'I think it's time we had a cool goddess ruling the world!'

'Quim, you are the authority on Classical antiquities, perhaps you can explain all about Athena to Lulu' said Dimitri, nibbling on a few ripe olives.

'Oh please. Let's not discuss marbles. I left those blasted statues behind in the museum. Boring company you know. Never have anything interesting to say!'

Loud guffaws echoed in the sultry sea air.

'Is it true that you have parts of the goddess on display at the museum in London?' asked Rupert, guzzling champagne.

A great deal of throat clearing preceded Quimby's response. 'The section of Athena's upper torso is on display in the Quimby Gallery. We have her foot, or I should say we *had* Athena's right foot on display although it appears to have gone missing, mysteriously disappeared a few months ago and we have been unable to locate it.' More throat clearing. 'We also had a piece of the goddess's arm.'

'What about her head?' asked Rupert. 'Do you have any idea where Athena's head is?'

'I haven't the faintest idea!' shot Lord Quimby, shrugging, obviously feeling the heat in his navy blazer. 'We don't know where her head is. One day it might turn up. Why do you ask? Do you have the marble tucked away in the hold, in a cubby on the yacht, perhaps?' Sarcasm was rising in his voice. 'I could take it home with me. How absolutely marvellous to have Athena's head on display in London, enhance our collection.' Quim scratched his head. 'You know it's strange but the museum here in Athens have not been able to locate her head, either. Athena's head seems to have vanished from the face of the earth. Along with her lower torso and...'

'Do you have any idea what Athena looked like,' asked Rupert, suddenly curious, 'I mean the goddess's marble head?'

'No, we don't know for certain but we have a very good idea,' said Quim, as he gulped his Hendrick's and tonic. 'Another, waiter please!'

'Well, that's very interesting,' said Rupert. 'The reason I ask is, I have had my eye on a Roman bust for quite some time, and let me tell you the sculpture is really quite exceptional. In fact I have been meaning to discuss this with you, see what your thoughts were.'

'Honey!' cried Lulu, 'you don't know a thing about marble statues!'

Rupert ignored his wife. 'I was in New York at the time. I was coming out of Rockefeller Center one day last autumn and happened upon the most magnificent bust that I have ever seen. Not that I have seen many Quim. The bust came up for auction at Lushington's last January. I placed a bid on it, however, the statue was removed from auction by a professor of Greek studies. I'd be surprised if you didn't hear about the sale; the papers were full of it!'

'Really?' said Quim, however there was no further discussion as another guest came rushing up on deck.

'Francesca, darling!' Potch rushed to greet Francesca, planting kisses on both cheeks. 'I am so pleased you could come.

'Now, please, allow me to introduce my dear friends,' as he took her arm and waltzed her around the sun deck. 'I don't believe you've met my dear friend Rupert Longfield-Jones who was also a friend of Charles, and his delicious other half Lulu.'

'Delighted to meet you' said Francesca, smiling brightly.

'And, my new love, my darling Badiya, my princess.'

Francesca took Badiya's small hand in hers.

'I'm so thrilled to be here!' enthused Francesca, unable to contain her excitement, or was it relief, after taking the overnight bus all the way from Menton. Your yacht, or, should I say "Kallisti", is magnificent. What a lovely name for a yacht. Am I right, "Kallisti" means *most beautiful* in Greek?'

'Absolutely right!' Potch sounded chuffed. 'Spot on.'

'Can you speak Greek?'

'Good heaven's no,' replied Francesca, brushing her luxuriant mane from her eyes; an intoxicating combination of azure and deep blue of the sea.

'Enough talk about yachts!'

Potch, being his charming self, said 'Please, let's all sit down at the table. Enjoy the splendid view of the Acropolis, watch the sun set over the lofty Parthenon!'

'Hello Francesca,' said Lord Quimby looking as though he was trying to avoid a foul smell in the air, with a 'you-will-never-amount-to-anything' look, as he took Francesca's hand, kissing the air. 'How are you my dear?'

'Well, thank you Quim,' replied Francesca, resisting the urge to pull her hand back. Not the time for a family feud.

Quim glanced over Francesca's head, the way people do when bored with their company.

'Thank you for having us Potch. Max will be over the moon when he sees your helipad!'

'Perfect for a quick getaway,' said Rupert, from the bar stool.

'Bring a glass of champagne for my guest!' Dimitri bellowed.

The birthday party continued. Food just kept coming. Canapés, Greek olives, taramasalata, every tantalising morsel imaginable was offered on magnificent silver trays.

'Where is that handsome son of yours?' asked Potch, padding towards the dining table in his bare feet.

'I passed Max and Harry in the launch as I left the harbour.'

Rupert slouched on his bar stool, asking himself why he'd never had the privilege of meeting Charles' stunningly beautiful wife at some time.

'Should be here soon,' said Badiya, her smouldering deep brown eyes flashing in the bright sun. 'Helen is so excited, She can't wait to see Max and Harry again; it's been a year since their last visit to Athens.'

'Of course, this year is very special with the opening of the New Acropolis Museum,' said Dimitri eying his three iPhones, blinking non-stop. 'Helen has worked so hard to restore the marble statue of Athena. In fact, all the marbles. She despairs, knowing that her beloved statues are elsewhere, without any hope of the marbles ever being returned to Athens in time for the grand opening of the museum next month. Helen told me how many tonnes of plaster-of-Paris had been used to make casts. It is staggering. People do not understand the labour involved in making the reproductions when there is no need for it. To say nothing of the cost involved!'

Potch looked towards the Parthenon bathed in glorious sunlight. 'For Helen, not having the marbles is soul destroying.'

'You cannot possibly understand what it means to have something so precious taken away,' Badiya offered, softly, with her head bowed, staring at her hands neatly folded in her lap.

'Please! Don't get me going!' cried Lulu, waving her fingers painted in bright orange shellac wildly about like daggers capable of gouging cyclops' eye out.

'Please darling. Not here!' cried Rupert. 'Not now!'

'I will *never*, and I mean *never* be the same again since my jewels were stolen last year. My diamond engagement ring, my grandmother's sapphire engagement ring, my grandmother's tiara... all precious family jewels, gone.'

At this point Lulu burst into tears and sobbing hysterically, dug into her bag for a tissue. Wiping her nose she blubbered, 'The problem is that my jewels can never be replaced. Never!'

Then, Lulu from La La Land had the most profound thought ever as she gazed at the Parthenon. 'Perhaps this is how Helen feels about Athena's missing parts.'

Everyone on board the sundeck fell silent – even the crew.

Lulu had spoken the truth. Socrates, who had spent his lifetime in the pursuit of truth would be proud of this silly American woman who unknowingly had spoken the truth.

'It's not the same thing!' Lord Quimby offered hotly, looking constipated.

'It is exactly the same thing,' said Rupert, huffily. 'Lulu's jewels meant everything to her. They were precious keepsakes. Lulu's jewels represent who she is. Furthermore, until they were stolen I had never seen Lulu without her jewels. She even wore a diamond necklace in the bath!'

'The last time I wore Mommy's tiara was at the Mayflower Ball. Now, I don't want to go to the ball. My jewels were worth millions. Honey, how much did you say my diamonds were worth?' asked Lulu, sniffling.

Rupert shrugged. He didn't like to elaborate.

At this point in the conversation Lulu glanced at the Parthenon in the setting sun. She laughed. 'Whereas I doubt very much that the stones from the Poplios...oh you know the Papilon...the building on the hill has any value at all. It looks like a pile of old stones to me, nothing more than a lot of old rocks. I like Athena, though!'

The wit coming from Lulu was extraordinary.

'Athena Rocks! The Pantheon rocks. Athena is my kind of woman. She has class. Something I've always dreamed of having!'

'Well, I certainly care, Mrs Longfield-Jones. Helen cares. Harry cares more now than he used to,' said Max as he strode on to the sundeck; a young Adonis in navy blazer, crisp white shirt, Cambridge tie, cream Chinos and top-siders. Max smoothed back his mop of thick brown hair flopping over his eye, while a member of the crew followed close behind lugging heavy rucksacks up on deck.

'Max!' cried Potch. 'Good to see you young man. Make yourself comfortable!' Potch was the perfect host, hospitality meant everything to him. After all, he was Greek.

Max made the rounds, shaking hands, kissing the ladies; he may have had his shortcomings but his manners were impeccable.

There was a lull in the conversation when Helen and Harry suddenly appeared, straggling up onto the sundeck, just in time to hear Max...

'I overheard what you said Mrs Longfield-Jones on my way upstairs.' Max had been dreaming of this moment for months. He had rehearsed every word over and over in his mind. King's College unbound. Shelley...here goes... He winked at Helen.

'I have a question for you. As we stand in sight of the most iconic structure in the world, the one building in our Western world that is perfect. Absolute perfection. As Edward Hollis said in his book, "it is what architecture was, is and should be". Although there isn't a lot left of it, how much more empowering would the Parthenon be with its marbles?'

'Good question!' Potch banged on the table.

'Allow me, if you will, to quote from Thucydides,' said Max with authority, using his tutorial voice. 'He said that Athens became the school, not only of the Hellas but of the whole Western world, and the Parthenon has been a model of architecture ever since.'

'Nonsense!' said Quim. 'Ancient Greece was one thing, modern Greece is quite another.'

'Think about it?' Max's deep voice was getting deeper; he hadn't expected to see his uncle. He was determined to get his point across. Desperate to enlighten he added, 'The eighteenth-century dilettante believed the Parthenon was a model for all civilised art and became the symbol of Grecian liberty.'

'I am thinking about it!' Rupert's wine glass suddenly went flying overboard, disappearing into the deep blue sea as he kept right on talking, 'The facade on the bank of England, the facade on the Museum of Classical Antiquities, the Stock Exchange on Wall Street, the Brandenburg Gate in Berlin, the White House for Christ's sake have all been copied from the Parthenon. Although, I must confess,

I never thought about all this before. I guess we really do owe a lot to those brilliant men, ancient Greek or not!'

'Grecian liberty is a bit like our Statue of Liberty,' said Francesca enthusiastically. 'I can't possibly imagine what the American people would do without their lady!'

'We would have a world war on our hands!'

'Just think, for a moment, if you will,' said Badiya, 'what would happen if the Greeks pinched a brick from the Statue of Liberty?'

'War, I tell you, there would be war!' shouted Potch, being his passionate self, always keen to debate. 'There would be war if we stole a light bulb from the Statue of Liberty!'

'What if the Greeks helped themselves to the Crown Jewels?' asked Francesca. 'Would the theft cause a world war?'

'No there wouldn't be a war. We would ask for them back, that's all,' said one of Potch's English guests. We are British. We have manners.'

'What if the Greeks refused?'

'You wouldn't. You are too civilised,' said Harry.

Lulu offered, 'I remember reading an article in the newspaper about the Queen, her strong affection for her jewels. They mean a lot to her, especially the diamond tiara belonging to Queen Victoria. I can relate to this affection for one's jewels. Therefore, the Greeks have my support, and my sympathy, because, I understand how the people of Greece must feel: grief-stricken!'

'There's something else that I believe you may find a bit strange,' said Max. 'We believe that the Greek marbles have souls. Ask anyone who reads Classics at Cambridge!'

'Please, Max! Enough. Sit down!' His uncle gave his nephew a curt nod, wanting to shut him up. 'Don't be ridiculous!'

'The bloody Greek stones,' growled Lord Quimby. 'I can't abide the lot!'

'Careful what you say, Quim, or I'll have you thrown overboard.'

'We are all Greek,' enthused Max as he stood at the end of the table. 'We are all Greek!'

'We most certainly are not!' from none other than Lord Quimby.

'Potch is Greek. Helen is Greek. Most of the crew are Greek and hands up who else is Greek?'

'Well, I most certainly am not!' Lord Quimby laughed nervously.

'Well I beg to differ. I am Greek and I am proud of it. May I add, so are you uncle,' said Max, as everyone on deck fell silent.

'Bollocks!' Lord Quimby shot.

'I have proof!' Max extracted a collection of crumpled letters from his blazer pocket.

'We are both Greek, Uncle. Shall I read you a letter that I found at the house in St James's Square to prove my theory?'

Lord Quimby, who until this point had been standing by the railing enjoying the light breeze, slumped down on a nearby sun-lounger.

'Please, allow me to enlighten you.' A bit of good old-fashioned Greek rhetoric wouldn't go amiss Max thought, as he plunged in...

'The love story goes something like this: My great, great, great, grandfather, Maximilian Henry Perceval fell in love with a beautiful Greek girl, a flower seller, whom he rescued from a terrible fate, right here at Piraeus, exactly where we are now. The young woman was about to be sewn up in a canvas sack by the Turks, thrown into the sea for being wrongly accused of theft. This story has a happy ending. Maximilian married the flower seller in Athens at the Capuchine

Monastery, and their first son was my great, great grandfather. Uncle, does this not prove that we are Greek?'

'At least half Greek,' cried Potch.

'Shelley says we are all Greek and I agree.'

'Byron also had a great affection for all things Greek.'

'So did Ovid!' Harry shouted. Harry liked to shout. He said he shouted because he was an American and they shouted because they wanted to be heard.

Max wasn't shouting. 'Wait! There are more letters that I found inside Murgatroyd.

'Murgatroyd? Who on earth is Murgatroyd?' asked Lord Quimby.

'Murgatroyd is cool, really cool,' exclaimed Harry, collapsing onto a sun-lounger, his huge arms dangling over the side. 'I am sure you'll all get to know him soon. I think Murgatroyd deserves a T-shirt. In the meantime, however, I'll say no more, 'cause I'm on holiday!'

'I thought you might enjoy hearing the truth about the theft of the Parthenon marbles as I have here correspondence between the 9th Lord Quimby and his London agent, Mr Dashiell Hamilton.'

'Where the devil did you get those?' spat Quim.

'At the house.'

'I have my Lord the pleasure of announcing to you the possession of the eighth metope, the one of the centaur carrying off the woman. This piece has caused much trouble in all respects, and I have even been obliged to be a little barbarous.

Dear Dashiell,

I should wish to have examples of the Acropolis, actual objects of each thing, and architectural ornament

- of each cornice, each frieze, each capital of the decorated ceilings, of the fluted columns - specimens of the different architectural orders, and the variant forms of the orders - of the metopes and the like, and as much as possible. Finally, in the way of sculptures, medals and curious marbles that can be discovered by means of assiduous and indefatigable excavation. This excavation ought to be pushed on as much as possible, its success be what it may.

'There is another letter, dated, 1802. It was written by Don Battista Belisario concerning the removal of the centrepiece of the east frieze and reads...

Milord,

We will not be able to continue as we are in want of longer saws. Our saws have broken and are stuck in the metope. The Athenians appear displeased. Let's get this part of the demolition over as quickly as possible. I am sickened by this terrible deed.

'Now, what do you think?' asked Max. 'Have you changed your mind? Do you still think the Quimby Marbles should be returned to Greece?'

'Absolutely not!' said an English guest. 'We rescued the marbles from further destruction by the Turks!'

'Greece is ripe for revolution!' said another. 'Civil war could break out at any moment in this damn country. What if we returned the marbles and the Neo Nazis plundered the museum and stole them!'

'Why on earth would they do that?' Lulu asked.

'For exactly the same reason the French stormed the Bastille!'

'You mean just for the hell of it!'

'Your uncle would be a hero if he returned even one of the marbles to Greece!' said Helen. 'Lord Quimby, why not send the marbles back?'

Helen didn't wait for his reply. This was her chance to speak her mind. 'Whenever I visit the Museum of Classical Antiquities I watch the tourists swarming into the Quimby Gallery with their mobiles and their earphones and guide books and do you know what I think Lord Quimby? I don't believe that the majority of the people who visit the gallery understand what the marbles are all about. Even more to the point. It matters not whether the statues are original or not. What I'm trying to say is this: the marbles could be reproductions and no one would even know the difference or care. To most, the marbles are just enormous chunks of carved stone, stuck to the walls of the museum.

'The last time I visited the museum I despaired, because the statues looked sad and forlorn. Museums are such gloomy places. It made me weep. Any why do you keep our beloved Kore alone in another room? She looks so sad. Marble statues were designed to be outside in the open air, in the sunlight. When the sun shines through the marble it brings the stone to life. Mrs Longfield-Jones, imagine the Statue of Liberty stuck inside a building. The set-up of the frieze is wrong, according to Mary Beard, it is inside out.

'We sculptors despair, because many of the marble statues' body parts are in different parts of the world. For example, Iris' head is in Athens but her torso is in London. Forgive me, but can you possibly imagine how unsettling that is for a Greek goddess?

'Why, it's enough to give a goddess a headache!'

Everyone laughed.

Helen continued. 'We are too polite. We are suffering from lack of confidence. We are so afraid of upsetting the British and the Germans who bailed us out financially that we wouldn't say boo to a goose!'

Max rushed to her aid. 'Remember when the Stone of Destiny was in London and what a bloody great fuss the Scots made about it? Have you ever seen it? It's just a great lump of stone, yet nothing would do. The Scots insisted the stone be returned to Scotland. There isn't even an ounce of adornment on the stone. Nothing. No carving. No inscription!'

'The problem is,' said Lord Quimby, 'If you will allow me to explain, if our museum gives the marbles back to Greece every country on earth will want their treasures back, and then what? The floodgates will open and the museums will be empty of their treasure!'

'With respect Sir, I beg to disagree,' breathed Helen. 'Let me make this very clear. We are not asking for all our marbles to be returned. Only the marbles from the Parthenon, with the exception of Kore of course. We have offered to replace the Parthenon marbles with other marbles from ancient Greece. We have lots of artefacts we would be willing to swap.

'What you really don't understand is this: every chunk of stone from the Parthenon is of vital importance to the Parthenon because it is an integral part of the temple itself. The very fabric of the building if you like. Compare what I am saying to the dome in St Peter's Basilica in Rome. Take away a brick and the entire edifice crumbles. Remember: the Acropolis is a World Heritage site but sadly, there is so little remaining of our heritage!'

'So what?' said another. 'Every country in the world has been plundered at one time or another.'

'Imagine living and working in Athens, as I do, and as you go about your daily life, glimpse the Parthenon high on the outcrop of the Acropolis. It's impossible not to live in Athens and not see the Parthenon as it looms over the city. What happens is you are constantly reminded of the fact that someone has something that rightly belongs to you and won't give it back. It makes you angry. It makes your children angry. And, gradually this anger turns to despair, because there is nothing you, yourself can do about it. The despair turns to anger, anger clothed in hatred. You feel as though you have lost your soul and every single time you gaze up at the Parthenon, you realise so much valuable time and money is being spent, money we don't have, on recreating that which is in your museum in London. Yet, you know you cannot do a thing about it. It's diabolical. Despair eats away at the centre of your being. Like a cancer. I believe this is the reason there is so much corruption in Athens, because we no longer care. We have lost hope. Pandora is no longer on our list. Her box once filled is now empty.'

'What have we got to lose?' Rupert said. 'Come on Quim, Helen's right. Why not give it a try?'

It was Lulu's turn. 'For once I agree with my husband. Why not give the pieces of Athena back to the museum, the Greek people, Quim?'

'Give the caryatid back to us. The statue is a favourite among the school children!' Helen was now shouting.

'Why is this issue such a problem?' asked Max, glaring hard at his uncle. 'Will it start a third world war, a revolution? Will the Tower of London fall down or the FTSE collapse?

'I read somewhere about the value of returning or restoring China's heritage and how it brought nations together,' said Max. 'I watched a programme on TV about the island of Sicily, and how the people longed to have their statue of Persephone returned to their city. Eventually all her broken pieces were returned from different parts of the world and re-assembled. The people of Sicily rejoiced. They danced in the streets. She has become a main tourist attraction. The people regained a vital part of their heritage. You can't take away something that doesn't belong to you. It's theft!'

'What do you think the Queen would do if the situation was reversed?' asked Badiya. 'Or, has anyone ever asked Her Majesty what she thinks? Why not ask Prince Philip what he thinks, he's half Greek!'

'I know exactly what I would do!' Lulu cried. 'I understand what it feels like to lose everything you hold dear. Because I have lost what I consider to be my heritage, I understand how the Greek people feel. So I would like to join your cause. I have lots of highfalutin American friends. Michelle Obama, Arianna Huffington, Steven Spielberg, Oprah Winfrey, honey you name them, I know them.

'It's time to get us Americans on board. I'd give everything I own to have my jewels back. So thief, whoever you are, you can have our house in the Hamptons, our house in Scotland, our penthouse in New York and our house in Grand Cayman, just return my mama's diamond tiara because Mama blames me for losing it. We haven't spoken since I told her about the theft. My life will never be the same, will it honey?'

Lulu was on a roll. 'My baby (meaning Harry) tells me that the plastic plaques in our guest bathroom are Greek. I am only too happy to send the wall hangings back because I can't stand the darn things. I'll even pay for delivery!'

Max looked at Helen. Helen winked at Harry. Three Cheshire cats.

'We will take all the marbles you have!' cried Helen.

Lulu clapped her hands gleefully. 'This is the best news ever!' She looked at her husband, demanding, 'Honey? Arrange transport!'

Everyone at the table clinked their glasses.

'Let's hope this is the beginning of the reuniting of the Parthenon's marbles to Greece.' Helen's tears said it all.

However there was one person on the sundeck who was not amused.

'Uncle, where are you going?' Max asked, as his uncle strode off in a huff.

'I'm going to my cabin, for a rest.'

'Before you go Uncle, may I say, frankly, I don't know how you have the nerve to even come to Athens. How on earth can you stand here, gazing at the Parthenon, knowing that when the new Acropolis Museum opens there will be globs of ugly plaster where the missing pieces should be and you are responsible. You should be ashamed of yourself, Uncle.

'Because I am ashamed to call myself an Englishman!' Max said in a loud voice so all could hear, however, Lord Quimby just kept on walking. 'I am ashamed to call myself a Quimby!'

Max was shaking as he watched his uncle slink off, like a thief caught in the act, which was in fact the truth.

Meanwhile, the debate on deck continued.

'Has anyone ever considered that the Greeks might not be in this bloody awful financial situation if the marbles hadn't been pinched in the first place?' asked Francesca. 'Perhaps the Greeks lost their reason to live when they lost their marbles, the very life-blood and soul of

Greece was bled dry by waring invaders. How much can people take before they have nothing left to live for?

'I know how it feels to lose everything. And I mean everything!' exclaimed Francesca, her beautiful face flushed with emotion. 'I have lost my money, my home, my husband, my pride, my ambition, hope; and I can tell you, when you have lost all that, you have nothing left. And yes, I would agree, when you lose all that you hold dear, you lose your soul. When you lose your soul, you no longer care. So I can see now, why the Greeks got themselves in this pickle because they no longer care. Being under Ottoman rule for hundreds of years didn't help. Imagine, England under German rule. Say, the Nazis had won the war. Being dictated to by the German Chancellor cannot be pleasant, after thousands of Greeks gave their lives during the Second World War. Talk about rubbing salt into a festering wound. Having a German telling you what to do must really be a bitter pill to swallow. We wouldn't like it would we...although, perhaps we are too?'

'Yes. This may be the reason corruption has taken over in Greece, Francesca.'

Francesca continued, 'The Parthenon has become a metaphor. The temple represents two and a half thousand years of democracy and when the Parthenon crumbles our entire democratic world may be crumbling too. We have the power to do something about this terrible injustice, however, we are all cowards, because we stand back and do nothing about it!'

'What about this for a hypothesis? 'Why not ask the Greeks how they feel about the return of their marbles?'

'Better yet, why not ask the world? Ask the Americans. Ask Obama. And the Canadians and the South Africans. Ask everyone you meet. Ask the children. Shout from the rafters, from the deck of the ship.

'Stand in the crow's nest and shout as loud as you can. Then, only then, will you have your answer.'

'Ask the Pope. What do you think the pontiff would say?'

'Ask the Dalai Lama!'

'This is not a political issue. It is a moral one. And, the answer lies in truth. The absolute truth is, that it no longer matters whether the marbles were pinched or plundered or scraped or painted, or whether there are marbles in the Louvre or the Vatican or Copenhagen or Rome or London, or at the bottom of the bloody Aegean Sea. The truth is that the marbles belong to Greece. That's it. Beauty is truth, truth beauty and that's all you need to know!' demanded Max. 'Keats where are you!'

'Let me tell you something you may not know,' said Helen, as she stood close to Max, hugging his arm.

'The late Nikos Pantazopoulos, my professor at the Aristotle University, passed on to us an observation derived from great knowledge and profound study: the view that Western civilisation rests on three pillars: the Acropolis, the Capitoline and Calvary. "The Acropolis symbolises intellect and beauty, the Capitoline order and law, and Calvary faith and religion". Is there anyone present wishing to debate this?

'I see tears brushed away every day. As I, one of the Parthenon sculptors, set about trying to recreate the impossible. And, let me also say, that I would give my life,' tears were streaming down her face, 'do you hear me – my life if I thought it would provoke the return of the marbles to Greece!'

Dimitri rushed to his daughter's side, time to intervene. After all, it was his only daughter's special day.

'Darling, don't you think it's time to open the rest of your birthday presents?' Dimitri nodded to the waiter.

The waiter rolled the trolley towards the table. He couldn't wait to see what was inside; the presents had come out of the heaviest backpacks he had ever carried on board.

'You only have a few more gifts to open, darling. Then you can cut your cake.'

Helen's birthday presents were piled on the trolley.

'I think I shall open the biggest first!'

'Here. Allow me to help,' offered Max knowing how heavy the box was. It was all he could do to lift it without invoking interest.

Helen opened her card first, although she was reluctant to share Max's loving wishes with anyone. She was desperately in love with Max but it was still a secret, for now.

'Thank you Menelaus,' said Helen, smiling, using his ancient Greek name. 'Thank you.' Then, she tore open the cardboard box with Cadbury's Custard Creams printed on the lid (definitely not Tiffany. Not the usual birthday wrapping for a millionairess). She dug down, anxious to see what lay wrapped in newspaper.

Helen screamed.

'Oh my god!' Oh my god, Max! Helen was ecstatic. She screeched, 'It can't be...Athena's right foot!'

Max was awarded the biggest kiss imaginable. She hugged Max for all he was worth. 'Menelaus you got it!'

Once she had calmed down Helen said to all her guests seated at the table, 'This is the most important moment of my life!'

'Good lord!' Lord Quimby had returned from his cabin and was strolling up on deck.

'Max! What on earth have you done?' obviously unable to comprehend. 'You stole the marble from the showcase in the museum? How could you Max? How could you!' Lord Quimby was livid!'

'Quite easily, Uncle, I have a mole.'

'You are going to jail. I am calling the police!'

'You can't do that!' Dimitri was getting very red in the face. 'You bloody English! Time you started thinking like a Greek. Don't you understand what it means to be passionate about something Quim? Passion is everything. If you are without passion when you die in Greece you go to Hades!'

Lord Quimby looked out to sea. He was lost for words.

Max was ready to attack. He was a fencer. He had been preparing himself for months, even years.

'How can I steal what doesn't belong to you? Athena's foot does not belong to you or me or to any of us, nor should I say, the Museum of Classical Antiquities. Athena's foot is not ours nor has it ever been ours. Athena's foot belongs to the Greek people, Uncle. In fact all the marbles in the Quimby Gallery belong to the people of Greece.'

'Well. We will certainly see about that!' shot Lord Quimby as he paced back and forth on the deck. 'Waiter, please, a large brandy!'

At that moment Harry, enthused, jumped up from his sun-lounger and rushing over to the trolley, presented his gift to Helen.

'Surprise. This is a little something from the Shambles!'

Helen ripped open her present, hastily wrapped in brown paper and bubble-wrap, tied with a Cambridge University scarf.

'Harry!' Helen gasped. 'Harry where on earth did you get this?'

'Oh gosh Helen, you mean the doorstop?'

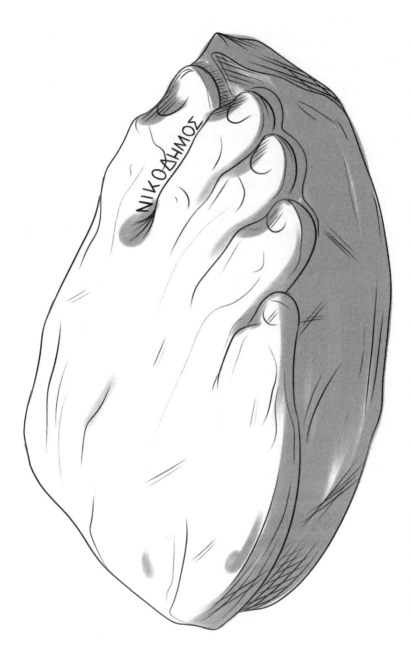

Plate XXI: Athena's right foot was carved and then signed by Nikodimos himself in Athens, fifth century BC. It was later discovered amidst the rubble on the Acropolis by Max in 1802. The foot was the first Parthenon marble to leave the Museum of Classical Antiquities in London when it was pinched by a Quimby descendant – the first stone to return to Greece.

'Don't tease! This is not a doorstop Harry This small chunk of marble is the most important chunk of stone in the world!'

Helen looked around the table, at the sea of blank faces.

'You must be wondering what all the fuss is about? Such a nondescript piece of stone, however, this piece of marble has one of the most important provenances in the history of the ancient world. We have been searching the world for pieces of Athena's aegis and now finally we have one small piece of it.

'I can't wait to show the marbles to the sculptors at the Acropolis Museum!' Helen was so excited she turned to her father, '*Pateras*, please forgive me, I don't wish to appear rude, however, I'm so excited, I really must take the stones to the museum. The sculptors will go crazy!'

'Max! Harry! Come on, I need you to help carry my birthday presents!'

'I can't thank you all enough for coming and for the lovely gifts,' said Helen, while standing knee deep in a sea of gift boxes.

'What about your cake?' asked Dimitri, obviously thrilled to see his daughter so very happy.

'We can have our cake later. We're going to the Parthenon *Pateras*,' said Helen heading towards the stairs. 'We'll take the launch.'

'Enjoy yourselves!' Dimitri added, cautiously, 'Take care darling, you know how dangerous the streets are. Stay well away from Syntagma Square as the protesters have been holding demonstrations there all week.'

'I know *Pateras*!' replied Helen smiling brightly. 'Don't worry, Max and Harry will keep me safe.

'Helen, why don't you take Max and Harry to the bank afterwards, to see the spectacular view of the Parthenon from the rooftop!' Dimitri suggested.

'Take care honey!' gushed Lulu. 'I watched the news this morning on TV and riots are expected to break out again.'

'Be careful Max!' Francesca added, kissing her son on the cheek. She never told Max how much she worried about him, though she prayed nightly for the gods to keep him safe.

'We'll call you from Athens, Sir,' Max shouted happily over his shoulder. 'We wouldn't miss the midnight cruise for anything!'

'We're not in the mood to go clubbing in the Plaka!' said Helen as all three hurried down the steps with the marbles tucked under their arms, their soft-soled shoes squeaking on the oiled teak.

—◯ ◯—

All the guests who came on board that night were in a celebratory mood, which wasn't difficult to understand as the view from the Kallisti was truly amazing. Romance filled the air as the most enormous full moon rose over the Parthenon, and a veil of glimmering light wrapped itself around the Acropolis.

'Just look at the violet light!' exclaimed Rupert Longfield-Jones, with his arms in the air. 'Why, it's extraordinary!'

'What an amazing sight!'

'Truly and utterly spellbinding!'

Those standing on the sky deck were mesmerised.

It was a spectacular moment. However, in an instant the moment had passed, the violet light surrendering to the darkness of the night.

Francesca wandered off. There were so many cosy couples she felt more out of place than ever. *Why on earth did I come?* Francesca asked herself, wanting to disappear, suddenly feeling the need to be alone as romance was no longer on her radar. Anyway, she wanted to discover the Kallisti for herself, so now was her chance. Thank god she had worn crêpe-soled shoes, Francesca thought, as she padded softly on the teak deck, gathering her wrap around her and strolling towards the bow of the boat. It was difficult not to be caught up in the moment; a heady combination of all the things she thought truly sublime in life. The view of the Acropolis was breathtaking. The Kallisti, ravishing. How long had she been leaning over the railing, lost in thought gazing out to sea, with the wine-dark sea slapping lazily against the hull before she realised she was not alone?

'The most redeeming feature about Kallisti is she has so many damn decks that if one so desires, one has the option of being alone,' Rupert whispered softly in Francesca's ear.

'Exactly!' Francesca turned her head, gazing up into the dark blue eyes of Harry's step-father. 'Bliss, sheer bliss!'

They stood together leaning over the polished brass railing, spellbound by the skyscape. 'Have you ever in your life seen anything more beautiful?' asked Francesca, studying Rupert's profile in the grey light.

'No. Frankly, I don't think I have,' replied Rupert somewhat in awe of the view, although he was not referring to the sea.

'The discussion about the Parthenon is an interesting one, though, don't you agree?' asked Rupert.

'Absolutely!' exclaimed Francesca. 'Max is passionate about the return of the marbles.'

'I wasn't before today, but I most certainly am now,' replied Rupert, musing that he could be seduced by this charming woman.

'Let me ask you, what would you do if you found a Greek marble in your back garden? What if the statue was worth millions and if you sold it the money would solve all your financial problems?'

'Sell! Sell! You would be a bloody fool not too!'

'Of course you would sell Rupert, you are a successful hedge fund manager. You understand the value of money. Well, so do I.

'Just for argument's sake, let us say the Greek statue proved to be a marble from the Parthenon. Would you sell it or give it back to the Greeks?' Francesca hastened, gently touching the sleeve of Rupert's linen jacket, 'and, say the prospective buyer was Chinese or a wealthy Arab from the Near East.'

'Francesca, I doubt the Chinese give a toss about the marbles from the Parthenon. I doubt the Arabs have any affection for bits of marble either.'

'Can you possibly imagine visiting Dubai, Rupert, and finding a Greek marble on display in the grand foyer of one of their sumptuous hotels, what would you think, knowing that the museum here is crying out for their marbles?'

'Well, the museum isn't getting their hands on mine. I have a marble on board. Care to have a look? It's a metope and it hangs over my bed in my stateroom!'

Francesca and Rupert swung round.

'Bloody hell!' Rupert flinched. 'You are planning to give the metope back to the museum aren't you Potch?'

'Why should I?' replied Dimitri, who had now joined them on the deck. 'The metope is the only thing I own of *real* value. Helen and I have a deal. When you Brits send our marbles back I'll give my metope back. Until that day comes, which I strongly doubt will be soon, the metope stays put. My girl loves it. Don't you darling!'

Badiya was snuggled up in Dimitri's arms giggling coyly, 'Of course darling!'

'Time to return to the bar!' Dimitri was in fine form. 'I ordered a case of Crystal and it needs drinking!'

They strolled along the deck together, Dimitri doing all the talking.

'As you can imagine the metope is a sore point. Helen and I argue about the fate of the metope every time she comes on board. She cares more about that damn marble than she cares about her old dad.

'My daughter has everything money can buy but all she really cares about are the Parthenon marbles. What she said is true by the way. She is Greek and we are a passionate lot. Helen believes that the marbles are a force to be reckoned with. That nothing on earth will prevent their return to Greece, where they belong. She believes the stones are empowered in some magical way, and, to her, the statues are real, living things and not inanimate objects, as we see them, as stones. Helen equates her passion for marbles to how I feel about my yacht. She says Kallisti has become my mistress. She's right of course. Even though the yacht is made of wood and steel, and, may I add, marble. Inanimate objects they may well be, be it a ship or a house or the bloody Parthenon!'

As the barman poured champagne, toasts were offered.

'Now, please, let's celebrate!

'Here's to life! Here's to love! Let's raise a toast to Helen and to Max and one day soon may the Parthenon marbles return to Greece!'

—◌র ৪৹—

Captain Balanos was alone at the helm station that night, waiting to leave port. While everyone on board was snug in their stateroom, preparing for the midnight cruise others were no doubt sleeping off the booze. He was anxious to set sail, although Helen and her friends had yet to return from Athens. The weather was perfect. The sea was gin-clear. There was a full moon to guide them to their final destination, Patmos. The captain glanced at the controls. Pushed a few buttons. Everything was in order. He wasn't really listening when the news bulletin flashed onto the TV screen.

'At nine o'clock this evening a bomb exploded inside a branch of the Athens' Central Bank. We are not sure how many people have perished trying to escape through the fire escape in the roof.'

Captain Balanos collapsed onto the leather seat unable to breathe. He felt as though he had been hit by a bullet as he sat listening to the newsman standing at the scene.

'Oh, God!' Captain Balanos caught sight of Harry being wheeled out of the bank on a stretcher and placed in an ambulance. He looked dead. His face was black and his clothes were in shreds. Fire trucks, ambulances, police sirens screamed in the background.

Then, he watched two bodies being taken out of the bank in gruesome black body bags.

The newsman said, 'I am able to confirm that two young people died tonight in the explosion!'

Captain Balanos rushed to the toilet where he was violently sick.

—⚬⚭—

'Mr Papadopolous. Sir. Wake up!' The captain was shaking Dimitri's shoulder, finding it difficult to waken him after so much champagne. 'Sir, Sir, please! Wake up!'

'What is it Balanos?'

'There has been a terrible fire Sir, at the bank Sir. A bomb exploded inside the bank about an hour ago Sir!' Tears were streaming down Captain Balanos's face.

'What?' Dimitri paled.

'I just received a call from the security service at the bank.' Captain Balanos collapsed onto Dimitri's bed. 'Helen and Max were upstairs on the roof when the bomb went off. They couldn't escape... it's too awful Sir...the launch is waiting...you must leave at once!'

'Max's mother is in her stateroom...!'

'Harry was taken out of the bank on a stretcher – I saw him on TV.'

'Wake Rupert and Lulu, tell them to meet me on deck. They will want to come with me.'

'What about Lord Quimby Sir?'

'Yes...yes, of course, go to him at once.'

'Yes Sir.'

Chapter Thirty-Seven
Shattered Desolation

Lord Quimby returned to London immediately after Max's funeral had taken place in an ancient cemetery in central Athens. Pippa was waiting for him upon his arrival at Heathrow with more disturbing news.

'We are all very sorry for your loss,' said Pippa, with a tissue held tightly to her nose. 'I can't believe what's happened Sir. None of us can.'

'Tragic Pippa,' said Lord Quimby, looking grim, his jaw squared, his scalp tight. 'Tragic!'

'There was no need to meet me Pippa' said Lord Quimby, curtly. 'I can find my way home you know.'

Pippa was in a forgiving mood. Grief changed people. 'Lord Q, while you were away a rather bizarre incident took place in the Quimby Gallery and it is so preposterous that, well Sir, we really need you to come along to the museum at once. I have a car waiting.'

—⊂⊃—

'I am so sorry to hear of your loss Lord Quimby!' Holloway came rushing towards His Lordship. He was shaking his head. 'I am so dreadfully sorry to hear about Max's death.'

'Yes. Yes.' Lord Quimby looked positively grey as he strode into the Quimby Gallery.

'You will not believe what happened during your absence, Sir.

'This way, come this way,' said Holloway, guiding Lord Quimby over to a shrouded plinth.

'Well Sir,' said Holloway, as he pulled the cloth from the statue. 'Take a look at this.'

'Good lord!' Lord Quimby staggered backwards. His large hands grabbing his face as he stared at the shattered remains of the horse's head. 'Good heaven's Holloway, someone tried to destroy the statue? The nose of Selene's horse is completely gone!

'This is shocking Holloway...what happened?'

'We don't know Sir,' said Holloway.

'What do you mean you don't know?'

'It's a complete mystery Sir.'

'Were the police called in?'

'Yes, Sir. The police came right away. They left shortly after as there didn't appear to be any sign of wrongdoing. The stone shattered. It wasn't blown up or chopped up. Nothing.'

'It doesn't make sense!'

'I know Sir. We are all baffled by what happened.' Holloway started chewing his fingernails. 'It's almost as though some force inside the statue was trying to escape. I have heard Sir, that the marbles are enchanted. So, this would make sense.'

'Rubbish Holloway!'

'The marble looks awful without its nose. Grotesque!'

471

'When did this dreadful thing happen, Holloway?'

'It happened while you were away in Athens Sir.'

'By all accounts the marble shattered on 5 May, we expect, sometime around midnight, while the night-shift workers were having their tea break.'

Lord Quimby's stoicism remained intact, as he realised the statue had shattered the night Max and Helen died in the blaze.

'This is a travesty!' Holloway exclaimed, his face reflecting the colour of stone. 'Selene's horse was the most popular marble in the Quimby Gallery.'

'It was also Max's favourite,' Lord Quimby stated, flatly.

'What are you going to tell the Greek press office, Sir? The Greek Ambassador will be furious. We are the custodians of the Greek marbles are we not? The statues are supposed to be safe in England!'

'I haven't the faintest idea Holloway,' said Lord Quimby, nodding his head, repeating himself, 'I haven't the faintest idea.

'Please arrange to have the statue removed at once,' said Lord Quimby.

'There is another matter Milord.'

'What is it?'

'Well Sir, there's been a woman on the phone. She's been calling every day. She works for a skip hire company in Watford. Her name is Mrs Alice Lightbody. She said that she found several statues in the skips. Seems she recognised one of busts, if you can imagine Lord Q, because the marble head was wearing a winged hat. Mrs Lightbody went on to say that she wasn't sure what to do with the bust, because she wasn't an expert on marbles, but, she would be happy to bring the head into the museum for us to take a look. She didn't fancy taking the bust on the bus, however, because the marble head is extremely heavy but perhaps, Mr Lightbody could drive it in, in his van.'

Lord Quimby had a blank expression on his face. For the second time in his life he was lost for words.

'What should I say to Mrs Lightbody?'

'Tell her to send the head to the museum in Athens. Let the curator there sort it out.'

'Very well Milord.'

'We'll pay for shipping.'

'Thank you Sir!'

Nothing more was said.

Lord Quimby took his leave of the Museum of Classical Antiquities. He was in no mood for trivia. He was devastated, although he never showed it. Max's death had been a terrible blow. Now, this. It wasn't only the statue that was shattered. His job was on the line.

Lord Quimby walked out the door of the museum. He was in a reflective mood. The tragic death of his nephew had shattered his world. Max was the last in line. The Quimby dynasty had ended with his death.

Lord Quimby considered himself to be a man of honour and so he *must* do the honourable thing. He was, after all, an Englishman. He was a Trustee of the Museum of Classical Antiquities, but, not for much longer. Not after this last blow. There was one thing he could do, as Director. He still had the power to persuade the Board to have the marbles returned to Greece. The absolute truth was that that is where the marbles belonged and no one could dispute it, most of all himself. Even more revealing, he could no longer abide the sight of the marbles. The pain associated with the Quimby Marbles was too great. The Parthenon marbles should never have come to England in the first place. There was one further truth, however, that he would never reveal: that all of the marbles in the gallery, including the shattered statue of Selene's horse were fake.

—⟐ ⟑—

Life had become a blur. Rupert Longfield-Jones had great difficulty recounting a single thing he had said that was worthwhile in the last fortnight. The one thing he *did* know, however, was deep down in his soul, life, as he had known it, would never be the same again. That two precious lives had been snuffed out, just like that, was unfathomable. Max and Helen never stood a chance while trying to escape the raging inferno in Athens' Central Bank. Her father's bank. Potch's bank for Christ's sake! Rupert Longfield-Jones no longer believed in God and resolved to refrain from referring to the Almighty ever again. If there was a god, which he doubted, God would never have allowed such a terrible tragedy to happen. And, because the appalling tragedy did happen he chose not to believe in God. Simple as that.

United in grief they were not. Lulu had not spoken to him since the funerals. His wife blamed him for allowing her baby to go ashore in the first place. She blamed Rupert for everything that had happened in Athens. What else was new? After a terrible row she had taken Harry who was still recovering from his injuries out of the hospital, insisting on going home. Rupert had no idea where she actually was because they had so many damn homes. She also didn't answer her phone. Not that it mattered, but he worried about her.

Rupert had taken the next flight to New York. All he wanted to do was walk the dogs on the beach in the Hamptons.

While he was in New York the contractor had called from Scotland, advising him that he was desperately needed at the Shambles. Rupert wanted to see how the refurbishment was progressing anyway. No. That was a lie. What he really wanted was to walk to the local pub, indulge in a million wee drams, drown himself in single malt; dull the pain in his gut.

Would the pain ever go away?

The chopper levelled off, circling in the night sky, preparing to set down on the front lawn.

'Thanks Charlie,' Rupert had to shout to be heard.

Charlie spoke through the intercom, 'I'll pick you up at seven o'clock tomorrow morning.'

Rupert stepped on to the squishy ground, ran across the lawn avoiding being sucked into the down-draught, as the enormous blades of the chopper sliced through the warm night air. He waved goodbye to Charlie as he hurried towards the grand entrance to the house, an elaborate compendium of colossal fluted Doric columns – reminding him of the mighty Parthenon in Greece. He couldn't escape.

This isn't going to be easy.

The exterior of the house was nearing completion. The front of the house was finished. The skips had finally been removed from the rotunda. The Shambles was perfect in every way; a dream without sorrow or sadness. The black and white harlequin marble floor gleamed in the moonlight streaking through the clerestory windows high above his head. The walls were lined in Jacquard silk tapestries, imported from France, costing the earth. The plasterers had finished the ceiling, a masterpiece of artwork stretching up three flights of stairs. A gateway to heaven – bloody heaven no longer existed.

Rupert walked from room to room. Late afternoon shadows gathered, like phantom ghosts. His body weighed a ton. Was he dragging lead weights on his feet? The main salons were nearing completion. Although most of the salons in the west wing of the house remained in a state of chaos. A wasteland of broken dreams, Rupert thought bitterly as he caught sight of his latest purchase, 'Caught in a Storm' resting against the wall, waiting to be hung. Rupert ignored the painting. He kept on walking until he found himself alone in the kitchen, sitting cross-legged on the floor with his back to the wall. Ground Zero.

What on earth had he been thinking of when he bought the Shambles? Was his ego really *that* big? He didn't do drugs. He wasn't on cocaine. He must have been high on something to buy a house as enormous as the Shambles to house three people. Or was it two people? Or one? He could always fill the house with servants although people didn't have servants any more; they had 'help'. The Shambles would make a great hotel. A Hilton. Perhaps he should sell it.

The kitchen was straight out of *Architectural Digest,* a palatial *tour-de-force* of imported marble, English oak, satin-finished stainless steel and highly polished brass. In the last month the cupboards had been installed. The imported Carrara marble worktops went on for miles. There was only one thing out of place. A large manila envelope had been left on the island – that much sought-after centre in kitchens. Rupert rose to his feet. His legs had gone numb. He assumed the envelope was an invoice from the building contractor. Why was his wife's handwriting on the front?

Rupert tore open the envelop scanning the page. Lulu had been to the Shambles.

Rupert

I returned to collect my things. I am going home to California I could never be happy in Britain I hate the rain I am a sunshine girl remember. I hate this house. There is something macabre about the Shambles, a graveyard for disembodied ghosts, just like all those ghostly statues Quim left here, to haunt us. I have organised the shipment of the marbles to Greece. Every time I see marble I weep. I can't stop weeping Rupert.

Max and Helen lost their lives for something they both strongly believed in. It's a shame that neither of us have something other than money to believe in. The nothingness that comes with extreme wealth overwhelms me. I am searching for something money can't buy, something much greater.

I guess it's time to say goodbye. I will always love you Rupert. My lawyer in LA will contact you directly.

Don't worry honey; I don't want the damn house.

Rupert had a severe pain in his gut. He had five houses and no home. Edgar Allan Poe said something about many mansions in his father's house. Well, he had too many mansions and no house to call home. All his houses were empty. His heart was empty. And he had completely and utterly lost his soul, if he had ever been in possession of a soul? What was missing? Commodities. He bought and sold commodities. Rupert searched through the inner chambers of his lucid mind. 'Love!' Love was the missing commodity and then...the vision of a lovely woman standing beside him on the Kallisti came rushing back.

—◌ ℘—

As golden sun rose over the lofty Parthenon a wealthy Greek shipping tycoon could be seen standing on the top deck of his yacht gazing out to sea. He was casually dressed in a ratty T-shirt with Athena printed on the front, baggy sweat pants and bare feet which wasn't uncommon among the uber-chic elite. Six months had passed since Dimitri Papadopolous had buried his beautiful daughter, yet, he still could not come to terms with what had happened. He could no longer live with himself. The guilt he was suffering because of Helen's death was insurmountable; so was the shame. This, above all, made it impossible for him to grieve. He wasn't suicidal. Had he been so inclined he would have jumped overboard on 5 May.

Dimitri had called in the movers.

He could no longer sleep in his bed in his stateroom with the metope hanging over it. Every damn time he entered his stateroom he felt nothing but shame. Dimitri had never understood the meaning of the word before and yet shame was now eating away at his soul, destroying his life.

As he waited for the movers to leave the yacht he drummed his fingers on the brass rail, continually berating himself for not supporting Helen's cause to fund her campaign to have the Parthenon marbles removed from the Museum of Classical Antiquities in London and returned to Greece. It was a moot point and it haunted him. His beautiful daughter had been taken from him and now all that remained was a broken heart. For the last six months he had tried to escape from his wretchedness by sailing around the world. Spent millions on frivolous nothings. He could not rid himself of the fact that he was a shallow human being. The only thing he knew how to do was spend money. Why hadn't he done something *really* worthwhile in his life? This is where his shame and his shallowness fused into an eternal life of hell. Damnation came to mind. He had turned his back on his daughter and his people and now he could no longer live with the guilt.

You must repent you bastard.

Dimitri clutched the railing, watching the movers dragging the enormous crate along the deck, scratching the teak. At one time he would have made a fuss – now, he no longer cared. It had taken four men all morning to remove the metope from the wall in his stateroom as it was so extremely heavy. He guessed perhaps half a ton in weight. Dimitri turned his head, sobbing like *Zorba the Greek*. His legs had turned to jelly as the crated stone was dragged down the gangplank onto a flatbed vehicle, en route to the Acropolis Museum. He couldn't wait to be rid of the metope, although he doubted the removal of the marble would soothe his wretched soul. That was the problem: how to make peace with his soul.

Kallisti was the next to go. He had decided to put the money from the sale of the yacht towards a worthwhile cause, for once. He had set up a foundation in Helen's name, as he wanted to carry on fighting for her cause: to promote the return of the marbles to Athens. He had also started a charity to support young people to become stone-carvers. Helen would have liked that. He had bought a property near the quay, across the harbour in Piraeus, a shed, really, not far from Harry's place, who had taken over Helen's T-shirt business.

It was 5 May and that evening Dimitri was presenting a prize of £25 000 to a student from King's College Cambridge for outstanding achievement in the Classics department. Dimitri mused, would this outrageous display of benevolence absolve him of his shame? He doubted it, Dimitri thought, bitterly. Perhaps an anonymous offer to purchase the Greek marbles in the Quimby Gallery would ease his pain. Should he make the trustees of the Museum of Classical Antiquities in London an offer they could not refuse? Now, there was a thought.

Chapter Thirty-Eight
The Homecoming
Six Months Later

The British Airways cargo plane was the next to land on the runway that morning. Excitement filled the air as a platoon of armed guards greeted the plane, lifted the colossal wooden crate out of the hold, lowering it onto a flatbed truck trimmed with blue and white bunting, the colour of the Greek flag. Then the vehicle proceeded slowly across the tarmac, along a red carpet befitting a head of state. The crate was stamped 'Athens, Greece'. As the band played the national anthem two soldiers unrolled the Greek flag, placing it reverently over the crate. The flag could not have been more poignant; the blue representing the sea and the sky, and the white, representing the purity and cleansing of the human soul.

The crowd went wild. The story had been leaked to the press. Hence, a high security fence had had to be erected to keep the joyful throng at bay. Thousands of people had been waiting since dawn to catch a glimpse of the caryatid. Harry was there too, standing amidst a sea of flag-waving Greeks. Unable to believe that every person standing next to him was wearing Helen's T-shirt with '*Kore's Come Home!*' printed on the front. A middle-aged Frenchman had his face pressed against the wire fence. He was standing very tall, as though he were a sergeant in the French Foreign Legion. Jean-Pierre was the proudest man in the world as he represented the French government, sent to Athens on a mission of great importance. The President of France had elected him to accompany the marbles from the Department of Greek and Roman Antiquities in the Louvre to Greece. This was a great honour. Jean-Pierre had a secret that he couldn't reveal to anyone, and it was this: he was the only man on earth who understood that the marbles had finally been released from exile and had come home to their rightful place in antiquity. He was a happy man. He was also greatly relieved as there would be no more hauntings at the Louvre.

Thousands of people were taking selfies while others were throwing garlands of flowers over the fence onto the passing vehicle as it made its way slowly through the airport gates. People from all over the world had come to Athens that day to watch the spectacle. Every hotel room in Athens was booked. The economy was on an upturn. The crowds lining the streets watched in awe as the cavalcade of important dignitaries and government officials made their way slowly through the streets of Athens towards the new Acropolis Museum. After all, the people of Athens had waited for this moment for over two hundred years. They deserved to dance wildly in the streets. The news of the event had gone global. The world's press had taken the homecoming of Kore to the people.

The marble that arrived in Athens that day was the first of many to follow, as other European countries had agreed to return the much-sought marbles. Sections of Athena's aegis were being returned

Plate XXII: Kore is second from left; she was brutally hacked out of the temple by Lord Quimby and now stands alone and weeping in the Museum of Classical Antiquities in London. She longs to return to Athens, to be reunited with her sisters. She is the first marble statue to be returned.

from Germany and Denmark. That evening the Prime Minister was hosting a state banquet to honour the occasion. Many esteemed guests had been invited. There was one special lady; an American who was to receive an award for her outstanding contribution to the people of Greece. Her name was Mrs Longfield-Jones and she had single-handedly rallied the troops. Through her generosity of spirit she had taken the story to the world. Lulu was being escorted to the banquet by Harry who now lived permanently in Athens. When not in his shed printing T-shirts, Harry could be found in the Plaka selling his latest shirt with Murgatroyd printed on the front, or roaming the Acropolis barefoot.

The statue of Athena Parthenon had, in Max's words, been 'glued back together again!' Thanks, in part, to an elderly gentleman from Berlin called Opa who had decided to honour his grandson by sending Athena's torso home to Athens. He had never had any affection for the statue. Enormous sections of the Parthenon Frieze were being sent special delivery from a house in rural Scotland. Lord Quimby, the out-going Director of the Museum of Classical Antiquities in London had become a national hero. His statue was being unveiled that evening in the foyer of the Acropolis Museum. Sadly, Lord Quimby had sent his apologies.

An Englishwoman was also standing in the crowd that day. She came from Watford. Mrs Lightbody had become a local hero and had had her picture in the local newspaper many times since discovering the head of Hermes in one of her husband's skips. She had sent the marble head to Greece, never in her wildest dreams expecting such a response. However, the Curator of Antiquities at the Acropolis Museum in Athens wrote to her, informing Mrs Lightbody that the bust was indeed authentic, in other words, 'the real thing!'

THE HOMECOMING

This day had particular significance for the school children in Athens, as they had been given a special treat. The pupils had been given the day off to attend a very notable event taking place at the museum. Needless to say they could not contain their excitement as the students were allowed to watch the statue of their beloved Kore being exhumed. The children were allowed to touch the statue and were so excited that they even hugged and kissed the stone. Many brought bouquets of violets for the statue. Everyone in attendance at the museum that day cried tears of joy, as the marble statue had finally returned home to be with her sisters.

Chapter Thirty-Nine
Wounded Echo

Francesca had been sitting in her favourite chair, nestled in the corner of the greenhouse. It was the same chair she ate her supper in, and her lunch, and her breakfast. It was the same chair she slept in, snoozed in, wept tears of grief in and where she debated the meaning of life and death. The truth was all she wanted to do was sit in her chair.

Unable to sleep, Francesca had tried reading *Being Shelley* by Ann Wroe, thinking a book of poetry might put her to sleep. How wrong could she be? She had suffered from insomnia for the last year and didn't believe she would ever sleep peacefully again. The well-thumbed paperback that lay open in her lap had obviously been a favourite of Max's because almost every page had paragraphs underlined in red ink.

Francesca had spent the last year struggling to come to terms with her son's death and had failed miserably. Her loss, she found almost crippling. Having an analytical mind continued to be her undoing, because she was unable to rationalise Max's death and had therefore resigned herself to a life of grief.

Yesterday afternoon, however, she had unexpectedly come upon the book in Max's things and hadn't been able to put it down again. Yes, she had read all night; better than thrashing in her bed, angrily punching her pillow, crying herself to sleep. Francesca glanced down at the words written on the page, reading aloud to herself.

'Shelley's Hellenism wasn't only about the making of a modern Greek state, but also a prescription for the moral condition of human society everywhere and of civilisation itself.'

She flipped through the pages, stopping on page 143 where the lines had been underlined three times in red.

'He imagined how, when Greece first came to be, the forms of its statues already lay there.'

How profound. Francesca was fascinated by the thought.

On another page she read, 'In the dim interior light the statues stood, crowding, white and still, like ghosts...to drink in the spirit of their forms.'

She found more in Shelley's poem, 'Queen Mab'; 'the heroine Ianthe, her spirit lulled in sleep or translated in death, was fair/as breathing marble.'

Another underlined passage, from 'Revolt of Islam'; 'the bodies of young women lay piled, as if not dead, but slumbering quietly, like forms which sculptors carve, then love to agony.'

Max had scribbled, 'as I love Helen to agony!'

Yet, another truth had been revealed. Her son was besotted with Helen and she hadn't even known. Was that why Helen and Max had perished together, because they had experienced such great love? Another question unanswered, thought Francesca, miserably.

She was fascinated by the fact that Max had underlined so many sentences, concluding that Max had been trying to understand what the marbles really meant, not only to the Greeks but to the world.

She read another underlined passage, '...entranced him, because her Grecian hair and pale skin and the faultless lines of her profile, were those of a marble image of loveliness come alive.' (My Helen of Troy) Max had printed in the page.

The last few lines in the book had several red lines scratched deep in the page, as though Max never wanted to forget.

'Plato in the Republic had taught; that beyond the world's illusions, those shadows men saw on the walls of their prison-cave lay the unchanging realm of what was real and what was true.'

This, Francesca had read at least a thousand times. Finding it impossible to imagine Plato had written such poignant words over two thousand years ago. She imagined the shadow on her cave to be her grief and this, above all, prevented her from seeing beyond her prison cell, as she could not rid herself of the shadow of grief. However, what lay beyond the wall was real and true. Max had looked beyond the wall. He could see beyond life's illusions. Max struggled to find truth in everything he did. She knew this. Love went beyond the wall. Max's love of life, life itself, his love for Helen went beyond the prison wall and now, in death, his spirit lived on, in the stones, at the Parthenon in Athens. Like all great men.

Francesca sat curled up in her chair watching golden sunlight blaze a trail of magenta across the eastern sky, reminding her of her last visit to Athens, standing on the bow of the Kallisti with a man by her side. She pulled back her thoughts.

Don't go there you fool.

Francesca put the book down on the arm of the chair and rushing outside trod through the brown, withered bracken, standing knee-deep among the overgrown weeds in her garden. It was time to say goodbye. Her life at La Redousse had come to an end. Like everything else in her life. She had packed her belongings, knowing that this moment was coming. Not that she had anything left of value. The most valuable thing in her life had been snatched away, she thought bitterly, as she strolled deeper into the garden, watching a helicopter swirling overhead. It wasn't unusual on the French Riviera. Francesca didn't socialise with Monaco's super-rich, she couldn't afford to. Rich people didn't understand donkeys. She assumed the pilot had made a mistake.

The blasted chopper, much larger than most was preparing to land.

The down-draught nearly swept her away as she stood on the path waiting. Once the blades had stopped the captain opened his door, slid out and racing around the chopper in the swirling debris from the garden, opened the passenger door and out stepped Rupert Longfield-Jones.

Did he have to be so frightfully good looking?

He reminded her of Pierce Brosnan as he ran towards her, his dark hair catching in the wind, immaculately dressed as always in nautical attire, chinos and deck shoes; no doubt straight off Dimitri's yacht.

'Francesca!' Rupert thrust out his hand. 'I'm so glad I caught you.'

'I was about to leave,' replied Francesca, her voice flat, hollow, as she took his hand.

'Are you leaving?' asked Rupert, waving his arm in the direction of the house.

'Yes. La Redousse is officially up for sale. There is no one to leave it to, now.' Her voice trailed off. She didn't want to admit that it was a relief to be going, that she was haunted by happy memories bent on strangling her to death.

Rupert looked uneasy. 'Where will you go?'

'I'm going to Paris. I'm taking an apartment on the Left Bank with fabulous views over the Seine. It will be good to have a change of scene...get away.'

'Forgive me for dropping by on such short notice,' said Rupert, smiling brightly, thinking Francesca looked as though she could use a little humour.

Francesca did not respond.

'I've come to discuss a matter of great importance with you.' As he spoke he realised that the *matter* was staring him in the face.

Rupert caught sight of the cases on the drive. He could see the marble head of Athena through the packing case. In fact, he could see her eyes staring directly at him, into the deep recess of his empty soul.

'Are you taking Athena with you?'

'Yes.'

'It's been over a year since Lushington's pulled Athena from the sale. The impact must have been catastrophic for you, I know, because Lulu told me. I had no idea the statue belonged to you Francesca.

'However, in the last six months I have been in contact with the New Acropolis Museum in Athens. I've even been to visit the museum, to see the work going on, and I must say I am terribly impressed. Helen was a truly gifted sculptor. The head of the department has been an inspiration. His name is Nikolaos. He told me he comes from a family of sculptors who carved the marbles in the Parthenon thousands of years ago. On my last visit Nikolaos gave me something that he wanted you to have.' Rupert extracted a small velvet pouch from his coat pocket.

'Nikolaos said that this belonged to one of the most brilliant sculptors of all; his name was Menelaus, which is ancient Greek for Maximilian. He wanted you to have this. It is a small lead weight used by the sculptor himself. Can you believe it Francesca? I hope you don't mind but I had it made into a key ring for you and gave the original to the museum. I hope you like it. Isn't it extraordinary, Max and Menelaus both mean the same!'

Francesca took the small relic in her hand.

'Rupert! There's a tortoise embossed on the top!'

'I know,' said Rupert, frowning, 'I don't really know what that's all about.'

'I do!' Francesca was beaming 'It's Murgatroyd!'

'Murgatroyd? Who on earth is he?'

'I'll explain later. It's a long story!'

'Well, there is something else that I wished to discuss with you.' Rupert smiled at Francesca, overwhelmed by the resemblance between the statue and Francesca, as they both had striking classical features.

'I would like to make you an offer for the bust, difficult, I know, because she is priceless. I have no idea what Athena is worth because Lushington's refused to give me a proper valuation. I've had to rely on my own resources. I have a cheque in my pocket that I think might be a fair amount. Although, I insist that my offer be kept secret.' Rupert removed the envelope from his back pocket and presented it to Francesca.

Francesca peeked inside the envelope. She could see the amount written on the body of the cheque.

'If you agree that the amount is sufficient, then, what I would like to suggest is that I take Athena for a ride in my new chopper. You can come too if you wish. I'm not keeping you from anything Francesca?'

Francesca was struggling; 'Yes...yes...of course...'

'What do you intend to do with Athena?' asked Francesca, feeling anger rising. 'Tart up Dimitri's yacht or display her in your garden in the Hamptons? Take her back to New York where she would feel like a stranger in a foreign land?'

'Most definitely not!' replied Rupert, understanding how grief-stricken Francesca must be.

'I have decided that there is only thing to do with Athena and that is to give her to back to the people of Greece.'

'Rupert, that makes no sense at all!' Francesca was grieving but she could still think straight. 'Why on earth would you do such a thing, to pay over-the-top for Athena and then give her to the museum?'

'The Acropolis Museum in Athens will be delighted to have Athena's head. I have learned that it has an interesting history. Records show that the bust was discovered in a well in 1815 in the garden of Don Giovanni Battista Belisario. He had been Lord Quimby's clerk of works, and, so the story goes, he went mad. Because, according to the story the marble made such a racket it drove him insane. The story is unbelievable. Apparently, the marble bust of Athena carried on something frightful, until the people who bought the house had to have her removed from the well. So, Francesca, these marbles have a life-force all of their own. The Parthenon's marbles insist on being returned to their homeland and that is exactly what needs to happen.

'And because...' said Rupert, grabbing hold of Francesca's arm, gently guiding her over to the chopper, 'because, I may have got more than I bargained for when I bid for Athena.' Rupert touched Francesca's cheek. 'I hope I got two goddesses. Two of the most beautiful women in the world and because I am not a greedy man I feel it's only right to part with one, however, I would very much like to hold on to the other for as long as possible.'

Rupert didn't wait for her to reply.

He leapt up the steps, into the chopper. The pain in his gut was gone. The emptiness in his soul was gone. Joy had come back into his life. He had discovered something precious and for once it had nothing whatsoever to do with the almighty dollar and everything to do with love and giving something back.

Francesca stepped up into the chopper and within minutes Charlie was whisking the happy threesome towards Athens. She reached for Rupert's hand, unable to believe he was sitting next to her. And, as she glanced out the window of the chopper a little of the pain and the sorrow she had suffered in the last year lifted. Francesca could feel her spirit rise towards the heavens, towards Olympus. Max and Helen should be with them. They would be so excited to know that the bust of Athena was going home. But, then again, perhaps they already knew.

Chapter Forty
Menelaus, End of the Legend

On the second anniversary of her son's tragic death, Francesca and Rupert Longfield-Jones returned to Athens. Their visit was twofold. They were invited to be honoured guests at a dedication ceremony taking place that evening at the Acropolis Museum, in honour of Max's great contribution to the people of Greece. However, their first priority was to visit her son's grave as Max's headstone had been erected in the ancient Kerameikos Cemetery in central Athens. And, so, on 5 May Rupert and Francesca walked through the busy streets of Athens towards the final resting place of the Athenians of old.

'Darling, isn't it wonderful,' said Francesca, gripping onto Rupert's arm, 'that the Greek government offered to have Max's body interred here in Athens?'

'I am humbled by their generosity,' said Rupert, 'to think that the cemetery has been closed for two thousand years.'

'There is a calmness and a serenity about the place,' said Francesca, 'unlike any other on earth.'

Hand in hand they walked towards the stoa, with a paper bag tucked under Rupert's arm, passing several funerary inscriptions in

494

the wall, failing to see a small owl hiding in the undergrowth, not far from where Max lay buried.

Francesca stopped for a few moments, needing all her strength to continue.

'Francesca,' whispered Rupert, taking her hand. 'Look at this!'

She studied the stele, beautifully carved in stone.

Rupert whispered in a low voice, as one does in a cemetery. 'Even though the stele was carved over two thousand years ago you can still see the outline of a young boy holding a mallet and chisel in his hands. Look Francesca. The boy is standing in front of a marble carving of a Lapith and a centaur.'

'The metope is the same one as I have seen on the Parthenon's marble frieze.'

'I wonder who the handsome young man is holding a lyre.'

They couldn't understand the words however an attendant standing nearby offered to translate. He said,

This commemorate plaque is dedicated to Menelaus

The brilliant young stone-carver

Who died tragically, while carving the metopes on the Parthenon frieze.

Although his body was never found

He became a hero, a legend to the Athenian people

'Thank you,' said Francesca, softy, and in silence they carried on down the path leading to Max's grave standing in the shade of an ancient cypress tree, amidst a plethora of exotic wildflowers growing between the ancient grave stones.

CHAPTER FORTY

They had come for a reason.

Rupert very gingerly opened the paper bag. It was only right that the tortoise shell be returned to Athens. After staring at the empty shell for the last two years they decided it was time for Murgatroyd to be with Max.

'Isn't it odd darling!' said Rupert, lifting the tortoise shell out of the bag. 'Murgatroyd no longer exists, yet we act as though the tortoise is still a living creature inside its shell. Illusion is a potent thing, my darling,' said Rupert, holding Francesca tenderly in his arms, wanting to keep her close, always.

'Murgatroyd has become such an important part of our family,' said Francesca as she placed the shell on her son's grave. 'Without Murgatroyd we would never have learned the truth, that the Quimby family are in fact, half Greek!'

Francesca ran her hand over the shell. 'Murgatroyd's shell feels exactly like stone Rupert.'

'Perhaps we are all made of stone,' said Rupert, brushing tears from his eyes. As he read the inscription in Greek carved in the headstone.

This block of stone

Taken from the Parthenon Frieze

Is to commemorate the life of

Maximilian Henry Charles Perceval

Francesca, overwhelmed, said, 'The marble headstone represents the very essence of the people of Greece. I am the proudest mother on earth. Max gave his life for something he strongly believed in.

'I can feel Max's presence here with us. I believe it was his destiny to spend an eternity in Athens, Rupert. To be forever close to his beloved Parthenon and Helen. Max simply adored all things Greek. Hence, the reason for reading the Classics. Perhaps Max was more Greek than we can possibly imagine.'

It was time to say goodbye and at that moment Francesca suddenly felt at peace, at one with the flowers and the trees and the earth and the stone.

Acknowledgements

Alex Benakis, Tom Waterton-Smith, Fiona Marsh, Tony Mulliken, Titus Odedun, Heather Boisseau, Clare Christian, Ron, Whelan, Joey Everett, Carol Anderson and Kathy Steer.

Thanks also to Eleni Cubitt, founder of the British Committee for the Reunification of the Parthenon Marbles.

Reading List

Being Shelley: The Poet's Search for Himself Ann Wroe (Jonathan Cape, 2008)

Metamorphoses Ovid (Penguin Classics, 1955)

The Odyssey Homer (Penguin Classics, 1997)

Reflections on the Paintings and Sculptures of the Greeks Johann Winckelmann (Nabu Press, 2011)